FALLING
A LOVE STORY

JANE GREEN

LARGE
PRINT

First published in Great Britain 2016
by
Macmillan
an imprint of Pan Macmillan

First Isis Edition
published 2017
by arrangement with
Pan Macmillan

A catalogue record for this book is available
from the British Library.

ISBN 978–1–78541–413–8 (hb)
ISBN 978–1–78541–419–0 (pb)

Published by
F. A. Thorpe (Publishing)
Anstey, Leicestershire

Set by Words & Graphics Ltd.
Anstey, Leicestershire
Printed and bound in Great Britain by
T. J. International Ltd., Padstow, Cornwall

This book is printed on acid-free paper

FALLING

Five years ago, Emma Montague left behind the strict confines of her upper-crust English life and moved to New York City, where she immediately found success in the world of finance. But her soulless, cut-throat, all-consuming job only led to another life she didn't want. Answering an online ad, Emma finds a tiny beach cottage to rent in the small town of Westport, Connecticut. It's the perfect DIY project — if Emma's new landlord, Dominic, is agreeable to the small changes she yearns to make. A local handyman with a six-year-old son, Dominic is a world away from the men Emma should be interested in; but he's comfortable in his own skin, quiet, and kind. And slowly, over a shared garden, time spent with his son, and late-night conversations, she finds herself falling in love . . .

SPECIAL MESSAGE TO READERS

THE ULVERSCROFT FOUNDATION
(registered UK charity number 264873)
was established in 1972 to provide funds for
research, diagnosis and treatment of eye diseases.
Examples of major projects funded by
the Ulverscroft Foundation are:-

- The Children's Eye Unit at Moorfields Eye Hospital, London
- The Ulverscroft Children's Eye Unit at Great Ormond Street Hospital for Sick Children
- Funding research into eye diseases and treatment at the Department of Ophthalmology, University of Leicester
- The Ulverscroft Vision Research Group, Institute of Child Health
- Twin operating theatres at the Western Ophthalmic Hospital, London
- The Chair of Ophthalmology at the Royal Australian College of Ophthalmologists

You can help further the work of the Foundation
by making a donation or leaving a legacy.
Every contribution is gratefully received. If you
would like to help support the Foundation or
require further information, please contact:

THE ULVERSCROFT FOUNDATION
The Green, Bradgate Road, Anstey
Leicester LE7 7FU, England
Tel: (0116) 236 4325

website: www.foundation.ulverscroft.com

ACT ONE

CHAPTER
ONE

"It's lovely," she lies, in her most gracious of voices, looking around at the tired wood panelling lining the walls of the living room, floor to ceiling. As she looks down, her gaze lands on well-worn salmon-pink shagpile carpeting and she quickly conceals her horror.

Emma wonders if this house might not be beyond even her capabilities to transform. Perhaps the landlord would let her paint it? Surely he would let her paint it — who wouldn't want to lighten up this room, so dark it feels more like a cave? She would paint it for free, and pull up that carpet. Maybe she would be lucky and find a hardwood floor underneath; even if it was merely concrete, surely it wouldn't cost too much to stick down some inexpensive sisal.

This room could be transformed, she determines. Lipstick on a pig is her speciality.

Her landlord, or potential landlord, smiles. "Hey, I know it's not everyone's taste today," he says. "Why do people want everything to be grey and modern?"

Emma is surprised by his comment, surprised frankly by his interest in making small talk. "I hate that look," Emma offers. It happens that she does agree, quite passionately, in fact. "None of those decorated houses feel like real homes."

"Exactly!" he says in delight. "This is a home."

Struck by his words, by the obvious sincerity with which they are spoken, she turns to look at her potential landlord for the first time. She can't help but feel struck by the sight of him. He is not too tall, only a few inches taller than her, with skin tanned by the sun and an easy smile that seems to put her at ease. It isn't so much that she finds him attractive, but rather that there is something familiar about him, a recognition, a sense of having somehow met him before.

Perhaps because she has remained silent, he goes on to add, "At least, it was a home. My grandparents lived here for forty years."

Yes, thinks Emma, *it looks like it. It smells like it, too*. The air is fusty. Of course old people had lived here. That explains the wood panelling and the floral wallpaper in the family room; it also explains the salmon-pink carpet and avocado-green bathroom suite with matching tiles.

"How would you feel about me putting . . . " Emma pauses, wondering how to say this diplomatically. She doesn't want to jump in and tell him she'd like to tear everything out and start again. He probably doesn't want to change anything; his voice had softened when he mentioned his grandparents. She has an odd reluctance to offend him, and senses she'll need to take this slowly if she wants this house. ". . . a woman's touch on the house?"

"A woman's touch!" The landlord smiles and nods approvingly. "That's exactly what I've been saying this house needs for years. A woman's touch."

She follows him into the kitchen at the back of the house and her heart sinks slightly. It hasn't been touched since the fifties, rough wood cabinets bumpy with layers of white paint, although pretty black iron hardware. Formica worktops with large cracks, and linoleum floors. A stove that is so ancient it's fashionable again, and, surprisingly, a large modern stainless-steel fridge.

Emma looks at the fridge and raises an eyebrow as she looks over at the landlord.

Damn, she thinks. What was his name again? Donald? Derek? Something like that.

"The old fridge gave up last year," he explains. "The tenants picked out this one. And I paid for it," he adds quickly, as if to reassure her that he is a good landlord, on top of everything, ready to jump in and deal with problems.

"Great," says Emma, wandering over to the back door and peering out through the glass onto a fenced-in garden, or what could be a garden if the weeds were cleared. "Can I go outside?" she asks, already out the door.

He follows her out, apologizing for the weeds. They both stand there as Emma looks around, her imagination already firing. There are two filthy peeling rattan chairs stacked off to the side, surrounded by boxes and baskets: in other words, rubbish.

5

The landlord turns to look and immediately apologizes. "I haven't been out here," he explains. "Obviously all of that will be gone. I can replace those chairs with new ones."

Emma is again struck by him. His eagerness to please doesn't seem solely mercenary. He wants her to know that he cares about the house and yard. "Do I get to choose what kinds of chairs the new ones are? Like the fridge?" Emma says.

"As long as they're not too expensive."

"I am the expert at renovating on a shoestring." She smiles.

"You're my kind of woman." He laughs, as Emma flushes slightly and turns away. A flirtatious landlord is the last thing she wants right now. "Sorry." He apologizes immediately, realizing his mistake. "I was kidding. But I'm happy for you to choose things as long as they're within the budget."

Emma looks up at the sky, noting the sun, looking at the shadows to try to figure out which way the garden faces. "South-west," she guesses, and he turns to her with a smile.

"You're a sun worshipper?"

"With this pale English skin?" She laughs and shakes her head. "I turn into one giant freckle in the sun. But I am a gardener. At least, a frustrated one. For years and years, I lived in flats in London dreaming of having a garden of my own. Then for the last five years I've been on the top of a high-rise in Battery Park." Good lord. Why is she suddenly giving him her life story?

"Ah, so you're a city girl."

"Not by choice."

"You're ready to be out here?"

"Ready to be steps from the beach, in a gorgeous town where the pace of life is relaxed and the pressure is off? No. Definitely not."

He laughs. "I've lived here my whole life, and wouldn't move anywhere else. How did you find Westport?"

"I have a friend who lives here, who I used to work with. She moved out three years ago after she had a baby, and she loves it. I've been out to visit her quite a few times, and something about this place feels right. I never thought I'd be able to move out here permanently, but . . . I needed to make some big changes in my life. Moving somewhere like this, with a quieter pace of life, seemed like a good first step."

"I saw on your application you're a banker. That's quite a commute."

"Actually," Emma says, "I took a package. I'm now officially unemployed, albeit with a very nice severance. I hope that won't be a problem?"

"As long as you pay your rent, nothing's a problem. What are you going to do here in town?"

Emma is struck again by the sincerity of his interest. He is not just making small talk, she is sure of it. He's looking at her, making her feel like he cares about what she'll say next. She shakes her head. "Thankfully, I have enough to have a little bit of breathing space. I don't really know. I've always had a dream about doing something with the home. Interior design, gardening,

7

that sort of thing. I've been doing an online course to get the official qualification. Now all I need are clients."

"And a house to do up."

"And a garden to transform. Preferably one that faces south-west." She grins as she looks around the garden.

He grins, too. "Then you've found it. It seems that you and this house were meant to be. Although, you couldn't do anything major to it without consulting with me."

"Of course." Emma laughs politely. She couldn't move in *unless* she did something major with the house. As it is, it's completely awful, but stepping back to take it in, even with all its flaws, she thinks she could turn this into a charming beach cottage.

The landlord seems like a nice guy. He may be resistant to her changes at first, but she surmises that she could ask forgiveness rather than permission for most things. If he walked into this room and found the wood painted a lovely chalky white, the floors covered with sisal, the single light bulb replaced with a pretty glass pendant light, surely he would be thrilled. Who *wouldn't* be thrilled at someone transforming their house for nothing? He would undoubtedly get more money for it next time he decides to rent it out.

The truth is that Emma Montague isn't looking for somewhere permanent just yet. She's just looking for a place to call home for the next year or so. A year to try to recover from the last five years of working in finance in New York. A year to try to figure out what kind of life she wants to live. For five years she has lived a life that wasn't hers. Five years of utter exhaustion; five years of keeping her head down and working like the devil, putting away enough money to be able to afford to do what she is doing now, leaving the rat race and pursuing her dream. Her goal is to figure out what her dream is. Right now she only knows that the first step is to find a world and a life that feels likes her own; a life in which she finally feels she belongs.

It starts with a house. She is itching to buy, but it is more sensible to rent, making sure this is where she wants to live. Still, the rentals down by the beach, here in Westport, Connecticut, are mostly prohibitive for a single girl with a budget, even an ex-banker. The last thing she wants to do is blow all her savings on rent.

This house, this dated, fusty house, is entirely within her budget, precisely because it *is* so dated and fusty. It is the perfect size — two bedrooms with a living room, kitchen, and family room that would make a perfect office.

And best of all there is a garden, or rather more than enough space for one. She can finally plant vegetables. She can put a gravel path down the middle, can grow tomatoes, cucumbers, and lettuce, plant roses and clematis over the fence at the back. She imagines a long, rustic table, a small group of friends sitting around, bottles of rose, and candles interspersed with galvanized steel pots of lavender running down the centre. Laughter. Happy faces. Everyone lit by the glow of summer and love.

Emma shakes her head to bring herself back to earth. She knows only one person — her friend Sophie

Munster — here in Westport. She has no other local friends she can invite to sit around the table, and since she's something of an introvert, it may take a little while to find them. But she will find them.

Although a bit of a loner, she is loyal, and fun, when she finds people with whom she is comfortable. She is thinking of taking up yoga, and maybe knitting. There are evening classes at the local yarn shop, Sophie says. They should both go. Sophie grew up here, although she went away to boarding school. She has friends from grade school, though, and seems to know almost everyone in town. Surely it's only a matter of time before Emma's fantasy of summer evenings comes true.

For as long as she can remember, Emma Montague has had a fascination with America. Growing up in her upper-crust family in Somerset, England, sent off to boarding school, then moving to London after university to enter the world of banking, she had the persistent belief that this was not supposed to be her life.

As a little girl, she had never quite felt she fitted in. She was loved and treasured, but her boisterous, overbearing mother and loving but somewhat beleaguered and introverted father didn't quite know how to connect with their quiet, studious child. The place she felt happiest, the place she found her solace and joy, was in the pages of books.

She read all the time. It was so much easier than dealing with the chaos of her playmates during breaktimes. She was close to one or two of her classmates, but she only liked seeing them one at a time. Otherwise, she was happier with her books. She was the child with the torch under the duvet late into every night. She would breeze through a book in a day and a half, then read it six more times.

She fell in love with America through the pages of these books. Her dull, patrician life in Somerset felt very staid compared to the lives of Jo and her sisters in *Little Women*, and Katy in the What Katy Did series. She devoured the stories of Laura Ingalls Wilder and dreamed of having a farm out in the middle of nowhere, growing all her own vegetables, raising her own animals.

Life then got in the way, sweeping her up into the cut-throat world of London finance, not because she had a passion for finance, but because it was what all the girls were doing at that time. First London, then New York. Finally, now that she has extricated herself, it looks like she has a shot at the kind of life she might actually want to live.

Westport, Connecticut, may not be Walton's Mountain, but there are enough trees for her to pretend, and the beauty of the beach on the doorstep is something she now realizes she has always wanted.

When she was living in Manhattan she would go running along the river every day before work. The sunlight glinting off the water brought a calm and peace to every morning. She hadn't known how much she wanted to be by the water until Sophie drove her to Compo Beach for a walk one weekend. That was the moment she knew this was where she wanted to be.

There had been a tremendous expectation for the life Emma was supposed to have led, at least from her parents. And she had tried to fit into the life they had designed for her. Namely, to work at a pretend job for a few years to enable her to meet the right kind of husband, before quickly getting pregnant, giving up work, and going on to raise three or four beautiful children in a lovely stone manse in Somerset. Preferably near her parents. Have a couple of dogs, Gordon setters or pointers, possibly golden retrievers; have lots of local women friends who come for coffee. Get involved in the village fair and perhaps, given her love of books, institute a reading mentoring programme in the less well-off town twenty minutes away.

Emma knew the path well, as it was the path so many of her childhood friends had taken. At thirty-seven, she is the only one still unmarried, apart from Imogen Cutliffe, who is one of the leading lights of British screen and stage and about to star as the lead in a film starring Bradley Cooper. Emma is the only one who continued to work and rise up the corporate ladder, putting all her focus on making money. It wasn't that she cared about money for the sake of money, rather it was the only path out: making enough money to retire from banking in her thirties, and the freedom to pursue her dream. If she could figure out what her dream was.

She hadn't known her life was going to turn out like this. For a long time she imagined she would indeed follow the path her parents expected of her. She dated Rufus Fairfax for years throughout her twenties, not because she loved him, but because her parents loved him and he seemed to tick all the right boxes. He was a banker in the firm where she worked, he was handsome (although he had not an ounce of sex appeal, as far as she was concerned), and he was of the right stock. Clever, but not very funny; in fact, he was achingly dull. But they looked so good together! They seemed to fit so perfectly together that everyone assumed they would get married from the moment they started going out. And Emma had presumed everyone was right, that everyone knew something she did not, and she was the one who must have been wrong.

She determined to make it work. She and Rufus spent their weekdays in London, both of them burning the candle at both ends, and their weekends in the country, usually staying with friends in crumbling old piles that were impossibly draughty, with terrible food and lots of drink to distract from the fact that everyone was freezing cold and permanently starving.

Rufus had a huge group of friends from boarding school that Emma always found rather awful. They were shockingly loud, and arrogant, fuelled by absurdly expensive bottles of wine that they ordered in restaurants to prove they could afford them. They shouted inside jokes from when they were all thirteen, their wives and girlfriends sitting with smiles plastered on their faces, pretending to be amused.

Emma started leaving these evenings early, claiming headaches and making her way up to bed during those country weekends, earplugs tucked into her overnight bag to help her sleep through the inevitable banging and shouting in the early hours of the morning when the party eventually broke up.

None of this fazed Rufus, who proposed to her four times. The first time, he did so after a romantic dinner at Hakkasan, having gazed at her over the course of the evening with a hopeful kind of love that Emma found slightly discomfiting. Each time, Emma said she just wasn't quite ready. Eventually, five years ago, Rufus issued an ultimatum: if she wouldn't marry him, he would find someone else who would, and with a great dramatic flounce, he packed up his things and left their Kensington flat. Emma knew he thought she would beg him to come back within a week or so, but from the minute he was gone, she felt nothing other than tremendous relief.

She had been playing the part of adoring girlfriend, probably — hopefully — soon-to-be wife, for so long that she had forgotten how liberating it was to simply be herself. She saw girlfriends from university she hadn't seen for ages because Rufus disapproved of their drinking ("Darling, there's nothing quite so ghastly as a woman publicly drunk"). She got into bed at seven thirty p.m. with hummus and chips for dinner, and spent hours watching terrible reality television that Rufus would never have condoned.

She was happy, and happier still when she was called in to her superior's office and asked if she would consider taking up a position with the bank in New York. They were starting a new private wealth management operation, specifically for English expatriates living on the East Coast of the United States, and they needed someone to head client relations.

They would put together a package, they said. All moving expenses would be paid. She would be set up in an apartment, and there would be a healthy relocation allowance. They offered all of this as if to sweeten the deal, as if Emma weren't using everything she had, sitting in her office in her oh-so-staid black Givenchy skirt and Manolo Blahnik d'Orsay heels (the perfect combination of elegant and sexy), not to break out in a scream of joy and twirl around the room, punching the air and whooping in a mad happy dance.

It was the fresh start she had been longing for, and better still, in New York! The place she had always imagined living! Well, perhaps not quite New York City. She preferred to see herself in rural Vermont, or Maine, but at least it was across the pond, and she would get a green card, and at some point surely, surely, she'd make it out of the city and into the farmhouse of her dreams.

This is not the farmhouse of her dreams. This isn't even the beach cottage of her dreams. But it could be. With just a little bit of work, if her oddly welcoming landlord acquiesced, she could transform this into something, if not quite magnificent, at least beachy, and airy, and filled with charm.

They walk back through the house, Emma trying to see through the wallpaper, the linoleum, the salmon-pink flat shagpile carpet, as the landlord shows her out.

"It was great to meet you, Emma," he says, meeting her gaze with a friendly smile and shaking her hand with a grip so firm she crumples slightly before flexing her fingers.

"Ouch!" she says, laughing.

"I'm so sorry!" he says, clearly mortified.

"It's fine." She smiles. What a friendly man he is. "It's just, I wasn't expecting that."

"I'm Italian," he says, by way of explanation, which makes no sense to Emma whatsoever. "My family is known for its handshakes."

"Really?" She peers at him.

"No. I'll work on it. Do you want to think about the house and let me know when you've made a decision?"

"That sounds great," she says, wishing she could remember his name.

"Dominic," he says, as if reading her mind.

"Dominic," she says confidently, as if she had remembered all the time. "Thank you so much. I'll be in touch."

"I can't believe you didn't invite me!" Sophie walks back into the kitchen, having put her soon-to-be two-year-old down for a nap. "I would have loved to see it. Which house is it again?"

"The grey one with the overgrown garden?" says Emma, scooping up a handful of Goldfish crackers from the bowl Sophie's son, Jackson, hadn't touched. "On Compo. About four in. Maybe six. I don't know. Close to the end of the road."

"But it was awful?"

"It wasn't *awful*. It's just that it wasn't great. But I've looked at everything online, and if I want something great it's going to cost me at least twice as much. It seems ridiculous to pay so much money on rent, especially since I don't know what I'm going to be doing or where I'm going to land. I'd much rather be frugal, or at least moderately frugal, and rent something I can turn into my own." She sighs. "If he doesn't let me change the inside I'll just do it and say I'm sorry afterwards. At least we've established that he's definitely fine with me putting a garden in. And I could put a gorgeous garden in."

"That won't help you much in winter."

"No, but it will give me something to look forward to. And can we not talk about winter yet? It's June, for heaven's sake. The last thing I want to think about is snow."

Sophie shakes her head. "I can't believe you're actually going to be moving out here!" She grins suddenly. "This is the most exciting thing that's ever happened to me."

"Apart from marrying Rob and having Jackson, you mean?"

"Well, yes. Apart from that. But it will be just like old times when we worked together. We can hang out every day. Imagine if we could get Hilary Trader to come and live here, too. God, we'd have fun. We're going to have fun anyway, even if it's just you and me. Do you need a second opinion about the house? Because I'm really happy to go see it if you need me to."

"Oh, you're sweet," says Emma, blanching in horror at the thought of her friend, in her immaculate, brand-new, pseudo-modern farmhouse, every wall horizontally planked with perfect high-gloss white wood, her kitchen a panorama of white marble and grey cabinets, every chandelier hanging from the ten-foot ceilings a perfect cluster of crystal globes dripping from polished nickel fixtures, walking into the grimy little cottage by the beach.

"You would hate it," Emma says. "You would think it the most disgusting house you have ever seen."

Sophie looks offended. "Why would you say that? Just because I live in a new house doesn't mean I can't appreciate older homes."

"Darling, this house isn't just old, it's dead. I have huge plans for it if I decide to take it, and I'm not even sure about that. But I honestly don't think, even you, with your glorious taste, would be able to see through the brown flowery wallpaper and threadbare salmon carpet."

Sophie wrinkles her pretty little nose. "That sounds gross."

Emma laughs. "It is. But all that can be changed. I'm going to see a couple more rentals later this afternoon and, hopefully, by the end of the day, I will have made a decision."

CHAPTER
TWO

Her phone rings just as Emma has put the last box down in the living room of her new home. She sighs looking at the screen, ready to divert it to voicemail. But she can't actually divert it, for her mother knows that if she gets voicemail after fewer than about seven rings, it is because Emma is choosing not to answer the phone. She silences the ringer instead.

The last person Emma wants to talk to is her mother. The last person Emma *ever* wants to talk to is her mother. But it's been a while, and better to get it out of the way, do her good deed for the day.

She thinks about Sophie, whose mother, Teddy (short for Theodora), lives in Westport and is as close to Sophie as a sister. Sophie always says she doesn't need a lot of friends, although she does in fact have tons of friends, most of whom she has known her entire life. She says this because her mother is her best friend, and Emma always smiles and says how lucky she is, not understanding how such a thing is possible.

The thought of *her* mother, Georgina Montague (born Georgia but changed to Georgina shortly after realizing her newly embarked relationship with Simon

Montague was serious), being her best friend is nothing short of hilarious.

Emma has never felt particularly comfortable around her mother. In fact, she finds herself shrinking into corners to allow her mother to take centre stage. She has always been aware that with her quieter personality and her occasional need for solitude, she is a source of both bewilderment and irritation to her mother. Her mother wants to be closer, too, she knows, wishing for the kind of daughter who goes shopping with her, accompanies her to fund-raisers, and provides her with the grandchildren she so desperately wants.

In many ways, moving across the Atlantic was the best thing for Emma and her mother. They don't have much in common, and their different personalities often result in Georgina unwittingly belittling Emma. Her barbs seem to be couched in tremendous good humour, or so it appears, unless you are paying the closest of attention.

Their relationship was better while Emma was with Rufus. Emma's parents adored Rufus, naturally, and still haven't quite got over the fact that Emma broke up the relationship. Rufus married the next little blond thing to come along, eight months after he and Emma broke up. Emma was stunned when her parents were invited to the wedding.

She presumed they wouldn't go, but they did, declaring it a high old time, with excellent grub and a darling bride who couldn't wait to start making babies with good old Rufus, who seemed over the moon.

Emma did what she always did when her parents unknowingly offended or upset her. She said goodbye as if nothing was wrong, then took a break from them. In the past, those breaks had sometimes lasted for six months or more. But they didn't notice. Her mother left numerous messages, not seeming to realize that anything was wrong, or perhaps hoping that if she pretended nothing was wrong it might entice her daughter back.

The hurt would heal — it always did — and Emma would eventually get back in touch, and there would be no mention of her going AWOL for six months, or however long it had taken to nurse her wounded feelings. Her mother cheerfully blundered through life, never noticing the bombs she threw around her (for Emma was not the only one to find her overbearing and insensitive), cheerfully carrying on as if life was peachy.

"Hi, Mum."

"Hello, darling!" booms her mother's voice over the phone. "Just checking in with you. Isn't the big moving day coming up? Daddy and I were wondering if you needed help. It's a bit busy over here with all the summer festivals coming up, and you know how Daddy likes to enter his vegetables in the village fete, but we could absolutely jump on a plane if you need us. It's very hard moving on your own, though I know you've done it before, darling. But you were in your twenties then, and I don't want you to put your back out. Plus I'm terribly good at organizing, as you know, and I'm worried that you have no one to help you."

21

In the room filled with nothing but boxes, Emma shakes her head. Her mother will take any opportunity to point out her single status. It used to upset her, but she has learned to let the comments wash over her head.

"It's fine, Mum," says Emma, knowing how much her mother hates being called Mum, infinitely preferring what she sees as the far more palatable "Mummy".

"I changed the date of the move, so I'm already in my new place, actually," she says, looking around the room defeatedly at the number of boxes. It's not as if she were downsizing. She had lived relatively anonymously in her flat in Battery Park, a small one-bedroom that she had always thought of as pleasantly minimalist.

She'd had no idea that her books would take up so many boxes. Nor her artwork, now stacked in three piles against the wall. Where did all this stuff come from?

Dominic had had the dreadful salmon carpet professionally cleaned, and had regrouted the bathroom. The new bright-white grouting did little to help the avocado-green tiles, but at least Emma thought she could bear to step into the shower.

After looking at other far more lovely, but pricier options in neighbouring towns, her only choice if she wanted to stay both solvent and by the beach was this one. She had phoned Dominic the next day to confirm. He sounded delighted, that unusual sincerity in his voice again — but on the other hand, who wouldn't be delighted with one quiet tenant with lots of books and no dogs? Two weeks later, she was preparing to head out, having given up her sparkling New York City apartment for . . . this.

"Darling! You should have said! How is the new place? Is it gorgeous? Do you love it?"

Emma suppresses a snort. "Not exactly. I think the best way to describe it is that it has a tremendous amount of potential."

"That sounds like a perfect project for you," says Georgina. "What can we send you for a housewarming present? What about a lovely teapot? Or a set of bowls? Actually, I have those lovely green bowls from Grandmère" — when had Grandma become "Grandmère", Emma thinks wryly — "which would be perfect for a young, well . . . youngish girl on her own. Why don't I send those?"

Emma instantly pictures the bowls, a faded green milk glass, possibly pretty once, now scratched and stained after years of use.

"It's okay, Mum," she says. "I don't need a housewarming present. At least, not yet. Let me get settled, then I'll let you know what I need."

CHAPTER
THREE

A dull thud on the front door makes Emma jump. She can't imagine who could possibly be visiting her. She puts down a stack of books, eyeing the door nervously. "Hello?" she calls, as her hand hovers over the door handle.

"Hey," she hears from outside. "It's Dominic DiFranco. I wondered if you needed some help."

Opening the door, Emma is simultaneously grateful and slightly nervous. Is it normal for the landlord to show up whenever he feels like it? She looks over his shoulder but there is no car in her driveway.

"Where do you live?" she asks. "Did you walk over here?"

"It seemed silly to drive," says Dominic, gesturing to a large red pickup truck in the driveway next door. "Given that I live next door."

"You do? Why didn't you say anything?"

"What if it had freaked you out?" he says.

"What if it's freaking me out now?"

"Is it?"

"A little." Emma frowns. This is something he should have mentioned. Surely this is relevant. She knows nothing about him, she realizes, thinking how unbalanced that is.

"Don't let it. I inherited both of these houses from my grandparents when they died. They lived in this one, and rented out the one I now live in. I do the opposite. I live next door with my kid, Jesse. It helps to supplement my meagre income as bartender-slash-carpenter."

"You have a kid? Sweet. How old is he?"

"Six. He's the coolest. You'll meet him soon. I'm surprised he hasn't poked his nose in already to meet the new neighbour."

"Thank you for the warning! I'll look out for him. So you're a bartender? That's cool. Where do you work?"

"The Fat Hen?" He looks at her, expecting a reaction.

She stares at him, not sure what she is supposed to say. "Great."

"You don't know it?"

Emma starts to laugh. "How would I know it? I've been living in town for, oh" — she looks at her watch — "approximately four hours and thirty-six minutes."

"We've been on Guy Fieri's show." His chest puffs up proudly. "*Diners, Drive-Ins and Dives*?"

His pride is endearing. Emma smiles as she watches him, certain now that whoever said all men are little boys at heart was right. "Should I have seen it?"

He gasps. "Yes! Yes, you should have seen it! It's the greatest show ever invented."

He's sweet, she realizes. A big kid. "I'm not a big television watcher," Emma admits reluctantly.

"How about the games?"

"What games?"

"Weekend sports. Baseball. Basketball. Come on. You've got to watch football, at least?"

"Nope." Emma shakes her head and laughs. "I'm so sorry, but not even football." She peers at him. "When you say football, do you actually mean American football? Or *real* football?"

"You mean soccer? Soccer is soccer and football is football. What's American football?"

The teasing is fun. She hasn't had a sparky, teasing conversation for a very long time, she realizes. Her old colleagues took themselves too seriously to engage in conversations like this. "American football? It's like rugby for wimps. With helmets and padding."

"Oh, ha ha," says Dominic, shaking his head. "I think maybe we should take the topic of sports off the table. You should come down to the Fat Hen, though. I'm working tonight. I'll get you a good seat at the bar and make sure you're looked after." He leans forward, lowering his voice conspiratorially. "First shot's on me."

"Shot!" Emma barks with laughter. "Good lord! Do I look like a shot girl to you?"

"Everyone looks like a shot girl to me. What's the point of drinking if you don't start off with a shot? Tell you what. I'll help haul boxes for you if you promise to come and have a drink at the Hen tonight. It's the perfect introduction to town. The real Westport. Not the prettied-up, perfect version."

Emma appraises him. Of course he doesn't like the prettied-up, perfect version of anything. How could he?

Everything about this man is real. *Integrity*, she finds herself thinking. *He has integrity.* "I suppose we'll find out tonight which I prefer," she says, challenging him gently on his preconception of her. "And thank you, I would love some help with the boxes. I've got far more books than I realized and I'm not sure where to put them."

Dominic looks around the living room. "You want me to build some shelves in here? I could make some beautiful built-in cabinets."

"Actually, I wouldn't mind some in there." She points to the family room. "I was thinking of having that as a little library-cum-office. Would you be able to build some shelves in there? I was just about to order some of those stepladder bookshelves, but having built-ins would be even better."

"Sure. All part of the service. No charge." He smiles at her. "I can run to Home Depot today and pick up the wood. I'll just have to take measurements."

"You would really do it? I was kind of joking. I didn't actually think you'd say yes."

Dominic frowns. "Why would you joke about that?"

"Because it would be unthinkably rude to actually ask for something so huge. Are you completely serious? Because I'd totally understand if you aren't." Part of her feels guilty. She barely knows him, and yet she trusts him. If he means it, she wants him to do it.

"I'm totally serious."

"Thank you," she says. "Truly. This is amazing." She is smiling widely, unable to quite believe his kindness. "Can I just ask one tiny thing?"

"What?"

"If you're going to build bookshelves, wouldn't it be better to remove the carpet first? You don't want shelves sitting on the carpet. If I pull it up while you're gone, we can re-cut it to fit around the shelves. That will give a much more professional finish."

Dominic looks at the carpet, thinking, before nodding. "Okay. Sure. You pull the carpet up and we can refit it when the shelves are done."

"Fantastic!" Emma's face is alight with pleasure that her plan to get rid of the hideous carpet has been put in motion so soon. "Let's get these boxes stacked up against the wall so at least we can get the rest of the furniture in."

CHAPTER
FOUR

"You're right, this is . . . fine for a temporary place to live," says Sophie, walking through the house and trying not to show how much she hates it. "I mean, I really can't see what it's going to look like with all the boxes everywhere. And . . . that terrible wood."

"I know. The wood. Isn't it awful? I'm dying to paint it all, but I need to move slowly. I've already got the landlord to agree to take the carpet up, which will then mysteriously disappear. 'Oh bugger! Those bloody rubbish disposal men took it by mistake. I only propped it up against the wall outside because there was no room for it inside. Oh, I'm so sorry. How about I replace it with some lovely fresh, new, clean sisal? My treat. To make up for my mistake.'"

Sophie laughs. "Poor landlord. He won't know what's hit him. So what's the story with him? Is he cute?"

Emma starts to laugh. "Absolutely not. First of all, have you not heard the expression about not doing your dirty business on your own doorstep?"

"Are you kidding? Where better? He could slip through the sliding doors at night and have his wicked way with you. So, is he cute?"

"Sophie, no. First of all, he's not my type at all"

"What's your type?"

"Not him."

"Methinks the lady doth protest too much."

"I promise you, Sophie. He's not for me. But he seems like a lovely guy and he did help me move all the boxes." Emma sits up as she hears the sound of a car. "In fact, here he is after his Home Depot run. So now you'll get to see for yourself."

Sophie joins Emma to look out the window, giving a low wolf whistle as Dominic climbs out of his truck and goes to the back, hauling planks of wood off the flatbed.

"Are you kidding?" she says. "He's ridiculously sexy."

"Not going to happen," says Emma. "We couldn't be more different."

"You don't have to marry him, but a summer fling would be an excellent idea. Whoa. Who is that?" A small boy, a miniature version of Dominic who looks to be about six years old but sports a Mohican, climbs out of the passenger seat and walks to the back of the truck to help.

"That," says Emma, "is his son. Jesse. Yet another reason not to get involved."

"What's the story there?" Sophie is intrigued. "Divorced?"

"I have no idea. Honestly, Sophie, I've just met him. I certainly don't want to start peppering the poor man with questions. He's my landlord, after all, and he lives next door. I don't want him to think I have any ulterior motives. I just want us to . . . be friends." She pauses. "I did say I'd go and have a drink at the Fat Hen with him tonight, though."

Sophie turns to her, open-mouthed. "Oh my God! Are you kidding? You're having a date with him already?"

"It's not a date. He's the bartender there. He's just trying to make me feel at home. He's not trying to get into my knickers."

"What?"

"It's an English expression. Never mind. Why don't you come with me?"

"And gate-crash your date? I don't think so! What are you wearing?"

"This!" Emma gestures down at her old clothes. "Oh, go on. Come. It will be much more fun if you're there."

"I guess Rob could put Jackson to bed. It will give me a chance to get the lowdown on Sexy Dominic and the small son."

Emma gives her a long, hard gaze. "I shouldn't have invited you, should I?"

"Too late now. How about I pick you up at seven?"

CHAPTER
FIVE

The Fat Hen parking lot, just off Riverside Avenue, is filled with pickup trucks, motorcycles, and the odd Audi and Range Rover. As Sophie parks the car, she explains to Emma that it is indeed a Westport institution, home to bikers from all over the state, as well as a popular spot for the brave hedge-fund manager who likes to experience the rough-and-ready of the real world from time to time. It's known for having the best burgers for miles, as well as live music three times a week, and karaoke on Mondays.

Neon signs adorn the walls, throwing glowing light into the otherwise dark space. A long bar runs along one wall, packed three deep, with a small restaurant area at the back. It is loud and raucous, filled with a mix of regulars and people stopping in to experience the famous joint.

And it is probably the last place on earth Emma would ever choose to go. Her world, at least the world she has most recently left in New York City, is filled with genteel cocktail bars. In her world, she orders French martinis, Prosecco cocktails with St Germain, Negroni Royales. She perches on bar stools surrounded by handsome, clean-cut men in sharp suits who eye her as soon as she walks in, considering whether to talk to her. This scene is about as far away from that world as you can get, and even though she willingly left all that behind, she's a little intimidated by what greets her here.

Emma grins as she pushes through the throng of people at the bar, trying to catch Dominic's eye to let him know she's arrived. Her blond, naturally curly hair is scooped up in a clip at the back of her head, with a few tendrils hanging loose. She's wearing an oversized white shirt and dark jeans, with flat espadrilles on her feet, only because she figured flip-flops probably weren't right for a night out, even to the Fat Hen. The only jewellery she wears is a large gold cuff on her right wrist, the last gift she gave to herself when she left the bank, and the last time she would spend serious money on something so utterly frivolous. She hasn't taken it off since.

Sophie is with her, rather more done up. Sophie has known about the Fat Hen all her life, but she hasn't ever been to the bar before, although Rob has. He warned her she was a little too dressed up, but Sophie ignored him. She dressed for herself, she'd told her husband, not for the bar she was going to, and so she had, wearing towering platforms, white jeans, a flowing shirt. With dangling earrings and blow-dried hair, she gets admiring glances from the men at the bar as she walks in, as tall and slim as a model, and so very much more glamorous than most of the women here.

Dominic is chatting with a group at the other end of the bar, and as he looks over, he notices Sophie first, then lights up as he sees Emma.

"Hey!" He comes over with a grin, clearly thrilled they are here, thrilled to show off his workplace. "You made it!"

"I did." Emma finds she has to shout. "This is my friend Sophie."

They shake hands as Dominic turns to a couple of guys sitting on stools. "Hey! Get a move on, and let these ladies sit down."

"No, no, it's fine," Emma starts to say, but the men immediately stand up and offer their stools. Smiling a grateful thanks, she and Sophie sit down as Dominic pours them a couple of shots and slides them over.

"*Salut*," he says, pouring himself one, too. The three of them down the shots in unison. "Welcome to the neighbourhood." He smiles, instantly refilling their glasses.

"Bugger," says Emma, as she lifts the glass to her mouth. "We're not going to be driving home after this, are we?"

"That, my darling," says Sophie, downing the second drink, "is what Uber is for."

Dominic, overhearing, snorts as he shakes his head. "You bankers," he says. "Uber!"

"I'm not a banker," Sophie says defensively, although she's smiling. "Any more. If I were, I wouldn't be here, would I?"

"Good point," says Dominic. "Another shot?"

"No!" Emma interjects. "No more shots. Let's have proper drinks. I'll have a vodka martini, straight up, with olives. Sophie?"

"Vodka and grapefruit juice."

"Coming right up, ladies."

Sophie leans towards Emma as Dominic turns to pour the drinks. "He is very cute," she says. "If I weren't married . . . "

"Thankfully you are, and thankfully, I am not you."

Sophie looks up as Dominic approaches. "So, Dominic. I saw your very cute son today. How old is he?"

Dominic's face breaks into a smile at the mention of his son. "He just turned six, and thank you. He is very cute, I agree. Jesse. Light of my life."

"Do you have a sitter?"

"I have a few. A friend's daughter often comes over when I'm working, then there's a high school student around the corner, and I have an old friend who fills in if I can't find anyone else. They're all great with him. He's the kind of kid who will go to anyone."

"Where's his mom? Is she in town?"

Emma tries to catch Sophie's eye to give her a warning look — this feels far too intrusive to ask someone she doesn't know — but Dominic is unfazed.

"His mom took off just after he was born. She didn't want a kid, but by the time she found out she was pregnant it was too late. She had him, then left when he was about four months old."

Sophie's mouth opens in shock. "Are you serious? She's not in touch with you at all?"

Dominic shrugs. "Nope. I tried. I used to email her pictures of Jesse and updates about what he was up to, but then the emails started bouncing back. We haven't heard from her in years."

Emma is disarmed by his candour about something so personal. Sophie, meanwhile, can't hide her shock. "So you're raising him all by yourself? Are your parents around? Do they help?"

"Nooo!" Dominic laughs. "I mean, they're around, but we don't see them too much. They're in Trumbull, but they're kind of busy doing their own thing."

"So you're, like, the perfect man?" Sophie, Emma realizes, is drunk. Not sloppy drunk, but uninhibited drunk, as she leans across the bar, smiling.

Dominic looks at Emma. "I like your friend," he says.

"This is what happens to her when she downs three drinks in as many minutes," says Emma, wondering how it is that she is managing to hold her drink so much better than Sophie.

"Is she married?"

"Very much so. With a very large and strong husband. The jealous kind. You know the type."

Dominic shakes his head and whistles. "I shouldn't have poured you guys all those shots, should I? Is he going to show up and punch me?"

"Only if you're very unlucky."

"Will you two stop talking about me as if I'm not here?" Sophie says. "Anyway. I am married and very happily, but Emma isn't. Emma is very definitely single, and isn't she gorgeous, Dominic? Don't you think she's pretty?" Sophie raises her eyebrows a few times, gesturing towards Emma with her head. "I just want you to know that if you were interested, you would have my blessing."

"That's very kind of you," says Dominic, laughing, as Emma turns a bright red and silently wishes the floor would miraculously open up and swallow her whole. "But I don't think it would be a good idea. Landlord, tenant, that whole thing. It can get messy. Also, I'm . . . seeing someone."

"Okay?" Emma rolls her eyes at her friend. "Can you just stop now?"

Sophie throws her hands up in the air. "Okay, okay! Forgive me for trying to do some good in the world. So. Who are you dating? Is she cute?"

Dominic just shakes his head and laughs, excusing himself as he goes to serve a group of women at the other end of the bar.

"He really is cute. And nice. Did you notice? He's really nice," Sophie says, turning to look at Emma and seeing that she is mortified. "I didn't mean to embarrass you. Sorry."

"I think maybe after we've finished these drinks it's time to go home."

"No way!" says Sophie. "This is the most fun I've had in years."

Emma makes it a habit not to get drunk, but this evening she's well on the way. At the very least, she has bypassed tipsy and moved firmly into that slightly more serious, happy stage of intoxication. She has a very large glass of water alongside her martini, which she is sipping regularly.

She doesn't like being drunk because she doesn't like being out of control. It has been such a long time since she's been in a situation like this that she's forgotten how much fun it is. She isn't plastered, not nearly as drunk as Sophie, but she is giggly and loose, and having fun with all the men in the bar — so many men! so friendly! — who are talking to them. She is having fun with the fact that Dominic is keeping an eye out for them and warning off any men he doesn't like the look of.

It's been a while since Emma had fun. It has definitely been a while since she has been anywhere where men have given her an appreciative glance.

For a while, when she first moved to New York, fresh out of her long-term relationship with Rufus, she dated non-stop. Everything was so exciting — the men! the bars! the way strangers would walk straight up to her in a restaurant and hand her their business card.

It didn't take long for her to realize how empty that was. Every man she dated inevitably ended up having a long list of other women he was taking out on the side. She had never heard of the word *exclusive* in terms of dating. Apparently, it was an American thing. Emma had always presumed that if, after around four or five dates, you liked each other and you ended up in bed together, you were "going out". Who would ever imagine that a person would be doing the same with someone else, or indeed, a number of someone elses? Well, everyone in New York, it seemed. Everyone but her.

It never felt like an even playing field. For every man Emma was interested in, there were at least three tall, skinny, leggy model-types who flung their Keratin'd hair around and smiled their perfect, white-toothed piranha smiles while elbowing Emma out of the way.

She couldn't compete with such high-maintenance gorgeousness, nor did she want to. At work, she put on her uniform — the designer uniform that all the female bankers were expected to wear: the Givenchy, the Dior, the Jimmy Choos, the Manolo Blahniks. She blow-dried her hair and expertly applied make-up every morning before leaving her apartment for work. But as soon as she got home she tore everything off and slipped into jeans and a T-shirt, scrubbing her face, pulling her hair back into a messy bun. On the weekends she let her curls burst free.

But every time she went out for dinner with one of the men she had met when she was done up for work, or at a client meeting, she knew she had to maintain the image or they would lose interest. After a while, she didn't want to pretend any more. After a while, it just seemed easier to *not* date. And even though all of her work colleagues thought she was crazy moving out to the suburbs as a single, childless woman — *Westport! But you're not married! You're never going to meet anyone in Westport! What are you going to do in Westport?* — she knew she stood a better chance of meeting a real person there, someone who wasn't obsessed with a perfect trophy girlfriend hanging off his arm. More than that, she realized that in the life she wanted to live, meeting a man just wasn't the most important thing.

There were other things that Emma wanted to accomplish, things other than a picture-perfect relationship that may have been hollow beneath all the flash and charm. A business of her own that fuelled her creativity. A peaceful life. She dreamed of sitting in her own garden surrounded by hydrangeas, sipping a glass of wine and breathing in the salty air; going for daily walks along the beach; renting a kayak and taking it out on the water. She wanted to be living her life, finding friends, and if someone happened to come along whom she found interesting, then great. She wasn't going to go looking for him.

She was perfectly happy building a new life by herself.

In fact, the last thing she needed was a man to complicate things. Although, with a couple of drinks under her belt, there was nothing wrong with the tiniest bit of flirting. Was there?

Later in the evening, a girl comes into the Hen and Emma sees every man in the bar appraise her as she sashays through the crowd with a very plain friend. She walks right through the crowd, stopping several stools down from where Emma and Sophie are sitting.

"Dom!" She leans over the bar, pulls Dominic in with a proprietorial hand around the back of his neck, and gives him a long kiss on the lips.

"Wow." Sophie leans towards Emma with a frown. "That's the girlfriend? How disappointing."

She is pretty, Emma thinks, pretty beneath all the makeup. Her hair is very blond, and very hairsprayed. Her eyelashes are false, her T-shirt tight and low-cut. She's sexy as hell.

"Why? She's a bombshell," says Emma.

"She looks like she just walked out of Ruby's Two."

"What the hell is Ruby's Two?"

"It's where the girls are."

Emma continues to look bemused.

"A strip club! It's where all our hedge-fund husbands go for their boys' nights out. And trust me, it's not exactly . . . not exactly sophisticated."

"Are you calling his girlfriend cheap?"

"Yes!" slurs Sophie delightedly. "That's exactly what I'm calling her. She's nothing compared to you. And without the make-up she's probably as rough as anything."

"You're mean when you're drunk." Emma sits back, looking at her friend in astonishment, narrowing her eyes to try to focus more clearly.

"I'm not mean. I'm just more honest. Seriously."

Before Emma can respond, Dominic comes over with the blond girl. "Ladies, I'd like you to meet Gina."

Sophie puts on her most gracious smile. "So nice to meet you," she says, as Emma admires her capacity to switch gears so quickly. "I'm Sophie."

"How do you do?" Emma extends a hand to Gina. "I'm Emma."

Gina's smile is polite, if not warm. "Which one of you is the tenant?"

"Me." Emma raises a hand. "I just moved in this morning."

"I guess we'll be seeing a lot of each other," she says eventually. "I stay over a lot next door."

"Great," says Emma. "You'll have to pop in for a cup of tea."

"Right," says Gina, who mumbles vaguely — something along the lines of how nice it is to have met her — then walks off to the other end of the bar.

"Not exactly warm and fuzzy." Sophie pretends to whisper this, but she is within earshot of Dominic.

"I'm sorry." He turns to face them. "She's a nice girl underneath, but not much of a woman's woman. It's just insecurity."

"Why is she insecure?" Emma is perplexed. "She's gorgeous."

Dominic shrugs. "Isn't it a female thing?"

They all turn to see Gina, at the other end of the bar, who smiles at them before beckoning Dominic over. It's clear he has no choice.

"Gotta go," he mutters.

"Wuss," mutters Sophie, as Emma just shakes her head and laughs. "You know why she just did that, right? Claimed her territory?" says Sophie, as Gina slides her arms around Dominic again, from the other side of the bar, and kisses him deeply. "She's threatened by you."

"Why on earth would she be threatened by me?"

"Because . . . I don't know. There's something. I think he might like you."

"Don't be ridiculous," says Emma. "Never have there been two people less compatible than my landlord and myself. Just because neither of us is married doesn't mean we're going to jump into bed together." She doesn't know why she feels the sudden need to

42

defend herself, to insist that there is no possibility of anything happening, when she is beginning to notice she feels happy whenever he is around.

"It might be fun."

"I'm not planning on finding out. Don't you think it's time we made a move to go home?"

CHAPTER
SIX

It takes a while for Emma to open her eyes. She isn't sure where she is at first. The room is brighter than she is used to, and it smells different. Her head is pounding. As she swims up to consciousness, she cracks open one eye to see the light flooding in through the French doors in the bedroom.

Ah. It comes back to her. She is in the rental house. There are boxes everywhere. The light is flooding in through the sheer white Ikea blinds on either side of the windows. She hadn't drawn them last night, not that it would have made a difference — they wouldn't keep out the brightness of this summer's day.

Last night. Oh God. The drinking. She makes her way to the bathroom, ripping open a box and digging through it until she finds a bottle of painkillers. Tipping two tablets into her hand, she leans over and puts her mouth to the tap, swallowing the pills with a mouthful of lukewarm water before walking back to bed and sinking into the covers with a moan.

Emma doesn't remember the last time she had a hangover. However bad she is feeling, though, Sophie must surely be feeling worse. Sophie didn't drink any water, and Sophie was hammered. Emma pats the bedcovers for her phone, and, squinting at the screen, she taps out a text.

You alive?

The dots appear, before one word. **No.**

Emma grins and puts the phone down, closing her eyes to wait for the painkillers to take effect, trying to remember what happened last night. Dominic had been sweet and solicitous, looking after them at the bar, pouring them drinks on the house far longer than he should have. His girlfriend, Gina. Bitchy. Probably not who she would see him with only because he seems so nice, and she seemed . . . insecure and rude.

Nothing terrible happened, she is sure. And it was fun, even though it's not something she wants to do on a regular basis. Someone asked for her number; she can't remember who. She only remembers giving it to him, with one digit off.

An hour later, having dozed off again, Emma wakes, this time feeling guilty. There is so much to do today, so many boxes to unpack, so much organizing. She pads into the kitchen to dig out a jar of instant coffee from one of the boxes. (She hates instant coffee but always has some on hand in case of emergencies.) As she hauls the boxes from the high pile in the corner, there is a knock on the door. She's not as alarmed as she was the first time this happened, but she still can't help but wonder who could be knocking on the door.

"Hello?" Emma calls from the kitchen.

"It's Dominic," comes the voice. "I've come to start working on the shelves."

45

Emma catches sight of herself in the door of the microwave. She's in men's boxer shorts and an oversized T-shirt, with her hair a tangled, frizzy mess. Shit. She doesn't particularly want to be seen like this, but she is stuck. She runs to the bedroom, grabs an elastic band off the bedside table and scrapes her hair back into a bun, then goes to the door, opening it a crack and peeking her head through.

"I'm not even dressed," she says. "Can you give me five minutes? I had no idea you'd be here so early."

"It's eleven o'clock," says Dominic. "Bit too much drinking last night?"

She blushes, but laughs. "Thanks to you constantly refilling, yes."

"Here." He hands her a cup of coffee through the door. "I thought you might need this."

"Good God! Are you the greatest landlord ever?"

"I aim to please," he says.

"Thank you. This is amazing. Can I just put some clothes on? Give me five minutes. Is that okay?"

"See you in five minutes."

Emma runs to the bathroom and looks at her face in the mirror. Her eyes are puffy, her skin greyish. She washes her face and splashes it several times with icy cold water, pinching her cheeks to bring some colour back into them. Her make-up bag sits on the dresser; she looks at it, but no. It would be ridiculous to put make-up on. Maybe just the tiniest bit of concealer to hide the shadows under her eyes.

Her clothes are still packed, but she finds a clean T-shirt and denim shorts. A roll of deodorant — the shower will have to wait — a spritz of perfume, and a shake-out of her hair before gathering it back again, and she is, if not her best self, at least presentable.

Not that it should matter in the slightest, she tells herself. But she wants to redeem herself after last night.

She's soon back to open the door again. But when she does so, she's greeted by a surprise.

"Hello."

There is a small person next to Dominic, holding a toolbox. Emma crouches down to look him in the eye. She isn't very used to small people. Most of the women she worked with in New York were single, and those who were married tended to keep their families and work lives separate. Emma hasn't spent very much time with children at all. She sees Sophie's son, Jackson, from time to time but he is so young, and her time with him sporadic.

It's not that she doesn't like children, it's that she never feels entirely comfortable around them. She wonders whether it's better to talk to them the way she hears other adults talk to them — in a singsong voice, like a child herself — or to talk to them as if they are adults themselves.

Because she is never sure who to be or how to act, she is convinced this awkwardness makes her someone whom children will dislike. She once read that it is good to crouch down to look children in the eye so they see you as being on their same level. Hence her crouching now.

"I'm Emma," she says, holding out her hand to shake his. "You must be Jesse."

Jesse doesn't say anything, but he takes her hand, even though he doesn't look her in the eye. Emma wishes she had something fun to tempt him out of his shell. A dog! A cat! Any kind of small animal. But she has nothing other than herself to offer. "I like your haircut," she says lamely. "Is it a Mohican?"

Jesse looks at her then. "Mohawk. It's called a Mohawk," he says gravely, as if he were the teacher and she the student.

Emma nods. "In England, where I come from, I think we used to call them Mohicans, but Mohawk it is." She's aware that she is babbling and worries that she's sounding stupid, so she stands up, gesturing them both inside. "I guess you're going to help your dad?" she says eventually, as Jesse nods and marches past her, lugging the toolbox with him and setting it down in the little room that will be a library, before opening it and extracting a tape measure.

Emma leaves them to it. They are measuring, and sawing, and sanding. It all seems very professional. Every now and then she hears Dominic talking to his son, as if he were a colleague and not his child. He asks Jesse's opinion, and waits to hear what he has to say, appearing to seriously consider everything the child offers.

"Should I put this shelf here or here?" she hears.

"Put it higher so she can fit big picture books on it, too," says Jesse.

"Great idea," says Dominic. "I bet she has a lot of picture books."

48

Emma experiences a slight pang when she hears this. She doesn't actually have many picture books, but she does have an awful lot of hardback novels, and more than a few coffee-table books. She is tempted to go in and check on their progress but doesn't want to interfere. Perhaps she should make them some fresh lemonade.

Emma busies herself in the kitchen, squeezing lemons, adding sugar, then unpacking her pots and pans, the pantry items, putting everything away. Halfway through one of the boxes, she finds her wireless speaker and sets up her playlist on her phone to play the sounds of summer.

Seconds later the voice of Jack Johnson fills the air. Emma sings along, moving through the tiny galley kitchen. For the first time in a long time, she feels the burdens of work, of banking, the stresses and pressures of the career treadmill, beginning to lift. As she continues to unpack, she swells with the thought that this is her life now. That she has a future filled with all kinds of possibilities. A wave of excitement builds deep inside.

Dominic comes out of the library and stands in the doorway. It takes Emma a little while to sense that she is being watched; she flushes a bright shade of red when she sees him.

"You look happy," he says.

"It must be this house. I think it's having a magical effect on me."

"It's living by the beach. It has a magical effect on everyone. It's why I would never leave. I think it's the light, but it feels different from anywhere else in town.

Living down here reminds me of growing up. Kids are out on bikes, free-range. Like time has stood still." He pauses. "Want to come see the shelves? We're almost done."

"Sure. I made you lemonade." Emma puts down the dish-cloth, picks up a pitcher and glasses, and follows him into the library. She takes a deep breath before looking at what he has built. The shelves are ever so slightly sloping to the right. Not all of them, but at least two. There are giant seams at the top, and although they will clearly do the job of holding books, they are hardly a thing of beauty.

"Fantastic," says Emma, mustering every dramatic skill she has ever possessed. "I can't believe you've done this in just a few hours. Wow! These are brilliant."

"I'm pretty good at making things," says Dominic, proudly.

"My dad can build anything," says Jesse, proudly.

"You are clearly a man of many talents," says Emma, as her brain furiously ticks, figuring out how she's going to fix the sloping shelves and seams.

"Want me to start loading the books on them?" says Dominic, good-naturedly. "I can put the carpet back, too, if you'd like."

"No, no, it's fine," says Emma quickly. "I'm going to paint the shelves and I haven't decided what colour, so I'll put the carpet back after I've painted. Thank you so much for this. It's amazing."

"No problem," says Dominic. "I'm going to run over to the deli and grab something to eat for Jesse and me. Can I get you something?"

50

"I'm fine," says Emma. Actually, she's starving but she doesn't want to ask anything more of Dominic. "But thank you. For everything. Maybe you guys can come over for dinner one night this week so I can thank you properly."

"That would be great," says Dominic, although Jesse narrows his eyes slightly and says nothing, Emma notices, realizing that Jesse may like her as a neighbour, but he may not feel the same way about a friend who might get in the way of his time with his father. "Speaking of dinner," Dominic continues, "I'm having some friends over on Wednesday for a barbecue. Good people. You should come. You can bring your friend Sophie if you'd like." With that, Dominic and Jesse gather up their tools and say goodbye.

Two hours later, Emma returns from the hardware shop with mouldings, moulding pins, filler, sanding blocks, primer, and paint. The boxes left to unpack will have to wait. The shelves are only a few millimetres off, but Emma knows it will be all she focuses on every time she looks at them. She can nail pins into the back and lift the shelves to straighten them; put the moulding onto the fronts of the shelves to disguise everything else. She will fill the gaps with caulk, prime them, and paint them a glossy pale greige. All subtly done, so they are perfect and it won't look like she went back to "fix" Dominic's hard work.

She will turn them into something beautiful. This is what she does. This is what she is good at. And there is nothing she loves more than a challenge.

51

CHAPTER
SEVEN

"I've made delicious cake," says the extremely well-groomed and flawlessly made-up woman who ushers Dominic inside, where a perfect lemon almond cake sits atop a white china plate stand. Cans of fizzy drink are stacked on the worktop, next to a silver ice bucket filled with ice, glasses, and whimsical napkins with an illustration of a glass of wine and text: *It's 5 o'clock somewhere!*

"And I have cookies and fruit for the kids. Hi, Jesse!" Lynn says, as she leans down and gives Jesse a high five. "Weldon's in the playroom, sweetie. You want a juice box or some cookies before you go?"

Jesse shakes his head before running up the stairs to the room above the garage that was once a spare room but has now been converted into a playroom, complete with a basketball hoop for a passion Weldon's dad very much hopes he will soon develop.

Dominic sits down on the stool at the worktop, looking around. "This house is beautiful," he says to Lynn, getting up quickly to examine the open shelving on one side of the kitchen. "I love these shelves."

"They aren't new!" Lynn says.

"I know, but I never noticed them. I just built shelves for a new tenant so I'm noticing shelves in a way I hadn't before."

"I didn't know you were handy."

"There are a lot of things you don't know about me," says Dominic.

"Really?" Lynn raises an eyebrow. "Want to tell me more?"

Dominic blushes. He had no intention of flirting with Lynn, the mother of Jesse's best friend since preschool. He knows Weldon's dad, even though he doesn't see him much, since Tom commutes into the city every day. Tom is more of a weekend dad, the kind who throws himself into coaching Little League and driving his kids everywhere at the weekend, because during the week he's lucky if he even gets to see them.

Dominic has lived in this town his entire life. He grew up going to school with the kids of policemen, garbage collectors, actors, and writers. He grew up in a time when everyone knew everyone else, when there were few class distinctions, when nobody cared how much money anyone had, or how big your house was. Very few families even lived in big houses back then. Now the McMansions in town have reached absurd proportions, much like the one he is sitting in now.

Dominic remembers the house that was here before. The Bennett house. He used to go to school with the Bennett kids. He got stoned, many times, in their unfinished basement, while the laundry tumbled around and around in the giant old machines on one side of the room.

That house is long gone. Lynn and Tom squeezed within the boundary lines a giant gabled manse that stretches out, almost meeting the edges of the plot. There is room for a small pool, with a high white fence to keep the neighbours out.

The floors of the giant house are a bleached driftwood grey, shiny chandeliers hanging wherever you look. Beautiful furniture has been tastefully arranged by a decorator, huge clamshells filled with tall white orchids, shelves dotted with the odd vase, a shagreen box, three artfully stacked coffee-table books. Everywhere there are vast gaps of empty space. Dominic has often wondered if there is a junk room somewhere, a small cosy space that houses all the *stuff*, a room that feels like part of a home. Because this isn't a home. This is a magazine spread. He often finds himself wondering how Lynn and Tom actually live in this space rather than tiptoeing around trying to keep everything perfect.

More and more frequently, Dominic finds himself around families like this. The husbands are gone most of the week, the wives rattling around in these giant, beautiful, soulless houses. He is aware that as one of the few fathers present, he is something of an . . . attraction? Distraction? He is aware — and it has taken him a very long time to fully realize this — that with his golden Italian-American complexion, his thick dark hair, his big brown eyes, and, okay, he'll go there, his butt (every girlfriend he has ever had has gone on and on about his butt), he's a welcome addition to the Mommy and Me groups.

If he hadn't gotten involved with the parents of other children, he would have gone out of his mind with boredom when Jesse was young. It wasn't that he didn't adore his son, but there were only so many days he could take him to the playground, or the bookshop, or the museum, or the maritime aquarium in Norwalk. The jellyfish were beautiful, but only for the first two hundred times. After that, even the seahorses got old.

Having a young, handsome, single man in regular attendance was the most exciting thing that had ever happened at the Mommy and Me groups. A couple of women were standoffish and rude, never looking at him, barely responding when he said hello. They were the worst kind of *new Westport*, he felt: horribly entitled snobs. Later, though, he discovered that both those women had huge crushes on him (not that they would ever have done anything about it) and couldn't bring themselves to even meet his eye lest they turn beetroot red.

Regardless, Dominic found he loved the groups. He loved how the women gossiped, how they knew everything about everyone in town and had no compunction about sharing what they knew "within these four walls only". The women would look at each other solemnly, crossing their hearts that they would never tell anyone. But Dominic knew they would spill the beans about everything they'd learned as soon as they left the driveway.

He loved that he got to see beyond their black Range Rovers and gigantic, multi-carat diamond studs, to realize their insecurities and their fears. He also got to see their kindness, and their humour, and their willingness to help anyone in their community. He got to learn who they were before they became power mommies.

It was only a matter of time before Dominic fell for one of them. They all made such a fuss — flirting, welcoming him with open arms, teasing him, loving seeing him blush. They loved that he fixed things, that he was "good with his hands". He'd walk into their houses for playdates and notice broken light fixtures, or shelves that needed putting up, or doors that didn't close properly, and he'd grab his toolbox from the truck and get to work. No charge, naturally, while the women simpered and smiled, thrilled at having a man around who knew what to do.

Amy was different. She didn't flirt, and didn't tease, although she did talk. They started organizing their own playdates outside of the Mommy and Me group, and after a few weeks she confessed her unhappiness. She was trapped in the wrong life, she said. She was desperately lonely, she said. She and her husband had nothing in common, other than their daughter, Sara. She was convinced her husband was having an affair with a young colleague in his office who Amy had just discovered was accompanying him on all his business trips.

Dominic tried to be a good friend, to listen and advise without getting too involved. Amy could talk to Dominic, she said, because he was a man and understood her feelings in a way her girlfriends couldn't. Then they stopped talking about Amy's problems, and started talking about themselves. They found themselves smiling every time they saw each other. Amy would open her front door, beaming, and Dominic would find that he couldn't stop beaming in return.

They were both high on the other's company, on what neither of them acknowledged out loud was an unspoken attraction. Acting on it, Dominic knew, was a terrible idea. It wasn't that he hadn't had affairs with married women in the past — he hadn't always been the thoughtful, considerate man he was today — but it would only lead to heartache for everyone involved. It wasn't as if Amy was his soulmate.

There were times, though, late at night, when he couldn't stop thinking about her, wondering whether perhaps she *was* the woman he was supposed to be with. He would tell himself that he only felt that because she was unavailable. He had always been drawn to the unavailable because it wasn't real, it posed no real threat, it could only ever be an exciting fantasy.

And then something did end up happening. It couldn't *not* have happened. It was only a matter of time, no matter what Dominic may have tried telling himself. They had dropped the kids off at a gym class and were waiting together in her car. They had done this many times before, but that day, neither of them could look at the other, and all Dominic could think about was touching her. The conversation had halted, and without thinking about it, without planning it, they were kissing, and it was electric, and amazing, and passionate, and life-changing.

Or it could have been, had Amy's husband not announced, two days later, that he was being transferred to Chicago and they were all moving. It was for the best, said Dominic, who was simultaneously devastated and relieved.

He had learned his lesson. However much he might flirt, however much some of these mothers might flirt back, he wasn't going to get emotionally involved again.

"So who's the new tenant?" says Lynn, cutting him a generous slice of cake, but none for herself. "I'm off the carbs," she announces, sliding the plate over to him. "You can clearly eat whatever you want, but it's Paleo all the way for me right now."

"You look great," says Dominic, because it's what he is supposed to say, although she does look great. Who wouldn't look great, he thinks, with daily workouts and hours of pampering?

"Really?" Lynn is delighted. "Okay." She leans forward conspiratorially. "I'm only telling you this because I trust you and I know you'll be honest with me. I haven't told anyone else, not even my husband, so you have to swear not to say anything."

This is why I love these playdates, thinks Dominic, delighting in being, once again, an honorary mom. "Swear," he says solemnly.

"Okay. I went to the dermatologist last week. I got the works."

"What does that mean, the works? Botox?"

"Oh, honey, Botox was just the beginning. I had Botox, Restylane, Sculptra, and Thermage. I had my lips reshaped and my crow's feet removed. Look!" She pouts and turns her head slightly to one side. "Cheekbones! I've never had cheekbones in my life!"

"You do look fantastic!" says Dominic, recognizing his place in these friendships — he's the handsome guy who makes these women feel good about themselves, brings a little bit of excitement into their lives without ever crossing the line. "If you weren't married I would — "

"You would!" Lynn bursts into peals of delighted laughter before squeezing his arm in a completely nonsexual but appreciative way. At least, that's what he hopes. "So tell me about the tenant. Is she young and hot?"

Dominic takes a bite of cake as he thinks about how to respond. The truth is, there is something about Emma that is enormously compelling, even though he would never think to describe her as young and hot. It's not that she isn't either of those things, but her qualities are understated. She is attractive, yes, in her mid-thirties, he guesses, and seemingly industrious and clever; a good person.

But finding someone attractive is not the same as being attracted to her. It was great that she came to the bar the other night, and she was cute and funny when she was slightly drunk, and that English accent of hers is adorable, but there's nothing more. He just likes her. She's someone he can see being the perfect tenant — reliable about paying the rent, pleasant to have around. But other than that, she's really not his type.

Gina, on the other hand? Gina is his type. Physically, at least. Italian American like him, she's fiery as hell, and smoking hot. She gives him shit all the time, but in a way that is completely familiar to him, and honestly, it might be the hottest sex he's ever had. Gina is up for it all the time, and there's nothing she won't say or do. She's definitely not the girl he's going to marry — she's never done anything beyond spending the night and is always gone before his son is awake — but for right now, he's having fun, making no promises. It seems to work for both of them.

"The tenant seems great," he says, pushing Gina, or rather Gina's mouth, out of his head. "I don't really know her. English. Quiet. Retired banker. I try not to get too close."

"That sounds like the perfect approach," says Lynn, who places her hand on his arm again and squeezes it just a second too long.

CHAPTER
EIGHT

Patience has never been a virtue of Emma's. She wants the house to look gorgeous, cosy, and welcoming, but immediately. She doesn't want to sit around waiting for primer to dry before she commits to more sanding, more coats of paint, and still more sanding after that. The prep never seems to end.

Finally, the shelves are done, and dry. There was so much paint left over that she carried on painting the orangey brown wood panelling on the walls. She is nervous about Dominic's reaction but can always strip it if he hates it. Would he hate it? How could he hate it? Look how much better it looks already! Look how this room has been transformed with just a coat of paint!

Her glass desk is perfect at the end, a small love seat in a slub linen pushed to one side, piled with printed cushions and a cashmere throw. White ceramic Chinese stools offer occasional seating, sitting atop the new sisal carpet that stretches to each corner. It is officially the cosiest, prettiest office ever, with an orchid sitting on the desk next to a bleached wooden lamp that cost next to nothing.

The rest of the cottage is still dark and dismal, but this room? This room! Emma pulled off the white slatted blinds, most of which were broken, and stapled a large piece of sheer canvas over the window. It is completely private and allows a soft light to filter through. And simple linen curtains hang on either side, hiding the staples and framing the window.

It is gorgeous, she thinks, every time she walks in. She sits on the sofa, looking around the room and admiring the transformation she has wrought in such a short space of time.

Even the vertical planking no longer bothers her. Now it is a glossy pale grey, and four large black-and-white prints of delicate flowers cover most of the wall.

She picks up her phone to check the time. Almost five. Dominic said his barbecue was kicking off at five — time for the quickest of showers and some clean clothes in order to meet his friends.

Reluctantly, she uncurls herself from the sofa and heads out of the one perfect room in the house, gingerly walking over the brown carpet in the hallway to make her way to the bathroom.

Emma has never enjoyed walking into parties alone where she doesn't know anyone. She has never been particularly good at small talk, although she manages to hold her own after years of working in the city and attending social events that would be good for business.

She had never liked those kinds of parties, or truthfully, any parties at all. She was much better on a one-on-one basis, or with small groups of people she knew well and felt comfortable with.

Much the same thing used to happen at each party she attended in her years of living in New York. It was either in some fabulous apartment in New York — a loft in the East Village, a classic eight-room apartment on the Upper East Side — or at someone's weekend house, whether a shingle house in Southampton or a renovated farm in Millbrook. The women would all be beautifully dressed (white linen shifts in the Hamptons; jeans, heels, and gauzy tops in both the city and the country), and would all shriek with excitement upon seeing each other, gabbing furiously as the husbands converged around the drinks, usually served from a permanent bar tucked into a small nook somewhere in the apartment or house.

The men would drink single malts and straight vodkas, while the women invariably chose some cute, pretty signature cocktail for the night. As the evening progressed the women would keep to their side of the space, and the men would keep to the other.

Occasionally the twain would meet, particularly if a sit-down dinner was involved, but even then, the men would shout to each other across the table, leaving Emma bewildered at their lack of manners. There'd been more dinners than she could count where she'd sat next to a man she hadn't met, and peppered him with questions about himself, only so she didn't have to sit in an uncomfortable silence. She was never obtrusive, but polite and gracious, only to have him break off mid-conversation to shout something to a friend sitting across the table.

Either that, or Emma would eventually run out of questions, and then, instead of asking her anything about herself or initiating any other subject of any kind, her dinner partner would just carry on eating in silence, leaving Emma chewing her chicken, or short ribs, wondering how early she could leave without causing offence.

Emma's mother may have been a nightmare, but she was a stickler for manners, for being gracious, and always — almost always — immaculately behaved. What would she have done in these situations, Emma used to think, imagining her mother turning to her father and saying, with a sniff, "NQOCD." *Not quite our class, dear.* It was quite as awful an expression as "not PLU," which her mother used frequently — *not people like us* — but, of course, Emma's mother never realized that these expressions were only ever used tongue-in-cheek, never seriously.

Emma thought back to one party in particular, in East Hampton. She'd been dating a man named Evan, the only man she knew at a party filled with the usual mix of braying bankers and their trophy wives, who showed off their worth with crocodile clutches and heavy gold men's watches dragging down their tiny wrists.

The dinner was interminable. She sat next to an imperious know-it-all, and afterwards, when they all retired to the vast conservatory, she almost sank with relief at the prospect of a quick escape.

After the meal, the men disappeared, apparently to the barn, which housed whatever it is men like to do late at night, leaving Emma in a room filled with women she didn't know, none of whom had spoken to her all night.

She excused herself politely, removed her heels, and slipped silently out the back door, walking back to the house they were staying in. She gratefully crawled into bed and was fast asleep by the time Evan joined her, hours later, so drunk that his snoring woke her and kept her awake for the rest of the night. She ended things as soon as they arrived back in New York.

As Emma approaches Dominic's cottage next door, she shakes her head to clear the memories. Parties are decidedly not her thing, but a barbecue in the garden at her landlord's house ... at least there will be no pressure to perform. At least the crowd won't consist of self-absorbed bankers and intimidatingly gorgeous and perfect women.

At least there is that.

She pushes open the gate that separates the two gardens, hearing the buzz of happy chatter and children's squeals. A group of people are standing around a trestle table covered in a red-and-white checked tablecloth, with bottles of wine and soda, and a big aluminium bucket filled with ice and cans of beer wedged underneath.

The table is covered with platters of crisps and dips, giant bowls of pretzels, and M&Ms mixed with popcorn. Children grab handfuls of the snacks when their parents aren't looking and run back and forth between them and a great big inflatable pool and slide at the bottom of the garden, not wanting to miss a second of the fun.

"Daddy! Daddy!" Jesse's at the top of the slide, yelling for his father. "We need more water! We need the hose!"

"Okay, buddy!" Emma sees Dominic put his beer down and grab the hose, pulling it back down to the slide. "Coming right up." He turns and sees Emma, and grins broadly.

"You made it! I'm so pleased. Help yourself to a drink — I'll just finish this off, then I'll come and introduce you to everyone. Hey, AJ?" A tall man at the other end of the garden looks up. "This is Emma, who I was telling you about. My tenant."

"Emma!" As AJ shouts her name, everyone turns to look at her, with smiles and waves. Emma walks over, shakes hands with people as she tries to remember everyone she's introduced to — AJ and Deb, Joey, Frank, Kevin, Tina, Johnny, Andrea and Victor — before someone hands her a cold beer and she takes a grateful swig.

"The English tenant," AJ says, a great big bear of a man with a huge smile behind his thick beard. "How's your landlord treating you?"

"So far, so good. But ask me again in another week."

"Dominic says you were a big-time banker. How do you like our slow life out in the suburbs? He says you're retired."

Emma laughs. "That makes me feel like a pensioner. I'm not retired; I couldn't afford to retire. But — well, I've retired from banking, I suppose. So far I'm loving it. No stress, no pressure, no working all hours of the day and night. I'm in heaven, although I can't do this forever. I'm just taking a short break before I decide what to do next."

"And how did you find Dominic?"

"Craigslist."

"Really? Now that's a great story."

"It is? There's no great story there. I just answered an ad for a rental house, and . . . voilà."

AJ shrugs and winks knowingly. "It's not a great story *yet*."

"What do you mean?" Emma feels a faint blush coming on, as he unselfconsciously teases her. "There's no romance. Anyway, he's dating someone."

AJ laughs good-naturedly. "Gina's not someone you *date*. She's someone you . . . do other stuff with. I'm sorry, I'm just teasing you. You're single, Dominic says, and you seem like a great girl. What's wrong with wanting my friend to be happy?"

Emma laughs. "That's very sweet, but it's a terrible idea. What if it all went horribly wrong and I had to move out? What if we ended up hating each other and then had to continue living next door, with me having to ask him to fix the tap every time it broke? Terrible idea. The worst."

"What if you ended up falling madly in love and discovered you were each other's soul mates?" AJ says, as a woman walks over and leans tenderly against his shoulder. Emma realizes she must be Deb, who was introduced to her along with AJ. Now Deb shakes her head with an exasperated smile at Emma.

"Is he teasing you? I'm sorry. It's what my husband does. It's like some bizarre initiation rite he has to go through with all the women Dominic's interested in."

"Oh. That's okay. Dominic's not interested in me. It's not what you think. I'm just the tenant."

"He's not? Are you sure?" Deb asked.

"Very sure." Emma laughs, excusing herself to go into the kitchen. How bizarre of his friends to be so preoccupied with the idea of her dating him. She felt she had to get away from the scrutiny. Perhaps she can help with the food.

"Can you baste the ribs?" says a woman, struggling to pull a lasagne out of the oven. "I'm Andrea. Andrea Leung. We met earlier?"

"Of course," says Emma. "Are you from around here?"

"We live in Massachusetts, actually, but we're here visiting friends. Penelope?" She turns suddenly, calling out to a sweet little girl sitting at the kitchen table. "Run outside and check on Grace and Victoria." She turns back to Emma. "Sorry. Just needed to check they're not getting into trouble."

"Of course. How do you know Dominic?" Emma asks, to be polite more than anything else.

"I don't. My husband, Victor, went to school with AJ, and we're staying with them, so he brought us. He seems lovely, though. You're lucky." She smiles, turning on her heel to take the food outside before Emma can close her mouth, which had dropped open in surprise at the comment, or have a chance to correct her. But she has to wonder what is going on. Why does everyone assume she has some kind of romantic connection with Dominic?

She turns back to the ribs, basting them with the sauce, ready to put them in the oven as Jesse runs into the kitchen, feet soaking wet from the slide. With a yelp and a loud cry, he goes skidding into the kitchen table, banging his head, collapsing in a small heap on the floor.

"Jesse!" Emma races over and feels his head. "Are you okay?"

Jesse is furiously trying to blink back tears as he nods. "I'm okay," he says in a small voice, trying very hard not to cry.

"Let me feel," says Emma, hoping he doesn't cry, because she has absolutely no idea what to do with a crying child. She runs her hand over the side of Jesse's head, where she can already feel a bump forming. "Oh dear," she says. "You've got a big one."

"A big what?"

"A big, ginormous volcano erupting out of your head."

"It hurts." He blinks back more tears.

"Can I rub it for you? Sometimes that helps. And we can put some ice on it, too. How does that sound?"

"Okay," he says, as Emma rubs his head just the way her mother used to rub hers. Leaving him for a second, she goes to the freezer and pulls out a bag of frozen corn that looks like it's been living in there for years. And just behind it, she spies a box of frozen Fudgsicle lollies.

"Okay." She goes back and drops down onto the floor next to Jesse, the bag of corn in one hand, a Fudgsicle in the other. "The corn's for your head, the Fudgsicle's for your mouth. You know chocolate is the very best thing for bumps and bruises, right?"

"No," says Jesse. But he reaches for the Fudgsicle as Emma holds the frozen corn to his head. Just then Dominic walks in, his face sinking when he sees his son's tear-stained face.

"Buddy! What happened?" he says, rushing over to pick Jesse up.

"I'm okay," says Jesse, who is more interested in sucking the Fudgsicle than in discussing his wound. "I skidded on the kitchen floor."

"Wet feet," explains Emma.

"Emma looked after me. I feel better now," he says, as Dominic winces when he feels the bump, before putting him down on the floor.

"No running with wet feet," says Dominic sternly. "What did I tell you?"

"Sorry, Dad. Can I go back to the slide?"

"Only if you walk."

"'Kay," says Jesse, Fudgsicle in his mouth, as he turns and runs out of the kitchen.

"No running!" shout Dominic and Emma together. Then they look at each other and laugh.

"Sorry," says Emma, who finds herself holding the bag of corn again. "I hope you weren't saving the corn for anything special. It's clearly vintage." She turns the bag over to look for a sell-by date. "Goodness, sell by the fourteenth of October, 2010. This could be worth

70

some serious money. Have you considered contacting *Antiques Roadshow?*"

"It's frozen," says Dominic, who is smiling through his embarrassment. "The sell-by dates don't matter in the freezer."

Emma wrinkles her nose with a laugh. "I think five years is pushing it."

"You thought I was going to *eat* it? Oh, you're funny. That corn is only there for bumps on the head. That's why I bought it."

"Of course you did. What else is in there, I wonder, that is purely for medicinal purposes?"

"This," says Dominic, pulling a bottle of vodka out of the freezer. "Want some? Go on. It's after five. Live a little."

"You're a horrible influence when it comes to alcohol," says Emma, although she doesn't protest as Dominic reaches for a couple of glasses and pours them each some vodka on ice.

"It's summer. We're at a party. We're not getting drunk; we're just having a drink. Here. Cheers," he says.

Emma realizes that she hasn't stopped smiling since Dominic walked into the room. "Cheers," she says back, then downs the vodka in one.

"We should totally get together for a girls' night out," says Deb, AJ's wife, later in the evening as they are sitting around, messily gnawing on ribs and coleslaw, reaching for the large pile of wet wipes in the middle of the table. "That would be so much fun. What do you

71

think? I'm still on the kids' vacation time, so I'm making the most of it before school starts."

"I'd love to," says Emma, thinking how much she actually would, how every single one of Dominic's friends has been welcoming and warm, without an ounce of competitiveness. Gina isn't here — she wonders why for a moment, and then dismisses the thought, happy simply to have spent time in such pleasant, relaxed company. These are the kinds of people Emma would never have met in her New York banking world, and she feels relieved again to be where she is now.

They are teachers, builders, personal trainers. The people, she thinks ironically, who work for the people she once worked with. They are real, fun to be with, and completely down-to-earth. A few weeks ago she wouldn't have fitted in, she thinks. Or they would not have accepted her, not in her short skirts and high heels. But sitting here today, wearing jeans and flip-flops, her hands sticky from the ribs, laughing as the afternoon turns to dusk, she is nothing other than the tenant, fitting right in.

AJ wanders over. "Dominic said he built shelves for you. How did he do?"

"They're fantastic," lies Emma. Although it is true, the shelves do look pretty fantastic now, after her ministrations.

"Really?" Both AJ and Deb look dubious. Deb lowers her voice. "He's a great guy but a master carpenter he's not. He built us a bench for our foyer and it collapsed the first time AJ sat on it."

72

"Hey." Dominic comes over. "I heard that. That's got nothing to do with the bench. That's AJ's beer gut." He reaches over in an attempt to pat it, but AJ wrestles him away.

"All I can say is don't give up the night job," says AJ with a guffaw.

"I built beautiful shelves for Emma, didn't I?" says Dominic, turning to Emma for confirmation.

"You did." Emma nods.

"Even if they fall down if you put anything on them?" AJ laughs.

"You don't believe me? Come and see. You don't mind, Emma, right?"

Crap, thinks Emma. *He doesn't know I've thrown the carpet out. He doesn't know I've painted his beloved orange wood-panelled walls. He doesn't know I've chucked the broken white slatted blinds. Why did I open my mouth?*

"Sure," says Emma, with some hesitation. "But the house is a bit of a mess. I don't know that today's a good time . . . "

"I don't care about that. Come on, I need to prove to these guys that I can build a decent set of shelves."

Emma closes her eyes for just a second. *Ask forgiveness*, she thinks. *Apologize once he's seen it, and hope to God he appreciates what it looks like now.*

Please do not let him be angry.

They walk across the garden, through the gate, Emma trying not to sink into a pool of guilt and misery. She thinks about whether to prepare him, about what she should say, but suddenly they are at the door, and

73

then inside the house, and then, all of them, standing in the doorway of the office.

"Oh my God!" says Deb. "This is *gorgeous*."

"Wow!" says AJ. He stands there silently for a moment. "I take it all back. Man, this room looks fantastic. Wow, Dominic. You did an awesome job."

"Thanks," says Dominic, his brow furrowing as he frowns at the room.

"I'm really sorry," Emma says to Dominic, under her breath. "I got a bit carried away with the paint. I was only going to do the shelves, but then I got some on the walls and I was only going to paint a section but it looked weird so I ended up doing the whole thing. I'm really sorry," she says again. She arranges her features into an expression of apology as she looks at him, but he doesn't look back at her. He's too busy looking around the room.

"What happened to the carpet?" he says, after a pause.

"Ah. The carpet. I put it outside while I was painting because there were so many boxes on the floor that I kept tripping over it, and the bin men took it. I mean, I presume they took it by mistake, because when I went to bring it back in the next day, it had disappeared."

"I love this rug!" says Deb. "Is this sisal? This is so fantastic."

"Where are the blinds?" asks Dominic.

Emma finally takes a stand. "I threw them away," she says firmly. "Dominic, most of those slats were snapped in half. They had to be chucked."

74

"They did," says AJ, looking at his old friend. "I came into this house before you rented it to Emma, and those blinds looked like crap. So did the carpet. In fact, the rest of the carpet *still* looks like crap. This room now looks like something out of a magazine. You should be paying her to do this. You'd probably get more rent if she did over the whole house."

Emma smiles her relief and gratitude at him.

"He's right," says Deb, turning to Emma. "You know, I'd love some help with our house. Is that something you would do? Would you be able to come over and advise me?"

Emma, beaming, says, "Sure, I'd love to," then sneaks a look at Dominic.

"Oh, come on, Dominic," she says. "You have to admit the room looks better. I am really sorry about the carpet. And the blinds. And especially about painting the wall. But look how bright it is now. Don't you think it's lovely?"

"I just didn't expect this," Dominic says eventually. "This house has been the same since my grandparents lived here. I liked that it was the same, because it reminded me of them and when they lived here."

"Dude." AJ shakes his head. "This house has looked like shit for years. I knew your grandparents, may they rest in peace, and back then this house looked fine. But now? I don't even know how you manage to rent this place, it's so dated. You should let Emma update the whole thing. She obviously has fantastic taste. She should do this professionally." Turning to Emma, he asks, "Have you considered it?"

"It's definitely something I'm thinking about," says Emma. "But it's early days. I need to get settled here first, but someday soon I might get serious about it."

"As a contractor I could introduce you to at least two people right now who need your help. You let me know if you want me to make the introductions, because you've really got talent."

Emma swells with pride. She has always loved turning a house into a home, creating a warm, elegant, cosy space, but the dream of turning that into a business has never been anything more than that — a dream. Dominic's upset is forgotten at the prospect of AJ finding first clients for Emma, and as they all walk back to Dominic's house, Deb chattering about how they could redo the kitchen and redecorate the family room, Emma thinks she should just tell AJ she'll meet whoever he wants her to meet. What is she waiting for?

Dominic's been quiet as they've all trooped back. They are about to go through the garden gate when he takes a deep breath and turns to her.

"You've done a beautiful job," he says. "I'm sorry I was a bit weird about it. I didn't expect you to have changed the house so much."

"Oh God, I'm sorry. It was really selfish of me. I didn't think you would be upset. I kept thinking you would be thrilled at how good it looked, but I never considered your emotional attachment to the house as it was, or the implications of all the changes I made. I didn't mean to do anything to upset you."

"You didn't," he says. "I was a little shocked at first, but honestly, you've done a beautiful job. I can't believe you did all of that by yourself. It looks incredible." Then he frowns. "What the hell did you do to the shelves? I swear they didn't look like that when I left the other day."

"Oh, just some mouldings I nailed on to make them look thicker. I think it's a more modern look."

"Well, they're great. I can't take any of the credit."

Emma smiles. "A little bit of the credit. You can definitely take a little of the credit. We make a good team."

He looks at her with a small smile, the tiniest hint of a raised eyebrow, not saying anything, just looking at her. Emma finds herself flushing pink, and looking away. That isn't what she meant, she thinks. She doesn't quite know what to say next. Saying anything else will only make it worse.

"Better get back," says Dominic, pushing the gate open and stepping aside to let Emma through. As she passes, he guides her by placing a hand, very gently, on the small of her back. As she feels his hand there, the strangest feeling comes over her, from the tips of her toes to the top of her head.

Safe, she finds herself thinking. *I have come home.*

CHAPTER
NINE

Emma wakes up early the next morning, crawls out of bed to make some coffee, then brings it back with her, slipping between the sheets again, revelling in the luxury of a lazy morning.

All those years she dashed out of bed, went running, on a literal or proverbial treadmill from the minute her feet hit the floor to the minute her head hit the pillow later that night. How she is loving the lack of stress, the fact that she has nowhere to be, no one to report to, nothing to do other than lie between these sheets and sip coffee, watching the sunlight filtering in through the sheer curtains: another beautiful day in paradise.

The phone buzzes on the bedside table next to her, and Emma reaches over to see who's calling. Her mother.

"Hello, darling," she hears through the phone. "I hope I'm not disturbing you. I know it's early, but you're always so busy."

"Not so much since moving out to the suburbs," says Emma. "It's fine. How are you?"

"Very excited, darling! Guess what?"

"You won the lottery?"

"Don't be silly, darling. No. But Cousin George is engaged."

"Oh, that's great. I didn't know he was seeing anyone, though." Emma barely remembers Cousin George. He's younger than she is by a good few years. She remembers him as a feminine and rather pretty boy. And almost certainly gay, she had thought, although, given her mother's news, clearly incorrectly. As a child she babysat and played with him on the rare occasions he and his parents visited them. He is a cousin of her father's, whose family is more aristocratic than her mother's. Hence her mother's involvement, for she distanced herself from her side of the family, embarrassed by their distinct middle-classness.

"He's been going out with the Honourable Henrietta Chapman," says Emma's mother, as Emma mentally rolls her eyes. No one but her mother would bother putting in the *Honourable* bit, but of course she has to repeat every title she comes across, as if doing so will somehow elevate her in the eyes of the world.

"That's nice," says Emma.

"It is nice," her mother replies. "It's wonderful, and I have offered to throw them the engagement party here at Brigham Hall."

Brigham Hall didn't use to have a name. It didn't use to be called anything other than home. But years ago, Emma's mother decided that every smart family lived in an old stately home with a name, and therefore their own old, not terribly stately home must have one, too. Weeks were spent trying out possibilities. Should it be a Manor? A Farm? A House? The name Brigham appeared to have been pulled out of thin air, although Emma's mother claimed it was from her own mother's side of the family. Brigham House sounded like an orphanage, they all decided. Brigham Farm was nice, except it wasn't really a farm, they just had a few acres and a couple of sheds, which didn't really count. Brigham Manor was very nice, too, thought Emma's mother, but her husband thought it too grand, too pretentious. So Brigham Hall it became, complete with personalized stationery and an embosser for the envelopes.

"Put it in your diary, darling, because you're expected to be there."

Emma resists a bark of indignant laughter. "Expected to be there? What does that mean?"

"It means that all the family are coming, and you haven't been home in over a year. Everyone's asking for you. Especially George."

Emma sputters with laughter. "Why on earth would George be asking for me? I haven't seen him in years."

"Exactly. That's the point. He very much wants you to meet the Honourable Henrietta. He still says you're his favourite cousin."

"I'm sure that's not true. He barely knows me. And Mum, you really don't have to call her 'the Honourable' every time you mention her. I'm not sure it's really the done thing." *Ouch.* Emma's mother has never taken criticism well, but better, thinks Emma, for her mother to hear it from her than from anyone else.

80

"I didn't . . . I mean, I know you don't actually use that term. I'm only saying it for you." Her mother stammers slightly, embarrassed at being caught out.

"Naturally," says Emma. "I don't know if I can make it, though. It's such a long way and it's not like George and I are close. What's the date?"

"September the fifth," says her mother. "Not too long. Write it down, and do your best. Darling, I know you have a busy life and I know it's far to come, but it would mean a lot to all of us. Especially me and your father. He misses you and he's not doing so well."

Emma's heart skips a beat. "What do you mean? Is he sick?"

"He has a touch of gout again, and you know what a bear he is when he's not feeling well. He'd love to see you, darling. Try to make it. I know you will."

Emma sighs. "I really don't know. Let's talk nearer the time. I'll do my best." She knows she won't, however, knows already that she will come up with an excuse, any excuse to avoid a great big family reunion.

"Didn't you get the invitation? I sent it last week. I'm surprised you haven't received it by now."

"I haven't been out to the mailbox in days," says Emma, realizing as she speaks that it's true. "It's probably in there. I'll go and check now."

"All right, darling," says her mother. "Let me know when your flight gets in and we'll send someone to pick you up."

Emma doesn't bother telling her mother that chances are she won't be coming. She merely says goodbye, putting it out of her mind.

It really has been days since Emma has checked the mail. This business of not working is great, but it's also disastrous for any kind of routine. It would be so easy to just while away the days drinking coffee in bed, renovating the house, and binge-watching TV series on Netflix, as she has been doing evening after evening, alone in her little house.

But a promise to her mother cannot be broken, she thinks to herself with a small smile. She'll just retrieve the invitation and then jump into the shower. She pushes open the door and trots over the lawn, still damp from the morning dew, to the mailbox. As she does so, the front door next door opens and Dominic walks out.

Shit. Emma is in her sleeping shorts and a baggy T-shirt, which is far too sheer to be worn without a bra, as she is wearing it now. And her hair! Oh God. She hasn't touched it since she woke up. Despite not having had the misfortune of seeing herself in the mirror, she's pretty certain it will look the way it always looks when she wakes up, before she has had a chance to shake it out or scrape it back: flat on one side, sticking up at the back and on top, tight curls at the nape of her neck where the night sweats have got her.

And, oh no — oh God, please, no! Last night, at Dominic's party, the drinks kept flowing, and while she hadn't drunk enough to be hungover now (thank God, because it could be so very much worse), it was bad enough that last night she fell into bed without washing off her make-up, which means there is undoubtedly mascara smudged halfway down her cheeks.

She's not supposed to see anyone. It's 7:32 in the morning, for God's sake. She's supposed to run to the mailbox, grab the irritatingly large stack of catalogues and handful of bills, and get back behind the safety of her front door without being spotted. Now Dominic is waving hello with a big smile, and — oh God! No! He's walking over. Emma grabs the mail and clutches it to her chest to hide the fact that her T-shirt is nearly transparent just as she realizes that she hasn't shaved her legs for days.

She slides a hand through her hair, attempting to shake it out slightly as she smiles a hello, backing slowly towards the house, hoping she can get away with the smile and nothing more.

"Hey!"

Nope. Dominic is almost upon her, and no hole in the ground is opening up to swallow her, so she is just going to have to brazen it out. Maybe she will get lucky; maybe he wears contact lenses and will have forgotten to put them in. Maybe a miracle will happen.

Why, she thinks, for a fleeting second, does she even care?

She watches him curiously, half expecting him to recoil with horror at what she looks like, but his smile is as natural and open as it always is.

"You're up so early," he says, as Emma takes a step backwards, realizing — and how could this possibly be any worse than it already is — that she hasn't yet brushed her teeth. So not only did she not remove her make-up last night, she didn't brush her teeth either. Her breath is so stale she can taste it.

"Early riser," she says, attempting to speak without letting any breath out of her mouth, so her words sound vaguely strangled.

"Wasn't that a fun party last night? My friends thought you were great."

"Thank you." Emma shoots a desperate look at her front door, so near, and yet so far. "I thought they were great. You're up early, too."

"Yeah. Jesse's sitter cancelled and I have a doctor's appointment at nine. I've been phoning around the sitters to find someone."

"Did you?"

"Not yet."

"I can look after him," Emma finds herself saying, without meaning to. "I mean, I'm right next door. It's totally fine. You can send him over whenever you want."

Dominic's face lights up. "Really? You wouldn't mind? That would be awesome."

"It's no problem. What does he like to do?"

"Jesse's the easiest kid in the world. He'll do anything. You can stick him in front of the television and he'll be happy. Or on the computer — he'll gladly play Minecraft for days on end."

"Can I take him out? I mean, if I have any errands or anything, would he come?"

"That would be great. Let me put the car seat in your car just in case. Wow. Thank you, Emma. This is saving my life."

"It's nothing. The least I can do. Just bring him over whenever you're ready. I'm going to get dressed, okay?" she says, finally making it to the safety of her house.

Only once she has successfully escaped her front lawn does she remember that she's not exactly a natural when it comes to small children. She loves teenagers, with their strong opinions and sense of moral outrage, loves children when they are old enough to have an adult conversation. But a six-year-old? Why did she offer to babysit a little boy she barely knows, when she has no idea how to talk to children his age? What on earth could she possibly have been thinking, other than how to get away as quickly as possible?

But Dominic had brought his son over and left. Jesse, now that he is here, seems entirely comfortable. He walked in, went straight to the sofa, where he sat down with his iPad mini, and has barely said a word for the past hour.

Emma has made herself busy with what she is calling work, although it's hardly that compared to what she is used to. She has Pic Stitched together a photograph of her office/library, the before and after shots, and is posting them online. She has put them on a local Facebook page and the classified sections of local websites, along with copy that offers inexpensive interior design services.

She wishes she had more photographs, more rooms that she had designed. While Jesse is busy playing online games, Emma examines the cabinets in the kitchen, standing in the doorway for a while, looking around. She has a moment of feeling guilty for not engaging with Jesse more, trying to talk to him or find something they could do together. But looking at his complete absorption in whatever is on the screen of his iPad, she decides he is fine, probably happier to be ignored by her. She turns back to the kitchen cabinets. She could easily spray-paint them white after taking the doors off, giving the room an open-shelf look. She could add the leftover moulding from the library onto these shelves to thicken them up, make them look more substantial.

It's a pity there are no splashbacks on the kitchen worktop. The Formica surfaces are among the ugliest things she has ever seen. She goes back into the library, stopping for a second to admire her work — such a pretty room! — before sitting at her computer to search for some kind of plastic worktop sheeting. There must be something. Some kind of sticky-back plastic or contact paper that will mask those worktops.

She finds something online, rolls of sticky plastic printed to look like marble — contact paper. It isn't expensive, and she buys two rolls, recognizing the nervous thrill she always gets from buying something online — it is likely to be either disastrous or the greatest thing she has ever seen. But it's cheap, so she'll find out which it is in about three days.

The blank wall facing the window needs something. Open wooden shelves like the ones she re-pinned on Pinterest the other day. Maybe a small butcher block island underneath, but narrow, enough to provide another work surface and some storage but not crowd the room.

She pulls her tape measure out from a drawer and makes measurements, noting them down in her phone. She's so inspired, she hates having to sit still. She turns back towards the boy on the couch.

"Jesse?" She has to ask three times before he looks up, so absorbed is he in his iPad. "Do you want to come to Home Depot with me?"

"Sure," he says, jumping up, eyes still glued to the screen. "That's my dad's favourite shop."

"Great. We could go somewhere else, too. Maybe grab some ice cream?"

Jesse's eyes are big. "Before lunch?"

"If you don't tell, I won't tell"

"Deal!" he says, high-fiving her as they walk out the door.

Emma runs through a number of beginner conversations as she steers the car up Compo and onto the Post Road. She could ask Jesse about school, what grade he's in, what his favourite subjects are, but she instinctively knows how boring that would be. She remembers a friend who had a routine with little kids. He would ask them what job they had and whether they were married, whether they had any children, and they would invariably burst out laughing.

Emma thinks about what would happen if she asked Jesse if he's married, cringing in horror at how ridiculous she would sound. She can already picture his sideways glance of disdain.

She turns on the radio instead, scrolling through until she finds 95.9 The Fox, grateful for Steely Dan, amazed that Jesse starts singing along right away. He knows all the words, more than her, even, and she starts to laugh.

"How do you know this?"

"This is what my dad and I listen to all the time."

"Steely Dan?"

"All the old music. Neil Young. Lynyrd Skynyrd. The Allman Brothers."

"You're a pretty cool little kid." Emma laughs. She feels amazed at how relaxed and open he seems with her after their silent morning together. "You know that, right?"

"Yup," nods Jesse. "I know. Hey, did you ever go to the Humane Society?"

"What's the Humane Society?"

"It's where you go to rescue animals."

"I haven't. I don't have any animals. Which is a shame. I'd kind of love something to keep me company, but I'm not sure I could handle a dog."

"I love animals," Jesse says, staring at her with great seriousness and intensity. "I wanted a cat for my birthday, but Dad is worried it will get run over. I don't know why. Our neighbours have three cats and they've lived here for ages and they're fine, and they live outside and inside, too."

"So he won't allow you a cat?"

Jesse shakes his head with such a solemn look on his face that a ridiculous idea blooms in Emma's head. Surprised, she shakes herself, trying to dispel it. Of course Emma shouldn't get a cat. For starters, she has no idea if animals are even allowed in her lease. Although, surely, given that she is babysitting Jesse today, her friendship with Dominic has reached a level where she could persuade him to say yes, even if the lease said no.

Now that she realizes she's talking herself into it, she stops to wonder why the prospect of a cat suddenly seems appealing. She'd never considered having an animal before. Is it for her, or is it to try to endear herself to Jesse? And why would she want to be doing that, anyway?

Because he's a kid, she thinks. *And he's my neighbour. Because he's sweet, and doesn't have a mother, and wants a cat. And if I got one, we could share it.*

She doesn't stop to be shocked by her own thoughts. Instead, she finds herself saying, "Shall we go and have a look?" After a pregnant pause, she adds, "Just to see."

Jesse nods, grinning widely. By the look on his face, she can tell the two of them are now in this potentially naughty outing together.

When they arrive at the shelter, Emma is really planning to just look. She thinks they can get away with wandering the corridors gazing at the animals, maybe playing with one or two, but leaving empty-handed a few minutes later.

She didn't expect the shelter to have kittens, much less a tiny tabby female who is the last one left. She didn't expect the kitten to curl up in her hands, nudging Emma's chin over and over as her whole body shakes with purring. Then Jesse sits cross-legged on the floor, the cat crawling all over him, up his shirt, as he heaves with giggles and nuzzles the tiny creature.

"If we got her," Emma says, "not that we're going to, but if we did, what would be a good name for a kitten like this?"

"I would call her Hobbes," says Jesse.

"Hobbs like the clothing shop?" Emma thinks about her mainstay in London.

Jesse frowns. "No. Like the comic *Calvin and Hobbes*. The tiger. She's kind of like a tiny brown tiger."

She laughs. "I like it." And then, not quite believing the words that came out of her mouth — what has happened to the good girl, with all those years of banking in her past? — she says, "Should we?" Even as she speaks, she realizes that it isn't really a "we" question. This cat would be hers. But she can't help acknowledging she'd be willing and happy to share her with Jesse for as long as she lives next door to him.

"For real?" His eyes grow big.

"Do you think your dad would go nuts if I brought home a kitten?"

"No!" he breathes, his eyes still large. "We had a lady live there two years ago who had two cats, and the last person had a big dog. He would be fine! For real, though? We can get this kitten?"

"Hobbes. Yes. We'll have to get a litter tray at Home Depot, and a cat flap." Then she feels the moment fill her with a warm glow. "I haven't had a cat since I was a child. This is actually very exciting!" she says, as Hobbes crawls on top of her foot and looks up at her with a plaintive mew.

90

"Gosh, you are gorgeous, Hobbes," she says, scooping the kitten up and burying her nose in her soft fur. Then she turns to Jesse. "Let's do it!" she says. "But let's leave her here while we go to the shop to get everything we need, and we'll pick her up on the way home."

In the end, what shocks her most isn't her impetuous decision, but rather that she finds herself standing in the aisle of the shelter with a small child hugging her legs, his eyes closed and a huge smile on his face.

Before long, she and Jesse are in the car, post Home Depot, the back filled with shelves, brackets, long thin boxes of thin veneer tongue-and-groove wood planks for the kitchen floor, cat litter tray and litter, cat flap and kitten food, and one cardboard box punctured with lines of round holes, from which Hobbes squeaks all the way home.

Dominic's truck is in the driveway when they pull in next door.

"Uh-oh," says Emma, with a wave of regret. She was trying to do something nice for Jesse, as well as for herself, but she really should have checked with him beforehand — he is her landlord, after all. All of this only seems to be striking her now.

"Do you really think it's okay?" she asks Jesse.

"I think he'll be fine," Jesse says, in a worryingly mature manner for a six-year-old. "Anyway, once he sees Hobbes, he's going to fall in love. Like we did."

"Let's hope so," says Emma, as Dominic walks out the front door and comes over to the car with a big smile on his face.

"Hey, buddy!" He gives Jesse a high five as he looks at the packed car. "You look like you need some help unpacking your vehicle, ma'am," he says to Emma with mock formality. Then he frowns as Hobbes's unmistakable mewling comes from inside the box.

"I'm really sorry," says Emma, and she immediately starts babbling. "We're hoping you're going to be okay with this and I realize I should have checked with you first but — "

But Jesse stops her by bursting out with, "We got a kitten!" Before Dominic can react, before he has a chance even to speak, Jesse pulls open the box and grabs the tiny Hobbes and places her in his father's hands.

Dominic's face instantly softens. He looks down, startled, before burying his nose in the kitten's fur, just as Emma had. The kitten starts to purr like an engine, clearly making her own bid for Dominic's compliance.

Emma catches Jesse's eye. *Bold move,* she mouths approvingly.

Jesse shrugs, as if he can always be relied on to know the right thing to do when it comes to his father.

"Whose kitten is this?" says Dominic. "It's adorable, but I mean, I don't know . . . Jesse, we need to talk about this."

"It's not mine. It's Emma's. But she said she'd share it with me. And it's not an it, it's a her. Her name is Hobbes and she's really Emma's, but mine, too. And we bought a cat flap and Emma says I can come over anytime and play with the kitten, and please, Dad, say it's okay? Please? It's the only thing I've ever really, really wanted."

Dominic pauses. But not for as long as Emma might have expected. "Okay," he says, his eyes still lit up at the tiny kitten in his hands. "She's adorable. Hobbes. Sorry. Hobbes is adorable." He raises an eyebrow at Jesse, who nods in delight. "Hobbes as in *Calvin and Hobbes*?"

Jesse nods, and Dominic glances at Emma. "Figures," he says to her. "His favourite comic strip for years." Now he meets her gaze squarely. "I'm fine with you having a cat. I guess. I don't really have a choice, do I?"

Emma doesn't know what to say, but he doesn't look angry.

Then he surprises her by saying, "Do you want me to put the cat flap in for you?"

"That would be fantastic" She suddenly feels shy, touched by his easy acceptance of her impulsive cat-rescuing. "Thank you."

"You're welcome." His tone now is quiet, and more serious, too. "Thank you for looking after Jesse. Obviously the two of you had a good time."

"It was the best," says Jesse. "And we stopped for ice cream on — " His face falls and he turns towards the houses. "I mean, nothing. We didn't have ice cream. We drove by the ice cream place and said maybe we'd come back after lunch. Right?" He turns to Emma with a warning glance.

"Absolutely," says Emma, who doesn't point out the chocolate drips all the way down his red T-shirt, drips that his father is looking at right now with wry amusement.

"So you didn't have any ice cream, huh?" Dominic says.

"Nope." Jesse shakes his head with great vigour. "I know I'm not allowed to eat ice cream until after lunch."

"So those brown stains on your T-shirt? Is that . . . " Dominic leans forward and examines them. "Coffee? Have you been drinking coffee?"

"I just let him have a tiny sip," says Emma. "I'm so sorry. He spilled my coffee all down his T-shirt. Right, Jesse?"

"I'm really sorry, Dad. It was hot and I spilled."

Dominic grins. "It's okay, buddy. Come on. Let's get Hobbes inside and get this cat flap installed. And it seems there may be some new shelves that need putting up?"

The rest of the day is punctuated by the intermittent sounds of the drill as Dominic installs the cat flap in the back door, before putting the shelves up in the kitchen, Emma handing him each drill bit or bracket as he needs it. Jesse spends his time playing with the kitten, rolling up strips of aluminium foil into balls and shrieking with delight as Hobbes bats them into the corners of the room, sliding across the floor as she skids towards them.

"If I'd known a kitten would make him forget about the iPad," Dominic says, whispering under his breath, "I would have gotten him one years ago."

Emma smiles as she unwraps hardware and hands it to him. "It's not about what happened," she says. "It's what happens next." She blushes slightly, realizing how this comment, one of her standard lines, could be misinterpreted.

"So what happens next in your life?" says Dominic, reaching up to position a shelf. His T-shirt rides up, exposing the tanned skin on his stomach and waist, and Emma, flushed with guilt for noticing, quickly looks away.

"What do you mean? Work? Well, I just posted some stuff today about helping people out with interior design. Hopefully that will lead to something."

Dominic glances at her with a grin. "I didn't mean work. How does a woman like you end up single? Who's the unlucky guy who let you get away?"

From anyone else, Emma would think it was a leading question, but from Dominic, who is so comfortable with who he is, it is entirely natural that he would say whatever is on his mind. "Do you say that to all your tenants?" Emma laughs. "Is that your way of flirting with me?"

"Only a little," says Dominic. "I can't help it. I'm Italian. It's my way of making friends. But seriously, you seem like you should be married with a couple of kids, baking chocolate chip cookies for the school bake sale."

"You know, I really think you should have quit while you were ahead," says Emma. "You went straight from saying I was cute to comparing me to a suburban housewife from the last century."

"Listen, some of these local housewives are hot. I'm telling you, I would never say anything derogatory about housewives."

"So it was a compliment?"

"Absolutely. But you are single, right? I assumed you were, only because there are no comings and goings here."

Emma sighs. "One of the downsides of having your landlord live next door."

"Maybe, but look at the upsides!" He gestures to the shelves.

"Granted. No, there are no men right now. There have been too many recent changes in my life for me to focus on relationships. I just need to settle into my new life before I'm ready for that stuff."

"When you are ready, you just let me know. I'll tell you all the places to go to meet the single men, which nights, and what to avoid."

"The Fat Hen?" She is joking, but she feels a slight pang. Suddenly she's not sure she wants Dominic to send her off to meet the single men.

"Nah. You don't want to meet men at the Hen. Not the kind of men you'd want to spend quality time with. I might be the bartender, but in all honesty I'd have to say that."

Emma pauses, not sure she should be asking, but she wants to know; now seems like the perfect time. "How about you? You're dating Gina?" She tries to make the question seem casual. Light. As if she doesn't much care.

"Dating." He seems to muse over the word. "I hadn't even really thought of it as dating. Gina isn't really someone you date. I guess you could just say we're hanging out together. We've known each other a long time. It's . . . fun."

"Sometimes the relationships that grow out of long friendships are the very best of all," says Emma.

Dominic laughs. "This is definitely not a relationship. I'm not even sure that it's fun a lot of the time. Gina is one tough woman, but . . . " He shrugs. "It is what it is."

"What does that mean?"

"It means it's fine for right now. Neither of us wants anything more serious."

"Men always say that. But I find invariably the women do want something more serious. A man always thinks that he's on the same page as the woman he's with, then wonders why she's so devastated when he says, 'Let's both go back to being friends.'"

Dominic is amused. "You sound like you have bitter experience."

"No," she says. "It's just that I think you're wrong about Gina. I think she's more interested in you than you think. She definitely seemed interested enough to be unfriendly to other women."

"You?"

"And Sophie."

"Don't take it personally. Gina doesn't like women. Especially if they're pretty. If you weighed four hundred pounds she would have loved you."

Emma laughs as her phone buzzes, a text from Sophie, which she excuses herself to read, realizing that it isn't just her phone buzzing, but her whole body. Is she imagining it, or is there real chemistry between them? She hadn't expected it, wasn't looking for it, but now that it is here, it seems to be making her feel more alive; at any rate, it is making her smile.

Rob's on a last-minute trip and my mom's babysitting Jackson. Want to go out tonight?

Emma reads the text and thinks to herself, *Yes.* She does need a night out. There are only so many nights binge-watching shows on Netflix that a girl can take. She needs to go out with a friend and have a couple of drinks and have some fun.

"Dominic? You know how you just said you'd tell me the fun places to go in town? I don't think I'm quite ready to go hunting for a man, but I am ready for a girls' night out, and you clearly know all the right places. If we wanted to have some fun, where would we go?"

"That was quick!" he says, before insisting she get her phone back out and make a list of all the places they should go.

CHAPTER
TEN

It is a gorgeous, balmy summer night. Emma asked Jesse to kitty-sit while she's out, and already she can hear him crooning at Hobbes to try to entice her from behind the sofa as Emma finishes getting ready.

She is wearing a white floaty dress that shows off her tan. Her hair is down, tumbling around her shoulders in beachy waves. Skinny gold hoops are in her ears, and a long beaded necklace with a tiny seed pearl tassel falls to her waist. She has sprayed a shimmery golden oil on her shoulders, her chest, and down her arms, and is glowing as she steps into the living room before leaving to pick up Sophie.

"Wow," says Dominic, seemingly stunned into silence as he looks at her approvingly. She didn't expect Dominic to be there. Jesse had wolfed down a grilled cheese sandwich in her kitchen before crawling across the living room to extract Hobbes from behind the sofa, never mentioning that his dad might be dropping in. She knew Dominic would come over after she left to watch Jesse but thought he'd wait until she was gone. She was aware of a vague disappointment that he wouldn't see her looking so pretty. She knows she looks pretty only because she feels pretty, prettier than she has felt in ages, and she registers a tiny thrill that he is seeing her looking her absolute best. Why she cares about what Dominic thinks is not something she is willing to think about just yet.

"I'm just bringing Jesse his juice box," says Dominic, sitting on her sofa and looking away, gesturing to the small box on the table before looking back at her with a slight shake of his head. "You look amazing."

"Thank you!" If Emma wasn't glowing before, she lights up at the compliment. She grabs a small straw clutch and slips her feet into strappy wedges. "Is this the right look for the place you recommended?"

"You're going to blow them away."

Emma smiles her way out of the house, into the car, over to Sophie's house, and all the way to Southport, the smile, the buzz, the glow never leaving her.

"Why are you so gorgeous and smiley?" asks Sophie when she gets in the car.

"I don't know," says Emma. "I'm just happy."

And she is.

"I don't get it," Sophie keeps saying, glancing over at her friend as they drive over to the bar. "Did you do something?"

"What do you mean, did I do something? Like what?"

"I don't know. Did you have a facial? Did you change . . . I don't know, something? You look ridiculously gorgeous tonight."

Emma snuggles further down in her seat, unable to wipe the smile from her face. "I think it's leading a stress-free life. Honestly. I feel like a different person since I moved out here and gave up my job. Sophie, I love living by the beach. There's something about the light there that is completely and utterly magical. I wake up every morning feeling happy and . . . I think that's it. It's just my new life." She's not ready to admit, even to her closest friend, that she is starting to realize there is something about her landlord that she can't quite shake off. It isn't an obvious attraction, but the more she sees him, the more he seems to be growing on her. His kindness, his comfort in his skin, his ease in the world. All of it makes Emma feel safe.

Sophie peers at her with disbelief. "Are you sure you're not in love or something? Is there anything you want to tell me?"

Emma frowns. "There isn't," she says, after a pause. "But there is. I know that doesn't make sense, but I think I might be feeling something for Dominic. I'm just not quite sure what it is."

Sophie's eyes widen. "What does that mean? You're attracted to him? Not that I'm surprised, but I didn't think you were interested. God knows you've spent enough time telling me you're not."

"I wasn't. I don't know what this is. I just feel . . . calm . . . when he's around. And I find myself smiling in anticipation at the thought of seeing him. I like seeing him. I'm starting to want to see him more and more. And I really don't know what any of this means."

Sophie leans back. "I knew it. The very fact that you kept saying he wasn't your type at all means he's your type. Of course he's your type. He's *everyone's* type. He's like, manliness personified."

"What's the matter with you?" says Emma, laughing. "*Manliness personified?* Have you been taking drugs? He's not manliness personified!" She cracks up. "He builds a terrible bookshelf, for your information. Although I do admit the kitchen shelves were slightly better, and the cat flap is really quite good."

"Cat flap?"

"Ah, yes," says Emma. "I knew there was something else I hadn't told you. Jesse and I got a cat today."

Sophie starts to laugh. "Jesse and I? Okay. That's it. You're already part of the family."

"I'm really not," says Emma. "I just babysat him today and we went to the Humane Society and ended up with a cat. I feel for this little kid. He's very grown-up for his age, you know — he's only six — and he clearly adores his father. I can't imagine what he's been through, being abandoned by his mother." Her face is serious, almost tearful as she thinks about Jesse, his closeness to his father, the incredibly close relationship they have.

"Did you find out any more about what happened?"

"Not yet. But I'm sure I will. I'm sure it's good for him to have a woman around who does nice things for him."

"Unlike that awful woman his dad's banging?"

"Sophie, don't be crass. But yes." She smiles. "Unlike that awful woman his dad's banging. Apparently, however, that relationship is not serious."

Sophie shoots her a sideways glance. "He told you that? Well, of course he did. How could it be serious when he has a beautiful, talented, single woman living next door who makes that girl look like an old tramp? He's totally falling for you."

"Okay, stop," says Emma. "Seriously. I love you but I'm not ready to predict the future. He's lovely, and I'm happy, and we need to sit back and just let this unfold the way it is supposed to." She gives her friend a hard stare. "*If* it is supposed to. Meanwhile, let's go and have some fun. What are we drinking?"

CHAPTER
ELEVEN

A large crowd of people fills the forecourt of the restaurant, beautiful people lounging on the rattan sofas dotted around the small square, the bar at one side five deep in men with dark tans, and women in floaty sundresses and high-heeled sandals. There is a buzz of laughter, excitement, and potential filling the air as Sophie and Emma thread their way through to get a drink.

This is awful, thinks Emma, catching the eye of an older man with an open shirt through which a copious amount of chest hair pokes out. He raises his glass in a toast, with what she can only interpret as a lascivious self-congratulatory smile. Everything about him seems sleazy. Emma looks away, rethinking the whole idea of a night out in what appears to be the worst kind of singles bar.

Emma has never done the singles scene. As someone who does not like crowds, and who is not actively looking for excitement, she cannot compete with the kind of women who now surround her. Emma is pretty, but she knows she is a *quiet* pretty; she is more girl-next-door than sex siren. As Sophie muscles her way to the bar, Emma steps back slightly and looks around. The laughter here is a little too loud, the men a little too tanned, the women a little too *done*. All cleavage, and legs, and teeth, and necks thrown back to expose golden clavicles. Blow-dried hair, glossy and long, curled at the ends to bounce on bare, brown shoulders; legs lean and muscled from hot yoga and Pilates, fingers heavy with cocktail rings glistening in the fading light.

Small globes twinkle overhead, strings of tiny fairy lights woven through white hydrangea trees in giant square planters. There is an air of possibility, as if anything could happen here. Indeed, as Emma backs away from the cluster at the bar, another man lays a hand on her arm as he moves past her. She looks up as he smiles and winks in a way that makes her want to run home, crawl under the covers, and never go out again.

"Isn't this fun?" says Sophie, eventually reappearing with two French martinis as they find the last available sofa and settle down. "I never go out to places like this any more. God, being married is boring. You're so lucky."

Emma looks at her as if she is entirely nuts. "You actually think this meat market is more appealing than curling up in bed with the man you love? Oh my God, Sophie, have you lost your marbles? Do you not smell the air of utter desperation?"

"Nope," Sophie says happily, looking around. "I think this is fun. Two men told me I was beautiful while I was waiting at the bar, and a third asked for my number. Honestly, I haven't had this much attention for years. I should come here more often."

"Which men?" demands Emma.

"Just some guys."

"Was one of them wearing an open-necked shirt with a mat of curly chest hair?"

Sophie pauses. "Maybe." She looks around with a frown. "Isn't everyone here wearing an open-necked shirt with a mat of curly chest hair?"

Emma bursts out laughing. "Come on, Soph, you have to admit this is pretty awful. You would have to be desperate to come here on a regular basis."

"I think it's great. If I weren't married this is totally where I'd come."

"You're only saying that because you *are* married, so it's fun. If you actually were single and this were about the only option available for you to meet some potential suitors, you'd kill yourself. The only decent men in this place have wedding rings on, and that's not good either. That guy over there" — she points to a tall, good-looking man in red trousers and a blue polo shirt — "the one all over the skinny blonde with the big boobs? He's got a wedding ring, and I'll bet you my pension she's most definitely not his wife."

"Don't be such a Debbie Downer. Come on, play the game. If you could have a date with anyone standing in this courtyard right now, who would you choose?" Sophie sips her drink as she challenges Emma, who looks around with a slight grimace.

"There really isn't anyone."

"I know, I know, because the cute landlord isn't here . . . " Emma shoots her a warning look. "Okay! Sorry! Of the available men in this courtyard right now, if you absolutely had to pick someone to go on a date with, who would you pick? And by the way, before you say chemistry isn't something you can predict and you don't go out with people based on what they look like blah blah blah, I already know all of that. But you have to pick someone. Just for the record, if I had to pick someone, I would choose the guy in the red pants and the blue shirt."

"Ew!" Emma shakes her head. "He is so full of himself. That's not my type at all."

"He's not full of himself. He's confident. He's probably a trader who lives in a great big gabled new house in Greens Farms with four small children and a wife who thinks he's in a business meeting right now. I didn't say I'd marry him, but he's my type. So who would you pick?"

"If I absolutely had to . . . " Emma looks around, her eyes finally landing on a man deep in conversation with a friend, short brown hair, slightly geeky glasses, no interest, it seems, in the women around him. "Him."

"Really? Him?"

"Yes. He looks interesting. And normal. He looks like an architect or a graphic designer."

"He does. And he actually looks like a nice guy. No wedding band, either. Just saying." Sophie takes a big swig of her martini, then stands up. "I'm just going to the bathroom."

Emma continues people-watching while Sophie is gone, wanting to feel a little less uncomfortable than she does. She tries not to catch anyone's eye, for even though she is single, she doesn't want to look single, doesn't want anyone here to think she's the sort of woman who comes to a place like this in the hope of meeting someone.

Sophie is gone for a long time. Emma gets out her phone and busies herself scrolling through her Facebook news feed, when suddenly Sophie is back, clearing her throat, and introducing her to the guy with the glasses Emma had pointed out, and Doug, his friend.

"I just started chatting with these guys," says Sophie, "and this is Jeff. He's a real estate agent. I told him that you were renting but were probably going to start looking to buy something in a few months, so I thought I should introduce you." Sophie makes big eyes at Emma as the men step forward and shake her hand.

"Here," says Sophie, pulling a chair forward. "Join us. Sit down."

When Sophie finally sits, Emma leans towards her and says, under her breath, "Girls' night?"

"Single friend needs sex?" says Sophie, equally quietly, as she smiles brightly, raising her voice to a normal level. "Emma? Jeff is divorced and lives very close to you at Compo Beach."

"Really?" says Emma, forcing a smile, for small talk was not something she had anticipated on her girls' night out. "What street?"

108

"Appletree Trail?" says Jeff, as Emma shakes her head.

"I don't know it. I'm sorry. I've only lived here for about five minutes."

"Where's your place?"

She explains as Jeff's face lights up. "Dominic's house? I love that house. Now *those* are two properties that are going to be worth some real money. I can't believe he hasn't sold them yet and cashed in. Every real estate developer in town wants those houses."

"Really? What's so special about them?" asks Emma.

"One's on a double lot. If you combine them, you can build a big house and a pool. That's pretty rare down by the beach, unless you're on one of the private roads. I've talked to Dominic about selling for years, but he won't do it."

"How do you know Dominic?"

"We were at school together. I've known him forever."

Emma is starting to feel more comfortable. The fact that he knows Dominic means he must be a good guy. "Do you know his son, Jesse?"

Jeff nods. "He and my nephew, Chad, are pretty friendly. They're in the same class at school." He smiles. "Big first-graders come September."

And Emma risks asking the question she hasn't been able to ask anyone else, not even Dominic. "Did you know Jesse's mother?"

Jeff laughs. "Oh yes. Everyone knows Jesse's mother. I've known her and Dominic for most of my life. We all grew up together. Stacy is . . . huge fun, but a party girl. Not the type who ever wanted to settle down. She's a holy handful."

"What does that mean?" Emma couldn't help asking.

"Stacy's a wild one. I don't know, I kind of thought she was crazy, but Dominic's always liked a bit of crazy."

Emma opens her eyes wide. "That doesn't sound good."

Jeff shrugs. "He is such a great guy. He would do anything for anyone, and we all love him, but he's always been a disaster with women. His parents were totally nuts. I remember going to his house as a kid and his parents would literally be screaming at each other. One time when I was there, his mom cracked his dad over the head with a frying pan and there was blood everywhere. The police were always going over there. Dominic grew up in crazy drama, and for years he's dated the kind of women who like crazy drama, and then he wonders why he gets hurt. Stacy was never really interested in him. I mean, she liked that she had him wrapped around her little finger, but there was no way she was the type to settle down. She was a huge partier, and — Oh, I shouldn't say this. This is gossip." He trails off.

"My lips are sealed," encourages Emma.

"She wasn't exactly the faithful type. Stacy was never faithful to anyone, and then she got pregnant, and she didn't find out until it was too late. So she had the baby, and boom! Took off. Dominic woke up one day because the baby was crying and he discovered that Stacy had literally run away in the middle of the night.

110

And that was it. I don't think he's ever heard from her again."

"Oh my God. That's really awful. But she must come home at some point, to visit or something? She doesn't know Jesse? What about her family? She must be in touch with some people, surely?"

"There are a couple of girls in town who know where she is, but they're loyal to her and won't say. Apparently she doesn't want to be found. I heard she moved to Alaska, but who the hell knows. So Dominic is raising that kid by himself."

"He's a great kid."

"He is. So, what brings you to Westport? What's your story?"

"I don't really have a story. I was working in banking, gave it up, and just moved out here for a quieter life."

"So you did what they all dream of doing and managed to get off the treadmill."

"I did."

"Boyfriend? Husband?"

"None of the above."

Jeff nods thoughtfully. "Hm. Interesting. So maybe you and I could go look at houses sometime? If you're actually interested in buying something."

"I'd love to," says Emma.

"And maybe we could grab dinner or something afterward?"

"Oh! That would be nice," says Emma. He is nice-looking, and perfectly pleasant, but there does not seem to be an ounce of chemistry between them. She thinks of Dominic. She likes Jeff. She very much likes that he's not a banker type. But she doesn't like him as much as Dominic. She doesn't trust him the way she trusts Dominic. She pushes thoughts of Dominic aside, bringing her focus back to Jeff. She had no idea she was about to be asked on a date, given how little they have talked. Perhaps she's wrong, perhaps it's not a date. The only thing they have established they have in common is Dominic, and that doesn't really count.

"What are you guys talking about?" says Sophie, who has been engrossed in conversation with Doug.

"We're planning house hunting and maybe dinner," says Jeff.

"Ooh, a date! So quickly! I like your style."

"Thank you," he says, before checking his watch. "Damn. We have a dinner. We have to go, unfortunately. It was so nice meeting you. Here." He roots around in his wallet, pulling out a business card. "Call me and we'll set up that date."

"Oh. Okay," says Emma, eyeing the card suspiciously. This isn't how it is supposed to happen, surely? Granted, it has been a while since she dated, but isn't he supposed to take her number? Or her email, at the very least? Isn't he supposed to be the one who gets in touch with her rather than the other way around?

As Jeff and Doug walk away, she fingers the card and turns to Sophie with a frown. "Call me old-fashioned, but isn't he supposed to take my number if it actually is a date? This feels like business. I think he only suggested dinner because he thinks he might get a house sale out of it."

Sophie shakes her head. "I don't know. I have no idea how dating works these days. Honestly, I think it's probably okay. You don't have to call him, though. I'd email him and leave the ball firmly in his court. You can just say it was nice to meet him. Was he nice? Are you interested?"

"I don't know," says Emma. "He was pretty forward, but all we talked about was Dominic. He knows him pretty well, and he filled me in on some of his history."

"Oooh. Gossip! Let me get us more martinis. Then I want to hear all about it."

The house is quiet. Jesse is on the sofa, fast asleep, a blanket over him, and Hobbes curled up in the crook of his neck. Emma pauses, smiling at the scene of domestic bliss, when she sees the glow of a candle in the garden.

Opening the sliding doors, she steps out to find Dominic, sitting in an Adirondack chair with a glass of what looks like it might be whiskey, earphones firmly in place, his eyes closed. He doesn't see her until she is right in front of him, and when he does, he opens his eyes and jumps.

"I'm so sorry!" Emma says, lowering herself into the chair next to him with a smile. "I didn't know you were sleeping. I didn't mean to give you a fright."

"I wasn't sleeping. I was listening to some music, and I didn't want to wake Jesse. Did you have fun?"

Emma frowns. "I'm not sure I'd call it fun. It's a bit of a 'scene'. Sophie loved it."

"You didn't?"

"I'm more of a quiet, glass-of-wine-in-a-corner kind of girl. We met someone who knows you, though. A real estate agent. Jeff Mulligan?"

Dominic smiles. "Yeah. Another townie. I've known him forever. Small world, huh?" He peers at Emma. "I think I know everyone in town. So, did he ask you out?"

Emma feels herself blush. "I'm not sure. He suggested dinner, but he didn't take my number."

"Did he give you his business card?"

"Yes!" She laughs. "So I don't quite know what he meant by dinner. I think he sees me as a prospective client."

"Jeff sees everyone as a prospective client. Which doesn't mean he won't also see you as a prospective something else. Although I'll admit I wouldn't have thought he's your type."

"No? What do you think my type is?" Emma leans forward to see him better. It's so dark, his features light up every now and then as the candle flickers in the breeze.

"I don't know," Dominic says slowly. "Why don't you tell me?" The candlelight glints in his eyes as he looks at her, as he leans towards her, never taking his eyes from her face. Emma's heart skips, then stops. They stare at each other, not speaking, the garden completely silent, as a cat yowls from the garden opposite, breaking the spell.

"I'd . . . better go inside," she says softly.

Dominic sits back, the moment gone, both of them wondering what has just happened; what might have happened had the cat not stolen that moment away.

114

Emma can't stop smiling. She locks the front door feeling as if she is walking on air. What did it mean? What *does* it mean? None of this should make sense; this is not the kind of man she thought she would fall for. Even that sentence sounds ridiculous. What kind of man *did* she think she would fall for? A banker? A hedge-fund manager? One of the tanned men at the bar tonight, buoyed by alcohol and their own narcissistic sense of self-importance? Jeff? She shudders.

Has she fallen for Dominic? Has *he* fallen for *her?* That moment, in the garden, when they stopped speaking, when they just stared at each other as Emma's heart skipped a beat before racing wildly. Wasn't that the moment he was supposed to kiss her? She could feel it, could sense it in the air, the intimacy, the chemistry, the excitement, but then, the cat. He had pulled away.

There was something there. She felt it. She is old enough and experienced enough to recognize chemistry, even in the most unexpected of places. She does like him. Every time she sees him, she feels happy. Sometimes when she's in the house, and she hears his truck pull in the driveway, without even realizing she is doing it, she starts to smile. She doesn't know when this started. She thinks of him guiding her through the garden gate the other night, his hand on the small of her back, the feeling of safety that came over her. She feels safe with him. He is the kind of man who would look after her. He is the kind of man who *is* looking after her. *Look at how he takes care of Jesse.* She is still smiling as she thinks of him building her shelves, helping her out in the kitchen, and just now, in the garden, almost . . . almost . . . kissing her.

Could she see herself with a man like Dominic? A few months ago she would have said no. Not because he wasn't a city boy, but because they come from such different worlds. She thinks of the world she comes from, the world she moved across the Atlantic to escape. The formality and pretentiousness of her aspirational mother, the expectations everyone held for her, expectations that led her into banking in the first place. And during those New York years, all the parties, the one-upmanship, how relieved she is to have escaped to a quieter life.

"Stop!" she says out loud, realizing how ridiculous it is to project into the future, to think about what kind of a life she might have with Dominic. This isn't what she does, what she has ever done. She has never been the sort of woman to dream about getting married. On girls' nights out, in her twenties, even when she was with Rufus and knew the path down which she was supposed to be travelling, she was never comfortable having the conversations the girls sometimes had: where they would get married, what kind of flowers they would have, what — oh, how many times did she listen to this one — the dress would be like.

Emma was never interested. She shakes her head now to dislodge her thoughts. Why is she even thinking about whether she could see herself and Dominic together? It's not like she's looking for a relationship with anyone. The fact that he makes her feel good is irrelevant, surely. She has bigger things to focus on — living purposefully and on her own terms, perhaps for the first time ever in her life.

Twenty minutes later she is brushing her teeth when she hears a car pulling up outside the house. Padding into the library, toothbrush still in her mouth, she leaves the lights off to peer through the window, knowing she can't be seen. Who could it be, so late at night?

A Jeep is in Dominic's driveway. Emma stands to one side and watches as the lights go off and the car door opens. And out steps Gina, who pauses for a minute to shake her hair out. Emma's heart sinks.

Of course. That was why he left. Gina was coming over. Emma got it completely wrong. He wasn't about to kiss her. That was all in her imagination. Why would he have kissed her when he has Gina?

Feeling stupid, and disproportionately sad over something so silly, Emma goes back into the bathroom to rinse her mouth, then crawls into bed. She tries to distract her sorrows with a few pages of the book on her bedside table. But it doesn't work. Eventually, finally, she falls asleep.

CHAPTER
TWELVE

The Jeep is gone by the time Emma wakes up, earlier than she normally would, only because Hobbes pads along her pillow, purring, curling herself up in the crook of Emma's neck, and licking her chin with a rough, raspy tongue.

Emma nuzzles Hobbes for a while, going over everything that happened the night before with Dominic. The talking, the sharing, the intimacy.

This morning she finds herself embarrassed. He has a girlfriend; she needs to push him out of her head, at least in any capacity other than helpful landlord.

I will be friendly and polite, but a little cool, she thinks. *I will ensure that he does not think his tenant is interested, that if I was a little flirty last night, or a little too revealing, it was just because I was a little drunk, not because I have a crush on him, or anything ridiculous like that.*

As she thinks this, she pictures him in his jeans and T-shirts, pictures his dimples when he smiles, the way he pushes his hair back when it falls into his eyes as he's working, and she finds that she is smiling to herself. Horrified, she wipes the smile off her face as she hears a noise.

118

"Hello?" She jumps out of bed and runs into the living room, to find Jesse standing in the middle of the room, still bleary-eyed with sleep.

"Jesse? How did you get in?" She is careful to lock all the doors every night, city girl that she is. She frowns, clearly remembering having locked both the front door and the back last night, after Dominic left.

Jesse grins. "Cat flap."

Emma can't help but smile. "Ah! The infamous cat flap!"

Jesse drops down to the floor and easily slips through the flap to the other side, popping up to wave at her through the glass of the window, before coming back through.

"Well, you're a boy of many talents, aren't you? Have you come to see Hobbes? You did a wonderful job of looking after her last night. She was so happy when I came home."

"Can I feed her?" says Jesse, spying Hobbes in the corridor and running over to get her, which sends her darting under the bed in fear.

"Yes. And be gentle. Move slowly so she doesn't think you want to play a game of chase, and she'll come to you. Have you had breakfast?"

Jesse shakes his head.

"How about I make pancakes?"

Jesse's face lights up, and Emma walks into the kitchen, makes a fresh pot of coffee, checks for eggs, flour, and milk, and gets to work.

At some point while she is spooning homemade pancake batter into the frying pan, Emma decides that she is not going to stress about making conversation with a six-year-old. In fact, she's not even going to try. She is going to let Jesse lead the way. If he doesn't speak, she will make herself busy doing something on the computer. Making conversation with a six-year-old, finding common ground, is altogether too anxiety-inducing for someone who doesn't consider herself good with children. With that decided, she slides a few of the finished pancakes onto a plate for Jesse, puts them on the table, and heads back into the kitchen to clean up.

"Where are yours?" says Jesse.

"I might eat some later," calls Emma, sponge already in hand.

"Oh." Jesse pauses. "But then they'll be cold."

"Good point," says Emma. She puts down the sponge, puts two more pancakes on a plate for herself, and sets it down opposite Jesse and sits.

"Is it okay for us to eat together?" she asks.

Jesse nods happily as Emma suppresses a smile.

"These are good," he says in surprise, taking a huge bite, talking as he chews.

"It's vanilla extract," confesses Emma. "It's the secret ingredient. Can you close your mouth when you chew because . . . *ew!* I can see all the food in there." Much to her surprise, Jesse instantly closes his mouth. "And I added a bit of sugar," she continues. "You're not supposed to, but frankly I think everything's better with a little sugar added to it. I'm a bit of a sugar addict, you know."

"I love sugar, too," says Jesse, his mouth again open and full. "You know what my favourite sandwiches are?"

"No. Can I guess?"

Jesse nods.

"Pesto chicken, Fontina cheese, and tomato?"

He makes a face.

"Chicken, dill, and mustard sauce? Roast beef and horseradish? Gravlax and dill?"

Jesse clearly has no idea what she is talking about, but Emma is having fun. She could go on all day, thinking up exotic sandwiches a six-year-old would never have heard of, let alone tasted.

"Sugar," he interrupts her, with a whisper and a devilish grin.

"What?" Emma feigns horror.

"I do it when my dad's sleeping."

"I know you expect me to be shocked," says Emma, "but that's what my mother had as a treat after the war. White bread, thick butter, and sugar."

"Butter?" Jesse is intrigued.

"Oh yes. She says it's all about the butter." Emma leans forward and drops her voice. "I could make one now, one with butter, one without. We could both sample them so we can decide which kind is better. What do you think?"

Jesse nods vigorously, as Emma pushes her chair back to go to the kitchen, grateful she had the foresight to buy a fresh loaf of bread yesterday. It isn't the processed sliced white bread that her mother loves, but it will have to do. She cuts four thin slices, removes their crusts, and slathers thick slabs of cold butter, straight from the fridge, on two of the slices.

She pulls the silver sugar shaker out of the cupboard, smiling as she always does when she uses it. It is a ridiculous thing for a single girl to own, she knows, the kind of old-fashioned object no one has any more, and certainly not someone with no husband or children. But her mother gave it to her, and it was a remnant of her childhood, and it always makes her think of her childhood home when she uses it. She gives each piece of bread a liberal sprinkling of sugar, then another, and then presses each pair of slices together to make two sandwiches, and cuts each in half again for her and Jesse to sample.

He has pushed the plate of pancakes away in anticipation of this forbidden treat. They each pick up a butterless sandwich and take one bite, staring into each other's eyes, Emma forcing herself not to grimace at the overwhelming sweetness.

"It's good," says Jesse, mouth filled with bread and sugar, as he grins.

"Next," says Emma, handing him the sandwich smeared with butter. Jesse takes a bite, then closes his eyes, a slow smile spreading on his face as Emma takes her own bite. She has heard her mother wax lyrical about sugar sandwiches since she was a tiny girl but has never before tried one herself.

"Oh, wow," Emma says, her tongue searching out the grains of sugar and thick creamy butter mixed in with the yeasty dough. "That is delicious."

122

"Mmmmmm!" says Jesse, wolfing down the rest of the sandwich. "Butter!"

"I never thought I'd like it, but that was amazing. I'm guessing you don't want the rest of your pancakes?"

"I do!" Jesse pulls the plate back and carries on with his official breakfast. "Do you think Hobbes would like sugar sandwiches?" he asks Emma.

"Only if they were coated in cat food," she says.

"What is cat food made of?" asks Jesse.

"I have absolutely no idea. It says turkey in gravy and beef, but who knows what else."

"Can I see if she likes pancakes?"

"Okay. But I don't think she will"

Jesse pulls off a tiny piece and puts it on the floor in front of Hobbes's nose. Hobbes sniffs it, then, to Jesse's delight, bats it across the room, running after it, trying to pull it out from under the chair with her paw.

There is a knock on the back door, startling Emma, who looks up to see Dominic's face in the glass.

Oh God. Again. At least she doesn't have mascara smudged under her eyes. Still, why does this man have to keep seeing her at her worst? *Why should it matter?* she reminds herself. *Friendly but cool tenant,* she thinks, beckoning him in.

Friendly but cool.

"What's going on here?" says Dominic, as relaxed and easy in his skin as he always is.

What was I expecting? wonders Emma. *Some kind of weird morning-after-the-night-before? Nothing happened. Look! He isn't behaving any differently, which means I don't have to get weird.* She takes a breath and tries to relax, even though it's hard to look at him, particularly given that smile, which causes a small flip in her stomach. She looks away.

"I'm just making breakfast for Jesse," she says, making big eyes at her young breakfast companion, trying vainly to telegraph that he hide the last of the sugar sandwiches.

"Is there enough for me? I'm starving." Dominic walks over and picks up Emma's sugar sandwich. "What is this? Egg?" Before anyone can say anything he pops the whole thing in his mouth.

"Oh my God, this is good! What the hell is this? It tastes like sugar!"

Jesse grins.

"It's a sugar sandwich. With butter," says Emma, reluctantly. "I'm so sorry. It's all my fault. It's my mother's favourite treat and I had to introduce it to Jesse. But I'll hypnotize him and make him forget he ever tasted it, I swear."

"Can you make me another one?" says Dominic, high-fiving Jesse, who whoops in delight, before reaching over and grabbing one of Jesse's pancakes. "I've got bacon in the fridge if we also need bacon," Dominic adds.

"Yes to the bacon." Emma's face is serious. She's both relieved Dominic isn't angry, and pleased at the suggestion of the three of them sharing breakfast. "Bacon is always needed. Go and get the bacon."

And before long they are all three sitting down at the table, to a feast of pancakes, more sugar sandwiches, and crispy bacon glazed with maple syrup (Dominic's idea). They sit, and laugh, and tell jokes, while Jesse gets Hobbes to try out everything to see what she likes (just the bacon).

Emma forgets that she saw Gina park her Jeep in Dominic's driveway late last night. She forgets that Dominic has a girlfriend, that she is supposed to be embarrassed to have given him any indication that she is interested in him. She forgets that she went to bed feeling lonely and sad. She is too busy having fun.

"You got something here," says Dominic, gesturing to his own lips as he looks at Emma.

Emma flushes a bright red, her hand flying to her mouth. "Did I get it?" she asks as she brushes her lips.

"No. Here." He reaches forward and brushes his fingers over the side of her bottom lip, and her breath catches as he looks in her eyes. "Got it," he says quietly, his smile fading. A second passes. Then Emma jumps up.

"I'm going to clear up," she says, and she can't look at him, knows that her face is bright red, that she is flushed from head to toe.

"I'm going to take Jesse to camp," says Dominic. "Come on, buddy. Let's go."

"No!" says Jesse. "I want to stay here and play with Hobbes."

"You've got to go to camp," Dominic says in his stern voice. He turns to Emma and adds, "And Emma has work to do, right?"

"I do," says Emma, the flush finally fading. "But, Jesse, I meant what I said. You can come over anytime.

125

Hobbes will be right here waiting for you when you get home from camp."

"Can I come over as soon as I get home?"

"Absolutely. The cat flap is now yours to use as you please."

"Look, Dad!" Jesse drops to the floor and scoots through the cat flap, waving delightedly from the other side.

"Oh God," groans Dominic. "I'm really sorry, Emma. I didn't think he'd be in and out of your house with the damn cat flap. I can tell him not to. I don't want him bothering you."

Emma finds herself slightly insulted by the suggestion that Jesse might be bothering her. "He's not bothering me," she says. "He's sweet. We had a lovely time before you arrived."

"Great. Thanks. How to make a guy feel wanted."

Emma laughs. "I didn't mean that! I just meant we were having fun — he's lovely."

"As long as *I'm* not unwanted, we're all good."

Don't blush, she thinks. *Don't blush, don't blush, don't blush.*

She knows he is watching her but she can't meet his eyes.

"We're all good," she says, not taking the bait. Not looking at him, willing herself to keep her cool.

"Okay. Jesse, let's go. See you later, Emma." And with a smile, he and Jesse are gone.

126

CHAPTER
THIRTEEN

Later that morning, when Emma's phone buzzes, she looks to see a number she doesn't recognize. She picks up to find a woman on the line who saw her ad on Craigslist offering interior design services.

They have recently moved to town, the woman says, and have purchased an older Colonial house on Marion Road. They don't have a big budget, and she has no idea how to decorate, no furniture, and really needs some help. She has been into a couple of local shops and spoken to the in-house decorators, but the furniture would be a fortune and she needs to keep the cost down.

She saw Emma's pictures on Craigslist and loved the style. She says it is exactly what she's looking for in their new house. Could Emma come and see it? Is there any chance she might be available that afternoon because she's itching to get started, and having an empty living room might be fun for the kids but she really, really wants to get some furniture in before Labor Day rolls around in early September, which isn't long, given that it's now mid-summer, and she's too scared to make those big decisions by herself.

Emma agrees to go over at two o'clock. Then she takes as many pictures as she can of her tiny galley kitchen, with its faux marble worktops and open wood shelving on rustic black brackets, before running out to the corner shop by the railway station to stock up on magazines. She hadn't expected to see a client so quickly and needs to cobble together some kind of portfolio, some indication of her style, and quickly.

She swings by Staples, picks up a ring-binder and plastic page covers, and spends a couple of hours clipping pages from magazines — *Coastal Living, Better Homes and Gardens, House & Garden, Elle Decor*. All are ruthlessly milled for examples of the style Emma loves. Before long, she loses herself completely in the task, letting go of her sense of time, of place, even of self, in a way that is almost magical. She certainly never felt this way working in the city.

This, she realizes, is what she does best. She can re-create any one of the rooms she sees on these pages for a fraction of the cost most designers would charge. She can walk into a shop like HomeGoods and bypass everything until she finds the one lamp, the one tray, the one mirror that is exactly, but *exactly* like the one in that gorgeous magazine spread, and the result will look just as good as a room created by a designer whose expertise costs a small fortune.

She can do this Fairfield County look — the white sofas, the turquoise accessories, the grey woods, the obligatory Buddhas everywhere you look — with her eyes closed. All she needs are the clients. If this woman

— Lisa is her name — works out, who knows where it might lead.

Thank you, God. Emma offers a silent prayer, grabbing her new ring-binder and a notebook in which to record all that Lisa is looking for. Taking a quick glance in the mirror, she pauses, noticing how different she looks from her banking days. For this meeting, she has gone for understated chic — dark jeans, ballet flats, a good linen shirt, and her ubiquitous chunky gold cuff. On her shoulder, a designer handbag — the one designer handbag — left over from her old life. She may not be interested in the labels any more, but it is good for potential clients to see that she is a woman who shares their good taste. She looks chic and understated. A little make-up and hair pulled back in an elegant chignon complete the look. *If I didn't know better,* she thinks, looking in the mirror, *I would say I was a seasoned interior designer. If I didn't know better, I would say I look like a woman who knows what she is doing.*

With that, she closes the door and sets off.

CHAPTER
FOURTEEN

The house is probably from the 1940s, Emma guesses, as she pulls up. Someone has added a curved portico over the front door, which adds character and charm, and there are pretty panelled window boxes on the first-floor windows, which would be lovely spilling over with lobelia and ivy, but are empty and forlorn.

The landscaping is tired. Half-naked yews, old enough to be huge, but mostly bare, apart from the top, flank the front doorsteps. Creeping fir, a weeping maple, various untended plants line the front of the house, and there is cracked tarmac on the driveway.

The house is pretty, or at least could be pretty, with a little bit of TLC, thinks Emma. She instantly imagines the quick fixes that could transform the front. Gravel the driveway, for starters. Pull out all the landscaping — those terrible old, bare yews — and replace it with something simple and clean. Boxwood balls perhaps, or a holly hedge.

Paint the front door a glossy grey; fill the window boxes; install large square iron planters on either side of the steps.

Lisa answers the doorbell as Emma looks around, making mental notes. She is Emma's age, with dark hair pulled back in a ponytail, a striped T-shirt and white jeans, bare feet, and a toddler on her hip.

"So nice to meet you!" She invites Emma in, handing the baby to a young au pair as they pass the living room, bare but for a brand-new huge sofa and dark wood coffee table, a couple of sad chairs pushed back against the wall. Beyond is the library, containing a glass desk and bookshelves, empty but for a few novels on one shelf.

"You do have some furniture," Emma comments, walking through the kitchen and noting the table and chairs — Restoration Hardware, she's sure — and the slipcovered sofa in the sunroom.

"Yes. But none of it makes this place feel like home," says Lisa. "I have no idea how to make a room the kind of place you want to spend time in. I thought getting the sofa and coffee table would make it inviting, but it still looks cold."

"At least you chose a great sofa and coffee table," says Emma, encouragingly. "There's so much we can do to dress it up. And the glass desk in the library is perfect — it's exactly what I would have chosen myself."

Lisa's face lights up. "Well, thank goodness I did something right. My husband's birthday is over Labor Day weekend, and I'm planning to throw him a party. It'll probably be outside in the yard, but I want everyone to see our house. We moved from the city a year ago and I'm totally embarrassed that the house still looks like this. I want it to be beautiful. And I have so little time to get it right before the party. Can we go see the rooms and I can tell you what I'm thinking?"

Emma follows Lisa into the living room and the library, then upstairs, hiding her nerves, hiding her fear that she will be found out as an amateur. Will Lisa be able to tell this is Emma's first job? But as she walks through the house, her confidence returns; she can see exactly what it needs to be transformed into a wonderful home: sisal rugs, sofas, a couple of chairs and side tables. Abstract paintings in coastal shades of blue and green, cushions, lamps, and trays. Window blinds. Emma could create gorgeous rooms here just by shopping for about three days, and there is no doubt in her mind that the result would be beautiful.

Lisa isn't asking Emma to spend hours in D & D Building gathering beautiful fabrics and wallpapers, putting them together on mood boards with sketches and photographs. She merely wants to give Emma a budget and send her off to local shops, where she will choose porcelain Buddhas, and crewel cushions, and mohair throws, and everything else she needs to create a finished, magazine-worthy house that Lisa can show off to her friends.

"You basically want me to shop for you," says Emma at one point, as they flick through the ring-binder she had put together, Lisa exclaiming over every single page.

"Yes!" says Lisa. "That's exactly what I want. I want you to send me pictures just to check that I like what you've chosen, although honestly, I don't even know what I like. That's the problem — I get so overwhelmed. I want to show you a picture of a living room and I want you to make mine look just like that, but within our budget."

"And that," says Emma delightedly, "is exactly what I can do. I've brought a file of designs. Why don't we look through and see if there are any rooms in there that you love? Or even parts of rooms that you love. Light fixtures or window blinds."

"Let's do it," says Lisa, opening the file again and sighing with pleasure at nearly every picture Emma has included.

"I love this," she says, over and over. "Oh my God, look at that fireplace!"

"We could do that pretty easily with your fireplace if you wanted," says Emma. "I have a handyman who could stucco over the brick and make it look like sandstone to give you that very modern, clean look. It wouldn't cost a lot and would give your living room a lovely contemporary feel."

"I love that idea!" Lisa turns to her. "Emma, you are the perfect person. I love every single room you've picked out in here."

Lisa's phone interrupts her with a buzz, and as she excuses herself to take the call, Emma stands up and wanders around, looking out the windows, thinking about where she might buy the furnishings she has in mind, if she is lucky enough to get the job.

Then Lisa comes back into the room. "I'm so sorry. That was my husband. He has a late meeting tonight." She rolls her eyes — clearly this is something that happens a lot. "We were supposed to be going to a farm dinner in Redding, but he has to cancel. I've got two tickets now to get rid of." She sighs. "You wouldn't be interested, would you? I'm never going to find anyone who can get a babysitter organized in time. It would be a shame to let the tickets go to waste."

"Really? Why don't you go with a friend?"

"To be honest, I'm kind of exhausted anyway," Lisa says. "I'd be much happier if I knew the tickets were being used."

"What exactly is a farm dinner? It sounds fascinating."

"Oh, it's a great concept. They do these a few times a year; each dinner features one of the hottest local chefs, and great wine, and they set up these long tables in the orchard. We went last year, not long after we moved here from the city, and it was amazing. The food was terrific, and we met some really nice people. I know we've only just met, but I'd love it if you took our place. Really. You should go."

"Are you absolutely sure?"

"Yes! Go. Just give them our names when you get there."

"Can I write you a cheque?"

"Don't worry about it. This is the beginning of what I hope will be a great working relationship. Send me a proposal with pricing so I can sit down with my husband and get back to you as soon as possible? Because seriously, I'm ready to get going on this, like, tomorrow."

"Done," Emma says with a laugh. "And thank you so much for the farm dinner tickets. I'll let you know how it goes."

Floating on air, Emma says goodbye and makes her way home.

"I can't come," says Sophie. "We're going out for dinner with a couple from my Mommy and Me group and we've already cancelled three times. I'd much rather go to a farm dinner with you, believe me, but I can't cancel on them again. I've spent the whole day praying she'll phone and say she's not feeling well or her husband's stuck in the office, but she just texted to say she can't wait to see us, and they've booked a table at the Whelk." Sophie sets down her mug of coffee and stretches out her legs as Jackson plays between her feet.

"Why are you going out for dinner with people you don't like?"

"I don't exactly not like them. I just don't think they're really our type. They've been pursuing us for months. Every time I see her, she says we have to get together with our husbands and go out for dinner, and I always smile and say, 'Yes! We must!' but I never follow up in the hope she'll just forget about it. Eventually I just had to bite the bullet and issue an invitation. Then I kept cancelling, thinking our plans would just fade away and she would forget about it, but she kept texting. Eventually I ran out of excuses, so we're just going to get it out of the way."

"So what am I going to do with these tickets? I'll have to give them to someone. Can *you* give them to someone? I don't even know anyone in this town other than you."

"How about sexy landlord?"

"Give Dominic the tickets?"

"No, silly. Ask him to go with you." Sophie rolls her eyes. "You know you want to. He'll be the perfect dinner companion. Go and knock on his door and ask him."

Emma groans. "I can't."

"Why not?"

"I just . . . it's overstepping."

"What on earth are you talking about? He invited you to his barbecue, and it sounds like the two of you are hanging out a ton. This is your way of paying him back. Why don't you just text him? Here. Give me your phone."

Without waiting for Emma to say yes, Sophie grabs it from the coffee table and scrolls through her screen of contacts until she finds Dominic.

"Hey, Dom," she types, looking up at Emma, who shakes her head vigorously in horror.

"He's not Dom," she says. "Dominic"

"Okay. Sorry. 'Hey, Dominic. Someone just gave me two tickets to a farm dinner in Redding tonight. Want to come?'"

"Don't say that," says Emma. "Say, 'Is there any chance you want to come?'"

"Why? So you can be all English and reserved and pretend you don't really want him to come? Too late. I pressed Send."

Emma groans. "It's too forward. Now I'm embarrassed."

"Oh . . . oh . . . "

"What?"

"The dots!" Sophie shouts. "He's responding already!"

"What does he say?"

"He says . . . " She pauses dramatically. " 'Yes! Sounds great!!!' " she reads from the screen. "Note the exclamation points," she adds with a wink. "Then he finishes with, 'I'll pick you up. What time?' "

"Pick me up? That's funny, since he lives next door. Tell him five."

"Done. Now I have to help you figure out what to wear for your date."

"It's not a date," grumbles Emma.

"Just because you extended the invitation doesn't mean it's not a date. And not only is it a date, it's your first date, technically."

Emma shakes her head. "Every time you call it a date it makes me freak out with nerves, and it sets the expectations so high I'm bound to have a horrible time. It's not really a date, is it? Isn't it just two new friends going out?"

Sophie stares at her friend. "I'm sorry, Emma. I didn't mean to freak you out, but I do think this is a date. I know you're nervous, but don't be. We've already established he's lovely. Now you just have to relax and be yourself. Oh, and look gorgeous." She grins. "Can I help you pick out what to wear for dinner on the farm? I'm thinking floral dress, with a fabulous straw cowboy hat."

Emma shakes her head with a laugh. "You're incorrigible. Okay. I will do my best to relax and be myself. As for the floral dress, that I have. But where am I going to get a fabulous straw cowboy hat?"

"My wardrobe. I'll drop it off in about an hour. You're going to look beautiful. Let's blow Dominic away!"

The dress is indeed floral, and floaty, with a vintage feel that Emma loves. She feels feminine and beautiful in this dress, which she fell in love with years ago in a tiny shop on Westbourne Grove, but has barely worn, because it has never felt quite her style.

Her hair is clipped back into a bun, tendrils hanging loose, with thin gold hoops in her ears and flat leather sandals on her feet. The tiniest bit of make-up, a woven raffia clutch, and the cowboy hat. She'd thought at first that the hat would be ridiculous, but even she has to admit it's perfect when she catches sight of herself in the mirror.

The doorbell rings. Dominic doesn't have to say anything for Emma to see that he approves. His eyes widen with a smile when he sees her, and he nods almost involuntarily.

"You look beautiful." He says this as he places a hand on the small of her back, again, to guide her out the door, and again, just like the last time he did it, Emma feels her nerves disappear. A feeling of absolute safety washes over her as she lets him guide her to the truck.

"This is definitely the right truck for a farm dinner," she says, as they pull out of the driveway. "You're going to feel right at home."

"I love a farm," says Dominic. "I worked on farms when I was a teenager. That was back when there were a ton of farms and farm stands around here. You wouldn't even have recognized this town back then. It really was a small New England town when I was growing up. Everyone on Main Street knew you, people kept tabs on you everywhere, even at the grocery store. If you misbehaved, the shopkeepers would call home and tell your mom."

"I wish it were like that now," says Emma. "I grew up in the country in England and it was much the same. I loved it, although of course back then I couldn't wait to leave and move to London."

"I would never want to live in the city," says Dominic. "Even though I don't always like how the town has changed, it's my home." He shrugs. "There isn't anywhere else I could imagine living. My parents moved up to a retirement community outside of Trumbull, but I have to say, I can't imagine ever leaving Westport, even though I never go to Main Street any more."

"What? No Brooks Brothers board shorts for you?" jokes Emma.

"Right. Because I look like a Brooks Brothers board shorts shorts kind of guy."

"You look very dapper tonight." She looks at him, in a button-down white shirt and jeans.

"I made an effort for you." He looks over at her and grins, and Emma smiles back, as her heart skips the tiniest of beats.

They turn up a dirt road and follow the hand-painted signs to *Dinner on the Farm Parking* through an open wooden gate, into a meadow filled with parked cars. They park and climb out, following another couple along a mown grass pathway through a wildflower meadow. A few minutes later they reach a large open field filled with people standing around sipping elderflower cocktails, helping themselves to hors d'oeuvres off trays borne by young, smiling women in linen aprons and chunky boots.

Dominic grabs two glasses off a tray, and they toast each other and take a sip.

"I had no idea this was a thing," says Dominic, looking around with a smile. "I like it, though. It makes me feel comfortable, at home. Just like we were talking about on the way here. Reminds me of what the town was like when I was growing up."

"Where do you think the actual dinner will be held?" Emma looks around but can't see any tables.

"Through there, maybe? See the sign to the orchard?" A passing waitress overhears and stops with a smile.

"The dinner? It is in the orchard but we don't let anyone over there until it's time. There's a whole theatre involved in getting the tables ready, and we wait to bring everyone in all at once."

140

"This is really nice," says Dominic happily, helping himself to a small spoon of shrimp with dill pesto and quinoa. "And delicious," he adds. His mouth is full as he speaks, and Emma laughs as she takes a spoon and tries the food herself.

It's not long before everyone is invited into the orchard. The scene they find there is beautiful. Four long trestle tables stretch between the apple trees, globe lights strung between the branches, votives in mason jars winding down the centre of each hessian-covered table, bamboo chairs lining each side.

The lights twinkle in the fading sunlight as waiters stand to one side, greeting the guests with smiles. Everyone first glimpses the magical setting, then looks for seats. Emma glances around, trying to spot people she hopes, prays, may be nice, chatty, fun for the night.

Before she can think too long, Emma and Dominic sit with two couples their age, who introduce themselves as soon as they sit down. Emma already has them pegged — she worked with people just like them in New York. The men, good-looking and clean cut, wear huge expensive watches on their wrists. She knows even without looking that they will each sport a Panerai, or a Rolex Daytona, and she flicks her eyes down to check, seeing that indeed one is a Panerai, the other an IWC. *Nailed it*, she thinks. *Bankers*.

The women are well groomed and friendly, but clearly not very interested in Emma. Out of politeness, she attempts to make small talk, asking them about their lives, their babies, where they worked before they had babies. Both of them are former bankers, undecided as to whether they will return to work. Emma knows in both cases they will not; she has worked with too many women like them, and she feels like she knows exactly how their lives will be laid out ahead of them. They have children and leave banking, thinking they will go back, but they will love being stay-at-home moms, even though a lot of the time they are bored. They will employ a nanny or au pair to take care of the boring parts — the endless trips to the children's museum, the aquarium, the soft play zone — and will spend their time getting back into shape and looking good enough to keep their husbands' interest. The children will grow, will start kindergarten, and the wives will get involved with charities, will tell people they used to be bankers, conferring on themselves a status they gave up to be full-time mothers, because they still want to be defined as something more than merely a wife.

When their children reach high school their friends will slowly start working again, and they will realize it is no longer a status symbol to be a stay-at-home mother. They will look for something not too taxing to fill their time. Good God, they will realize. Whatever did they do with all that time? They will work in local shops, or start businesses, or help out at the school library. Many will become real estate agents, although most will struggle to find clients in a town overrun by middle-aged women going into the real estate business once their children have started high school.

Oh yes. Emma knows these women well, thanks to Sophie and her vocal feelings about them. She can see their whole lives laid out in front of them in a way they will not be able to for years. As the women answer her questions, she wonders whether they will ask her anything about herself, but she is entirely unsurprised when they don't. Once she stops asking them about themselves, they grow quiet.

"I saw what just happened," Dominic says, dropping his voice so they can't hear. "They were as interested in you as their husbands were in me."

"Their husbands weren't interested in you?"

"Nah. I don't work at a hedge fund or bank. I told them I was a bartender and their eyes glazed over."

"But everyone loves the Fat Hen! Why didn't you tell them you worked there? You know they would have wanted you to be their new best friend if you'd told them."

"That's exactly why I didn't tell them," murmurs Dominic. "The Fat Hen has enough of those types. I definitely don't want to encourage any more."

"I'm sorry," whispers Emma. "I think we got stuck with the duds."

"We have each other," says Dominic. "And I couldn't be happier with the company I'm keeping tonight."

She flushes with pleasure, just as the feta and watermelon is set on the table, and she can distract herself with the food. They chat about this and that, until the plates are removed, when Dominic turns to her and asks, "How is it you don't have a boyfriend? I asked you before but you didn't give me a straight answer."

This time, she manages not to blush and commands herself to hear the question as one from a friend and not a flirtation. "I'm pretty self-sufficient," Emma answers. "Honestly, I'm not sure I'm a good girlfriend. I had a very long relationship when I was younger and everyone expected us to get married, but I think I'm a bit of a lone wolf. It's a terrible thing to admit, and not the thing you're supposed to say, but I'm perfectly happy being on my own. Why are you smiling?"

"Lone wolf," he says. "When I was a kid I used to be in a rock band and we called it the Lone Wolves because that's what everyone called me. The Lone Wolf."

"So you're independent, too?"

"It's different for a man. We're expected to be. But I don't know how easy it would be for me to share my life with anyone, either."

"Really? You seem so open. You seem exactly the kind of man who would, should, have a partner."

"Yeah. I know that's how it seems, but my model for marriage wasn't a great one."

Emma remembers what that real estate agent Jeff had said about Dominic's parents: the fighting, the drama, the violence.

"Your parents? Were they not happy?" She already knows the answer but wants to hear it first-hand from Dominic.

He laughs. "That might be the understatement of the century. They hate each other, but they're still married. I think my mom planned a huge bunch of kids, but after me she had a ton of miscarriages, and I think the whole thing was a huge disappointment to her. They're very Italian, which means there's always a lot of shouting, but in my family's case that comes with a lot of anger and a lot of . . . " He shakes his head. "This is boring."

"No. It's really not. I imagine that growing up in a family like that must have scarred you in some way, must have made you reluctant to get involved with anyone."

"I didn't think so when I was younger, but I realize now how often I was attracted to women who brought drama to a relationship. Everything I thought I wanted to avoid from my own childhood: the shouting, the anger, the turmoil? I always seemed to pick women who brought exactly that into my life."

"But not now?"

Dominic pauses. "I had a girlfriend once. I was about seventeen, and we would fight all the time. There was this one night when we were yelling at each other, and I was so angry, I swear to God it's the only time in my life I actually have come close to laying a hand on someone. I didn't. But I was scared that I was going to. And I realized then that if I didn't make a conscious choice to live differently, I was going to follow my parents' path. And I didn't want that. That night changed me completely. I learned that it's all a choice, and that choice is up to us. And then of course Jesse came along, and it's always different once you're a father. I'm different. Not only do I always have to put Jesse first, I've had to learn what it is to have a relationship. I know it's my kid, but it's the first real long-term relationship I've had as an adult. I've had to learn to be selfless. To put someone else before me. And I've had to try to teach Jesse that we're the only ones in control of our happiness. It's been a great lesson."

"So now you're ready for the woman of your dreams?" says Emma.

"Maybe." He looks at her. There is a long pause.

"Gina?"

"That's over," he says simply.

Emma fights the delighted grin that is itching to get out.

"Didn't I see her come over late last night?"

"She did. And I ended it."

"I'm so sorry."

Dominic stares at her. "*Are* you?"

She is quiet for a minute. "I don't know. Are you?"

"No. It was pointless. It wasn't going anywhere. It wasn't fair, either to her or to me." Dominic reaches for the basket of cornbread, takes two pieces, hands one to Emma. Without looking at her, he reaches for the butter and keeps his eyes down as he slathers some on his bread. "I found myself thinking about other . . . things," he finally says.

Emma's heart jumps. "Other things?"

Dominic looks up and gives her a slow smile. "Yes."

They make it through the lamb-and-date meatballs, the braised short ribs with succotash and roasted beetroot, through the burnt caramel ice cream with toffee apple slices. They make it through talking, and drinking, and laughing, and looking at no one but each other.

146

They make it through coffee, and fine, delicate ginger-and-lemon cookies, and mint tea with tiny chocolate biscotti.

They make it halfway up the mown pathway on the way back to the car park after dinner, couples behind them, couples in front.

"Look," says Dominic, pausing along the path and pointing out something glistening beyond the trees. "A pond. Shall we check it out?"

Emma nods, and as they step off the path and through the long grass, Dominic reaches out and takes her hand, and a warmth settles over her entire body as she feels his hand wrap hers.

They walk down to the pond, and stop when they reach the water, turning to each other at the same time. Emma is hardly able to breathe.

Dominic reaches out and places a hand on her cheek. And then she is in his arms, his mouth is on hers, her mouth opening as his arms wrap around her body and she sinks into something that feels so familiar, so right, that when they finally disengage, when they open their eyes and look at each other, her cheeks are wet with tears.

"Why are you crying?" Dominic asks, looking at her with wonder.

"I have no idea," she says, which is absolutely true.

They kiss at every red traffic light on the way home. They do not talk about what will happen once they get there until they pull into the driveway. Then Dominic

147

asks if she will wait in the car while he pays the babysitter and sends her home.

Emma sits in the car, astonished by what has happened. She watches Dominic, standing in the doorway paying the babysitter, feeling a jolt of lust in her loins, something she hasn't felt in a very long time. She's not even sure she has ever felt exactly this before.

She looks at him from inside the darkened car, tasting him still on her tongue, remembering from earlier in the evening what he feels like, the shape of his head, the texture of his hair, and a shudder runs through her body.

She wants to drink him in, eat him up. She wants to fold herself into him so tightly that the two of them become one. She wants to consume and be consumed, in a way so unlike the Emma she has always been, that when the babysitter leaves and she finally gets out of the car and joins him in the house, her legs are shaking.

"Sssshhh." Dominic puts his finger to his lips, indicating that Jesse is fast asleep, before pulling her back into his arms. They stand at the foot of the stairs, kissing, and when he takes her hand and motions her upstairs, she nods, and follows him up into the master bedroom, where he inches her back, until she falls backwards on the bed, laughing softly.

He dips his head down, kisses her neck, pushes the strap of her dress down, and the laughing stops, replaced with a sharp, ravenous intake of breath as she pulls his head back up, needing his mouth to be on hers.

Dominic kisses his way down her body, pulling her dress down, fumbling around her back to undo her bra and throw it across the room. He lingers on her breasts, slips a hand down inside her underwear, as she lets out a small, pleasurable moan. She reaches down to undo his jeans, unbuttons his shirt to feel his skin against hers.

She marvels at the intimacy of these acts, and how she feels so comfortable performing them. It should feel so strange, she thinks, guiding him into her, feeling him inside her as he props himself on his hands and gazes at her. But everything feels so right. So very different from before. From ever before.

The last time Emma had sex was through Tinder. She is not a Tinder girl, but everyone she knew was doing it, everyone said she had to do it. She thought, after a while, that she *should* try it. Though people used the app mostly for sex, surely there were some who found relationships unexpectedly, and if they did, why not her?

She was swiped by a handsome artist who lived downtown. Naturally. He was in his late twenties, and confessed to always being drawn to older women, which threw Emma slightly, for she didn't consider someone in her mid-thirties an older woman. They went to the bar of a basement restaurant in the West Village, where he was greeted by the hostess, the bartender, and even the manager, who came out from the back to give him a bro hug.

They sat at the bar and had dirty martinis, two for her, three for him. They talked about nothing very important, but he was good-looking, and young, and his interest in her made her feel desirable and beautiful. It had been a while since she had felt desirable and beautiful. Attention from the lecherous men with whom she worked didn't count — that was all part of the game.

She couldn't see herself with this Tinder man in any meaningful way, but the attention was flattering, and easy. Towards the end of her second martini, she began to feel like Mrs Robinson. How old must Mrs Robinson have been? Much older than thirty-five. In her late forties, at least, thought Emma, picturing Anne Bancroft in the film, her age indeterminate, a young and gorgeous Katharine Ross as Elaine. *She was much older than me*, thought Emma, looking at the bloom of smooth skin on the artist's cheek, *but I think I now know how she felt*.

"Want to come back to my place for a . . . coffee?" murmured the artist, after he had kissed her, at the bar, in full view of everyone, his tongue snaking into her mouth in a way that was both embarrassing and exciting.

She knew that coffee was not on the agenda, and she nodded. Why not? It would be something new for her.

Emma was not the sort of girl to have a one-night stand, had never, in fact, *had* a one-night stand. Emma was a good girl, a rule-follower. The only rule she had ever broken was not marrying Rufus. It was high time she did something unexpected.

So, yes, she would go back with him; yes, she knew coffee would be forgotten once they walked into his loft; no, they didn't have enormous chemistry. His kissing, in fact, was very . . . enthusiastic. *Too* enthusiastic. And wet. There was no build-up, no excitement, no anticipation; one minute his face was in front of hers, the next his tongue was plunging around her mouth. *That's okay*, she thought; that didn't mean the sex itself would be awful. Maybe it would be wonderful, despite the bad kissing. Why not have wonderful sex with someone young and handsome, and fun?

She should have listened to her feelings about the kiss. For she soon learned, a bad kisser was not a good start. A rough, wet, overenthusiastic kisser meant a rough, wet, overenthusiastic everything.

Emma did go back to his apartment, where he threw her on the bed in a way that he perhaps thought was dominant and sexy but was in fact the opposite. His tongue was too big, his touch too impersonal. There was no chemistry, and it was too late. Emma felt too guilty to get up and leave.

It was, thankfully, quick. She spent the few minutes it lasted thinking about a pair of shoes she had passed on the way to meet him, wondering whether they would go with a white dress she had hanging in her wardrobe. As soon as it was over he grabbed his iPhone from the bedside table and started reading texts. She watched as he hovered over the Tinder app, and she started laughing.

"You're actually going to swipe *now?* Seconds after you've finished having sex with someone?"

At least he had the grace to look embarrassed. She left, vowing not to have regrets. She had tried Tinder, and clearly it was not for her. The sex was definitely not for her.

Not long after, when she found herself out with a group of women, all talking about Tinder and their sexual escapades, she was gratified to discover she wasn't alone. Most of them were disappointed, complained that sex was a commodity, felt disposable. There was no intimacy, they agreed, and worse, no pretence or effort to give them pleasure.

And yet these women kept doing it, addicted to the swiping, to being swiped, to the possibility that one of the swipes might, just might, turn into something more. Not necessarily a relationship, but at the very least, great sex.

Not Emma, though. She deleted the app from her phone. No sex at all was better than selfish sex. She threw her energy into her work (and bought a small, discreet vibrator online).

Until now. Until Dominic, who has made her heart smile these past few weeks. She hasn't thought about him much, hasn't allowed herself to think about him, because the two of them seemed so mismatched, from such different cultures and classes, but there is no question she has a warm glow of happiness whenever he is around.

They have become friends, with an ease and openness that Emma isn't quite sure she has experienced before. With that friendship, she has found herself looking at him, with something she refuses to recognize as lust.

But it is lust. Oh God. It is definitely lust.

He doesn't stop looking at her as he moves inside her, Emma's legs wrapped around his back, her hands moving over his arms, his shoulders, his chest. He dips his head to kiss her, over and over, smiling, watching her face as she feels an orgasm beginning to build, tipping her head back and moaning as the feelings overtake her body, as he allows himself to be overtaken with her.

Afterwards, as she lies in his arms, Dominic talks. He tells her stories about his family, his friends, his hopes and dreams.

"I must go soon," she whispers, and he nods, and keeps on talking. He is still talking when she falls asleep.

ACT TWO

CHAPTER
FIFTEEN

It takes Emma a while to orient herself. Her eyes are closed as she fights her way upwards, out of the deepest of sleeps, with the vague awareness that something is different.

Everything is different.

The smell of the room is unfamiliar. She is pressed against something warm. Something breathing. Last night comes back to her in a flood, flashes of memories like Polaroids, flitting through her mind. The dinner. The kiss. The drive home. The strap of her dress being slipped off her shoulder. The hand moving . . . *oh!* There is a flicker deep down as she gasps ever so slightly and opens her eyes.

She didn't mean to fall asleep in Dominic's arms. She didn't mean to spend the night in Dominic's bed. She is pressed against him, or is he pressed against her? The two of them are in the middle of the bed, squeezed together. She can smell his cologne, the musky scent of his skin. She didn't think she liked cologne, but Dominic always smells delicious, even when he is building shelves, and she sniffs deeply now, drinking him in.

She wants to kiss him, to reach out and stroke him, but what if last night was a one-night stand? What if he wants nothing to do with her now? What if it is awkward, and awful, and they are not able to look at each other?

Damn, she thinks. *Why did I allow this to happen? Where am I going to live if it all goes horribly wrong?*

She turns her head and squeals in fright. Standing right by the side of the bed, up close, staring at her with narrowed eyes, is Jesse.

Oh *shit*.

She has no idea what to say. She wouldn't have wanted Jesse to know they were more than friends. She wouldn't have wanted him to know anything until she was sure there was anything to know.

"Hey," she whispers, pulling the covers up under her chin, attempting a natural smile as if it is completely normal to find the next-door neighbour in your father's bed. "How did you sleep?"

Oh God. Why did Jesse have to be standing here?

"Are you okay?" she whispers, when he doesn't answer. "We had a sleepover with your dad last night," she says lamely. "We didn't plan it but, obviously, I ended up staying over."

Jesse just stares at her.

"Why don't you have any clothes on?" he says eventually.

"It was so hot," she says. "I think maybe the air conditioning was broken. Was it hot in your room? No? It must just be in here, then. I do not want your father to see me with no clothes on, though. Would you mind passing me that dress on the floor over there so I can put something on before he wakes up?"

Jesse squints at Emma, deciding whether to believe her, knowing, she suspects, that her story doesn't quite add up, but eventually he gets the dress and throws it at her, quite unpleasantly she thinks, although she's in no position to say anything.

"What about Hobbes?" says Jesse. "Who's looking after Hobbes?"

"Why don't you go through the cat flap and check on her?" says Emma brightly. "I'll get dressed and maybe I'll make us some breakfast. How does that sound?"

Jesse shrugs but leaves the room. Emma hears the back door slam as he goes out into the garden on his way next door. She slips the covers back to get dressed, before an arm lays across her chest to stop her. She turns to see Dominic's eyes open, and for a second she is nervous about what he will say, until a slow smile spreads on his face.

"Morning," he says, pulling her gently towards him and kissing her. For all her concerns — about him, about Jesse — she can't help but giggle.

"Get off me!" She attempts to push him away, which only makes him squeeze her more tightly.

"This is great," he says. "This is like having my own teddy bear." And she finally relaxes in his arms, snuggling down in the bed, rolling over until she is looking into his eyes.

"Jesse came in," she says. "I'm so sorry. I honestly wasn't planning on staying the night, but I fell asleep, and when I woke up it was to see him standing next to the bed." She frowns a little. "I don't think he's happy."

"Why isn't he happy?" Dominic takes a strand of her hair between his fingers and twirls it around and around. "I love your hair, by the way," he says. "Curly hair turns me on."

Emma starts to laugh. "You're just saying that. Curly hair turns you on? I don't believe you."

"Okay. Let me revise. *Your* curly hair turns me on." He smiles. "Or maybe it's you that turns me on."

"I do?" Emma smiles back at him.

"You do. Everything about you. Your curly hair. Your English accent. Your hands . . . "

"My . . . hands?" Emma grins.

"You have the most delicate hands." He takes her hand in his, entwining her fingers with his own. "I noticed them right when you moved in. They're beautiful. You move them when you talk, in this really graceful way. It's like watching ballerina hands."

"You're weird," sputters Emma, although she is unspeakably flattered.

"Also, your body turns me on" — he raises an eyebrow — "big-time." He kisses her, and she relaxes into the kiss, so relieved this is still lovely, so relieved he isn't changing his mind, hasn't woken up to what he believes is a terrible mistake.

But she's still concerned about Jesse. She pushes Dominic away reluctantly. "Not now. Jesse's going to be back any second and I said I'd make breakfast. Is that okay?"

160

"It's more than okay. You're turning into quite the breakfast-maker, it seems. Lucky us. Lucky me."

After one more lingering kiss, Emma pulls on her dress. She watches Dominic watching her every move, with a lazy smile on his face. She smiles back before going downstairs.

Once there, she moves around the kitchen, finding bowls, plates, opening the fridge for the eggs and milk. She cuts slices from a loaf of sourdough bread, puts them into the toaster; beats the eggs and seasons them; melts butter in an old cast-iron skillet she finds at the back of a cupboard — as good as new after a very good wash.

This feels nice, she thinks. Cooking breakfast for Dominic and Jesse. Jesse clearly wasn't happy with her being in his father's bed, but why would he be? He's had his father to himself for his entire life; of course he doesn't want to share him. Not that Emma is looking to share him. Good *God*! She laughs out loud at the very thought. Still, it must have been disconcerting for him, and she understands that. Luckily, it won't last, thinks Emma. Look how she and Jesse bonded over Hobbes; look how much fun they had been having together before this morning. This is a tiny blip in what is clearly a friendship. She knows Jesse likes her, she can tell. He likes the fact that she talks to him like an adult; he doesn't have to know it's only because she doesn't know how to talk to children.

Breakfast will go a long way towards healing his shock at finding her there this morning. He's a little kid, after all. A little kid who has no mother, who will surely blossom with a spot of love and nurture. Of course his father adores him, Emma has no doubt of that, but Jesse needs a woman in his life to look after him, and right now, even if it's only temporary — God, why is she even thinking like this? — she can give him some of that maternal warmth. She will start by making him the most delicious eggs he has ever tasted.

Emma sets the table properly. She goes into the front garden and snips off five blue hydrangeas, setting them in water in a mason jar that she puts in the centre of the table. She lays the knives and forks at each place setting, with glasses of juice, the coffeepot in the middle on a coaster.

She places the toast on a napkin-covered plate, standing the slices up, as if they are in a hotel dining room. She finds grape jam in the fridge, and scoops some into a small ramekin, placing it on a small plate with a teaspoon.

She has no idea why she feels the need to create a scene of domestic bliss, only that she wants them both to sit down to something that is both delicious and beautiful. She wants this to feel special.

"Breakfast!" she calls, and hears Dominic clump down the stairs. Her stomach lurches as he walks in wearing boxer shorts and a navy T-shirt that rides up as he stretches. *You are gorgeous*, she thinks, gazing at him for a moment, savouring a feeling she now knows for certain she has never felt in quite this way before.

"I know what I want for breakfast." Dominic comes up behind her, murmurs into her neck, sliding his hands around her waist. Then the back door opens, forcing them to jump apart as if shocked.

"Breakfast!" Emma says to Jesse with false brightness. "Come and sit down!"

"I don't like these eggs." Jesse sits, sinking his head in his hand as he stabs at the eggs with his fork, a scowl on his face.

"These are scrambled eggs, English style," says Emma. "They're creamy and delicious. I promise you'll like them."

"They're really good," says Dominic, scooping some into his mouth, then turning to Emma. "Wow. These actually *are* really good. What did you do?"

"The secret is lots of butter, and very slow stirring over low heat so they cook slowly. It makes the eggs creamy rather than rubbery."

"Jesse, you'll really like them," says Dominic. "Come on. Try some."

Jesse reluctantly lifts a forkful to his mouth, grimacing as he chews, before jumping up and spitting them in the sink.

"Jesse!" says Dominic, with a laugh. "That's not very nice."

"They're gross!" says Jesse. "Slimy and disgusting."

"Come on, buddy. Sit down. You don't have to eat them, then. Have some toast."

Emma feels herself almost on the brink of tears but remains silent and tries to mentally talk herself out of it. *Don't be silly*, she tells herself. *He's only a child and he's punishing you for being here. Don't take it personally.*

She looks at Dominic, who is gazing at his son with unconditional love. *How can he not say something?* she thinks. *How can he laugh? Surely this is a learning opportunity.*

You may not like the food, she thinks, although she doesn't even believe that, for who would not like these creamy, buttery scrambled eggs? *But even if you don't, you don't jump up from the table and make a big song and dance about spitting it out.*

You put the fork down and say, "No, thank you. I'm not hungry."

Dominic is encouraging this bad behaviour. Instead of showing Jesse another way to cope with his distress, he is smiling at him indulgently, which will surely give him the wrong message, make him think his behaviour is acceptable.

It's a teaching opportunity, she thinks. And she will not let it pass.

"Jesse," she says gently, as Jesse crosses his arms in a sulk and refuses to look at her. "It's very rude to spit food out. I just went to a lot of trouble to cook you breakfast. You didn't have to eat it, but it would have been more polite to just say you didn't want it." He refuses to look at her. "Jesse, my feelings are very hurt."

He mutters something under his breath.

"What? I can't hear you."

"I don't care!" The words burst out of his mouth. "I don't care about you. I don't even want you here. Why are you here? Go back home! Go back to your house. We don't want you here!"

164

"Jesse," Dominic finally interjects. "That's not very nice. Say you're sorry."

"No," says Jesse, kicking the table leg, pushing the chair back, and running out of the room. As he heads upstairs his sobbing can be heard loud and jagged through the thin ceiling of the small house.

"I'd better go talk to him," says Dominic. "He'll be fine. He's never good with the idea of me having girlfriends. Wait here. I shouldn't be too long."

But Emma doesn't want to wait. Poor Jesse, she thinks. She understands why he would not be happy about the prospect of his father having girlfriends.

Is that what she is? she wonders. A girlfriend? It is far too early to use that term. A friend who is a girl, she thinks. That's what he meant. A friend who is a girl, a friend with, obviously, benefits. *Girlfriend*, in the loosest possible sense of the word.

She washes up quickly and quietly before letting herself out the back door and returning to the safety of her own home.

CHAPTER
SIXTEEN

Later that morning, Lisa phones, her voice high with excitement. Her husband has given her the go-ahead to get the house decorated on the budget they discussed, so she'd like Emma to get started right away. Should she accompany Emma to the shops? she asks. Emma senses she is nervous about giving up control, even though she doesn't want to do the hard part.

"You can," says Emma dubiously. "But it can be very hard to picture how things are going to work in the room until you see them all together. But don't worry, I won't buy anything that can't be returned if you don't like it, and I can always text you photos if you'd like. You have the big pieces already, all I really need to do is accessorize."

"Okay," says Lisa. "Don't worry about texting photos. I trust you. Do you think you'll be able to get it done by the end of next week?"

"It's tight, but I should be able to do it," says Emma. "Why don't I come over on Friday morning at nine to get the rooms set up. Does that sound okay?"

"Is there any chance you could come by on Thursday morning, instead?"

Emma realizes that she's going to need to get started right this minute. "Sure," she says to Lisa. "I'll see you then."

She starts with Pier 1, where she finds bamboo side tables that look far more expensive than they actually are. She adds three big faux orchids, knowing she will have to break the baskets they are glued into and find something else to put them in.

At the charity shop she finds two mid-century modern chairs, and a pair of white Foo dog lamps that have been sitting there for months. They are whimsical and fun, and she gets them for less than sticker price.

Just as she's leaving she finds a set of three huge black-and-white photographs, close-ups of flowers, grainy and gorgeous. The three would be perfect hung together, on the library wall.

On to HomeGoods for more lamps — she's always felt that pools of warm light do more than anything else to cosy up a space — a large sisal rug for the living room, and a grey-and-white geometric one for the library.

She picks up porcelain Buddhas and turquoise shagreen boxes. At West Elm, she buys both wooden and lacquered trays and chocolate-brown geometric poufs. At Pottery Barn, she finds more cushions, and throws, silver-rimmed candle holders, with huge three-wicked barrel candles to sit inside.

Her car is filled. She phones Lisa on the way home and asks if she can drop things off in her garage as she has no room in her house at the moment to store anything. She makes Lisa promise not to look at anything she has bought. Not yet.

But Lisa greets her as she pulls up, can't resist sneaking a peek into the bags as she helps Emma carry them inside. "Buddhas!" she says in delight. "I love the Buddhas. Oh, and look at those cushions! They're gorgeous."

"I'm on the right track, then?"

"Oh please, please, can we set some of it up now? I'll help. Please?"

Emma can't say no. She's dying to see it herself. But once Lisa has helped move the furniture to put the rug down, she banishes her upstairs, making her promise not to come down until it's all done.

She works quickly. The bags are put in the hallway as she drapes the throws over the back of the sofa, and piles the cushions on top. The trays are placed on the coffee table with the shagreen boxes. She needs a few stools, she thinks to herself. Maybe in porcelain. She can order them online tomorrow.

The tables look great, and the mid-century chairs, too. They could be re-covered, Emma thinks, in a thick linen, but for now, with cushions, they are fine. She switches on the lamps, takes some books that are already shelved and stacks them horizontally, looking at them with a discerning eye. She needs more, she realizes. So much more. Now she can see the gaps. Artwork for the wall. More objects. She can hang the artwork and the curtains on Thursday. Emma casts an expert eye around the room, making notes on a pad to remind her what else to buy. Lucite chairs for the office, she thinks, writing it down. An upholstered bench in front of the fire. Tables for either side of the fireplace. She'd seen two nice demilune tables at the charity shop but hadn't thought she had a place for them. Now she realizes she does.

"I can't wait any longer." Lisa has crept back into the room "Emma!" she cries delightedly. "It's *beautiful*. It looks like something out of a magazine!" She can't seem to wipe the smile off her face as she tiptoes around her own house, running her fingers along the sides of the trays, picking up the little sculptures on the bookshelves, admiring the vases. "I can't believe how different you've made it look!"

"Just you wait," says Emma. "I have more plans for these rooms."

"What do you think about more bookshelves?" Lisa pauses. "Not just for books, but I was thinking about maybe building some shelves in this corner to display stuff. Like one of the pictures in your file — do you remember? They were dark grey and glossy and absolutely beautiful. Do you think that would work?"

Lisa is talking about the bookshelves in her own house. "That would be stunning," Emma says. "I could draw something up for you to give to your carpenter."

Lisa's face falls. "I don't have a carpenter. Do you know anyone?"

Emma pauses. The bookshelves in her own house look beautiful, but only if you don't look too closely. Pull off her carefully nailed-on moulding and everything slants to the right. Could Dominic do a better job if she helped him? Would he do a better job with a spirit level and an assistant? She could be there to catch the mistakes. Surely this would be good for him, a job doing what he really loves to do.

"I do, actually," says Emma. "I can see if he's free right now to come and take a look."

"That would be fantastic," says Lisa. "I am so glad I found you, Emma. This is going to be great!"

Emma stands back as Dominic measures the wall, asking Lisa a series of very professional questions. Emma is quiet. It's probably not a great idea for Lisa to know she and Dominic have anything other than a professional relationship.

"Emma? Can you just show Dominic the picture in your file? I want shelves just like that."

"Absolutely." She turns to Dominic. "I can get those to you as soon as I get home," she says, and the twinkle in his eye brings a flashback of him moving inside her, smiling down at her, and for a second she loses her words. When she shakes her head to dislodge the thought, he is hiding a grin.

"Are you okay?" he says.

"I'm so sorry. I just got lost in thought for a second."

"Creative types!" laughs Lisa, seemingly oblivious to the sexual energy raging between them. "If Emma gets you the picture today, do you think you could start immediately? How long would it take?"

"I could get you something by next Friday."

"Can you make it next Thursday?"

"That's tight. I don't know."

Lisa lowers her eyes, looks up at him through her eye-lashes. "Pretty please?" she asks in a little-girl voice, and Emma suppresses a laugh.

Dominic sighs. "Seeing as you asked so nicely. Let me give you a price when I get home and figure out the cost of the materials and labour, and if it's good with you, I'll get going immediately. I should be able to have the shelves done in time. Like I said, it's tight, but I think I can do it."

"Thank you so much." Lisa's voice is almost back to normal. "Let me show you out."

As soon as the door closes behind Dominic, Lisa whirls back into the room with her hand on her heart. "Oh my God!" Lisa exclaims. "He's completely gorgeous. You didn't tell me your carpenter was so hot. He was so handsome I could hardly look at him."

"Really?" Emma wrinkles her nose. "I guess I don't really see it. You think he's handsome?"

"And tall. And sweet. *God!* It's a good thing I'm happily married or I'd be extremely tempted right about now." She peers at Emma. "Do you really not think he's *adorable*?"

Emma sighs. "Okay. Yes. I do think he's very handsome. But I can't let that get in the way of us working together."

"How do you know him?"

Emma thinks for a second, her mind trying to come up with a plausible explanation, but it doesn't feel right to lie to a client. She can tell the truth, just not, perhaps, the whole truth.

171

"I rent one of his cottages," she says. "He actually built those shelves in the picture you're talking about."

"Why didn't you say anything?"

"I didn't want you to think I was recommending a friend. If you want him to build them, I'm sure he has the time, and I can oversee them to make sure they're perfect."

"I'll oversee him anytime you want," says Lisa, and they both laugh. "Are you married?" she then asks, out of the blue. Emma blushes and shakes her head.

"Is he?"

"I know where you're going with this," warns Emma with a laugh.

"Seriously? Why not! If I were single and he was my landlord he could *fix my shelves* anytime he wanted."

"I don't know that we're terribly well matched," says Emma, aware suddenly of her well-spoken British accent. "And I'm not looking for anything at the moment." Which had been true, up until the moment Dominic kissed her. But certainly her first client wasn't the person she should be making any confessions to.

"The best things in life always find us when we're not looking for them," says Lisa, now serious. "Okay, I'll stop. But the two of you look good together. I could see it. And *I* would." She smiles. "If I were you."

CHAPTER
SEVENTEEN

By late that afternoon, she's back home. Everything she needs is at her fingertips. Emma sits at the computer, Hobbes on her lap, losing herself completely as she trawls websites, changes search terms, and zeroes in on all the accessories she needs to complete Lisa's house.

Just past six she hears the cat flap open, and seconds later Jesse is in her doorway. By the smile on his face, it looks as if he's got over his morning tantrum.

"Hey, Jesse." She pretends the last thing she heard him say about her was not that he wanted nothing to do with her.

"Hi," he says. "Have you seen Hobbes?"

"She's right here." Emma slides her chair back, gesturing to her lap. Jesse comes over and pets the cat. "Want to take her? Maybe the two of you can cuddle up on the sofa. I can put a movie on if you like."

"Sure," Jesse says. She notices now that he's carefully keeping his gaze on the kitten, and doing his best not to look at her at all.

She hands him Hobbes, gets up, and puts a movie on, grabbing a packet of M&Ms from the kitchen and pouring them into a bowl.

"Ssssh," she says, putting the bowl on the table in front of the sofa. "Don't tell your dad." She turns to go back into her office when Jesse speaks.

"I'm really sorry, Emma," he says. "For what I said. I didn't mean it."

Relieved, and moved, she turns carefully and sits next to him on the sofa. "That's okay, sweetie. I'm sorry I upset you."

They look at each other and Jesse nods, then giggles as Hobbes inches her way up his chest and starts to suck on his earlobe. Emma stands up, makes her way into the bathroom to wipe away her tears. It seems like everything is going to be all right.

A knock on her door brings her out of the bathroom, and she opens it, unsurprised to see Dominic standing on the doorstep.

"Hi, you." He leans forward to kiss her, but Emma turns it into a quick peck, whispering that Jesse is there. She doesn't want to upset the apple cart again.

"I wondered where he'd gotten to," says Dominic. "He can't see us. Give me a proper kiss. I deserve one after you were all weird with me this afternoon."

"I wasn't weird. I was being professional. I didn't want Lisa to suspect my reasons for recommending you." Dominic pulls her close as she loops her arms around his neck. "She thinks we look good together," says Emma when she pulls away.

"I knew I liked her." He lets her go and walks across the threshold, entering the cottage and heading over to where Jesse is lying on the sofa.

"Hey, buddy. I'm going to run out and get burgers and corn for dinner." He turns to Emma. "Want to join us? I'm just throwing stuff on the grill."

"Really?" says Emma, who hadn't much thought about dinner. She wasn't terribly hungry but presumed she would do what she had been doing almost every night and just throw together a salad from whatever she had in her fridge.

"Sure. If I buy salad stuff can you make it? Is it okay if I leave Jesse with you while I run up to the grocery store?"

"Salad stuff I have. And yes, of course Jesse is fine to stay here."

Dominic drops his voice. "Is he, though?"

"After this morning?" She drops her voice, checking that Jesse is glued to the TV. "He apologized."

"Good." He rolls his eyes. "Children." And off he goes.

When he gets back, they all gather at Dominic's house. Emma is careful not to touch Dominic all evening in front of Jesse. Every now and then Dominic will take her hand, or reach over for a kiss, but she doesn't want to upset Jesse, doesn't want to do anything that might disturb the detente they seem to have reached. She's still not sure she understands it, neither why Jesse got quite so upset nor why Dominic seems completely unaware that this might be an issue.

Dominic grills outside while Emma shucks the corn and gets a big pot of water to boil. She sets the table, getting a reluctant Jesse to help, while Dominic brings in a platter of food.

They crack open beers, even though Emma would normally drink wine. This year, in this house, in this town, with this man, an ice-cold bottle of beer has become summer personified. Everything about the evening is perfect.

Jesse is quiet but sweet. Towards the end of the evening, fireflies glimmer on and off in the darkening yard. When Jesse starts yawning, Dominic says it's time for bed.

Jesse starts whining that he wants to stay up, that he never goes to bed this early.

"You know what?" Emma says, when twenty minutes have passed and Dominic has clearly forgotten that he was supposed to be sending Jesse to bed, even though Jesse can barely keep his eyes open. "How about Hobbes has a sleep-over with you tonight?"

Jesse's face lights up. "In my room?"

"Sure. If your dad says yes." She looks at Dominic, who laughs, raising his hands, knowing he now doesn't have a hope in hell of saying anything *other* than yes.

"Why doesn't your dad take you up to bed while I go and get Hobbes. I can bring him in as soon as you've brushed your teeth."

"Do I have to brush my teeth?" Jesse says — but not to his dad, to Emma.

"Absolutely you do. Unless you want them all to fall out. Go on, go up now, and by the time you're done, Hobbes will be curled up on your pillow."

Dominic shoots her a grateful smile as he heads upstairs with his son. Emma watches them before heading next door to get Hobbes. *They need a woman*, she thinks. *The pair of them need someone like me.*

When Dominic comes back downstairs, he stands behind Emma at the sink and slips his arms around her waist. It is weird, she realizes, that it is *not* weird. There is no dancing around each other, trying to figure out what the other is thinking or feeling; there is no awkwardness, no trying to take it slow, no slight discomfort that exists at the beginning of a new relationship. How weird it is that they moved past that so quickly and completely.

Dominic seems quite unlike any man she has ever met, perhaps because he is not playing games. He seems completely open about how he feels about Emma, and doesn't particularly want to hide it from anyone. Even his own son. Emma has spent a large part of the evening attempting to fob off his amorous advances — because of Jesse, not because she wasn't ready and willing to receive them.

"Poor little guy," Dominic says as he nuzzles into her neck. "He's exhausted. No idea why. All that running around at camp, probably. Thank you for bringing the kitten. I honestly don't know how I would have got him into bed otherwise."

"It's a pleasure."

"You even got him to brush his teeth. I should be giving you a medal."

"I'm just relieved he's feeling better. That whole tantrum earlier really upset me."

"I know. I'm sorry. And I'm sorry we haven't had a chance to talk about it properly. If it makes you feel better, this time he's prepared."

Emma frowns. "What do you mean?"

"I told him you might sleep over again, that adults are allowed to have sleepovers, too, and that you are a special friend. I told him I really like you, and I want him to really like you, too. I also said that he and I would always be a team, and that no one would ever get in the way of that."

"And you think he's okay with that?" Emma can't wipe the smile off her face. He wants her to sleep over again! All of it said so easily, so simply. She doesn't know what to do with the feeling that gives her.

Other than enjoy it.

"I don't ever want you to think this relationship is only about sex," says Dominic, sliding his hands around to cup her breasts. "But the sex was so damn good last night, do you think it would be terrible if I picked you up and carried you upstairs to bed so we could do it again?"

"Yes!" Emma is horrified. "You can't pick me up! I'm way heavier than you thi — " She can't get any more out before Dominic has swept her up, not in a romance-novel kind of way, but hoisted over his shoulder. She yelps with laughter before remembering that they are both trying to get Jesse to fall asleep, so instead she thumps his back all the way up the stairs.

178

Is it possible, she thinks, lying in the dark, just able to see the outline of Dominic's body as he gently snores, *is it possible for something to get so very much better in twenty-four hours?*

And is it possible, she thinks, reaching out and stroking his arm over the sheet, feeling its contours, *to feel so strongly about someone I barely know? Someone I would never choose for myself? Someone I never would have thought would fit into my life or my world, at least not the life that's always been expected of me.*

There is something about Dominic. About all of this, that feels . . . right. From the moment he first put his hand on the small of her back, entirely innocently, a gentlemanly gesture to guide her through the garden gate, she felt she had come home.

What was it Lisa had said earlier today? That the best things in life always find us when we're not looking for them?

Now, more than ever, she knows that to be true. She barely even knows Dominic, but feels, for the first time, that she has found everything she has been looking for; this is where she fits in; this is where she belongs.

CHAPTER
EIGHTEEN

Dominic suggests the diner for breakfast the next morning, and Emma is relieved. She realizes she's been vaguely worried about confronting another scene with Jesse like the one at breakfast the day before. Although it is only a blip in a catalogue of lovely times together, she doesn't want to upset him again, and perhaps sitting together in a restaurant will make that less likely.

She gets dressed and goes to wash her face in the bathroom, where she finds Hobbes curled up fast asleep on the bath mat. Picking her up, she tiptoes downstairs and goes back home to brush her teeth and jump in the shower before meeting Dominic and Jesse outside by the truck.

It all feels so curious, she thinks, bouncing in the passenger seat of the truck as Dominic and Jesse loudly sing along to Neil Young, that this should feel so much like a family. Perhaps this is how every woman feels, dating a man with children. Perhaps this is how every woman feels when she has found what she didn't even know she was looking for. Emma should recognize family, for she was loved by her parents, but she didn't feel like she belonged, didn't feel she had the right family, even though they were clearly hers.

As for dating, they are not *dating*. Not exactly. They have only been on one date, to the farm dinner, and that wasn't really official. Nor has he mentioned taking her out. She is not sure what this is, other than fantastic sex, much laughter, and sweetness.

It may not have a label, but right now it feels lovely, and that is enough.

At the diner, Jesse is greeted by everyone, all of them commenting on how big he is, how grown-up. They tuck into a booth where Emma tries to order a fruit platter and rye toast, only to find Jesse insisting she needs to have pancakes instead, because the pancakes here are the best, and if she hasn't had them she is missing out.

Emma pauses. Pancakes drowning in syrup are the very last thing she wants right now, but she also wants to please Jesse, wants him to like her. If she has to eat a few pancakes to help that happen, she will sacrifice the fruit and toast.

Dominic tells stories throughout breakfast about Jesse, all of them funny, all of them delighting Jesse, though he has clearly heard them many times before.

"Tell Emma the one about my head splitting open like a watermelon!" He bounces excitedly on the banquette seat. "And the time you forgot me in the restaurant! Go on! Tell her!"

"I'm not sure I should, buddy," says Dominic. "I don't think those stories are good for my brand."

"Dad." Jesse raises an eyebrow at his father, who bursts out laughing and proceeds to fill the rest of breakfast with more stories of Jesse's childhood.

"Remember when you took the scissors out of the kitchen drawer and you decided to give yourself a haircut?" As Dominic recounts the tale, Jesse rocks back and forth with glee. He knows every word of this story but can't tear his eyes off his father, delighted at hearing his childhood over and over again.

"Oh man." Dominic shakes his head, laughing. "He cut huge chunks out of sections of his hair. It was terrible. He came in to show me with a big smile, thinking he'd given himself this great haircut, and he looked like he'd just stepped out of the circus ring. I had to shave it all off."

"But you left me a Mohawk!" Jesse shouts.

"Not that time. There wasn't enough hair."

Whatever Jesse was going through yesterday seems to be over, for the most part. He is as sweet with Emma as he was before he found her in his father's bed. When Dominic reaches for her hand as they walk out of the diner, Emma is glad to see that the flash of discomfort in Jesse's eyes passes quickly.

They drop Jesse at camp, then drive to Torno Lumber to buy materials for Lisa's shelves, before Emma goes off to buy more accessories for the house. She stops at Gold's for sandwiches for lunch, bringing them home to watch Dominic first construct the basic shelves in their backyard, leaping up from time to time to give him advice.

182

"I'm not sure that's completely level. It may be me, it probably is me, but can we just check it?"

They stop and check; stop and check; even when Emma is wrong, and she is wrong only once, they stop and check.

She brings her laptop outside, sitting under the shade of the apple tree while he saws, sands, and hammers. They stop, although only briefly, for a short but sweet lovemaking session after lunch.

One night, with a start, Emma realizes she has spent every night for the past week with Dominic. They haven't discussed it, but as each evening rolls on, they just both assume she will stay. And she has. She needs her own bed tonight, though. She has a lot to do tomorrow; they both have a lot to do, finishing up Lisa's house. And to be honest, she has to confess to herself that it will be good for her to have some space. Everything has happened so quickly, she feels a need to catch her breath, just to be sure it's all real.

After so many days away, Emma's house is a peaceful and welcome respite. But a lonely one. She pours herself a glass of wine and sits in the garden, where she immediately realizes she can hear Jesse laughing and Dominic calling him over to help with the grill, and her self-imposed exile seems ridiculous.

And yet she should have a night to herself. It can't be right to have this instant relationship in so short a time. Emma goes back inside, pours another glass of rosé, curls up on the sofa with Hobbes, and attempts to lose herself in a novel.

It doesn't work. She puts the book down every few paragraphs and picks up her phone, checking for emails, texts, any kind of distraction.

At ten o'clock, just as she is trawling through Netflix looking for a series she hasn't yet watched, Dominic texts her.

I miss you.

I miss you, too, she types, the smile wide on her face.

I'm going to bed now, he types. **I wanted to say good night.**

Good night, she types. **Sleep well.**

He sends an emoji kiss, and nothing else.

There is a part of her that had hoped he would suggest her coming over. She would have gone, even though she knows she needs the night alone. The relationships that burn brightest and fastest burn out the quickest, she reminds herself. She has learned this the hard way, with exciting friendships that failed.

A couple of years ago, at a party on the Upper West Side of Manhattan, Emma had watched as a very tall, rather stunning girl stalked in. She looked like a model, angular and chic, but it turned out she was actually a chef in a wonderful restaurant Emma had recently visited. The two of them spent the whole night chatting.

It felt immediately like they had known each other for years. It was one of those mutual girl crushes that women so often experience. They couldn't believe how much they had in common, how much they thought alike, how they were both interested in the same things, namely, interiors, food, design.

"We have to get together," said Anna, the girl, and they arranged to meet for lunch the next day. There were many lunches, coffees, dinners, and outings over the next few months. When they met one another's mutual friends they joked that they were each other's New Best Friends. But it was true: Emma hadn't found anyone in years who seemed to connect with her in quite the way Anna did.

The two of them went on adventures together, climbing into Anna's old VW Beetle convertible and driving out to fantastic farmers' markets in upstate New York, staying with friends of hers in Millbrook. Anna almost immediately became the best friend Emma had always wanted.

If she had been honest, she would have had to admit she didn't love Anna's friends. She found them pretentious and rather full of themselves. One of them, Albert, was the king of the malaprop. Emma would listen to him denigrate a fellow artist, using incorrect words in incorrect ways, and she would smile to herself as she sat there saying nothing.

She and Anna spent almost every weekend together, would text each other throughout the week and talk several times each night on the phone. Until, one day, Emma's text wasn't returned for a few hours. Anna eventually responded with an emoji unhappy face. She was sorry, she'd said; she'd been really busy.

Emma suggested coffee a few days later. Anna wrote back saying she had to work. She included a kissing emoji this time, as if that would make Emma feel loved.

Emma quickly discovered she felt like she was in a romantic relationship and the other person was backing off. She had no idea what she had done. They had become instant best friends, until the day they weren't.

She decided not to pursue Anna, certain that the friendship would get back on track as soon as her friend wasn't so busy. It was simply work-related, she told herself. This probably happened to Anna sometimes, and she just hadn't known her long enough to experience it before. So she waited, patiently . . .

Anna never contacted her again.

They ran into each other a few months later in a restaurant. She saw Anna, head close together with a girl Emma didn't recognize, two good-looking men sitting opposite them. And that was when she knew she had been replaced with another instant best friend.

It hurt tremendously. Emma wasn't used to being dumped. But she also had to admit the warning signs had been there, she had just failed to recognize them. Anna had regularly dismissed women she knew as being too high-maintenance, too bitchy, too needy. They had been friends, Anna had said about one or another woman she knew, until she realized they were awful. Emma lost count of the number of times she heard this. She thought that would never happen to her; she thought their friendship had been different.

She crafted texts many, many times. *If I did anything to upset you*, she wrote to Anna, *I would love to know;*

I'm so sorry if I said anything to offend you; I would never knowingly have done anything to jeopardize our friendship. But she never sent them. She deleted the number, which she had never known by heart, then blocked it. One night a few months after the previous encounter, she saw Anna again, this time sitting with another new friend at a different restaurant. This time, she went over, despite the pounding of her heart, and with a big smile, tapped Anna on the shoulder. She was friendly but slightly disinterested, cool but polite.

"Anna." She bent down to kiss her. "What a nice surprise to see you here. I saw the review in the *Times* the other week. Congratulations." She turned then and nodded to the other people around the table, now watching her curiously. Turning back to Anna, she said, "You look wonderful. So good to see you. Have a great evening," and with a wave she turned on her heel and walked out. She had known Anna would never realize how upset Emma had been when she disappeared, nor how discombobulating it was to see her now. But most of all, she had realized that Anna would never know how un-Emma it was for her to behave in the way she had just behaved, affecting an air of gracious disinterest. Because as close as she had thought she and Anna had been, she now knew they had really not known each other at all.

Emma was, at least, able to let go after that. She no longer worried about what she might have done to push Anna away. She had no idea whether Anna had tried to call after that chance meeting, thanks to blocking her number, but sometimes she liked to think she would have tried.

It had been just like a romance. The intensity, the delight at finding someone with so many shared interests, the way the mutual attraction had fizzled out. Emma hadn't been needy, or high-maintenance, or bitchy, but Anna was someone who moved through people, who gathered them easily because of her beauty and charisma, and discarded them just as easily and quickly. Perhaps it was from boredom, perhaps it was just because she was careless of any feelings but her own. All Emma was certain of was that she wouldn't jump into any friendships, or relationships, that quickly again.

However, here she is sleeping over every night with Dominic, for all intents and purposes, rushing things in a way that is bound to end badly. Yet there isn't the buzz of nervous excitement she has had before at the beginning of relationships. There is, instead, huge passion. But the relationship doesn't feel dangerous. She doesn't feel that she and Dominic are anxious about having found each other. If anything, their connection to each other feels calm, and safe, and — she doesn't even really want to think this it's so unlikely — *right*.

Nevertheless, she believes she needs this night off. She is glad she is in her crisp, cool sheets, glad that she can stretch a leg out to the other side of the bed when her own side gets too hot. She is glad that when she finds herself awake at two a.m., she can turn the light on and get back to sleep by reading, without worrying about waking anyone else up.

And at that early hour, before she has a chance to become absorbed in the book, she can lie in bed and think about all that has changed over the last week; the loveliness of not being alone, the fun it has been to get to know Jesse, to find herself cooking dinner for someone other than herself, to feel part of a family that is, this time, the right family for her.

Emma is awakened by the telephone. Sure it is Dominic, she is surprised to see *Unknown* on the screen. It's either withheld or overseas.

"Hello, darling," peals her mother's voice. "We haven't spoken for a while so I thought I'd check that you were still alive."

"I'm very much alive," says Emma, getting out of bed and padding to the kitchen to get some coffee on. "Alive and busy."

"Busy? Did you get another job? Oh, I'm so pleased, darling. Daddy and I have been worried about you, out in the country all by yourself with no one you know."

"I told you, it isn't the country. It's the *suburbs*, which is a different thing entirely. I'm surrounded by people, and I got my first decorating job last week." Of course, Emma knows her mother will refuse to acknowledge the word *suburb*, having spent her entire life attempting to erase her roots. She ignores Emma's mention of the word.

"Darling, that's wonderful!" she says. "Who is the job for?"

Emma smiles at her mother's question. What difference does it make who the job is for? It's not like her mother would know anyone in Westport. "It's for a woman my age who doesn't know how to decorate her house. I'm just doing two rooms, for now, but it's a start. She's thrilled."

"I'm so pleased for you. But I also called because I do want to make sure you've booked your flight for Cousin George's engagement. Remember? I'm throwing the party here at home?"

Oh, God. How had this so completely slipped her mind? "I'm so sorry, Mum, completely forgot. Give me the dates again and I'll see if I can work it out. It may be difficult, though," she lies. "I have a few more clients I'm meeting with, so it really depends on the work situation."

Her mother gives her the dates, as Emma's heart sinks, picturing a party at which she will know no one other than family members she hasn't seen in years. She realizes she will probably have nothing in common with any of them any more, if indeed she ever did. And with that thought, she can't help thinking about how comfortable she has felt with Dominic and Jesse.

"Mummy?" She resorts to "Mummy" only when she wants something, but a thought has just occurred to her. "Would it be okay if I maybe brought someone with me?"

Her mother is instantly suspicious. "What sort of someone?"

"My landlord, actually. He's terribly nice, and he's never been to England, but I'm sure he'd love to go. I have no idea whether he would come. It probably wouldn't work, but if he could, would that be okay?"

"Your landlord?" Her mother is shocked. "Darling, why on earth would you offer to bring your landlord to a family party in England? I know you're trying to prove you're a good tenant, but isn't this a bit *too too?*"

"We're sort of seeing each other," says Emma, reluctantly, for she really doesn't want her mother knowing anything about her life.

"Emma!" booms her mother in surprise. "Why didn't you say that in the beginning? Now I understand! But, darling, I'm not sure that a family party is the best place for him to meet everyone. And you haven't been living there very long. Isn't it a bit early to be thinking about bringing him to England to meet your family? I don't know, Emma. I'm not sure this would be the right time."

Emma says nothing. If Dominic can't go, she won't go either. If anything, it makes the decision easier.

Later that day, on the way to Lisa's, Emma mentions to Dominic that her mother has phoned. Emma's thinking about going to England, she tells him. Has he ever been?

"I've never left the country," he says. "I don't even have a passport."

"How can you not have a passport?" Emma, who has had a passport as far back as she can remember, is aghast.

"Why would I need a passport when I've never left the United States? My driver's licence is my ID."

"But what if you suddenly decided to hop over to, I don't know, Mexico, or the Caribbean for the weekend?"

Dominic turns and looks at her, shaking his head with a laugh. "Do you know me? Do I look like someone who would decide to hop over to the Caribbean for the weekend? Rhode Island? Yes. New Jersey? Yes. I've even been to Maine for the weekend, which I won't be doing again in a hurry because it was so far away. But the Caribbean? Never."

"I'm so sorry," says Emma. When she was growing up on the relatively tiny island of Britain, everyone she had ever met had a passport. It was so cheap and easy to hop on a ferry or a plane and go on holiday. The English lived for their holidays. Who wouldn't have a passport over there?

Of course someone like Dominic has never left the United States. Why would he need to? she thinks. America is so vast, you could spend your life picking different places to visit on holiday every year and you'd still never get to see the whole country.

"I'm an idiot," she says. "I'm sounding like a snob. It's just that in England almost everyone has a passport. Maybe you should get one? Maybe" — she takes a breath, hardly believing she's saying this — "we could all go away somewhere for a holiday sometime?"

"You're right. I should definitely have a passport," says Dominic. "Now that I have myself an English girlfriend. She's positively spiffing," he continues, in a really bad English accent as Emma groans.

192

"Please don't do that," she says. "That's the most horrible English accent I've ever heard."

"Toodles. Pip pip!" he says, as Emma shakes her head.

"No one in England ever says that," she says. "Seriously. Please stop. It's very difficult for me to continue being attracted to a man who sounds worse than Dick Van Dyke in *Mary Poppins*."

Dominic's face falls. "Really? I'm that bad?"

"Oh, Dominic," she says with a sweet smile. "You are so very much worse."

The shelves go up at Lisa's, and they are beautiful. More than beautiful; they are perfect. Dominic has done a great job.

Emma is slightly surprised, but relieved and delighted. She works right alongside him, priming, applying the first coat of paint. Tomorrow he will come back by himself to sand, and apply the second coat. Saturday will see the third coat, so Emma will be able to finish the room on Wednesday, by which time most, if not all, of the furniture she has ordered will have arrived.

"We make a good team," says Dominic, looking over at where she is painting. "I like this. You and I."

Emma smiles. She is liking it, too.

CHAPTER
NINETEEN

The weeks sail by, filled with ease, and fun, and a peace that Emma has never known before. One Saturday afternoon, after Dominic and Emma have spent the morning finally creating the garden Emma has long dreamed about, Dominic announces that AJ and Deb are coming for dinner that night. Does Emma have anyone she wants to ask? It might be fun to turn it into a small party.

She will invite Sophie and Rob, not knowing anyone else to ask. She worries, for a brief moment, that her friends might not have anything in common with Dominic's, but she pushes the thought away. This week has been so busy, finishing the decorating for Lisa, that she hasn't even had a chance to speak to Sophie. It will be nice for them to meet Dominic properly.

He is insisting on grilling his usual burgers, but Emma persuades him to try something a little different. "Not steak," she groans, after his first suggestion. "How about tuna?"

Dominic grimaces. "Do we have to have fish?"

"Who doesn't like fish? Okay, I can see that you don't particularly like fish, but I do. Most people do. I'll do a simple pasta with pesto to go along with it. I promise that everyone will love it. Maybe I'll do a shrimp ceviche to serve beforehand . . . "

"Why are you getting so fancy?" He peers at her. "Are your friends fancy?"

Emma laughs. "No, my friends are not fancy, but I want to do something nice. Let's do burgers with sourdough rolls, tuna and pesto, ceviche, and a tomato, mozzarella, and prosciutto salad. How's that? Unfancy enough for you?"

"I like the pro-zhiutt," says Dominic.

Emma stares at him. "*Prosciutto?*" she says.

"That's not how you pronounce it," says Dominic earnestly. "In Italy, they never pronounce the O. It's pronounced *proZHOOT, mohzaRELL, riCOTT.*"

"I'm sure that's not right," says Emma, who has been to Italy many times and has never heard anyone there ask her if she wanted some *proZHOOT* or *mohzaRELL.* "Maybe it's an American thing?" she says, finally, to appease him.

"Nah," says Dominic happily. "It's Italian. I can get the best *proZHOOT* ever. Want me to do the shopping? I can pick it up now if you want."

"That would be great," says Emma, giving up on pronunciation. "Do we have enough to drink? Shall I stop at the liquor shop?"

"Sounds good to me. Can you drop Jesse off at the School of Rock for his guitar lesson?"

"Sure," she says, but a slight feeling of dread settles on her. Despite the admittedly nice moments they've shared, she and Jesse have not yet quite found their groove again. At first, after that awful morning, she'd

195

thought he'd settled down. But in the past week or so, he has not been the sweet little boy he was before he realized that she and his father were more than just friends. Emma has noticed him becoming increasingly suspicious, and cool. She tries to convince herself that with time she can win him over for good, but she can't help feeling a little apprehensive. He loved her before, of course he will love her again, right? Still, the prospect of spending time with him on her own makes her nervous. What if he doesn't talk to her?

In the car on the way to his guitar lesson, her fears are realized. Jesse is silent, speaking only when necessary, and then in monosyllables.

"What songs are you learning at the School of Rock?" Emma turns her head to glance at him in the backseat, in a bid to engage him.

Jesse shrugs. "Don't know."

"Is it rock? Stuff I would know?"

"No." He refuses to look at her. After a while she gives up, reaching forward to turn on the radio, softly singing along until they reach their destination. As soon as they do, Jesse jumps out of the car without saying goodbye, leaving Emma both upset and angry.

How is a six-year-old allowed to behave like this? she wonders. Then she berates herself for not following him and forcing him to say goodbye. But she wouldn't have done that, she thinks. Couldn't have done that, lest it bring on another meltdown.

It's not good for a small child to have this much power, she thinks, aware that her mood has been brought down, that she is now obsessing about making Jesse happy.

She wishes she knew how.

That evening, setting up for the dinner she and Dominic have planned, Emma tries to settle the butterflies in her stomach. Will her friends like him? Will he like them? Why does she care so much?

"You look amazing," Sophie whispers in her ear as they hug on the doorstep, having merely texted for days. "Oh my God, are you totally in love?"

"Stop," says Emma, kissing Rob hello, then squealing in delight as she sees Sophie's mother, Teddy, emerging from the car with Jackson.

"Teddy, I haven't seen you in ages!"

"Is it okay to bring her?" says Sophie. "I knew we should have asked, but I totally forgot to text you and I know you love my mom."

"I'm thrilled," says Emma, giving Teddy a big hug. "How are you?"

"All the better for seeing you," says Teddy, as Jackson pulls on her long white braid. "Ouch. Jackson, sweetie. Be gentle with your old grandma."

"You're hardly old," says Emma. "You're the youngest fifty-something I know."

Teddy breaks into a big grin and leans forward to plant a kiss on Emma's cheek. "Fifty-something! I knew there was a reason I loved you."

"Come and meet the others," says Emma. "Let me get you all drinks."

"This looks fantastic." Sophie bypasses Emma's ceviche to lift the aluminium foil off a catering pan revealing a huge chicken parm, smothered in tomato sauce and dripping with cheese.

"Oh my God," swoons Sophie, picking a piece of cheese off the side. "Did you make this? This tastes incredible."

"I did not," says Emma. "I made all the other stuff, which Dominic said was far too healthy for his friends, so he insisted on making chicken parm. Please tell me you'll eat my ceviche?"

"He made this? All by himself?"

"He's an amazing chef, especially when it comes to Italian food, and all of it is insanely fattening, which means I'm going to weigh three hundred pounds by the end of the summer." She casts a look at the pan. "It may be worth it, though."

"I'll say it is." Sophie is almost drooling. "He cooks, too? Is he the perfect man?"

Teddy joins them, putting Jackson down and peering out the kitchen window. "Where is this perfect man of yours? Is he the rather macho bearded one by the grill?"

"No, that's his friend AJ."

"Of course it is. He's the handsome one by the table, then."

"Yes. That's Dominic. I'm not sure he's *my man* yet, though. Not really." Emma attempts a laugh.

Sophie shoots, her a sceptical look. "You're completely starry-eyed and you've been sleeping at his house every night. I'd say that pretty much makes it official."

"Sophie!" Emma blushes. "I just — " She lowers her voice. "His son doesn't seem completely happy about us being together, so I'm trying to be discreet about it. I don't want to rock the boat. I figure if we take it slowly, he'll have time to get used to it."

"I thought Jesse adored you?"

"Well, he's gone back and forth. We got along great at first, but not any more. Now he sometimes looks at me strangely. I'm afraid he thinks I'm the devil sent to steal his father away from him. I'm trying to prove that I have no intention of getting between the two of them."

"It'll be fine," Sophie says, shrugging off Emma's concern. "You're a wonderful person, and Jesse will realize you're a great addition to his family. He's incredibly lucky to have you. He should know that."

"He's six years old. I'm not sure he's capable of recognizing any of that. But he did like me before, so hopefully he'll get over this and we'll go back to being friends."

"You're the loveliest woman in the world. He'll get over it." Sophie gives her a hug, and asks, "Can I take anything outside?"

"Grab the crisps. Come and meet AJ and Deb. And, of course, Jesse."

When they get outside, they find that Jesse is busy with Dylan, a friend who has come over for a playdate. They are grabbing handfuls of popcorn from the table before cramming them in their mouths as they race around the garden.

Emma watches, wanting to tell them to slow down, not to fill up on popcorn, to leave room for the chicken parm and for the hot dogs Dominic is grilling. But she says nothing, reminding herself she is not Jesse's mother. She's noticed more and more that he sees her efforts to guide him as telling him off, and Jesse clearly doesn't believe she has the right to do that. Emma knows she doesn't have the right to do that, either.

Perhaps, in time, she will be able to exert more influence. She can see that Dominic is an amazing father, brimming with love, attention, and appreciation for his child. But he doesn't set boundaries the way she would, rarely setting Jesse straight if he is rude or behaving badly, which is not how Emma would parent.

Even though Emma is not a parent.

Teddy sits next to her on the Adirondack chair, toasting her with a frozen margarita in a plastic cup. They sit in companionable silence for a while, watching Dominic, A J, and Rob chatting by the grill, and Sophie and Deb animatedly discussing their shared obsession with Etsy.

"This is nice," says Teddy, after a while. "He is nice." She nods her head in Dominic's direction. "This is good for you. He's good for you."

Emma finds herself smiling as she nods. "Things are going well. It's early days but it feels good."

"Early days are irrelevant," Teddy says. "When it's right, it's right. Do you know, when I met my husband — Sophie's father — I came home that night and told

200

my mother I had met the man I was going to marry. He went home and said the same thing to his father. We had barely spoken, just seen each other across the room and shared one dance before the night was over, but both of us knew. Dominic may not be who you would have chosen for yourself, but here you are. It's quite clear the two of you have found something special in each other."

Emma looks at her curiously. "You can see that he isn't what I would have chosen for myself?"

"He's from a very different world than yours. Even I can see that. But he's a very good man. I see that, too. And he loves you." She looks steadily at Emma. "It would seem you love him, too."

Emma shakes her head. "I don't know that we're talking love yet. It's far too early."

"It may be too early for either of you to admit it, but it's there. I am something of a witch, Emma, and I can tell you that this is the man for you. You're going to live happily ever after." She smiles. "The son will come around."

"That's the challenging part," says Emma. "But I'm working on it."

Teddy goes off to talk to the others, and Emma notices Jesse is still tearing around the garden with Dylan, approaching their table for his third canned soda. Really, Emma's not surprised that he's acting like a crazy person, given that he's just consumed his weight in sugar. She watches him finish the drink and reach for another.

"Hey, Jesse, if you're thirsty, maybe you should have some water?"

Jesse barely pauses as he reaches for a fresh can from the galvanized bucket on the ground, and he doesn't even look at her as he swigs the beverage. He looks quite defiant, thinks Emma, who doesn't say another word.

"A Valium?" mutters Sophie, who has come up beside her and witnessed the whole exchange.

"You know what you need, Jesse?" Emma now calls out, loudly enough for Jesse to hear. "You need a trampoline." Jesse stops in his tracks and stares at her, his eyes widening as his mouth opens.

"I do." He starts nodding. "I do. I do need a trampoline."

"I think it would be a great thing for you to get rid of some of this energy."

"That and chucking the soda," mutters Sophie under her breath, although Emma hears her loud and clear.

"I think we should buy you one," says Emma. "A late birthday gift, seeing as I didn't know you when it actually was your birthday."

"Really?" Jesse is now hopping up and down. "Did you ask Dad? Did Dad say yes?"

Emma looks over at Dominic, who heard her raised voice when she made the suggestion and has been watching the exchange attentively ever since. "What do you think? Can I buy Jesse a trampoline?"

"I think that would be a great idea," Dominic says with a smile. "Jesse? What do you say?"

"Thank you!" shouts Jesse, running over and flinging his arms around Emma as her eyes, completely unexpectedly, fill with tears. Relieved, even thrilled, she hugs him back. It's not precisely how she would have chosen to pave the way back into his heart, even temporarily. But for now, it will do.

As the hours tick by, Emma realizes it is obvious to all that she and Dominic are a couple. Yet she also can't help but notice that Dominic has been careful not to kiss her or touch her all evening.

Perhaps he doesn't want his friends to know, she thinks, although Deb had sidled up to her earlier in the evening and whispered how thrilled she and AJ were that Emma and Dominic seemed to have such great chemistry. It is more likely, she knows, that he is being reserved for Jesse's sake. While at first he seemed oblivious to Jesse's resentment of her, they have discussed it enough since that first morning that Dominic is more sensitive to it now. Still, Emma tries not to let her imagination run riot with fantasies that his standoffishness is about something else.

Finally, towards the end of the evening, Dominic slips his arms around her waist from behind as she is talking to Sophie and Deb, and kisses her neck. She savours the feeling of his arms around her, even as she suspects this display is fuelled by alcohol.

"Now that's a bold move," says Deb, looking from one to the other. "We can definitely all see you've progressed from the landlord/tenant relationship now."

"No." Dominic shakes his head. "I do this with all my tenants."

"It's true," says Emma, leaning back into his body, marvelling at how solid and safe he feels. "It was in my lease."

They all laugh.

"Seriously, though," says Deb with delight. "The two of you are a couple?"

"We're a beginning," says Emma, and at the same time Dominic says, "Yes, we're a couple."

Emma pulls away and turns to look at him. "Are we? Are we a couple?"

"Aren't we?"

"We haven't even been on a date!" she says. "Well, except for that farm dinner — but that wasn't official because I invited you."

"That counts!" says Dominic. "Anyway, we've found plenty of other things to keep us busy . . . " He grins.

Sophie claps her hands over her ears. "Too much information," she says, before removing her hands. And then she glares at them in mock outrage. "What do you mean, you haven't been on an official date? A real, formal 'man asks a woman out' date? What have you been doing?" Then she laughs. "No, don't answer that! You must go on a date! It's terrible that it hasn't happened."

"It's all been a bit more organic than that," explains Emma. "We've just sort of fallen into a relationship. We've kind of gone beyond dating."

"Bullshit." Sophie turns to Dominic. "You need to take her out for dinner. You can drop Jesse off with us

204

and I'll babysit him. He can even sleep over." She winks. "Go somewhere nice. Wednesday night?"

"Sophie!" Emma starts to laugh. "I don't even know if I'm free on Wednesday night."

"Trust me," she says. "You're free." Then she looks at Dominic. "You don't work at the Hen until Thursday, right?"

"Right." Dominic grins.

"So now you both can go on your first official date. Take her somewhere you love. Don't go to a place that's trendy or cheap. You're welcome." She turns away with a smile. "Honey?" she calls out to Rob. "Can you bring me another glass of wine?"

"I don't even know anywhere trendy," Dominic says to Sophie. "What does that even mean?"

"It means somewhere that opened up in the last year that's filled with very glamorous people who are over-dressed and filled with their own fabulousness. They tend to be very loud. Don't take her anywhere like that."

"I don't know anywhere like that." Dominic feigns horror. "The restaurants I go to — when I go to restaurants at all — have been here forever. They're small. And cosy."

"Perfect. Take her somewhere like that."

CHAPTER
TWENTY

Love. Does he love me? Is this the real thing? Emma moves around the kitchen, cleaning up her house before she gets ready for her date, pausing with shock and surprise.

I love him, she thinks, her breath catching in her throat before a slow smile of wonder settles on her face. *I love him.*

She couldn't tell him. Wouldn't tell him. It would be too risky, would make her too vulnerable — what if he is frightened away?

She is certain, though, as she puts the dishcloth down and moves to the bathroom, that she does love him. For a long time now, Emma realizes, she has been worried about her capacity to love. She didn't love Rufus, the only other man she was supposed to have loved. She liked him very much, to be sure, but not in the way she needed in order to marry him. And her relationships in the years since have never blossomed into anything even close to what she's experiencing now.

Emma has never quite believed that love would happen for her. It certainly happened to others, perhaps just a few lucky people, but she had thought, had always known, she wouldn't be one of them. That kind of love wasn't going to happen to her, and she had accepted it.

And yet here she is. And it does seem to have happened. It is passionate, and sweeping, and dramatic, but in the most comfortable of ways.

I know you, she thinks, from the very beginning, when she first came to see the house. *I recognize you. Here you are.*

Their relationship is ease and safety. It is quiet recognition. It is going on their first date together, after weeks of sleeping together. It is so easily starting to spend all their time together, virtually living together, so easily finding herself no longer worrying about what she looks like first thing in the morning. She makes the effort to feel beautiful now, secure in the knowledge that she doesn't need to, that he likes her whatever she looks like, even with terrible bedhead and pillow marks on her cheek.

She remembers having read something once about a psychologist who had spent years studying married couples, and who was able to predict very quickly whether newly-weds would stay together and be happy or see their unions end in divorce. His predictions were unerringly accurate.

He'd discovered that successful marriages boiled down to kindness. Not necessarily the obvious kindness, like bringing someone a cup of coffee in bed, although that was a lovely sort of gesture, and important. But what he pointed to was the kindness of attention. When one partner asked a question of the other, or asked for an opinion, or wanted to talk about a problem, in a successful relationship the other partner always stopped to offer their full attention. By doing so, they met their partner's most fundamental emotional needs.

The article had stuck with Emma. And in the weeks since she's moved in, she hasn't been able to stop thinking about it. The couples in disastrous unions, this psychologist said, were constantly in fight-or-flight mode. They were verbally or sometimes physically combative, always preparing to attack or be attacked.

Looking back, her relationship with Rufus had indeed been combative. They would verbally spar, jousting with words and sarcasm.

The relationship with Dominic is different, not just because he is from such a different world. There is true kindness in their interactions. She thinks about how even when she met him that first day, looking at the house, he had listened to everything she said, really considered her words and responded. Dominic makes time for her, listens to her, is calm, and steady, and so grounded that he makes her feel calm, and steady, and grounded, too.

So this is love, she now thinks. *I was right*. It isn't a roller coaster of emotion, but rather a feeling of a kind of calm, a peacefulness.

And there is no doubt in her mind that she has come home.

Emma blow-dries her hair, then uses a curling iron to twist it into the loose curls that Dominic loves, the loose curls that make her feel feminine and beautiful.

She left his house this morning, telling him he couldn't come over until he was ready to pick her up for their date. She wants this to be a real date. She wants to feel excited, feel the thrill of anticipation, and she wants Dominic to feel it, too.

She has no idea where they are going, but Dominic said casual. Not too casual, though, she thinks. It is August already, almost the end of summer, and the evenings are warm. Warm enough for her to wear what she has chosen to wear all summer, one of the pretty linen shifts and loose printed tea dresses that make her feel feminine and pretty.

She chooses a strappy white linen dress tonight, to show off the deep, golden tan that has developed over the summer. Suede espadrilles with a small heel, a gold shark's-tooth necklace, and a sheer grey chiffon wrap.

The lightest touch of bronzer, highlighter on her cheek-bones, gloss on her lips. They may have been together just a short while, but Dominic has seen her first thing in the morning. He knows what she looks like without all the accoutrements. She doesn't need to dress up for him, but it is nice to dress up for herself. *He loves me with or without make-up.* And then, mid-thought, she stops.

I love him, she thinks again, getting up to leave.

The bar at Tarantino's is packed. Dominic greets a dark-haired man with a bro hug, and then they are led through the bar and into the restaurant.

"I reserved the quietest table we have," the man says, taking them to one in the window, and laughing because nowhere in the restaurant is it truly quiet. "What can I get you to drink? Dominic, you want your Tito's martini?"

"Always," Dominic says with a grin. "Emma?"

"Could I have a glass of Prosecco?"

"Coming right up."

Emma sits back and looks around at the bustling Italian restaurant. "I love it."

"I've been coming here forever," says Dominic. "Sophie told me to bring you to my favourite joint, and this is it."

"Do you know everyone in here?" Emma laughs as people look over to catch Dominic's eye and wave.

"Pretty much. The combination of being both Italian *and* a townie. My family lived right here, in Saugatuck, for years. I went to school with pretty much all the local business owners down here. It's a tight-knit community."

"What's Saugatuck?"

"A neighbourhood. The best neighbourhood." He winks.

"Have you ever wanted to live anywhere else?"

"Never. This is home. I like that wherever I go, I know people. The whole town is filled with memories for me. I remember tearing around on my bike with a pack of neighbourhood kids when I was young; I like that I grew up here when there was Bill's Smoke Store, and the Remarkable Book Store, and Sally's. I don't have any wanderlust in me. I guess we're very different that way."

210

"No," says Emma. "Obviously I left England for the United States, but honestly, I had never really felt at home there. Oh, don't get me wrong. My parents loved me. I'm much more like my dad than my mum — she doesn't understand me at all, and of course my dad was always at work while I was growing up, so I was left feeling like I must have been a changeling. Living in London wasn't much better, so I was happy for the transfer to New York. I lived in Manhattan for years, but I always knew it wasn't where I wanted to spend the rest of my life. I think I've found my place now. I'm really not sure I would ever want to go anywhere else."

"I think we find our place when we make a decision to do what's right for us rather than always keeping everyone else happy. From everything you've told me, it sounds like you spent your whole life following someone else's plan. This sounds like the first time you've respected yourself enough to do what is right for you. And you're right, that's when we find our place." He smiles.

Emma's heart lurches. *I love you,* she thinks, clamping her mouth shut in a tight smile to make sure the words don't escape. "Cheers." She raises her glass, instead, and takes a sip of her Prosecco.

"By the way," she says, "I forgot to tell you. I ordered the trampoline on Monday and it should be here in a couple of days. Do you think we can put it up together?"

"I wouldn't have you do it yourself. Not when we make such a great team. Listen, thank you for buying that for him. I know he's struggled with you and me a

211

bit, but hopefully it will all get better. I hope you haven't bought the trampoline to try to make him feel better about you, because I wouldn't want that."

"I've thought about that," says Emma. "I've worried myself about whether I'm subliminally trying to bribe him, but I don't know that I am. Honestly, he's just crazy about trampolines and every time we pass those kids in the house on the corner jumping up and down, he stares with such longing, it just breaks my heart. I really want to try to do something nice for him."

Dominic smiles. "You're right. He has been talking about a trampoline forever, and he does stare at those kids every time we drive past. I can't believe you noticed that."

"I can't believe you didn't buy him a trampoline earlier," she jokes.

"I was waiting for someone else to pay for it," he says. "Seriously, though, thank you. This is incredibly meaningful to me. And Jesse. That you would notice and then do something so nice."

"It's my pleasure," says Emma, as Dominic reaches over and strokes her hand. "I think he's such a great kid. This really isn't a bribe, but a part of me does hope that eventually he'll see I'm not a bad person."

"I don't think he thinks you're a bad person at all," says Dominic. "You have to remember it has only ever been him and me. I've been very careful to keep any relationships I've had away from him. Gina never spent the night, for example. He's really had no experience of seeing me with anyone on an ongoing basis."

"So why have you let him see *us?*" says Emma, in a tone of voice so light it doesn't give away what she is really thinking, hoping, wanting to hear.

"You know why," says Dominic.

"I do?" Her heart skips a beat.

"Is it too early to say it?"

"Say what?" says Emma, whose voice catches in her throat.

"That . . . this. Us. Feels . . . right. It does to you, too, doesn't it? Feel right?"

"Yes." Emma laughs to dispel her nervousness and her slight smudge of disappointment that he didn't say what she so wanted to hear. She pushes it aside.

Dominic's face is now serious. "I mean it, Emma. I don't know what it is about you . . . "

"Is it my English accent? My excellent teeth?" She bares them. "Is it my curls?"

Dominic laughs. "Why, yes. It is in fact all of those things, but more than that, it just feels . . . I don't know. Different. I feel safe with you. I love . . . being with you. It's the easiest, most comfortable relationship I've ever had."

"Is it a relationship, then?" Emma says.

"Isn't it?"

"Yes?"

"Yes!" He wipes an imaginary bead of sweat off his forehead. "I was getting worried."

The waiter approaches the table. "May I tell you about today's specials?"

"Thank God!" Emma looks at him. "Saved by the linguine."

The waiter frowns. "We don't have linguine today."

Emma shakes her head with a laugh. "Never mind. My mistake. Tell us what you do have."

The food has been eaten, the wine has been drunk, and Emma and Dominic have not stopped talking all night. She has heard his stories. And she has shared her own.

"Did you know you liked me as soon as you met me?" she teases, late in the meal.

"Almost as soon as I met you. I didn't walk away thinking, *Wow, that tenant is super hot.*" He laughs as Emma makes a comically disappointed face, growing serious before taking her hand. "It was more than that, Emma. I liked being with you, from that very first time. Even when you came to look at the house, I kept thinking about you. I was so worried you wouldn't take it! And after you signed the lease, I found I really looked forward to seeing you. When I'd leave my house and come out to the driveway, I would dawdle a little, hoping you'd come out and see me."

Emma is moved by his words, surprised that his feelings mirrored her own so exactly. The feelings that well up inside her are almost more than she can deal with, an explosion of happiness deep inside her belly. She has to lighten the mood, so she laughs again and says, "Oh God! I was doing the same thing. I'd hear your truck pull in and suddenly remember that I had to go to the mailbox."

"Remember when you went to get the mail early one morning and I came over to talk to you? Oh my God. Your face!"

"I was devastated. It was the one time I didn't want you to see me. I'd just rolled out of bed and I looked terrible."

"You looked adorable." Dominic's eyes twinkle at the memory. "I think that was the moment I really started to fall for you."

"Have you fallen for me, then?" *I love you*, she thinks.

He smiles. "Let's just say I like you."

"I like you, too," says Emma. "I really like you. I really, really like you a lot."

The smile leaves Dominic's face as he looks at her. "I love you," he says, serious now.

"Oh, thank God!" Emma bursts out, almost weeping with relief, before laughing at herself. "I'm sorry, Dominic. I'm so relieved to hear you say it. I love *you*. I love you, too."

Dominic leans forward and kisses her, pulling back for just a second to look at her, smiling into her eyes before kissing her again.

"I wasn't expecting this," says Dominic. "You. Us. All of it. I was happy to grow old with Jesse."

"I wasn't expecting it either." Emma laughs again, turning as they hear a burst of noise from the sidewalk outside.

They both watch a woman throw her head back with laughter as she's about to get into a large white Suburban. She looks over to the restaurant just as she gets in the car, and when Emma turns back to Dominic, the colour has drained from his face.

"Are you okay?" Emma rests her hand on Dominic's. "What's wrong?"

"That woman." He turns to her with an unfamiliar look in his eye, frowning. "That was . . . Stacy."

"Stacy?"

He's silent for a moment, looking dazed. "Jesse's mother."

"Oh my God." Emma's hands fly to her mouth. "She's in town?"

"It would seem so," says Dominic, now distant. Cold.

"I can't believe she's here and she hasn't been in touch. How can she not want to see Jesse?"

Dominic's face hardens as he calls the waiter over. "Can we have the cheque, please? We have to go."

Dominic doesn't talk all the way home. His jaw is clenched and twitching with anxiety. Emma sits staring down at the dashboard, unable to look at him, wanting this journey to be over as quickly as possible.

What just happened? she thinks. He just told her he loves her. How could seeing his ex-girlfriend derail him so? He had said Stacy hadn't meant much to him, other than giving him the greatest gift in the world in Jesse. If that is true, why is he so tense, so distracted, so clearly upset?

Emma stares out the window as they drive over the bridge, not even noticing the reflection of the lights in the water. Up until ten minutes ago, her life was perfect. What the hell just happened?

Can it have changed so quickly? In seconds? Was this all a terrible mistake? She turns her head from time

216

to time to look at Dominic. She is sure he knows she is looking at him, but instead of turning to look back, or reaching over to give her hand a reassuring squeeze, he stares stonily ahead, not saying a word.

"Is there something I can do to help?" Emma tries, halfway down Compo Road South. She wants to ask him why he's reacting so strongly, what his behaviour means, but she's frightened of the look on his face.

"I'm fine," says Dominic, who clearly isn't fine. Emma looks at his hands on the steering wheel, wondering if she should reach over and touch him, stroke his arm, squeeze his hand. But he has an impenetrable wall around him.

"Thank you for a lovely evening," says Emma, getting out of the truck in the driveway and hesitating. For a while now she has been going automatically to Dominic's house, brushing her teeth and washing her face in his bathroom at the top of the stairs, climbing into his bed, and falling asleep curled up in his arms.

"You're welcome," says Dominic, distractedly.

"I think maybe I should sleep at mine tonight," Emma says, which isn't what she wants at all. She wants him to snap out of whatever it is he's going through and put his arms around her. She wants him to apologize, tell her again that he loves her, that the words they'd said to each other at dinner and the happiness they'd found together were more important than anything Stacy might have meant to him or done to him.

But instead he says, "Sure. That's probably a good idea." Dominic gives her a perfunctory peck on the lips and turns to walk into his house. Clearly his mind is still elsewhere. She doubts he even realizes he is walking away from her. Emma stands as still as a stone, feeling like her entire world has collapsed.

She makes it inside, closes the door, and locks it before she realizes there are tears staining her cheeks. She tries to steady herself. *Just give him a few minutes*, she admonishes herself. Obviously it's a big deal for him to see her; he'd told her before that he had no idea where she was living or anything. *Just give him some time*. The poor man must be traumatized. If he would let her, she would try to comfort him, reassure him.

Dominic is sure to knock on the door eventually and apologize. How is it possible that one second he is telling her he loves her, and seconds later, when he glimpses his ex, he's changed his mind? It's not possible. It must be that he is upset, and if that's the case, he will come over. He would not deliberately leave her without an explanation for this long.

Her mind starts spinning again to darker thoughts, which grow darker as the night progresses and there is no word from Dominic. No reassuring text, no quick hug to let her know that he is okay, that what they have is still real.

In the early hours she sits straight up. What if he has realized he's still in love with Jesse's mother? What other explanation could there be for his behaviour?

Emma pictures the woman she saw so briefly from inside the restaurant. It had been hard to really see what she looked like. A redhead, slim, leather trousers and some kind of brightly coloured top. Was she pretty?

Hard to tell. Probably. Was she the kind of woman Emma could see Dominic with? Well, yes. She looked like all the women who hang around the bar at the Fat Hen and try to chat Dominic up. She looked like the kind of woman Emma would have imagined Dominic to be with, before she fell in love with him herself.

She is up all night, intermittently crying and feeling numb, exhaustion wreaking havoc with her emotions. She starts off concerned about Dominic, knowing he will come to talk to her, for isn't she his partner? His lover? Isn't she the woman he just tonight claimed to love?

But he doesn't come.

At four in the morning, exhausted and bewildered, she gives up trying to go to sleep and makes herself tea.

A few weeks ago, I was the most self-sufficient, independent woman in the world, she thinks. I had everything going for me. I had left the city and found a great little house and I didn't need anyone. I had finally accepted that I was better off on my own, that I didn't really fit in with other people, and that was fine. Good, even. This is exactly the kind of heartache and misery that comes with trusting someone else, looking to someone else to make you happy. I'm a loner. I've always been a loner, and I should never have tried to be someone else. This was my mistake in thinking I could have a relationship, that a connection, love, would make me happy. See how it ended up? I should have known better than to have given this much power to another person, allowed myself to get hurt in this way.

219

She replays the end of the evening over and over, as if watching the movie in her mind will somehow shed more light on the matter, offer some clarity, help her understand. The only conclusion she can draw is that Dominic has to still be in love with his ex. And she has come back. Which means Emma's relationship with Dominic is over. Which means that everything in her life has to change.

She can't stay here, in this house. She can't deal with the pain of living next door to him and seeing him every day.

At five in the morning she sits down at her desk and goes online to look at rental properties in the area. At five fifteen she stops, unable to believe she has to move again, unable to believe this is happening to her.

This is why I don't have proper relationships, she thinks. *This is why I have avoided falling for anyone all these years. This pain of ending is almost unbearable. How am I supposed to deal with it? How do I move through this and get back to being the whole person I was before I gave my heart away?*

At six, she picks up her phone and calls the very last person in the world she would normally think to call. But there is no one on this side of the Atlantic who would be awake.

Her mother picks up after two rings.

"Darling, what a lovely surprise. I was just about to leave for a tasting for the engagement. I've found the most wonderful caterer. She's doing these little crab choux pastries after I told her about the ones we had at the Connaught the other week, and the most divine mini roast beef and Yorkshire puds. I haven't got long, darling. Everything okay?"

"I'm fine," says Emma, as her voice cracks and a sob escapes.

"Darling! Are you crying? What's happened?"

There are a few seconds of muffled silence as Emma tries to stifle her sobs. "I'm sorry, Mummy. Just a bad day."

"Bugger the caterers," says her mother. "I've got all the time in the world. Why don't you tell me what's going on?"

"I'm just having a bad day," repeats Emma, who has never told her mother much about her personal life for fear of her mother's judgement. "I'm really fine. It's just a mild case of the blues."

"You know what you need?" says her mother.

"What?"

"A nice sweet cup of tea for starters," she says. Emma manages a smile. She had forgotten how her mother believes, like most Brits, that a nice sweet cup of tea is the cure-all for anything and everything. "And," her mother continues, "you need to come home and let Mummy and Daddy look after you. I know you said you probably weren't going to come to the engagement, but darling, there's nothing like being looked after at home when you're feeling down. I won't even ask you to come to the party if you don't feel like it. You can sleep in your own bedroom cuddling up with Ritalin."

"What's Ritalin?"

"Not what. Who. It's our new cat. She's completely bonkers. We called her Mittens originally, but we quickly changed it to Ritalin. She's mad all day long, and has driven the dogs potty, but at night she's very sweet and she loves to cuddle. I'll make you lots of cups of tea and Daddy's very good at pouring generous single malts. I'll make you shepherd's pie and trifle. You'll feel better in no time. Will you come, Emma? I don't know what's going on, darling, but I do know that being at home is the very best place to be when life isn't going the way you want it to."

"I'll think about it," says Emma with a sniff, grateful for her mother choosing to be loving and sweet. Emma had forgotten her mother could be loving and sweet. For the first time in perhaps forever, returning to her childhood home is starting to sound appealing.

"That's what you've been saying ever since I told you about the party. Why don't you just say yes? I can also update the numbers for the caterer."

"You're sure I don't have to be at the party if I don't feel like it?" says Emma dubiously, knowing that the last thing she will feel like doing is being paraded around in front of a group of family members she hasn't seen in years, and strangers she has no interest in meeting.

"Quite sure," says her mother.

"Okay," says Emma with a deep breath. "I'll come."

Her decision to visit England leaves her with a feeling of such relief that she decides the only way to get through the rest of the day is to get out of town. Showering quickly and dressing, she drives to the train station, averting her eyes from Tarantino's as she goes by, a swell of tears threatening to fall as she thinks about their evening last night, still unable to understand how something can change so drastically so quickly.

With a coffee-to-go cup in hand, she walks up the stairs to the platform and waits for the Metro-North into the city, no idea where she will go when she is there, knowing only that she wants to spend the entire day away from Dominic, away from Westport, away from memories that have become so painful overnight.

She puts earphones in on the train, and listens to podcasts from BBC Radio 4, all of them sweeping her back to a land she had been so determined to leave behind for the bigger, brighter lights of America, a land that now feels like the only place where she will find solace and refuge.

Even the voices are comforting. The English accents on the BBC are lulling her into a sea of daydreams. Was this a terrible mistake, moving to America? What if she packed up everything and went home? What would she do back there? Where would she live? Who would she see?

Emma has largely grown away from the friends she had when she was younger. They are Facebook friends now, which are not the same as real friendships at all. She scrolls through her news feed on a daily basis, curious to know what people are up to, what they look like, but with no desire to sit down with any of them in person.

Would she go back to London, perhaps? Brave her way through the crowds, the unfamiliar people? The last time she was there, for work, she found herself in restaurant after restaurant, café after café in the West End, surrounded by people who looked familiar, people she thought she ought to know, but didn't. It made her feel strangely displaced. In her old neighbourhood in New York City, she ran into at least three people she knew every time she left her apartment. She realized then that London wasn't home. Not any longer.

Where else in the UK might you go as a thirty-something single woman? If not London, where? Brighton? These days, it seems to have become spectacularly trendy. She doesn't know Brighton, only remembers visiting the pier with her grandparents when she was very young.

If she were to go back to England, her parents would want her back in Somerset. But could she live in the English countryside? Wouldn't she die of loneliness?

She wouldn't belong any more, she thinks. She has been away too long. Maybe, for now, as comforting as England seems, she just needs to focus on getting through the day. Maybe she shouldn't worry about the future. Maybe she should just focus on what she could do today to distract herself from thinking about last night.

At Grand Central Station, she walks around the main concourse like a tourist, head tipped back, looking — really looking — at the ceiling for the first time. She wanders through the passageway leading out to Lexington Avenue, stopping at all the stands, trying on jewellery, examining small artworks, buying a pair of delicate crystal earrings. All around her, people are rushing back and forth; she thinks how this used to be her, always rushing. She had always wanted to stop at these stands and look more closely at what they were selling, she just never had the time.

Her thoughts are all over the place . . . remembering when she used to work and had no time . . . wondering what she will do without Dominic . . . trying on earrings and thinking they would look lovely with the blue sundress, the blue sundress she wore last week when she and Dominic went to the farmers' market . . . oh, how she misses him . . . should she go to a museum? . . . Dominic . . . she's going to be a tourist for the day . . . please God let it not be over.

Tears spring in her eyes each time Dominic's name enters her head, but she refuses to give in to the deep sadness she feels, made worse by sheer exhaustion. Distraction has always been the best way Emma has known to avoid fear and sorrow, so she walks out of Grand Central and strides through the streets in no particular direction, until she finds herself outside the Guggenheim.

She enters the museum and spirals down from the top, stopping to take in the Calder mobile, the Klee paintings, the Kandinsky gallery. The art isn't soothing in the way she had hoped. Every time she stops to look at a picture, she finds her mind wandering back to the evening before.

On to Central Park — perhaps a walk will stop the thoughts crowding her mind. But the hordes of nannies and their charges only make her think of Jesse. She has grown so attached to him, despite the ups and downs of their connection. Seeing all these babies and small children only fills her with sorrow at not being able to continue to be part of his life.

She walks up Madison Avenue, window shopping. Expensive designer labels have never really been her thing. She indulged in them when she was working for the bank, only because she had to look the part, had to have the labels everyone else had. She would have been quite happy dressed head to toe from Zara, but everyone at work compared labels all the time, and the label you wore meant something.

She remembers the day just after she first moved to New York, when a female colleague complimented her on her shoes.

"Thank you," she had said, delighted. "They were only thirty dollars from Nine West." She thought she was sharing her bargain of the month with a friend who would be impressed with the deal, but instead she saw a look of disdain pass over her colleague's eyes.

"Oh," the other woman had said. "I thought they were Lanvin."

Emma went out the next day and bought the Lanvin pumps, an eerily close approximation of what she already owned. She bought the Hermès belts and scarves that everyone else wore, the Dior suits and dresses. She dressed in a way that was well beyond her years.

Her biggest clothing splurge was a Chanel jacket. She was accompanying a colleague to Chanel, intimidated at the quiet luxury of the shop, and at what she perceived to be the condescension of the sales assistants. Although afterwards she realized how nice they had been, that it was her own feelings of inadequacy that had made her so quick to judge them.

Her friend tried on a suit, and while Emma was waiting, she had slipped on a jacket. It was black and white, classic boucle, with an intricate trim of beads and ruffles. It was quite beautiful, if unlike anything she would ever wear.

Two sales assistants gasped and said it was the most perfect fit they had ever seen. Emma's colleague came out and said Emma absolutely had to have it.

"I don't think I'd ever wear it," Emma had protested.

"That's the kind of jacket you can wear to a gala, or throw over a T-shirt and jeans. Trust me. You'll live in it."

"Okay. Sold!" Emma had laughed, until she handed over her credit card, and picked up the receipt. The jacket had cost thousands and *thousands* of dollars. She blanched as she picked up the pen to sign the receipt with a shaking hand. It had never occurred to her to ask the price of the jacket. A few hundred dollars, she had presumed, because it was Chanel. A stretch, perhaps, but one could manage it. But a few thousand? She was too embarrassed to back out.

She did wear it, once, after which it sat in her wardrobe for the next year. Eventually she sold it through a high-end charity shop, making back a fraction of what it had cost her.

The thought of wearing it now is enough to make her laugh. Thank God she is out of that world, she thinks. Thank God she doesn't have to "label up" in order to fit in, or mask her insecurity about being perceived as *good enough*.

She walks up Madison past all of the shops she used to know so well: Chanel, Hermès, Stella McCartney, Dior. Their windows are filled with gorgeous chiffons and silks, thick cashmere sweaters for autumn, exquisite leather handbags as soft as butter. Emma couldn't care less. During these past few months in Westport she has loved pulling on a simple cotton dress, slipping on shorts and a T-shirt, living in flip-flops or sandals.

Everything about living there had been perfect, until she risked the life she was finally building for herself by getting involved with someone.

She stops at a small café, goes inside, sits down on the banquette against the wall to order an iced coffee. It is after lunch now, but she has no appetite. She hasn't eaten anything all day, but the thought of food makes her feel queasy.

She doesn't want to go home, but she needs to sleep. She supposes she could stay in a hotel for the night. She's not quite ready to hear what Dominic has to say; not quite ready for it to be over. She recognizes that part of her wanting to stay away is a hope that he will be shocked by her absence. If he thinks she has disappeared, will he reconsider whatever decision he might have made?

She feels childish thinking that way, but still, reflexively, she glances at her phone, even though she's switched it off. It would be too painful for her to check it every fifteen minutes, hoping for a call, a text.

The silence has been the most difficult thing of all. Dominic didn't come over and apologize after their awkward goodbye. He didn't wake up in the night, missing her, sending her a text. He left her on her own, all night long.

The phone starts whispering, begging her to turn it on. She stares at the black screen, her fingers moving, darting back and forth to the on button, sheer force of willpower eventually leading her to slip it back into her bag.

"They're terrible things, those mobile phones, aren't they?" says a voice next to her. It is a voice that is instantly recognizable, a voice that belongs to a typically patrician Upper East Side Lady Who Lunches, the kind who thrived in a bygone era. Emma turns to see an elderly woman, with silver hair extravagantly coiffed and waved in a way it doubtless has been since the sixties. Her arthritic curled fingers are weighed down by heavily jewelled chunky rings that Emma feels certain are real, or at the very least copies of real ones that are stored in a safety-deposit box.

There is a small dachshund on the seat next to her, wearing a smart quilted vest. The woman is wearing a Hermès scarf around her neck, a cream suit with large gold buttons, and neon-green Nike trainers.

Emma doesn't respond to her comment about mobile phones, merely smiles and nods in a way that she hopes will convey the message that she isn't in the mood for talking. She offers a tight smile before rooting around in her handbag, wishing for a magazine or book to show she is too busy immersed in other things to talk. But there is nothing there. No book or magazine has miraculously materialized in her bag in the last three minutes.

Emma sighs, taking a sip of her coffee, resolving to drink it quickly and leave, knowing that she is about to be pulled into a conversation with a stranger when the very last thing she wants to do is talk to anyone at all.

"I can't decide which one to use," says the woman, not taking the hint. "My iPhone, my iPad, or my BlackBerry."

Emma turns to look at the woman with an unwitting smile on her face. She has to be in her eighties. Emma's own mother, in her sixties, has very little idea how to use any of the new technology. In fact, her mother has only just made the transition from a flip phone because Emma's father has been complaining about how long it takes her to send a text, her fingers hovering over each number as she tries to figure it out. Emma smiles to herself now, remembering hearing from her dad that someone had downloaded Candy Crush on her mother's phone. Apparently now she's addicted, and plays it for hours every night in bed.

Her companion in the café has opened her handbag and draws out her three different devices. *Okay*, Emma thinks to herself, *I give up. I can drink an iced coffee in peace some other time.*

"That looks terribly complicated," she says. "Are you sure you need all of those things?"

230

"Not really," the woman replies. "The iPad is easiest for me to watch things on. I use the iPhone as my phone and calendar. But the BlackBerry is the easiest one for me to type on, and I do a lot of typing for my blog."

Emma's smile is now genuine. "You have a blog? That's wonderful. What do you blog about?"

"It's Confessions of an Old WASP. Or C.O.W." She chuckles a little. "I have quite a following, you know. Eight thousand unique hits a week."

"That's amazing. What do you write about?"

"My life. Often I reminisce about how it was in the old days, compared to now. I write about what happens each day, the things that make me stop and think, the people I talk to."

"Like me? Should I be worried?"

She leans forward. "It depends on whether you reveal anything interesting or not."

"How am I doing so far?"

"Very dull." She smiles. "But we've only just started. Clearly, you're not from here. I've always loved English accents. How long have you been in New York and would you ever go back home?"

"I've been here for almost five years, and I love it. I have loved it. I was here in Manhattan for most of that time but I've just moved out to the suburbs."

"Which suburbs? Westchester?"

"No. Connecticut. Westport."

"Why, that's lovely! I had great friends many years ago who had a wonderful house on, oh, what was it called . . . on the water. Grand mansions."

"Beachside Avenue?"

"Yes, that was it. Delightful people. They used to have dreamy parties in the summer on their grand lawn. It was extraordinarily Great Gatsby-ish, and terribly glamorous. Goodness. I haven't thought about them for years. I think, my dear, you may have just given me my next column. Who throws parties like that any more? People should!"

"I think people probably do throw parties still, they just aren't as elegant as they used to be," says Emma. "I'm the wrong person to ask, though. I've only recently moved there and I hardly know anyone. The only parties I've been to are barbecues at my boyfr — " She stops. She doesn't know whether he is her boyfriend. "My landlord's house. And they're not very glamorous."

The woman peers at Emma. "I'm Cece," she says.

"Emma. It's lovely to meet you."

"Emma. What a classic English name. Lovely. So . . . parties. Are the parties at your landlord's or your boyfriend's? I presume you started to say *boyfriend*. Or are they indeed one and the same thing?"

Emma swallows the lump that unexpectedly rises in her throat.

"Oh, my dear." Cece sits back. "I am so sorry. I didn't mean to say anything to upset you."

"It's fine," says Emma, although it clearly isn't. She blinks the tears away. "It really is. My landlord *was* my boyfriend. At least, I thought he was, but something happened last night and it seems to be over." She blinks again. "I'm so sorry." She laughs tremulously, wiping her eyes with a paper napkin. "I didn't mean to get emotional on you."

"Forgive me if I'm intruding with this question," says Cece. "But sometimes it is far easier to talk to a stranger than a friend. What happened last night? It may help to talk about it."

So Emma does. She tells this lovely older woman about the evening, and about Dominic: how they are from such different worlds but have found something lovely and special together, something that neither one of them expected, something that has made her feel safe and happy for the first time in her life.

She tells her about wanting to say *I love you*, how Dominic finally said it last night. She describes the both of them unexpectedly seeing his ex, the mother of his child, how he reacted, how he didn't talk to her for the rest of the evening.

She tells her how she spent the night alone, expecting to hear from him, expecting him to come to her side, apologize. She is only in the city today because she can't bear to hear that their relationship is over. She knew from the way the colour drained from his face last night, from his silence afterwards, that he is still in love with Stacy. That he has always been in love with Stacy. And while she has no idea whether Stacy is back temporarily or whether she is back for good, Emma cannot settle for being second best.

When she is finished, Cece pats her hand. "My dear," she says. "What a story, and what a difficult night you have had. I suspect you are exhausted. When we are tired, everything seems so very much worse.

May I tell you what I think, because I do have some thoughts?"

Emma nods.

"I think the greatest gifts we can give each other in a relationship are the gifts of kindness and communication. It seems that Dominic was unkind last night not to share with you what he was thinking, but he is a man, and most men are, as we know, somewhat limited. It may be that what you saw as unkindness was merely thoughtlessness. He was clearly discombobulated at seeing the mother of his child after so many years, but it may not be, as you have assumed, that he is still in love with her. It could be any number of things that upset him, and until you ask him, you won't know.

"In my experience, it is always better to confront these things. If you were to go home and ask him to explain, I'm quite sure he would give you clarification. I don't mean to offend you, Emma. I hardly know you, but it seems to me that you have created a drama in your head that may have nothing to do with reality."

"You don't think it's over, then?" It is the first time all day that Emma has allowed herself even a glimmer of hope.

"I don't know. But neither do you. And you won't know until you've spoken to him."

Emma is quiet for a long time. She stares at the woman, and notices for the first time, beneath her designer labels and big jewellery, what she hadn't noticed before: a kindness in her eyes. And, more than that, she notices that the woman meets her gaze directly, that she is paying attention, seeing Emma, and listening. Emma takes a deep breath. Perhaps she should have guessed that this woman would surprise her when she noticed the trainers on her feet. "You're right," says Emma. "Thank you." Then she hesitates. "You're not going to write about this, are you?"

"I probably will," says Cece. "But not in a way in which anything about you would be recognizable. What if I were to describe you as a delightful South African lady I met downtown who had recently moved to Rye? Would that be all right with you?"

"It would be fine," says Emma, smiling.

She leaves with Cece's business card and promises to read her blog and get in touch. Next time Emma's in the city, says Cece, she will take her out for lunch.

The simple human connection she's made with someone older and wiser has lifted her spirits. When Emma finally settles herself on the train heading back to Connecticut, she pulls out her phone and turns it back on with her heart pounding, praying for something from Dominic.

And there she finds what she's praying for.

Text after text after text. Asking where she is. Apologizing. Telling her he wants to explain. Asking her to call him as soon as she can.

CHAPTER
TWENTY-ONE

Dominic has not experienced serious anxiety for a very long time. The last time he found himself tensing up on a regular basis was when he was dating Stacy. She was pregnant, still drinking, not looking after herself, doing things he was convinced would hurt the baby.

He wanted to marry her back then. She was so exciting, so vibrant. They made a great-looking couple; they were such an *obvious* couple: the childhood classmates who would live happily ever after. It was hard for him to see any other outcome, any other path to walk along for the rest of his life.

And yet there was so much that wasn't working in their relationship. Her drinking, for starters. Could he really picture himself with a woman who was so careless about alcohol? If she were sober, if she could *get* sober, he knew they could make it work. If she calmed down, learned to control her explosive temper, didn't pick fights while under the influence, they could make it work.

There were at least two Stacys, he'd learned. Sober Stacy was sweet, funny, huge fun. Drunk Stacy was mean and angry and belittled him in front of anyone who would listen.

On the nights they didn't go out, she would curl into him on the sofa as they watched movies; she was playful, affectionate, and he would wrap his arms around her, imagining the family they would have. They had great conversations back then. Where would they live? Saugatuck? The beach? In their fantasy world, on Beachside Avenue. They discussed how many children they would have. (Two. A boy and a girl: Jesse and Sophia.) And what pets they would have. (A German shepherd for their son, and a cat for their daughter.) It all seemed so perfect. Too perfect to be real.

Every time Dominic relaxed, hoping this was the end of the madness, praying she wouldn't drink again, just as she had promised during those loving, sober moments, he would be disappointed.

Over time, the more frequently she drank, the nastier she became. She told him he was pointless, clumsy, and stupid. She didn't love him; he was a loser who was never going to do anything with his life. She said she hated him, she deserved better, she was only with him because she pitied him.

Dominic knew she didn't mean it, but the words hurt. The longer they were together, the more damage they did. And in time, he started to believe he was as worthless as she told him he was. All the lessons he had learned during his first bad relationship — the one in which he came close to physical violence — his decision to live mindfully, to make the right choices, went out the window.

Then Stacy got pregnant. It was an accident; she was using a sponge as contraception, and neither of them knew why or how it had failed. But it had happened, and at first it seemed to be a wake-up call for Stacy and he was convinced things would change. She cut down on her drinking, which gave him hope. But she didn't stop entirely, and before long he realized his belief that things would get better was just wishful thinking. Before too long, if anything, she became even more abusive. He had trapped her, she would insist; he was manipulative; he had somehow orchestrated the pregnancy in order to control her.

His anxiety grew throughout her pregnancy; he was so worried her behaviour was going to damage the baby. She stopped coming home entirely towards the end of it. She would tell him she was staying at Tanya's, or Lisa's, and he would call, or drop by with her pregnancy vitamins, and be told that she had just run out to get something from the gas station, or that she was staying there but hadn't arrived, or that she had decided to stay with another friend in Fairfield.

Dominic grew tired, exhausted not just by Stacy's antics but by his fears about the baby. That was all he could think about. As long as the baby was okay, nothing else mattered.

When Jesse emerged, he was perfect. His Apgar score was a perfect ten. Dominic couldn't believe not only his relief but the pure joy he felt when he first held his son in his arms.

He also assumed that having the baby would force Stacy to grow up. But she didn't care. She barely looked at Jesse when he was born. Once they got home, she went through the motions of mothering an infant, but it was obvious to everyone that she didn't bond with her baby. When Jesse woke crying in the night, it was Dominic who went to him. Always. Stacy didn't breast-feed. Dominic was the one who sterilized the bottles, warmed the formula, changed the baby, rocked him to sleep, worried when he cried.

One night, Stacy disappeared. She took everything that was hers and sneaked out in the middle of the night. No note. No explanation. Dominic didn't know whether to be devastated or relieved.

In some ways, it was easier. Having a relationship with Stacy was like having two children to take care of. He was constantly worried, angry, or scared. More than anything, he was terrified of what she might do to the baby. She had hit him only once, when drunk, but he knew it wouldn't be the last time. The thought of her raising a drunken hand to their son kept him awake at night, and he knew then he had to protect Jesse, could never leave him alone with her if she had been drinking.

When she finally left, he was relieved, although the thought of raising Jesse to adulthood as a single parent, of being the only adult in the house, was equally terrifying.

He knew then he would never live on anyone else's terms. That he would never again tolerate behaviour that was fuelled by rage, or alcohol; that he would never put his son, or himself, in that position again.

He had too much respect for himself. And he was able to make a choice. He would never make the wrong one again.

Relieved as he was that Stacy had gone, as he settled into daily life with his infant he kept thinking that she would get in touch. Jesse was her child. He could understand her walking away from *him*, but her own flesh and blood? He knew that she would have to eventually return.

But as time went on, and she didn't reappear, and he didn't hear a word from her, he began to wonder. He tried to find her, for Jesse's sake, always aware that Jesse was equal parts of both of them. That was when he discovered how completely she had vanished. Her parents didn't know where she was. Even her best friends claimed not to. He started searching on the Internet and couldn't find a trace of her anywhere. At one point, he considered hiring a private investigator to find her. But he really didn't have the money. And then he started to be honest with himself, and admit that while he felt obliged to look for her, he didn't really want to find her.

By the time Jesse was three, he started to ask about his mother. By then, he had noticed that most other kids had moms and he was the only one with a daddy and no mommy. Dominic explained that she'd had to leave, but it didn't mean she didn't love him, that one day she would be back to see the gorgeous son they had created.

As the years went by, he occasionally heard rumours that she had returned for a visit. Someone would say she had been spotted in town, or that a friend of a friend had talked to her. But he never believed that she could come back to town and not want to see her son.

240

So it was easy for him to dismiss the rumours. The Fat Hen had been her hangout. Mario's. The Black Duck. If she was in town, surely he would have run into her somewhere.

And after all these years, finally seeing her felt as if someone had taken a knife to his heart and twisted it. How could she be back in town and have made no attempt to reconnect with her son?

And what about Emma? He knew his reaction had rattled her, knew he needed to reassure her. He also knew that if he opened his mouth to speak, all that would come out would be a howl of pain. His perfect, wondrous little boy. How could Stacy not want to see him, to know him? She doesn't know he has her crooked smile and long fingers. How could she have abandoned her son the way she has?

This morning he couldn't wait to get to Sophie's to pick Jesse up from his sleepover. He lifted him up and held him close, squeezing him hard, kissing him all over.

"Dad!" Jesse wriggled out of his clasp, insisted on being put down, immediately running off towards the car, giggling. "Get off me."

Dominic couldn't stop looking at him as they drove home. His beautiful boy. With a mother who didn't want anything to do with him. How could she be here and not want to see who her son had grown up to be?

And so he has spent the afternoon on the phone. He has asked everyone he can think of where Stacy is. He has settled Jesse in with a sitter and driven to the Commuter Coffee Shop, Dunville's, AJ's hardware shop, the Fat Hen to ask if anyone has seen her. He has been to the Black Duck, and finally, he goes home. He may not be able to find Stacy, but he does know where to find Emma. If nothing else, she will make him feel better. She always does. Emma, who is so good for him. So good for Jesse. So good.

He had texted her that morning, eager to explain why he'd been so preoccupied and upset, longing to make things right. He'd had a terrible night's sleep. Last night he'd gone through the box that was stored at the back of the wardrobe, the box that contained all the old photos of him and Stacy. They were both different people back then, he'd realized, as he stared at the images. Different people living a different life.

He thought he had said goodbye to Stacy long ago, but seeing her brought back memories he'd buried, and pain he hadn't felt in years. And the only person who might be able to make him feel better wasn't around. Where *was* Emma? He had gone over there this morning, but the house was empty. It was only then that he realized how his behaviour the night before must have seemed to Emma, especially right after the conversation they had just had in the restaurant before they saw Stacy out the window.

He texted her multiple times but got no response. Had he screwed things up? She couldn't have done a runner — her things were still everywhere — but why else would she have disappeared? Why else would she have ignored his texts and messages all day?

And his anxiety, the kind he hadn't felt for so many years, came roaring back. That terrible, heart-jumping,

242

unsettled feeling, when you know that something in your life is terribly wrong, or about to go terribly wrong, and you don't know how you're going to fix it.

He loves Emma. He doesn't want to screw this up. He should have spoken to her last night; he realizes that now. But he'd been too blown away by seeing Stacy standing there in the middle of town, laughing like she hadn't a care in the world. He'd been too upset, his mind racing with everything Stacy's return could mean, his thoughts a jumble, his emotions so in turmoil he doesn't even remember the drive home from the restaurant now. He doesn't even remember the last thing he said to Emma.

But he does know Emma is the person he is supposed to be with. Not Stacy. Never Stacy. Or indeed any of the dramatic, volatile, unpredictable women he had dated before Emma.

She has brought a peace and calm to his life he hadn't known was possible. She makes him feel good. More than good, *loved*. It has taken him forty years to understand what it is to be loved. Now that he has found it, he can't lose it.

But now he can't find her.

Where *is* she? He checks his phone once again to see if she has responded to his texts, and when there is nothing there, his chest tightens; the pain only gets worse as the day goes on. He feels like he is barely able to breathe by the time he hears a car pull up next door. He jumps up and dashes out the door, certain Emma has finally returned; she would never just leave like that, never just walk out like Stacy . . . With a jolt he realizes it is not Emma's car he sees, but a white Suburban. The same white Suburban he saw last night. Outside the restaurant. His heart stops.

Stacy gets out of the car and stands beside it, looking at him with an unreadable expression on her face. Dominic just stares, not knowing what to say. He may have spent the day looking for her, but he never expected her to come looking for him.

"Hey," she says softly, slowly approaching. "Remember me?"

Dominic doesn't take his eyes off her until she is standing in front of him.

"You look good," she says, with the crooked smile that is so familiar to him it is almost heartbreaking. "It's been a while."

"Over six years," he says, after a pause.

"But who's counting." Stacy seems awkward.

Dominic just looks at her.

"Can we talk?" she says.

"Sure." He is staring at her intently now, trying to see if she will meet his gaze. "What do you have to say?"

"Can we maybe go inside?"

Jesse is still inside with the babysitter. It's the last place Dominic wants to go.

"We can go for a walk," he says. Stacy nods, and the two of them turn to set off towards the beach.

"I'm sorry," Stacy begins. "I should have said it years ago, but I didn't know how. I didn't know anything. I am sorry I abandoned both of you in the way that I did."

Dominic spent years imagining these very words coming from her mouth, but now that he is actually hearing them, he is stunned. He doesn't feel the relief he sometimes thought he would feel; he feels . . . confused. Angry. Conflicted.

"I know it doesn't help or make it better. I was not in a good place, and it has taken me a very long time to get to a good place. I really wish I could turn back the clock, and do things differently, but . . . " She trails off. "Dominic, I can't do anything other than apologize and try to show you that I've changed."

Show me? he thinks. *How is she going to show me? And what makes her think I even care? Saying she's sorry doesn't change anything.* He's too pissed off to respond to her. They walk in silence until Stacy speaks again.

"What's Jesse like?" she says.

Dominic stops walking and turns to her with a spark of anger in his eyes. "I don't know what you want me to say. You've been gone for six goddamn years and now you come back and want to know what your son is like? If you'd stuck around, you would know. If you'd made any attempt to get in touch with him in the past half dozen years, you would know."

"I know, Dominic. That's what I'm trying to tell you. I know you're right, and I'm sorry. I don't have an excuse. I was overwhelmed, and unprepared for motherhood. I was destroying myself with my drinking. I never intended to hurt you. I had to learn how to take care of myself."

Dominic can't control his fury. "You didn't hurt me," he spits. "I don't care any more that you left; my life is fine now. But you did hurt Jesse. And I do care about that. How could you leave your son? What kind of mother disappears and never ever gets in touch? Never even calls to see how her kid is doing? Never writes a letter, never sends a text, nothing? How dare you just show up and ask what he's like? How *dare* you?" He is shaking as he speaks, and he half expects Stacy — the Stacy he used to know — to spit her own fury right back at him, to come up with excuses, and accusations of her own. But to his shock, her face crumples as she starts to cry.

"You're right. You're right. There is nothing I can say in my defence. I didn't want to be a mother. I thought I could pretend I wasn't. I thought if I left and started a new life somewhere else, I could just forget about everything and everyone I'd left behind, including Jesse. But of course it doesn't work like that. There hasn't been a day that's gone by that I haven't thought about him. Dominic, I was drinking. I am an alcoholic. I know that now. But I am sober today, and I have been for two years. Long enough that I thought my life was getting better, that I could go on and try again. I knew you must have been disgusted with me, and wouldn't want to see me. But I had managed to find someone, and I was in a relationship that I thought was serious. I got pregnant, and at first I was so happy. I thought it was my second chance. I miscarried six months ago. Ever since then I haven't been able to stop thinking about the child I already have. I was finally able to realize what I had left behind, and I knew it was time for me to come back and get to know him."

"So you thought you'd just come back and pick up where you left off?"

"No. I get that I abandoned him. I know I don't have any right to walk back into his life and be his mother. That's not what I'm asking. But I would like a chance to get to know him. I would like to be . . . if not a mother, then someone like, I don't know, a favourite aunt."

Dominic has no idea what to say. This, of all things, is the last thing he expected Stacy to ever say to him. He had never imagined something like this happening and he has no idea how he feels about it. He closes his eyes for a few seconds to regroup. "Are you staying in Westport? Are you back for good?"

"I don't really know what I'm going to do in the long run. The relationship I was in . . . wasn't as serious as I had thought." She shrugs. "I'm a real estate agent now, in Florida. Fort Lauderdale. I have a good life there, but I needed to come back and see if I could meet Jesse."

"How long are you planning to be here?"

"Ten days."

Dominic nods. "Okay. Let me think about it. This is a lot to take in, and I have to think about Jesse. I don't know how he's going to react, and he's my priority."

"Of course. I know you're an amazing dad. You were always an amazing dad."

"Well, I didn't have much of a choice," says Dominic, surprising himself with the bitterness in his voice before he checks himself with a sigh. "I'm sorry. I shouldn't have said that. I'm glad you got your life straightened out. I need to figure this out with Jesse, and Emma."

"Emma?"

"My girlfriend."

"Serious?" Her eyes flash.

"Very. What happened with your boyfriend?"

Stacy looks away. "I sank into a depression after the miscarriage, and it turns out he wasn't such a great guy after all. He couldn't deal with it, so he dumped me for someone else. So." She turns back to him. "I'm single again, which means I'm also able to devote however much time I need to Jesse. Obviously I'm not here for long this time, but I can come back. I plan on coming back."

"I'll bear it in mind," says Dominic. "Listen, I had better get back. Here's my number. If you give me yours, I'll get in touch after I've thought about this. I need a little bit of time."

"Of course," she says sadly. "I understand. I know you want to protect Jesse, and I don't want to mess him up more than I have. I just want to be in his life. I'd love to see him before I go back to Florida, if you think that will be okay."

Dominic nods, and the both of them turn around at the same time to make their way back to the house. He can't quite figure out what he's feeling, now that she is actually here and offering to be a part of their son's life.

It seems to be some kind of mixture of sadness, regret, and relief. And the tiniest bit of fear.

"Thanks, Dommo," she says as they reach the house. They both stand awkwardly by her car as she reaches up and kisses his cheek. He stands stock-still, saying nothing, not even moving, as she gets in the car and drives away with a small wave.

No one has called him Dommo since Stacy. It sweeps him back to years ago, to the memory of what it felt like to be crazy in love, to think that the high of that crazy love was going to last forever. He doesn't feel anything for Stacy any more . . . but even so, that one word sets him off on an impromptu trip down memory lane, bringing back feelings he thought he had buried long ago.

He has no real emotional connection to these memories: Stacy as a young girl, sliding her hands into the rear pockets of his jeans; the two of them with part-time jobs delivering Chinese food for the Little Kitchen; Stacy drinking and shouting.

He shakes his head. He doesn't want to think about Stacy any more. Where is Emma?

He is still standing there when he spots Emma's car rounding the curve of the road and pulling into the driveway. He walks towards her to greet her, put his arms around her, apologize, but when she gets out of the car, she doesn't look him in the eye. Instead, she takes a step backwards, clearly uncomfortable.

"Hi," she says, meeting his eyes only briefly.

"Hey," he says awkwardly, not sure how to act in the face of her reserve. "How are you?"

"I'm okay," she says. And then she takes a deep breath and meets his eyes. "I think maybe we need to talk."

Dominic's heart plummets when he hears those words. They never mean anything good. Did she see Stacy? Did she see her reach up and kiss him on the cheek? *We need to talk* usually means *This is over.* It means *I have changed my mind.* It means *I may have told you last night that I loved you, but it was because of the wine, and I didn't mean it, and even if I did in the moment, I woke up this morning and knew all this — us — has been a terrible mistake.*

Dominic follows Emma into her house and stands before her in the living room, feeling slightly sick, as she puts her bag down, takes a deep breath, and turns towards him.

"I needed some time away to think today," she says. "I realize that you and I have probably rushed into things here. I wasn't looking for a relationship, and this . . . this thing . . . just crept up on me, on both of us. We probably took it much too quickly."

Dominic's face falls. He can't believe his worst fears are coming true.

"It's been lovely," Emma says, willing herself not to cry, "but I saw your face last night when you saw your ex." She can't seem to say the name *Stacy* out loud. "I know you probably aren't even aware of it, but I think you're not over her. There are things you need to resolve with her before you're ready for a relationship with someone else." She pauses, remembering the old lady in New York, and the advice she'd offered. "Is that what's going on for you?"

"Wait," Dominic says. "I don't understand. What's going on for *you*? What are you saying?"

"I'm saying we should maybe have some space while we figure this out. If your ex is back in town and you're still in love with her, you need to spend some time with her. I think you're amazing, Dominic, but I can't be second best in your life, and I want you to be happy. If she's the one who's going to make you happy, then you need to be with her."

Emma blinks away her tears. She crosses her arms, the way women do when they're trying to protect themselves from pain.

Dominic steps towards her, smiling.

"What?" Emma looks confused. "Why are you smiling?"

"I'm sorry," he says, as he takes another step towards her. As he continues to move, Emma steps backwards until her back is literally against the wall of the living room. "This is because you think I'm still in love with Stacy?"

"I watched your face last night when you saw her get into her car," says Emma. "I saw it in your eyes. You didn't say a word all the way home. You never bothered to say good night or come and see if I was okay." This time tears do spring into her eyes.

He finally stops smiling when he sees her tears. "That was shitty of me, Emma, and I am sorry. I was thrown by seeing Stacy last night, you're right. But not for the reasons you think. I was upset. I didn't sleep all

251

night, but not because of my feelings about Stacy. This is about Jesse, not me. To know that she's back in Westport? To see her after all these years when she walked out on our son without even a backward glance?" This time it is Dominic's eyes that fill with tears. "That's what I couldn't deal with."

"So . . . " Emma looks up at him. "You're not in love with her?"

"Are you kidding? Stacy is a nightmare. I'll admit, I was shocked last night when I saw her and realized she was actually back. For real. It was like a horror movie." Dominic smiles. "She's not the one I love. I'm in love with *you*. Completely." He puts his arms around Emma as she leans into his embrace. "Wholeheartedly. With everything I have. I love you, Emma. There is no one in the world I want to be with more than you. You make me happy, and calm, and just . . . better. You make me a better person."

Emma allows herself to be held, and all the discomfort and anxiety of the day slips away as if it had never existed. *Thank God*, she thinks. The pain of the last twenty-four hours was almost unbearable. If that's what relationships are like, she is better off without them. Except here she is, in Dominic's arms.

"I did see Stacy today, though," Dominic says, and he feels her body instantly stiffen.

"What?" She attempts to pull back, but he refuses to loosen his embrace.

"She came here because she wants to get to know Jesse." This time he does loosen his grip on Emma.

"She says she's sober now. She wants to get to know her son."

Emma stands back to face him, forcing herself to be calm, not to let her panic show. "Isn't this what you wanted?"

Dominic shakes his head with a sigh. "I don't know any more. All these years I was furious with her for walking out on him, but now that she says she wants to get to know him, I don't know what to do. What if she lets him down? She doesn't plan to move back here. She just wants to meet him. What if she's nothing but a huge disappointment?"

Emma takes a deep breath. "I don't know that you can stop it. If she's a huge disappointment, she's a huge disappointment. I think it's better that you let Jesse find out for himself. Maybe she really has changed and she can be a mother to him." As she speaks, Emma is stunned to find she almost chokes on the word. Jesse has a *mother*. All this time, she has harboured this secret hope that *she* will be his mother, that *she* will be the one to step into the void his real mother left. She never anticipated that Jesse's real mother would come back.

Dominic looks at her, his face serious. "This doesn't change anything," he says. "Well, obviously it changes things for Jesse, but not for us." He pauses. "I want to be sure you're hearing me, Emma."

She looks up into his eyes and nods. She just hopes he knows his own mind as well as he says he does.

"I love you, Emma," he says, leaning down and kissing her.

And this time, she lets herself believe him.

Later that evening, in the kitchen, Dominic's phone buzzes. He reaches over to grab it off the worktop where it's plugged in, charging, but not before Emma notices it's a text from Stacy.

He sighs. "She wants to know if I've thought about it and if she can meet up with Jesse this weekend." He looks up at her. "What do I do?"

"You should say yes," Emma replies. "She's only here for a few days. You should maybe let her take him to the playground or something."

"Really? You think that's a good idea?"

"You have to try," says Emma. "You'd never forgive yourself for cheating Jesse of this chance to meet his mother. And he deserves to know who she is, for good or ill. Maybe she will let him down again. But there's also the very real possibility here that Jesse could have a mother. That's what you've always wanted, isn't it?"

"Okay." He nods. "Okay. You're right. Playground. That's a great idea. I'll set it up."

"That sounds perfect," says Emma, but she feels slightly sick, knowing that Dominic should go, too. It would be insane to let Jesse go off with Stacy by himself, before he gets to know her. Still, she wishes she knew how to get rid of the creeping insecurity she has had since last night.

She knows she has nothing to worry about; she thinks, *hopes*, she has nothing to worry about.

Her disquieting sense of distrust now has nothing to do with Dominic. This is about Stacy, a woman who

254

may or may not have ulterior motives, a woman who may or may not still yield a power over Dominic. She is, after all, the mother of his child. If Dominic felt he ever had to choose, what choice would he make?

Emma shakes her head in an effort to physically dislodge her thoughts. *This is madness*, she tells herself. *Dominic hasn't given you any reason to doubt his love*. If anything, he's been refreshingly clear about his feelings. All she needs to do is follow Cece's advice and listen, pay attention to what he's saying, what he's doing. All she needs to do is stay present, and everything will be fine.

"Are you okay?" Dominic looks over at her as she nods and forces a smile. "This is hard for you, isn't it?"

"Not hard," she says. "But weird. I just didn't expect Jesse's mother to come back. It isn't something I was prepared for."

Dominic nods. "You and me both. I'm upset, too. All these years I wanted her to want to have a relationship with him, but now that she's here, I just feel anxious. It's going to be okay, though," he says, more to soothe himself than Emma, it seems. "Whatever happens, we'll figure it out. Maybe next week, after she's gone, you and I can go away for a night? Somewhere romantic?"

Emma is startled, remembering the phone call with her mother at the beginning of this endless day. How could she have so completely forgotten? And how can she now tell Dominic what she has done? "Dominic, I can't. I'm so sorry about what I've done. But, well . . . Do you remember I told you about my cousin getting

255

engaged, and my mother throwing him a party in England, how I probably wasn't going to go?"

Dominic nods.

"Well, the last time I spoke to my mother, she was still upset by my decision. I spoke to her again early this morning, when I was so upset, and she was worried about me, and told me she wanted me to go home. At the time, I thought she was right. So I changed my mind. I'm so sorry I forgot to tell you. I've already booked the flight."

"Oh. Wow. Okay," Dominic is surprised. "So when are you going?"

"Next week."

"For how long?"

"Just a few days."

Dominic pauses. "Why don't I come with you?"

Emma's eyes open in amazement. "Are you serious? You would really come to England?" She frowns. "But you don't have a passport."

"I do now."

"What?"

"Well, I got myself one after you seemed so horrified when I was building those shelves for Lisa. I thought maybe one day we could go away on vacation, so I got an expedited one as a surprise."

Emma starts to laugh. "You want to come and meet my whole family? You think you're ready for the craziness of my childhood home?" She imagines Dominic and her parents, and her laughter gets louder. "Actually, my childhood home isn't all that crazy, and my father's really quite normal, but my mother? Are you sure you're ready for my mother? I'm not sure *I'm* ready for this." It is impossible for Emma to hide her excitement. "Really? You really want to come?"

"She'll love me." Dominic grins. "Mothers always love me. I flirt a little, charm a little, and they fall head over heels in love." He laughs, then adds, "I do want to see where you grew up. And" — he narrows his eyes at her — "I want to see what you'll look like when you're old."

"Do not tell my mother you think she's old. She'll never let you in the house." As Emma laughs, she wonders what her mother will make of Dominic. She may well think he's charming. She will certainly think he is exotic, with his American accent, dark skin, big brown eyes, and strong arms.

"I very much want to meet your parents." Dominic steps back and leads Emma to the sofa, where they both sit, curled into each other. "I'm really serious about this, Emma. I'm serious about you. I know this is quick, and I know we've only had one proper date, but . . . I don't even know that I should say this . . . "

"Say it," encourages Emma softly.

"I feel like this is *it*." He looks at her, and she nods, a lump in her throat. "I can't believe how freaked out I got when I realized you were gone today. It really made me realize that I feel like I'm where I'm supposed to be with you, and I'm who I'm supposed to be. This all feels fated somehow, you moving in, us getting together. It feels *right*. I know you just said you thought we were rushing things, but I also know you understand what I'm talking about. So maybe we shouldn't jump

257

ahead and use . . . the M-word, or anything like that, but I see us together for a long time."

Emma nods, unable to speak.

"I mean, a really long time. A really, *really* long time. Maybe forever." He frowns. "I don't want to scare you off. Am I scaring you off?"

"You most definitely are not scaring me off," says Emma, leaning in to kiss him. "I've been terrified of saying it out loud. I feel exactly the same way. It feels preordained, even if you and I come from different worlds. I do feel I was meant to meet you, rent your house, for a reason. I do see us together for" — she laughs — "a really, really long time. And I would be thrilled if you came to England. As long as you prepare yourself for my mother."

"If she's anything like you, I'll adore her."

Emma lets out a bark of laughter. "She's *nothing* like me."

"Then I'll just pretend." He leans his head to kiss her properly, when they both jump apart at the sound of the cat flap.

"Where's Hobbes?" Jesse, just dropped off from a late playdate, let himself into the backyard to crawl through and head straight for the kitten in the corner. "Dad? Can we go to a movie tomorrow? Can we? Please? Pretty please?"

"Hmm. Let me think. I have a lot to do. I just took on a new job to make some cabinets for a nice lady across town." He watches his face fall. "But hey, buddy, don't worry, we're heading into the weekend. We can

258

definitely go see something. What do you think, Emma? Want to come with us?"

Emma looks at Jesse, expecting him to make a face, or scowl at her, or shake his head at his father. But instead, much to her surprise, he nods delightedly before running over and grabbing her hand.

"Come on, it'll be fun!"

"Okay," she says. "I'm in." And then, to Dominic, "Can I steal you for one second?" Jesse is already on the floor, playing with Hobbes, as Dominic allows himself to be led into the other room where Emma whispers quietly, "What about Stacy? Weren't you going to the playground with Stacy?"

"Doesn't this sound like a whole lot more fun? I'll text her and maybe Jesse and I will meet her for ice cream in the afternoon. How's that?"

"That sounds perfect," says Emma, wondering if Dominic believes her, if she is as convincing as she hopes.

CHAPTER
TWENTY-TWO

Emma stayed over again. It was as if the blip, if indeed a blip it was, had never happened. In the morning, they had a big breakfast together, then on Saturday they went to the movie Jesse selected. It was a wonderful day. A healing day.

After the movie, Jesse couldn't wait to show Emma the burger bar they always went to after a film. He told Emma which burger she needed to order, and how she needed to eat it — with no tomato, no cucumber, and extra mayo, which Dominic explained was kind of a rule in the family. All in all, for the first time since Jesse walked in and found her in his father's bed, Emma started to feel that they had turned a corner.

Every time she felt a worrying thought about Stacy creep in, she pushed it away. She knows Dominic texted her back, knows they are going to Sweet Frog for frozen yogurt later in the day, but she refuses to worry. The whole situation had exhausted her, emotionally and physically. The thought of Stacy re-entering their lives had seemed so terrifying, but now, after more consideration, Emma can see what a good thing this could be for Jesse. She could almost believe everything she had said to Dominic.

And after Jesse's seesawing emotions since he realized they were together, he seems to have finally accepted her. The three of them seem — she is almost too scared to say this, to even think it, but she can't deny it any longer — the three of them feel like a family.

After lunch they stop at the Athletic Shoe Factory to get Jesse some new trainers. Dominic wanders off into the shop next door as Emma supervises the fitting. The salesman unboxes the pair they'd picked out, and when Jesse tries them on, he tells him to stand up and "walk over to your mom".

Emma fully expects Jesse to correct him with a snap, to insist she isn't his mother, but Jesse says nothing, merely walks over to Emma, who finds her eyes stinging with happy, relieved tears.

They drive home, Emma enveloped in a warm glow of happiness. Now she is filling Hobbes's bowl with cat food. Dominic is upstairs talking to Jesse, no longer able to put off telling him about the London trip, which requires that they leave him behind so he doesn't miss school. It's not for long, Emma knows, but she's apprehensive about his reaction just the same.

The house is quiet. Emma enjoys the peace for a few minutes before she has to run next door and grab some eggs from her fridge. Just as she turns to go, she hears Jesse raise his voice. She pauses, listening, sorry, though unsurprised, that Jesse is upset. She hears Dominic murmuring in a low voice, although she can't make out what he is saying.

And then she hears Jesse's voice rise again. "I hate her," he says.

Emma knows it isn't true, yet it feels as if a knife is twisting in her heart.

"I hate her," he says again. "If she wasn't here, you wouldn't be going to England and I wish she wasn't here."

"Come on, buddy." Dominic's voice is soft, placating. "You know you don't hate Emma. I'm only going for a few days and you're going to have fun with Nonna and Papa."

"I'm not. You've never been away before and I don't even know Nonna and Papa. I don't want you to go. Emma can go by herself! Send her away! I don't want her here any more. Make her go."

"You don't mean that," says Dominic in what Emma has come to recognize as his *soothing* voice. "You love Emma. I know you do. And you love her being around."

"I do *not*!" screams Jesse, sobbing now. "I *hate* her. You and me are the team. She's not on our team and we don't need her and I don't want her. You keep bringing her on our team and I don't want her any more. Send *her* to England and you stay here with me."

"Buddy, I'm sorry you feel that way," Emma hears Dominic say. "I promise I won't be away for long, but I've already bought my ticket. I know you don't want Nonna and Papa to stay, but remember what happened last time they were here?"

"They've never stayed here."

262

"Yes, they have," says Dominic. "You were about four. They stayed for two nights when I went to a wedding in Rhode Island, and you had chocolate ice cream and cannoli for dinner every night."

There is a pause. A lowered voice. "I did?"

"Yes. You did," says Dominic. "And they took you to the toy shop and bought you whatever you wanted. That giant bear over there? That was what you wanted. Remember?"

Another pause. "Maybe."

"I bet they'll do that again. What's your favourite food in the world?"

"French fries." Jesse is reluctantly being pulled out of his hysteria.

"What else?"

"Chocolate ice cream."

"What else?"

"Chocolate chip cookies."

"I can pretty much guarantee that Nonna will give you French fries, chocolate ice cream, and chocolate chip cookies for breakfast, lunch, and dinner. You know what else?"

"What?"

"You know how you think your dad is the best cook in the world? Guess who taught him everything he knows? That's right. Nonna. You think my chicken parm is good, wait till you try Nonna's lasagne. Oh my God, Jesse, you will think you have died and gone to heaven."

There is a brief silence. "What does that mean? Is that bad?"

"No! It means it's good! It's amazing! It's the best thing you'll ever eat in your life. I'm jealous you're getting to eat all that amazing food and not me." He pauses, then frowns. "I don't know about the toy shop, though."

"What do you mean, you don't know?"

"Maybe I should tell them not to take you. All those things you don't want. Those *Star Wars* things. That Lego. The stuff you never talk about when you watch TV and see those ads."

Emma can practically hear Jesse smiling as his father teases him. "What I really want is a hoverboard."

"Then you better let Nonna and Papa stay here, because I'm not planning any trips to the toy shop soon, but I guarantee they *are*. Although . . . I think you may be a little young for a hoverboard."

"Okay," grumbles Jesse, whose heart is no longer in the protest. "Do you think they'll take me to Skyzone, too?"

"Most definitely. Why don't you and I make a list of all the fun stuff you're going to do when I'm away? And listen, buddy? There's something else I need to talk to you about, too."

"What is it?"

"Come sit down with me, buddy. I need to talk to you about your mother. You know how you sometimes ask me questions about her, and want to know what she's like?" There is a pause and Emma imagines Jesse's nod. "You know she hasn't lived here for a long time, but I just found out that she's back in town for a visit." He pauses again and Emma pictures Jesse's eyes

264

widening in surprise. "I know this is a lot for you, and it's totally fine if you don't want to see her. But she has asked me if she can meet you. She knows all about what a fantastic kid you are, and she wants to get to know you. But if you don't want to, that's absolutely fine. This is all up to you."

Jesse seems to be processing all this big information.

"If you want to, I thought maybe we could meet her for ice cream later today. What do you think?"

Emma holds her breath.

"Ice cream?" says Jesse. "Where?"

CHAPTER
TWENTY-THREE

Waiting for Dominic and Jesse to return from getting ice cream with Stacy is the longest hour and a half Emma can remember. She spends it outside in what she has finally transformed into a sweet little vegetable garden. Dominic had bought wood and made raised beds, filling them with soil dropped off by one of his landscaper friends.

It was too late to plant seeds, so Emma had run to the garden centre and bought the last of the straggly pumpkin plants and squashes, a few aubergine plants, and two tomato plants, just enough to give her some of the pleasure of picking her own vegetables.

She had put a large flowerpot in the middle of the garden, filling it with pink geraniums that spilled over the sides and made her think of the south of France, and there's a small stone bench that she perches on now, taking a break from pulling weeds.

Weeding is like a meditation for her. When she is bending over, digging around for the green invaders, pulling them up by the roots and forming small piles that she lifts into garbage bags, she is thinking of nothing, her brain entirely focused on clearing the beds. When she has weeded as much as she can, she gets the clippers from the garage and clips the boxwoods she had planted around the edges of the small garden into a small, perfect hedge.

She has barely thought about the fact that Dominic and Jesse are with Stacy. And they have been gone for quite a while.

As she sits on the bench, hot and sweaty, she hears a screen door slam. She looks up to see Dominic striding towards her.

"Hey," he says, bending down to give her a kiss. "I see you've been busy."

"I can't believe how many weeds there were after such a short period of time. I have to make a point of getting out here and weeding more often."

"Summer's over," says Dominic. "You won't have to worry about it for almost a year." He sits next to her on the bench before sighing.

"Everything okay?" says Emma. "How did it go?"

Dominic frowns and shakes his head. "I can't tell. Jesse was kind of quiet with her. She asked him a lot of questions about school, and what he likes to do, and he answered everything, but it wasn't like there was this big bonding moment."

"Surely you didn't expect that?" Emma looks at him in surprise. "Jesse must have been overwhelmed."

"He didn't seem overwhelmed. He seemed, if anything, bored."

"He's six years old. He probably had no idea how to express anything. Don't they say that little kids never react to big things in the way we expect? I'm sure there's a ton of stuff going on in that little mind of his, and you'll probably get to hear about it when you least expect it."

"Yeah, you're right. I do know that. I just thought he'd talk to me when we left. I asked him if he had any questions or wanted to ask me anything, and all he wanted to know was when the new *Star Wars* movie is coming out." Dominic starts to laugh. "That is not what I expected him to say."

Emma laughs, too. "He'll probably ask you about his mum on the way to school, or when you're giving him a bath or something."

"I hope so. I mean, I hope he talks about it sometime. The only thing he asked me was what to call her."

"What did you say?"

"I said to call her Stacy. I didn't know how else to answer the question. If after this quick trip she really stays in touch with him, and they form a relationship, then maybe he'll call her Mom someday, but I think that has to be his choice. She can't ask that of him, and I would feel weird telling him to call her that. What do you think? Do you think that's okay?"

"I think you did great," smiles Emma. "I would have said exactly the same thing."

"Thanks. She wants to pick him up on Monday and take him to the toy shop."

"Did you say yes?"

Dominic frowns. "I said I'd think about it. I'm worried that it's all happening too fast. She won't be here for long and I don't want to get him too attached too soon."

"He won't. It's only a couple of days. And it's the toy shop. Let her spoil him if she wants to, and let him get to know her. Nothing huge is going to happen in such a brief period of time. She's not going to be able to hurt him in a few days."

She takes Dominic's hand. "If you don't take the risk of allowing him to be loved by her, you're also keeping him from something momentous, something you said you've always wanted."

Dominic closes his eyes. "I know, I know. But wanting it when she wasn't around, when it was only an abstract concept, is very different from wanting it now that she's here and could hurt him again."

"It's like falling in love," says Emma. "You have to give it everything you have or you'll miss out on all of it, the highs and the lows. You have to close your eyes and jump, hoping that you'll be caught, that you'll emerge better for the experience." For a moment, Emma pauses, wondering when she had come to feel this way about love. She never believed any of this before. It was all new. It was Dominic. "You have to allow this to happen between Jesse and Stacy, however scared you are. You have to step back and allow him the experience of getting to know his mother."

"You're right. I know you're right. So I let her pick him up?"

"Yes. If you still feel weird about it, you can always go with them."

"I think I still feel weird about it."

"So accompany them. You'll feel better."

"You know what makes me feel better?" He smiles at her. "You. You always know exactly what to say. How did you get to be so smart?"

Emma smiles. "And you thought I was just a pretty face."

They spend Sunday working in the garden and watching Jesse have the time of his life on the trampoline. Not surprisingly, he falls asleep right after dinner, which is a great thing both because the next day is finally the first day of school and because it gives Emma and Dominic the kind of quiet night at home they treasure. A healing night.

The next day, after Jesse goes to school, Emma spends the morning working, posting new photos of her work online, while Dominic goes out on a carpentry job. Just after lunch, Emma takes a break to text Sophie.

I miss you! Want to have tea later today? How about Neat at four?

I miss you, sister! comes back, seconds later. **But, ugh, I've got a gym class with the boy this afternoon. How about tomorrow morning?**

Client meeting ☹ **Lunch?**

Can't. Ugh. Shall we text tomorrow and see if we can squeeze in something quick?

Sure! Emma fills a line with the kissing face emoji, then loads her car with returns she has to drop off, and mail she has to send, and sets off to do her errands, singing out loud to Jason Mraz as she makes her way up the Post Road.

She is driving across the bridge on the way to Whole Foods when she sees them, and her breath catches in her throat as she sits in traffic, unable to tear her eyes away.

Dominic is holding Jesse's left hand, Stacy his right. They are doing the one-two-three-swing with him, something Emma and Dominic have never thought to do with him themselves. Jesse seems too old for that, too big, far too mature to enjoy it, but there he is, being swung, and all three of them are laughing, looking like the most perfect, perfectly happy family you could ever wish to see.

Emma finishes her errands in a haze. She admonishes herself not to jump to conclusions; she resolves to listen, and pay attention, and thereby gets through the afternoon. She is cooking dinner when they get home. She is on her second glass of wine, with loud music on in the kitchen to try to distract her from her fears.

She hears the front door open and sees Jesse, a blur running upstairs to his room. Dominic looks happy, happier, she is sure, than she has seen him look in ages. Maybe ever.

She feels sick.

"How's my girl?" He bends to kiss her and she kisses him back, forcing a smile, trying to pretend that everything is fine. All she can think of is the image of the three of them, Jesse swinging between his two parents, delight on each of their faces.

"I'm fine. How did it go?"

"It was fine." Dominic shrugs. "Nothing dramatic. We had a good time. Jesse had a good time, and so far he hasn't asked me anything."

"I saw you, you know," she says, instantly reprimanding herself for mentioning it. She hadn't wanted to say anything, but the words, the feelings, wouldn't stay in.

"You did? Where?" There is nothing but innocent delight on his face.

"On the bridge. Swinging Jesse."

Dominic shakes his head. "Oh man. I told him he was too big and too grown-up, but it was Stacy's idea. And she was right. He loved it."

"I saw." Emma turns away.

"Emma? Honey? What's the matter?"

Emma shrugs miserably before turning back to face him. "I'm sorry. I hate myself for feeling this way. I saw the three of you together, and you looked like the perfect family." Her voice wobbles. "I'm the one who feels like the intruder now. I'm thrilled that Jesse has the chance to get to know his mum, but I'm scared, and I grew more scared after I saw you today. You looked . . . happy."

"I *was* happy," he says quietly, taking her hands. "I was happy because Jesse knowing his mother is something I've always wanted. This has nothing to do with me. I love you, Emma. You are the only woman I want to be with, ever. Even if there was something between me and Stacy, which there isn't, at all, but even if she thought, I don't know, that she'd come back to try to make it work with me, it wouldn't matter." He sighs. "How can I say it so you can hear me?"

Emma looks at him. "I don't know. I think it's just this stupid thing I'm going through. I feel better, though, hearing you say that." She gives him an embarrassed smile, allowing herself to be gathered in his arms. "And the wine helps."

"Okay, I'm glad you feel better. Because there's one more thing." He holds her tight. "Stacy has asked if Jesse can stay with her while we're away."

Emma steps back, furrowing her brow. "What? I thought she was leaving."

"She was. But she said she can change her flight to spend more time with Jesse."

"Do you feel safe enough leaving Jesse with her? He doesn't really know her."

Dominic nods. "I know. But he doesn't really know my parents, either. I don't know what to do. She asked him if he wanted to come stay with her and he seemed to think it was the best idea ever."

Emma is horrified. "She asked him? Without checking with you?"

"Jesse had volunteered that Nonna and Papa were going to stay with him when we were away and she offered."

"So what did you say?"

"I said we'd already made plans with my parents."

"And?"

"And she said plans could be changed."

"I don't like this," says Emma. "I think it's too much, too soon, and you can't be around to monitor what happens."

"I know. That's how I feel, too, but Jesse was so eager to be with her, and I keep thinking about what you said, about how sometimes you have to close your eyes and jump in."

"Not when it's unsafe. I didn't mean let him stay with her all that time on his own."

"She's sober now, Emma. I think she really is. And I've talked to other friends who know her, and they think she is, too. It's probably better than having him stay with my parents and their shouting. I think this might be a good thing, and I don't know how I can say no."

Emma sighs. "I can't tell you what to do, Dominic. If you think it's a good idea, then do it. I think it's a huge risk. She may be sober, but she hasn't shown herself to be responsible. Don't you want to give this some time, ease into this relationship slowly? Isn't that better for Jesse?"

"In an ideal world, of course that would be better for Jesse. But it's not ideal. I honestly don't know which is the lesser of two evils, Stacy or my parents. And I think Jesse will have a better time with Stacy. But it's more than that. I saw them together today. They seemed to be making a real connection. It made me feel like our trip was a good thing, I mean to give them a chance to spend a few days alone together. Maybe that's what they need to establish a real relationship. And ultimately isn't that what I want for him?"

"Okay," says Emma, resigned. "There's your answer. I hope she's good with him."

"If today was anything to go by, she's going to be great. I agree with everything you're feeling, but I can see she's changed, Emma. And it's not like she's a stranger. This is someone I've known practically my whole life. I'll be honest and say I haven't trusted her in the past, but I really do think it's going to be okay."

"Okay," says Emma, going back to chopping peppers, knowing she has no say, she has to keep quiet. "Okay."

The days pass in a flurry. Jesse is distant with Emma again, excited at the prospect of staying with Stacy. She is not surprised. She understands that he is simultaneously excited at the prospect of staying with the woman who is his mother, and angry at Emma for taking his father away. Emma understands. On some level, and certainly from a six-year-old's perspective, she *is* taking his father away. Not emotionally, and certainly not for very long, but this is the first time, other than a night in Rhode Island two years ago, that Dominic has left Jesse overnight.

She understands that this is a big deal, and not just for Jesse.

Dominic's whole life has revolved around his son. His guilt at being a single parent, at not being able to give Jesse the proper family life he deserves, has meant that Jesse is indulged. He is a child used to having his father at his beck and call always.

Dominic has not had a life because he has given it to Jesse. He's kept his relationships from Jesse, working hard to ensure that they neither impact nor infringe upon his life with his son in any way whatsoever.

Jesse has no idea that Dominic has even dated. Until now. And the woman his father is dating is taking him away.

The wicked stepmother, thinks Emma. *Isn't that the way these things work?* But wicked stepmothers rarely start out that way. A woman, a loving, kind, caring person, falls in love with a man who has children. She decides to work hard to earn the love of his children; surely they will respond to her overtures of kindness, affection, and warmth. She is a good person; all these children need in order to love her is a happy family, a stable and loving life.

She marries the man, ignoring the fact that the children are distressed, or angry, or in pain. They take the children shopping, redecorate their bedrooms, buy them toys, and accompany them to their favourite sports events in a bid to seduce them, but the children can tell they are being seduced, can smell the disingenuousness, and no amount of gadgets will give them their father's undivided attention again. Their dislike and distrust of the stepmother grows.

The children get more sullen and resentful. The step-mother grows more sullen and resentful. She has tried so hard! She has done everything for these ungrateful children! She has had enough of being nice. And thus, the wicked stepmother is born.

Emma knows how these things happen. She has read enough fairy tales, been friends with enough women who have stepmothers. She will not be one of those women. She will never try to get between Jesse and his father, will never try to take Dominic away from his son. And she will have patience with Jesse's feelings about her.

She's a good person, and kind. All Jesse needs is a stable, loving family. If Emma can give it to him, they will all, surely, live happily ever after.

Dominic comes downstairs, his hair wet from the shower, muttering in anger as he casts a dark look at his phone.

"What's the matter?"

"I knew it." He shakes his head. "I fucking knew it."

"Knew what?"

"Stacy. Just called to say she couldn't change her flight without it costing her hundreds of dollars that she doesn't have. So she's going back, and now I have to tell Jesse that once again she's let him down."

"When's she leaving?"

"Tomorrow."

"I'm sorry," says Emma. "That sucks."

"It really does. I really thought she had changed, but turns out she's as irresponsible as ever. I shouldn't have said yes. I should never have let her back in our lives."

CHAPTER
TWENTY-FOUR

"Whoa." Dominic lets out a low whistle in the Virgin Atlantic upper-class lounge. "This is *awesome!*"

Emma still has thousands of air miles from when she travelled with the bank. She would never have paid for these tickets, but she decided to upgrade, knowing that for Dominic, a man who has never even left the country, business class will be an experience he will never forget.

She finds a spare sofa in the lounge and curls up with a book, while Dominic goes off to explore. He has a head massage in the spa, and two dirty martinis in the bar, and orders a plate piled high with antipasti, which he brings back to the table for them to share.

"Is this really all free?" he leans forward and whispers.

"It's all included in the astronomical price of the ticket," Emma whispers back, amused and touched by his wide-eyed wonder at something she has taken for granted for so many years.

"Emma?"

She looks up to see Caroline, a girl she used to work with at the bank, a girl she hasn't seen since she left two years ago when she got pregnant.

"Caroline!" Emma stands up and gives the girl the obligatory air kiss on both cheeks before crouching down to admire a beautifully dressed toddler in what has to be the most top-of-the-range buggy she has ever seen. "Is this the baby? Oh my goodness!" Emma says. "He got so big!"

"That's Burke," says Caroline. "My husband is over there. Hunter. Did you ever meet him?"

"Not really," says Emma, who remembers being briefly introduced at their engagement party. He was a big tall golden preppy man, filled with the kind of confidence that comes from being raised in a family that has always had the best of everything. "Although I did meet him before you two got married. This is Dominic," she says, as Caroline casts a curious glance over him and extends her hand.

"Nice to meet you," she says.

"Hey." He smiles. "How are you doing?"

"Great. Thank you." She smiles politely before turning back to Emma. "So how is everything at work? I wish I could tell you I miss it, but I'm thrilled to be a stay-at-home mom." Caroline lets out a peal of laughter, as Emma remembers how she never really liked Caroline. She seemed pleasant enough, until you realized how competitive she was.

Whatever anyone had done, Caroline had done better. If someone came in with a new bag, Caroline showed up the next week with the more expensive version; when someone bought a house, Caroline would make sure everyone knew hers was bigger. Or more expensive. Or in a more prestigious town.

When she and Hunter got engaged, Emma suddenly remembers, Caroline showed up with a ring so big, she joked that she had pulled a muscle in her finger trying to hold it up.

She claimed it was Hunter's great-great-grandmother's diamond, which they had had reset. No one quite believed her. It could have been bought wholesale the day before on Forty-Seventh Street, but that didn't make for such a good story.

"I left the bank," says Emma. "A few months ago. Burnout!"

"Good for you," says Caroline. "So you're a lady of leisure, like me. Isn't it fun?"

Emma nods. "It is fun, although I'm starting my own interior design business."

"I had no idea interior design was your thing," says Caroline. "I ought to get you over to look at our house. I wanted to do it myself, but frankly ten thousand feet is a little overwhelming. Every time I start thinking about it, I get the cold sweats, so of course we're living in it with no wallpaper and not a single window blind anywhere. Can you imagine?"

"Deathly." Emma shakes her head, without a trace of irony. *Now I remember*, she thinks. *You are awful.*

"I'm the carpenter," Dominic offers. "If Emma helps you out, I come along as part of the deal and build a great bookcase."

Caroline closes her eyes for a second before shaking her head with an embarrassed laugh. "Oh God! I'm mortified. For a moment there I thought you were Emma's boyfriend. I'm so sorry. I couldn't quite make sense of the two of you together." She lets out another peal of laughter, oblivious to the looks on Emma's and Dominic's faces. "I'll definitely give you a call. Emma, do you have a card?"

You bitch, thinks Emma, fishing for a card, her heart pounding. *You fucking bitch*. She glances at Dominic, who also looks a little stunned, and knows she has to say something.

"Dominic *is* my boyfriend," she says eventually, her voice shaking. *Fuck it*. She's not going to give her the card. "And we work together."

"We sleep together, too," says Dominic, seeing Caroline's face fall. "Apparently I'm a fantastic fuck."

Caroline's mouth opens in a small O.

"So nice to see you," says Emma, gathering her things and standing up. "Enjoy your ten-thousand-foot monstrosity and the sunlight streaming through your curtainless windows." Summoning as much hauteur as she can manage, hauteur that may, in fact, put Caroline to shame, she glides off, with Dominic at her side.

"What a bitch," says Dominic. "Who the hell is she?"

"Someone I used to work with. I'd love to tell you she is unique in her cattiness, but sadly that kind of attitude is one of the reasons I had to leave banking. There were some wonderful people, but too many like that. I just can't play that stupid game of 'I have more money than you, therefore I'm better than you.'"

"I really wanted to say that I was also overwhelmed in my *twelve-thousand-foot* house, but I thought she might have knocked me out."

"She's far too polite to have knocked you out. She may have turned you to stone with a withering look, though."

"Eurgh." Dominic shudders. "Please tell me that if she ever manages to track you down, you won't work for her? Life is too damn short to be around people like that. Too much negative energy."

"I couldn't agree more. Shall we go to the gate and wait there? At least outside this first-class lounge with the masses, we won't have to see her again."

As they walk towards the gate, Dominic turns to her. "Your mother isn't anything like that, is she?" he says.

"Like Caroline? Why would you ask that?"

"I don't know. You said she was a roaring snob. If she's like that woman, this isn't going to go so well."

"Are you nervous?"

"Yes. What if they hate me? What if I hate them? What will happen to *us*?"

Emma stops walking and turns to face Dominic. "Well, my mother may be a roaring snob, but not remotely in the same way as Caroline. She's funny more than anything else. Once you understand that she's not to the manor born, her assumed superiority is hilarious. And she's not mean. Truly. My mother doesn't have a mean bone in her body."

"Do you think she'll like me?"

"I think it's impossible for anyone not to like you."

"That doesn't answer my question."

"Dominic, I can't speak for my mother. I am sure she will love you, but even if she doesn't, it doesn't matter. I love both of my parents, but I moved across

282

the Atlantic to get away from them. That should tell you everything you need to know about how much it matters to me whether they like you or not."

"But it matters to me."

"It shouldn't, *I* like you. I *love* you. Jesse loves you." She smiles. "That's all that matters."

"Okay, you're right." He nods. "You're right. I have no idea where this anxiety came from."

"It's all going to be fine," Emma says. Hoping very much that's true.

They call Jesse just before they get on the plane. Dominic describes everything to him in detail. The lounge! The massage! The free food! He promises to try to find a TARDIS for him from England.

"How is he?" Emma looks over at Dominic, who is frowning slightly, staring at his phone.

"He's okay. Quiet. I think he was really looking forward to staying with Stacy. Jesus." He shakes his head in disgust. "Poor little guy. And now he's stuck with my parents, and I don't know if this is a good idea."

"Which bit?"

"Getting my parents to stay with him. He doesn't really know them."

"Don't you always say you think they'd be better grandparents than parents?"

Dominic's laugh is bitter. "They are, but that doesn't mean they're any good."

"It's just a few days," Emma tries to reassure him. "I'm sure he'll be okay for just a few days. What specifically are you worried about?"

"I just haven't left him this long before. He said Nonna and Papa were having a fight. That's the thing I was worried about. That they'd get violent in front of him."

"Violent? What kind of violent?" For everything Dominic has told her about his parents, he hasn't explicitly described any violence. Then, with a start, she remembers the man she met at the start of the summer, when she was out with Sophie. Jeff. The real estate agent. The one who had known Dominic when he was little, when his parents were still living in town. Hadn't he said something about Dominic's mom cracking his dad over the head with a frying pan? Something like that. She hadn't paid much attention because it was . . . well, it was *before*.

It's only a few days, she reassures Dominic. It will be fine. However badly his parents had got on when they were young, they're still together, aren't they? Not to mention they're in their seventies, and would have undoubtedly calmed down.

Jesse is going to be fine.

CHAPTER
TWENTY-FIVE

"Muffin?" Georgina Montague shouts down the hallway to where her husband is trying to have a peaceful hour, tucked in the old battered wing chair in the library, with the paper and a small nip of scotch.

He sighs as he sets the newspaper down. They have been married forty years. For forty years he has pleaded with her not to roar through the house when she wants someone, and been duly ignored. If anything, he is convinced she now roars more loudly, just to spite him.

"In here." He raises his voice just a little bit, knowing she probably won't hear. He can't bring himself to shout, nor is he willing to get up and go to her. This chair is perfectly comfortable, Petey's nose is resting on his good foot, and the foot that is still recovering from gout is resting on the ottoman.

"Where are you, Muffin?" shouts Georgina, drawing closer, for he knows she knows exactly where he is, where he *always* is on a hot day. Or a cold day. Or a rainy day. The library, which is the only room in the house he considers "his". It's too warm for a fire today, more's the pity. He glances out the window at the unseasonable Indian summer and sighs. He never quite got the hang of gardening, and summer is only enjoyable for about four weeks. By mid-July he's always longing for jumpers, and thick socks, and hikes with their chocolate lab, Petey, pushing the leaves out of the way with his walking stick.

He is an autumn/winter person, he had decided long ago. Georgina, or Muffin, as he calls her — as they, in fact, have called each other for the best part of forty years — adores the summer.

He looks out of the library's French doors, sighing as he sees the large white marquee sitting on the lawn, tables and chairs stacked up on one side. When Georgina asked him if they could throw an engagement party for his nephew George, he thought she meant a bit of wine and a few nibbles in the living room. It's why he said yes. He thought it would be a relatively quiet affair.

There have been men shouting in his garden all day as they hoisted up the marquee, and lorries filled with equipment that they have put in the barn, turning it into what is apparently called a caterer's kitchen.

Simon Montague loves his wife. He doesn't love crowds. He can only tolerate the kind of parties at his house where, at a certain point, he is able to quietly disappear. He enjoys people very much, but only for limited periods of time, and only if he can escape by himself to recharge his batteries.

This library has always been his refuge, but it's not much of a refuge today, with all the activity right outside the door, the men shouting back and forth, the bursts of raucous laughter.

286

Why can't people be more respectful? he thinks sadly, waiting for Georgina to come pounding into the room.

"Thought I'd find you in here," she pants, resting in the doorway.

"Why were you shouting for me, then?"

"Habit," she says brightly, ignoring his irritation.

"Muffin," he says sadly, as another burst of laughter comes from outside. "Is it really too much to ask for people in our house to be quiet?"

"They're not in our house, darling. They're outside."

"But it's so disturbing! Every few seconds there's a burst of shouting or laughter. Why can't they do their job quietly?"

"They're almost finished," she says. "Don't be an old grouch, Muffin. I know you hate lots of people, but George and Henry are thrilled."

"You're calling her Henry now?"

"Apparently everyone calls her Henry. They'll be here in time for supper tonight. I know he can't wait to see you. And I've made a lovely beef Wellington for you." She smiles, seeing the look of pleasure on her husband's face. "With apple crumble for pudding. See? I'm trying to look after you amidst the madness."

"Party's tomorrow evening?"

"It is. Will you be sociable? Just for one night?"

"Just for one night," grumbles Simon. "But you mustn't do this again, Muffin. Truly. You know I only agreed to host an engagement party because I thought it would be small."

"Darling." Georgina leans over to give her husband a kiss on the cheek. "How long have we been married? When it comes to parties, when have I ever done anything by halves?" She smiles at him indulgently. "Are you able to run to the cellar and get that lovely wine? I'm putting out a plate of cheese and biscuits for when Emma arrives with her man. They should be here soon."

Simon takes his foot off the ottoman with great reluctance and heaves himself out of the comfort of his chair. "Know anything about this man?" he asks his wife as he slowly makes his way out of the room. "Is it serious?"

"I imagine it must be if she's bringing him home to meet us. I trust you'll be on your best behaviour with him?"

"Me?" He turns to look at his wife, aghast. "I have never been the one in this partnership that anyone has had to worry about." He lets out a bark of laughter. "Let's just hope he's looking after her. That's my only concern."

"Ssssh," says Georgina suddenly, her head cocked. "Oh my goodness! I think I just heard a car door. I think they must be here."

It has been ages since Emma has been to her parents' house. She has barely given England a second thought during her five years in the States. She has made a few sporadic trips back, but not to Somerset, only to London, for work, where she has stayed at the Four Seasons, dined at the best restaurants, had her parents

288

come up from the country to see her, and taken them out somewhere fabulous for dinner.

She hadn't been back to Brigham Hall since she left. She told people she was from a beautiful part of the world, but her heart didn't ache for her house, the fields, the narrow country lanes overgrown with lush hedges.

At least, it didn't ache until today, driving along those winding roads with Dominic, seeing everything through his eyes, passing charming thatched cottages and village streets lined with pretty stone buildings older than anything Dominic had ever seen in his life.

She drives the hire car expertly, even though it has been years since she drove on this side of the road. As they draw closer to Yeovil she remembers it all, and she laughs in pleasure as she points out pubs she used to frequent as a teenager, fields in which she snogged teenage boys, buses she used to take, sitting on the top deck in the seat at the front, puffing on cigarettes and blowing smoke out the side of her mouth in a way she thought at the time was ineffably cool.

"*Snogged?*" Dominic starts to laugh. "I've never heard anyone but Austin Powers use that word. I didn't think it was even real."

"It most certainly is real," says Emma. "You know what it means, right?"

"Sure. Having sex."

"No!" She laughs. "It most certainly does not mean having sex. Oh my God, you think I was having sex with teenage boys in fields? What kind of girl do you think I am?"

"My kind of girl?" he says.

"Well, I wasn't. Having sex in fields. *Snogging* is kissing. Proper kissing. French kissing."

"Do you mean with tongues?"

"Yes. With tongues."

"So . . . making out?"

"Yes, exactly. Making out."

"Hmmm. *Snogging*. I like that word. I'm going to call it snogging from now on. Do you want to go snogging with me?"

Emma cracks up. "I can't actually believe we're having this conversation. Anyway, that's not how you'd say it. You'd say, 'Fancy a snog?'"

"No way." Dominic starts laughing. "Is that really what you'd say? 'Fancy a snog?'"

"Yes, but it's not *snahg*." She starts to laugh. "It's *snog*. Short o."

"Snog. 'Fancy a snog?'"

"Are you asking?" Emma is still laughing.

"I'm asking."

"I'm dancing."

"What?" He stares at her.

"Never mind." Emma shakes her head, giggling. "It's an old joke. The boy who walks up to the girl and says, 'Are you dancing?' 'Are you asking?' 'I'm asking.' 'I'm dancing.'"

"I don't get it."

"No. It's an old saying. Must be an English thing."

"Shall we pull over into a field and *snog*? I'm feeling competitive with all those old boyfriends of yours. I'm not going to feel like I've had the full English experience until I've snogged someone in a field."

"When you say 'someone', do you mean anyone at all? Like, say, her?" Emma gestures to a sour-faced older woman on the pavement.

"No thanks. When I say someone, I mean you."

"I'll think about it," says Emma. Once they have passed through the village, she veers to the left and parks. "Come on." She gets out of the car and pulls Dominic out, too, pulling him behind a bush where she snakes her arms around his neck and passionately kisses him.

"Mmmm." Dominic starts to unbutton her jeans. "I could get used to this."

"Not now." She giggles. "I don't want nettle rash. Later. I promise you," she says. She gives him another kiss, before dragging him back to the car.

A mile, another mile and a half, a left, a right, and the car slows as Emma drives through the wooden gates and up a winding driveway, rounding a small copse of trees to reveal Brigham Hall, nestled in a gravel driveway, fields stretching all around it, the setting sun turning the pretty stone a glowing pinkish gold.

"Whoa." Dominic whistles, gazing at the house. Emma realizes with a start that it does look rather stately and grand, particularly to an American newcomer. She'd never thought of it that way when she lived here.

"You never told me you live in Downton Abbey."

"Hardly," Emma says. "This is nothing. It just looks grand from here. Wait until you get inside. It's all falling apart." She steps out of the car, pausing to really look at the stone Georgian house she has always taken for granted. Seeing it through Dominic's eyes, she recognizes how beautiful it is, how lucky she was to have grown up here.

As she stands by the car and Dominic busies himself with their bags, a chocolate lab suddenly emerges through the front door, his tail wagging furiously in delight. Emma flings her arms around him, covering him with kisses. As much as she has made America her home, this is home, too, she realizes. And for the first time since moving to New York all those years ago, she is happy to be here.

CHAPTER
TWENTY-SIX

"Hello?" Emma walks through the front door, Petey stuck to her heels, followed closely by Dominic, who puts their bags down in the hallway, next to the Wellington boots lined up under the coat rack.

The limestone floor is old and worn, dotted with aged Persian rugs, and a couple of riding hats sit on a console table. Dominic walks over and picks one up. "Who rides?"

"No one any more. I used to, but obviously I'm not here. That's my old hat, I think." She walks over and picks it up, smiling at the memory. "I kept a horse at a stable down the road. Pennyflake was his name. I adored him."

"Why are the hats out?"

Emma lowers her voice. "Same reason the wellies are lined up by the front door. It's what you do when you're a *yah* living in the country."

"A what?"

"A yah. Someone upper class, don't you know." She exaggerates the accent as Dominic shakes his head with a laugh.

"I thought we spoke the same language, but I guess not."

"That's exactly what I thought before I moved to America," says Emma, putting down the riding hat. "I kept asking where the shopping trolleys were kept, and was there a petrol station nearby. I couldn't understand why no one knew what I was talking about."

Dominic stares at her. "I'm not even going to ask," he says finally, as Emma laughs and walks over to give him a kiss.

"I love you." She looks into his eyes, seeing them crinkle as he smiles.

"I love you, too," he replies, and then both of them jump apart as Emma's mother walks into the hallway.

"There you are!" she booms, coming over with a smile, kissing Emma on each cheek before embracing her in a quick, tight hug. "I thought I heard a noise. Well, hello!" She releases her daughter and stands back to look Dominic up and down, before extending her hand. "You must be Emma's friend. I'm her mother. Georgina Montague. How do you do?"

"Good, thank you," says Dominic. "How are you?" He shakes her hand enthusiastically.

"Well, let's get you upstairs," she bustles. "Daddy's just in the cellar, but put your things away, then come down and we'll all have a little glass of something. Muffin?" She turns and bellows down the hallway. "Did you find the wine?"

"Your mother is terrifying," says Dominic, as soon as they are safely behind closed doors in Emma's old bedroom. He looks around, taking in the evidence of Emma's life, long before he came into it. "Why are there posters of boy bands on your wall still?"

294

"Because I basically haven't been back since I went to university. This is like stepping back in time."

"Who are they, anyway?"

"Take That."

Dominic looks blank.

"Huge band in Britain. That's Jason. He was my favourite."

"Cute," says Dominic, walking around the room and examining the gymkhana ribbons. "Your mom must treat this room like a shrine."

Emma bursts out laughing. "Are you joking? The only reason this room still looks exactly like it did when I left for university is that my mother has probably never set foot in it since. My parents' bedroom is in the other wing. She never comes up here. It was brilliant for parties. I could sneak tons of people up here and my mother never knew." She pauses. "Can I just say something about her being terrifying? You didn't mean that, did you? She really isn't terrifying at all, once you get to know her. She's just quite strong and imposing. You can handle her."

"Okay," says Dominic, although he sounds doubtful. "But if *she's* like that, what the hell is your father like?"

"He's a softie. My mother's the one who wears the trousers."

"You mean pants." He raises an eyebrow at her.

"When in England," she says, as he grabs her and pulls her onto the bed.

"Really good to meet you, sir," says Dominic, more respectful than Emma has ever seen him. He looks more sophisticated than she has ever seen him, and more uncomfortable. And terribly American, she thinks, in his chinos, blue button-down shirt, and trainers.

She looks at the trainers, then at her father's battered old brogues. Her mother will have noticed them immediately, disapprovingly. Trainers, she would say, are only for the gym. Thankfully, though, her mother is not casting disapproving glances at Dominic, but is instead busy bringing in the cheese platter, twittering on about someone's homemade peach chutney she had bought at one of the country fairs over the summer.

"Come and sit down," says her father. "The girls are drinking wine, but I'm on the scotch. Fancy a glass? I have an excellent single malt, too."

"Actually," Dominic says, "I'm more of a beer drinker. It's not that I don't like a glass of Jack every now and then, but this early in the evening I drink beer, sir."

"Hmm," says Emma's father, visibly pleased at being called *sir*. "I think we may have a couple of beers in the outside fridge." He stands up.

"Please, let me. If you tell me where they are, I can get them."

"That's very kind of you. Go through the kitchen into the gallery, then to the garage. There's a small fridge in there. I'm not sure what kind we have, but they should be on the top shelf."

"Is there anything I can get for you?"

"No, no. I'm quite all right with my nip here." He toasts him with a smile. When Dominic is safely out of the room, he turns to Emma.

296

"Very nice young man, your American," he says.

"He is nice, isn't he?" says Emma. "I'm glad you like him."

"I like the way he called me *sir*," says her father. "It reminds me of army days. Quite unusual to find a young person these days who has that sort of respect for the older generation. I approve, Emma."

"You hardly know him." Emma laughs. "Which is not to say I'm not delighted you approve. He's a lovely person. I know we're not here for long, but hopefully you'll get to know him a little."

"He's quite good-looking," booms her mother from the sofa. "Very glamorous and exotic with that suntan and that black hair. Where is his family from?"

"I believe Connecticut," says Emma, being deliberately obtuse. "Westport, originally, but now Trumbull."

Georgina's face is blank. "I mean, where is his family *from?* What country?"

"His grandparents were Italian," she says.

"Aha!" beams Georgina. "I thought I detected some Italian in there. We were just in Puglia, weren't we, Muffin? The most divine place. Where in Italy are they from? Has he spent a lot of time visiting his ancestral home?"

"I don't know. You'll have to ask him yourself about what region his family comes from. But this is the first time he's left America." As soon as the words are out of her mouth she regrets them, for her mother opens her mouth in dismay. Luckily, before she can say anything disparaging, they are interrupted by the sound of the doorbell.

"George and Henry are here," exclaims Georgina in delight, walking out of the room to get the door as Emma looks at her father in consternation.

"I thought it was just us," she says. "I thought the four of us were going to have dinner so you could get to know Dominic. I didn't know George and his fiancee were coming, too?"

Her father shrugs helplessly, placing a hand on her shoulder. "You know your mother, darling. She can't help it. She has this compulsion to invite everyone. What's that she always says? *The more the merrier?* I'm sorry. You know I would have preferred it to be just us. Not that I don't like my nephew very much, but it would have been so . . . George!" Her father composes a welcoming smile on his face as a young, handsome man walks into the living room, striding over to shake his hand effusively.

"Thank you again for doing this, Uncle Simon," George says. "It's so kind of you and Aunt G. I don't know how we'll ever thank you."

A large woman with a big smile and short blond hair bounds into the room, flinging her arms around Emma's father, who pales slightly as he pats her on the back, trying to extricate himself from her embrace. "Uncle Simon!" she says into his shoulder, pulling back but not releasing him. "As soon as we move into our new house we're having you both up to stay! That's how we'll thank you! Honestly, this is just so, so lovely of you."

She finally releases him, as both she and George turn to see Emma, standing behind them.

"Good God!" says George, peering at her. "Emma? Is that you? My favourite cousin?"

"It's me," says Emma, astonished to see George hasn't changed in the slightest since he was a child. He is still spectacularly pretty, with delicate aquiline features. He's also beautifully dressed in a pale green cashmere pullover tied around his shoulders, green-and-pink argyle socks, mouse-suede Oxfords. He looks like something out of another era, as if Brideshead had revisited Brigham Hall by way of *Chariots of Fire*. He has floppy blond hair that he brushes out of his eyes, and perfect white teeth that sparkle as he comes over to give Emma a hug that she really doesn't feel entitled to receive.

He steps back to look at Emma, still clasping her arms. "You look positively glowing," he says. "Aunt G says you're in love and we get to meet the lucky fellow. In the meantime" — he lets her go and steps back — "I'd like you to meet my beautiful fiancée, Henrietta."

"How do you do?" Emma holds out a hand only to find herself enveloped in a fierce hug. Henrietta is rather large. And, there's no other way to put it, rather manly. She has a huge smile, twinkling green eyes, and dimples. In a white shirt and beige trousers, with ballet flats on her feet, she is friendly and warm, and if Emma didn't know better, she might think Henrietta was perhaps a somewhat feminine bloke, with a penchant for ballet flats.

It is all very confusing, she thinks, as the door opens and Dominic steps back into the room, with an open can of beer in his hand.

"Well, hello," says George slowly, and, if Emma didn't know better, she would swear seductively. "You must be Emma's lucky man. I'm George. The little cousin."

"Hello," says Dominic, shaking his hand. "Hey." He waves to Henrietta. "I'm Dominic"

"Hello!" The wave wasn't enough for her, though. She bounds over and gives him a cheerful hug. "I'm Henry."

Dominic looks confused.

"Henry is short for Henrietta," explains Emma, while stifling a case of the giggles. "The engagement party is for George and Henrietta."

"Henry," corrects Henry.

"It's quite confusing," says Emma.

"I know. Everyone thinks George is marrying a man!" With that Henry throws her head back and lets out a belly laugh. Emma, Dominic, and Emma's father Simon all smile rather uncomfortably just as Georgina comes back in the room.

"Ah, here you are," she says merrily to the happy couple. She claps her hands and puts an arm around Henry's shoulders. "And you've met the wonderful Henry! Isn't she the most perfect addition to the family? Don't you adore her?" Henry turns as she and Georgina gaze affectionately at one another.

"Dominic?" Emma says loudly. "You wanted to borrow the computer? Let me just show you where it is. Back in a sec" She takes Dominic by the hand and leads him out. Once they are safely in the library, both of them collapse in nervous giggles.

"What's going on?" says Dominic. "I'm very confused. It must be an English thing, but is Henry a man or a woman? I think George is a man, although I'm not totally sure. And Henry is marrying George? Have I got that straight? Meanwhile, I think Henry's got the hots for your mother."

"Oh God." Emma snorts with laughter. "Don't. That's the most horrible thing I've ever heard."

"It's true. You know it's true. That's why you're laughing."

"Yes. Henry was looking at my mother rather adoringly." She winces. "You don't actually think she's got the hots for her, do you? Because that would be ever so slightly wrong."

"I don't know. Maybe it's an English thing but George seems gay, not that there's anything wrong with that, and Henry seems to be, well . . . a man. Which is maybe why George wants to marry her. Him."

"We're being awful," says Emma with another giggle. "We must stop. Although, I did always think George was gay," says Emma. "Which might explain his attraction to Henry."

"And me."

"Oh God! Yes! When you walked in, George looked like he had died and gone to heaven to find the hunky American of his dreams standing at the gates."

"I want to tell you that's the craziest thing I've ever heard, but yeah. That's pretty much what he looked like. You told me a little bit about your family, I know, but apparently you've kept the best part a secret!"

"I didn't know!" Emma laughs. "I haven't seen George properly since he was a little boy. When I heard he'd got engaged, I was a bit surprised. I guess for all these years I'd assumed wrong."

"Guess so."

"Guess so," echoes Emma. "Henry seems nice, though. In a very jolly hockey sticks kind of way."

"What does that mean?"

"English public schoolgirl. Super excited and enthusiastic about everything."

"When you say *schoolgirl*, you actually mean . . . "

"At least she's nice. Look, we'd better get back. If my mother becomes too impossible, we'd better have a plan of action. It won't do to dissolve in hysterics in front of everyone."

"We need a code word," says Dominic. "How about *birdcage*?"

"Oh, you're funny. Fine. *Birdcage* it is."

"If I say *birdcage*, that means you have to get me out of there, fast. Got it?"

"Got it," says Emma. Then she ruefully shakes her head at Dominic. "I really thought we were going to have a quiet evening when my parents could get to know you. I'm sorry."

"Don't be. It isn't what I expected either, but it's probably more fun."

"This cold pea soup is really good," says Dominic, as they sit around the dining room table.

"It's not meant to be cold," mutters Emma under her breath. "It's my mother's cooking."

"What?" says her mother, from the other end of the table.

"Dominic said the soup is cool," says George, winking at Dominic. "I think that's American slang for *delicious*."

"Oh, I'm so glad," says Georgina. "I was worried it wasn't quite hot enough. I do love to cook, but I'm not always so good with timing."

"She's right," says her husband jovially from the other end of the table. "Delicious food, always cold."

"Or overcooked," booms Georgina with a laugh. "I'm lucky you love my overcooked broccoli."

"Sounds delicious," says Dominic quietly, going back to his soup.

"So, Dominic" George lays down his spoon. "You look like you're in shockingly good shape. Is that from working out or is it something in the water over there?"

"I don't work out," says Dominic with a smile. "Not any more, anyway. I was a gym rat in my twenties, but now I mostly stay in shape with a lot of physical labour."

"Like what?"

"Dominic's a carpenter," says Emma. "He made the most beautiful bookshelves for my house."

"That's right," says George. "Now I remember. Your mother told me he's your landlord. That's handy. A hunky landlord who makes things." He shoots Emma an approving glance. "You certainly hit the jackpot."

"I don't just make things," Dominic says. "I work as a bartender, too."

"A what?" Georgina says, turning to Henry and saying under her breath, but loudly enough for everyone to hear, "I can't understand anything he says. It must be the accent. What did he say?"

"He said he works as a bartender," says Henry loudly.

"A bartender?" says Georgina, composing her features into the politest expression she can muster. "How . . . fun."

"*Fun* is not the word I'd use," Dominic says with a laugh. "That's where the muscles are from. I haul boxes of wine and liquor up and down from the cellar all day long."

"Nice," coos George, as Henry bursts out laughing.

"Stop teasing him," she tells George.

Emma and Dominic exchange confused glances.

Birdcage? mouths Dominic as Emma shakes her head and laughs.

"What about your family?" says Georgina. "What line of business are they in?"

"My dad worked in the restaurant business," says Dominic. "He was a cook."

"A chef!" Georgina perks up. There's something she can work with. "How nice! Maybe he can give me some tips on timing."

"That's not really — " Dominic starts to speak but Henry interrupts, much to Emma's relief. Emma doesn't care what kind of job Dominic's father had. She doesn't care if he was unemployed his entire life. But her mother would. And the less Georgina knows

304

about Dominic's family, the better. At least until she gets to know him, and fully accepts him into the family.

So Henry's interjection saves the day. "Emma!" she says brightly. "George says you love living in America! We were thinking about going over to the States for our honeymoon. I've always wanted to see New England. What do you think? Would you help us work out where to go?"

"Of course," says Emma, "I'd be happy to. I'm dying to hear all about the two of you. Where did you meet?"

"You tell it," says George, looking at Henry. "You always tell it so much better than me."

"It's terribly unromantic" Henry giggles. "It was in Tesco Metro. I had a group of friends coming for dinner, but I'd burnt the stew — complete accident, I didn't realize the burner was misaligned — so I was desperately trying to cobble together something passable at the last minute."

"One of her dinner guests was a chef," says George. "So she had to impress."

"Did your hands meet over the potatoes?" asks Emma.

"Almost!" Henry says. "I had paused by the cauliflower, trying to decide whether I ought to buy it, when George started talking to me."

"She was actually wearing a sweatshirt saying *Oxford University*."

"I didn't go to Oxford, though," says Henry. "Far too stupid!" And she starts laughing. "I did a cordon bleu course instead."

"Which means she is a far better cook than I will ever be, but we started talking about Oxford . . . " says George.

"And all my best friends went there, and George knew all of them, including two of the people coming for dinner."

"So I gave her my recipe for tandoori cauliflower, not knowing she was already an amazing cook . . . "

"And I invited him for dinner."

"And the rest," says George, reaching for Henry's hand, "is history."

"He never left." Henry rolls her eyes as George looks at her adoringly.

Emma shoots a look at Dominic as they give each other the tiniest of shrugs. Clearly they both got it very wrong.

"And now the two of you are about to embark on the journey of a lifetime, starting tomorrow night!" says Georgina, from the end of the table. "I'm utterly thrilled to be the one hosting your engagement party. The two of you are going to be gloriously happy forever."

"Thank you," says George. Then he shoots a fond look at Emma and Dominic. "Maybe there will be another announcement soon . . . "

"Oh, I don't know about *that*," Emma's mother says clearly, her hearing suddenly fine.

"I'll clear." Emma, bright red, jumps up, gathering plates and whisking them into the kitchen. She loads the plates into the dishwasher, aware her heart is pounding, embarrassed for Dominic, who surely must have heard her mother's remark, embarrassed for

306

herself. Dominic probably didn't understand. He may have assumed her mother was simply implying that it's too early in their relationship to be considering marriage. But Emma knows better. She knows her mother too well. It was a clear statement that Emma should not be marrying someone like that. That Dominic is beneath her.

A wave of dismay washes over her. This is why she left to take a job in New York. She didn't want to deal with her mother's bullshit any more, her passive-aggressive digs, her ridiculous snobbery.

I shouldn't have come back, she thinks. *It's so much easier when I see them on my turf, when they fly to New York for a week and I can take them to dinner, to a show, perhaps a lunch or tea and send them off sightseeing. But this? Being in my childhood home, having to deal with my mother's snobbery and not being able to escape, is awful.*

Emma places her hands on the kitchen worktop and steps back, looking at the floor, taking a few deep breaths. The sound of footsteps behind her startles her, and she looks up to see Dominic coming through the kitchen doorway, juggling a stack of plates.

"Are you okay?" he asks, concern in his eyes.

"I'm fine." She forces a smile. "It's just always a challenge, being home."

"Was it what your mom said? Not knowing about an announcement?"

Emma shrugs. "Kind of. It just seemed so unnecessary. I know we haven't been together long, but she didn't need to point it out."

Dominic smiles. "That wasn't what she was pointing out and you know it."

Emma swallows hard. "What do you mean?"

"Someone like you? Someone who grew up with *this*?" He gestures around the kitchen. "Someone like *you* does not end up with someone like *me*. Even I see that."

Emma stares at him as Dominic sighs.

"Look, I knew as soon as I met you that we are from very different worlds. I feel like I've stepped into the queen's palace here. Your parents can definitely see I don't belong. I'm okay with that, but yeah, the thought of you and me getting formally engaged and having a party here like the one your parents are throwing tomorrow is crazy. If my parents came, they would be so intimidated, they would get drunk and end up throwing up on one of the antique rugs."

Emma's face falls. "Are you saying you and I are pointless? That it can't go anywhere? That maybe we shouldn't be together?"

"What? No!" He steps towards her and places his hands on her arms. "God, no. I know that what you and I have is rare, and really special. I also know that we come from very different backgrounds, and not everybody's going to understand that. I get that your mom doesn't understand it. I get that most of the people who are going to show up tomorrow for the party aren't going to understand it, either. They're going to wonder what you're doing with a guy like me. But that's okay. I know what we're doing together, and you know what we're doing together. That's all that matters. You know that, right?"

Emma's eyes are filled with tears as she nods. "I do know that. I needed to hear it from you. Thank you." She sniffles again. "I'm sorry about my mother," she adds. "I was hoping she would behave better."

"Honey, I'm a bartender at the Fat Hen, remember? This is nothing. She says anything else, though, and I'll take her down. Boom!"

Emma starts to laugh as she allows herself to be pulled in for a hug, the anger, embarrassment, and angst all gone.

"What's going on in here?"

Emma smiles as her mother bustles in. "Nothing. We're just clearing up. We'll go and get the rest of the plates."

She takes Dominic's hand and leads him back to the dining room. She may have forgiven her mother for the time being, but the last thing she needs is to give her the opportunity to say anything else.

CHAPTER
TWENTY-SEVEN

"I could get used to this," says Dominic, settling back on the bench, nursing his pint of Guinness as a ploughman's lunch is set in front of him. "Beer, bread, and cheese. Does life get any better?"

"Cheers." Emma lifts her vodka and tonic in a toast to Dominic and her father, relieved that the three of them have managed to get away.

The caterers showed up late that morning, with teams of men to finish off the marquee. A lorry had trundled down the driveway even earlier, just after seven, dropping off vases filled with sweet peas and peonies, banging, clattering, shouting. The noise they'd made seemed entirely unreasonable, Emma felt, so early in the morning.

And Georgina bustled in and out of the house directing everyone, pretending to be stressed, although Emma knew she was loving every second.

Emma had grabbed some toast, made tea for herself and Dominic, and sneaked quietly back upstairs to bed, thinking it was the only peaceful place in the house. It quickly became apparent that there was no peaceful place in the house; the noise and banging could be heard everywhere. In the end Dominic and Emma got dressed and went for a walk.

It was noon by the time they approached the pub. Neither of them could face going back to the house, so they headed inside the eighteenth-century building. There, tucked into a corner with a stack of newspapers and a pint, was Emma's father.

"Dad? What are you doing here?"

He had put his paper down and groaned. "It's the noise. I can't bear it. Your mother's gone into overdrive and I had to get out. I've got enough here to read to keep me busy for hours."

"May we join you?"

His face lit up. "Of course."

The three of them toast each other and sip their drinks as Emma's father closes his eyes in pleasure. "I love your mother," he says, his eyes still closed, "but she does drive me up the wall."

"My father's an introvert," Emma says unnecessarily to Dominic, reaching over for a piece of his cheese. "And my mother, as you have probably realized, is an extrovert. It makes for an interesting partnership, don't you think, Dad?"

"Interesting is the polite way of putting it." He smiles.

"And I" — Emma gestures to herself — "just in case you haven't already guessed, take after my dad." For years, Emma realizes, as she speaks, she had thought she ought to be different. More like her mother, more outgoing, more ambitious, but suddenly she knows she is perfectly content to be like her dad; to be herself.

"It's funny," Dominic says. "You seem really outgoing. You're not shy at all."

"That's not really what introversion is about," says Emma. "Although everyone seems to think otherwise. Being an introvert really means you recharge your batteries by being alone. You can be sociable and outgoing and enjoy people, but only for limited amounts of time. Large groups and lots of stimulation exhaust an introvert. Literally, for every hour spent at a party, an introvert will need two hours on their own."

"I'm the opposite, clearly," Dominic says.

"Indeed you are," says Emma, smiling. "Definitely an extrovert. You're okay on your own, but when you're feeling drained or tired, you make yourself feel better by inviting a ton of people over, or going to work at the Fat Hen."

"It's true." Dominic nods as he sips his pint. "Does that mean an extrovert and an introvert shouldn't be together?"

Emma's father laughs. "You might think that from looking at Emma's mother and me, but no. I think it's rather good for you to marry the opposite. It brings balance to your life. If my wife didn't force me out from time to time, I'd never leave the house." He pauses thoughtfully. "I would actually be quite happy never leaving the house. But I also know that in order to live a full life, I have to have other experiences. It's good for me. And I wouldn't have it any other way. Except when she says she's throwing an engagement party and it turns out to be the equivalent of a wedding." He shakes his head in dismay.

312

"Speaking of, where are George and Henry today?" Emma asks.

"George has found some spa in Yeovil and has booked a massage." Simon says this without expression, leaving it to Emma to raise her eyebrows. "And Henry is accompanying him to get her hair and make-up done."

"Henry wears make-up?" asks Dominic.

"Not that I've seen," admits Emma's father. "But there it is. I'm also slightly unclear as to what exactly could be done with her hair. It's terribly short."

"Have you planned your escape route for tonight?" Emma teases her father.

"I was thinking about booking a room at the Summer House. Just in case the party's too noisy. Although we do have the box room at the front of the house," he adds. "I'm sure the bed in there is shockingly uncomfortable, but if I have to escape to a quiet spot, I think that's probably going to be the quietest I can find."

"What on earth is a box room?" says Dominic with a frown.

"It's a junk room," explains Emma. "It's the tiniest bedroom where you put everything that doesn't fit anywhere else." She turns to her father. "Can we join you?"

"That *will* be cosy." Her father laughs as they lean towards each other.

Dominic watches the two of them and sees, suddenly, how much they look alike, how similar they are.

Years ago, his mother had told him that when he met the girl he was going to marry, he should look at her mother to see how she would turn out. For some reason, that piece of advice stuck with him.

He remembers it now, thinking of Georgina Montague with a slight shudder. She was undeniably a handsome woman when young — Dominic has seen the old black-and-white photographs in silver frames that dot every surface — but she is a bit of a battle-axe now. Clearly she was never tiny in the way Emma is; her stoutness and imposing bosom add to her commanding air. Seeing Emma here, next to her father, Dominic breathes a sigh of relief. He is clearly the parent she takes after in every way.

Dominic's phone buzzes and he lights up when he sees it's Jesse calling. He excuses himself to take the call outside.

"I like him," says Simon Montague, when Dominic has left the room. "He seems like a lovely chap, and he quite clearly adores you."

Emma feels the warmth of happiness spread through her body. "Thank you, Dad. That means a lot to me." She pauses, knowing she shouldn't pose the question she's about to ask, but she can't keep the words in. "Does Mum like him?"

"She really doesn't know him," says her father diplomatically. "And you know your mother. She still thinks you're going to find yourself a nice English fellow and settle down in Somerset. Preferably a peer." He raises his eyebrows, then continues, "Your having found yourself a serious American boyfriend means there's a very real possibility that you'll never come back for good. And although you and your mother have had your . . . issues over the years, she loves you very much, and that's a bitter pill for her to swallow."

Emma sits back, surprised. She hadn't looked at it like that, hadn't ever considered the possibility that her mother wouldn't like Dominic because she fears he will take Emma away from her forever. Has she been too harsh on her mother? She is surprised to feel a wave of compassion.

Dominic walks back in, distracted.

"Is everything okay?"

He shrugs. "Jesse's okay. He's not loving his grandparents being there. I mean, he's thrilled they've taken him out and bought him toys, but he tells me they're screaming at each other all the time. He's stressed and upset." Dominic shakes his head. "I shouldn't have done it. I thought they might have calmed down, but it doesn't sound like a great situation."

Emma sinks down on her seat, filled with guilt and remorse. "I'm so sorry," she says. "It's only another couple of days. Do you think he'll be okay until then?"

"I guess," Dominic says. "I just feel guilty, and a little foolish to think they might have been different with him. I hope he is going to be okay."

"Listen," Emma reminds him. "You survived an entire childhood with them, and you turned out fine. However bad they are with each other, they're still loving with him, aren't they? And kids are resilient. He'll be okay."

"I won't do it again, though," Dominic says. "I can't have my parents look after him regularly. I mean, that's why they never have, and he doesn't really know them. I was always scared this would happen. I don't want him around that kind of shouting." He looks at Emma then. "At least with us he sees what a good relationship is."

"He does," says Emma, taking his hand. "He will forget this visit with his grandparents, but he won't forget the example we're setting for him. That's what counts."

It is Emma's turn to excuse herself. She goes to the bathroom and stares at herself in the mirror, smiling. Everything Dominic says, that they are setting an example for Jesse what a relationship can be, that he knows this is it, makes Emma happy. She knows this is different, knows this is for real. The only fly in the ointment is the childish need she still has for her parents' blessing.

She already has her father's — of that she is sure. But if she doesn't have her mother's approval, she can learn to live without it.

CHAPTER
TWENTY-EIGHT

"Oh God!" Georgina Montague throws her hands up in the air as she walks into the kitchen from the garden.

"What's going on?" Emma is doing up the ankle straps on her Manolo Blahniks, wishing she had brought evening flats rather than high suede Mary Janes. Now she will have to spend the entire evening tiptoeing around so that her heels won't sink into the lawn.

She is wearing a black silk dress she has had for years, her go-to cocktail dress for parties in New York, although it probably isn't what's worn for an English engagement party under a marquee in a garden. She owns a million floral tea dresses, any of which would have been perfect. Oh well. Emma sighs, seeing the first guests stride down the driveway in their pretty sundresses. They'll just have to presume that she has become completely New-York-ized over the past few years.

"What's the matter?" She looks at her mother as Dominic walks into the kitchen, breathtakingly handsome in a navy blazer and pale blue shirt.

"The barman's throwing up in the back loo," Georgina says. "Food poisoning, he says. He's been retching for the past hour and tells me he can't work at the party. I don't know what we're going to do!" She throws her hands up in the air again for dramatic impact. Then she pauses, and swivels neatly to settle her gaze on Dominic.

"Wait a moment," Georgina says. "Dominic. Didn't you say *you* were a barman?"

"Mum, come on. We're guests," says Emma. "It's not fair to ask him. Phone the caterer and ask them to send a replacement. And if they can't, people can just serve themselves."

"I have phoned the caterer," snaps her mother. "They don't have anyone else. Apparently it's one of the busiest Saturdays of the year. As for your suggestion we have people serve themselves?" She snorts with derision. "I don't think so. This isn't that kind of party, and our friends certainly aren't those kinds of people. We *must* have a barman." She stares at Dominic. The seconds tick by.

"It's fine." Dominic gives an easy shrug as he breaks Georgina's stare and looks at Emma. "Honestly. It's no problem. It's what I do. Do you have any signature drinks I need to know about?"

"I knew there would be something I'd forget. No! We don't have any signature drinks. Oh lord."

"Don't worry. Let me go out and see what you have. Maybe I can come up with something." Everything about his manner is reassuring. Emma watches her mother's shoulders visibly relax as she smiles at him graciously.

318

"Oh," she says, just before she turns to leave the kitchen. "You can borrow a white shirt from my husband. The trousers are fine." She casts an eye over his khaki trousers. "I would have preferred black but never mind."

Emma is suddenly furious. How dare her mother be so patronizing. How dare she treat Dominic like a member of the staff, especially when he's doing such a huge favour for her. But Dominic places a hand on her arm and holds her back until her mother disappears through the doors into the garden.

"It's okay, Emma," he says gently. "She's hugely stressed, obviously, and at a party this size, having a bartender get sick is a big deal. I'm happy to help. She's just trying to make sure the evening's perfect."

"Because she's so bloody insecure she thinks that a barman in the wrong trousers will make her look like a failure. Heaven forbid. My God. It's pathetic"

"Yes. It is. Which is why you need to feel sorry for her, not get angry. She can't help it. It's okay."

"Are you absolutely sure about this? Because honestly, at this point I would be quite happy to pack up our stuff and go to a hotel. I just don't know that we should stay."

"They're your parents," says Dominic. "And they're getting older, and they're not going to be here forever. You hardly ever see them. Let's just accept your mom's insecurities and forgive her. She can't help it. Remember, she's just doing the best she can with the knowledge that she has."

"When did you get so forgiving and generous? And wise?"

"I'm not sure I am. If it were my parents, I'd fucking kill them. But they're yours, so I'm able to be forgiving and see their good side."

"There's a good side?"

Dominic pauses as if he's thinking. "Well, your dad's awesome," he says finally, and Emma laughs.

"Come here." He takes her in his arms. "It's all going to be okay."

"Dominic?" They hear her mother calling from the gallery. "Are you coming? I have the shirt here for you."

"I promise to make you a very stiff drink," he says with a smile, kissing Emma before walking off to join Georgina and take care of the bar.

The marquee, or, as Dominic kept referring to it, much to her mother's chagrin, *tent*, is packed to bursting with the guests. George and Henry are moving through the crowds, greeting friends, being introduced to ancient family members Henry has never met.

Henry, it has to be said, looks not unlike a man in drag. She is wearing red lipstick, which is entirely the wrong colour for her, and heavy eye make-up that no beautician worth her salt would ever have chosen for her. Her hair has been curled, and now has a pink streak in it that Henry described with a hoot of laughter as "great fun!" She is wearing a belted green dress with a knee-length skirt that does absolutely nothing for her, and she has large sparkly multicoloured hoops in her ears.

Emma has greeted her relatives, family friends of her parents she hasn't seen for years, and people from the village she has known her entire life. She has had the same conversations over and over again: yes, America is exciting; no, she isn't married yet; the barman is her boyfriend, and he is helping out because the original barman has a stomach bug; yes, I think he's terribly handsome, too; no, I'm no longer with the bank.

She goes to the bar frequently, for constant refills and reassuring kisses, but Dominic is busy. She can't expect him to look after her as well as the other guests. So she moves to the other side of the marquee, wishing he weren't helping out, wishing he were by her side so she wouldn't be quite so bored.

"Em-ma," says a familiar singsong voice, and she turns, catching her breath, utterly stunned to see a tall, lanky man standing there, the top buttons of his shirt open to reveal the beginnings of a suntanned chest. A chest she used to know very well. A body she used to know almost as well as her own.

"Rufus." She forcibly replaces the surprise with a smile and gives him an air kiss on either cheek. "What a lovely surprise. No one told me you'd be here."

"I didn't know I'd be here myself." Rufus laughs. "I'm up staying with Kat and Jonti for the weekend. I had no idea they were attending an engagement party, much less one at the Montagues'. Of course, I insisted on gate-crashing."

"Oh. I hope my mother doesn't see you," says Emma, knowing how appalled her mother gets when people show up without an invitation.

"I'm not really gate-crashing," says Rufus. "I phoned her first. I told her I was up for the weekend and she invited me immediately."

Emma frowns. "When was this?"

"Yesterday morning. Clearly she didn't pass on the information." He laughs.

Emma finds herself looking at him, unable to believe she spent so many years with him. This was the man she woke up with every morning. She knows all his habits: the way he soaps himself in the shower, the way he shaves while grimacing into a tiny magnifying mirror stuck to the wall. He likes to sit on the loo for hours, reading the papers, sometimes with a glass of scotch on the window ledge next to him. He loves soft, creamy scrambled eggs for breakfast, with burnt wholegrain toast. He finds cruel humour hilarious. She knows the expression on his face when he orgasms. And what it takes to get him there.

She blinks. It has all come flooding back to her. She knows him so well, and here they are, making small talk, like strangers.

"I heard you got married and have children now," says Emma, awkwardly, not knowing what else to say. "Congratulations. How old are they?"

"I have Charlie, who's four, and Daisy, who's just turned two. They are adorable, naturally, as all small children are."

"And your wife? Is she here, too?"

Rufus grimaces. "Little bit of a problem at the moment."

Emma stares at him. "What do you mean?"

"We're on a little bit of a break. Having a few issues with . . . with our marriage."

Emma can't hide her look of surprise. "You're having issues? Aren't marriage and kids what you always wanted?"

"Well, yes. Absolutely. But my wife seemed to think I'd be home all the time once we had kids. She doesn't seem to understand that I can't change my schedule — all the after-work meetings I have to attend — just because I have children now."

Emma tilts her head. "Do you mean long drunken dinners with the boys four nights a week?"

Rufus gives her a sheepish smile. "You know me so well." He shrugs. "You always understood."

"I did, but I didn't like it. I never had a problem with you going out with the boys, it was just that the boys were so ghastly I never wanted to go."

"That's what my wife thinks, too. She would never dream of going, but she doesn't want me to go either, which is where the problem started."

"You're really allowing nights out with the boys to get in the way of your marriage when you have two tiny children?"

"Well, it's not just that," says Rufus. "You said I always wanted marriage and kids, which I did, but . . ." He pauses and looks away.

"What?" prompts Emma.

"I always wanted that with you," he says simply, without a trace of his signature sarcasm.

Emma doesn't respond. She has no idea what to say.

"Clearly we've both moved on." He shakes his head. "I think I may have made a terrible mistake. I married the first girl I met after we split up. I didn't really give us a chance to get to know each other, to find out if we were compatible. I just met her, we fell into this thing very quickly, and I proposed without really thinking it through."

"Oh God, Rufus. I'm sorry."

"Nothing to be sorry about. I just don't think we have very much in common."

"Other than your two children," Emma points out.

"Well, yes. Obviously it's not ideal circumstances, to have had the children. I did rather think I might have been making a terrible mistake when I showed up in church on our wedding day. I was quite drunk, you know. But I didn't know how not to go through with it. And she announced she was pregnant before I had a chance to confess my un-happiness, and how could I say anything after that?"

Emma reaches out and rubs his arm sympathetically. "I don't know what you do in a situation like that," she says. "It sounds impossible."

"It just got worse from there," he says, seemingly relieved to be able to talk about it. "We weren't friends. We weren't partners. We were two people who happened to have children, but we had nothing else in common. I didn't feel love when I looked at her. I felt resentment. And she felt the same way about me. Anyway, I'm sorry. I didn't mean to talk your ear off. I certainly didn't mean to complain. I moved into a flat in Notting Hill a couple of months ago and I'm making the best of things. How's your life? You look wonderful."

Emma smiles. "Thank you."

"No, I mean it," says Rufus. "You're absolutely glowing. America clearly suits you." He pauses. "I should never have let you go."

Emma laughs. "You didn't let me go, Rufus. I left. Or at least, it was my decision for us to split up."

"But I should have worked harder for you. I shouldn't have let you just walk away without fighting to try and get you back." He steps closer to her, looking meaningfully into her eyes, and Emma shrinks back. If she didn't know better she would be certain he was about to kiss her. Rufus pauses, Emma freezes, with no idea what to do, and the moment hangs in the air until they both hear his name being called.

"Rufus!"

Emma turns around to see her mother bearing down on them, delight in her eyes as she gives Rufus enthusiastic kisses on both cheeks. "What a gorgeous surprise!"

Emma turns to her. "You knew he was coming," she says, trying to keep the belligerence out of her voice.

"I completely forgot!" her mother replies, still smiling. "Gosh, you look handsome. Doesn't he look handsome, Emma?"

Emma nods uncomfortably.

"And is it true that you're a single man again? Oh, Rufus! I am so sorry." But she can scarcely hide her glee. "Emma, did you hear that? Rufus is single again!"

"I know," Emma says flatly. "We were just discussing it."

"Were you? Oh, it's lovely to see you, Rufus. And even lovelier to see the two of you together. I know, I know, I'm just an annoying old woman, but the two of you do still make the most beautiful couple."

Emma shakes her head with scorn as her mother innocently throws her hands in the air. "What? Don't glare at me just for pointing out the obvious. Emma's gone all *American* on us," she says, turning to Rufus. "She brought her American *boyfriend* here."

"Boyfriend?" Rufus raises an eyebrow. "I had no idea you had a boyfriend. Where is he?"

"Behind the bar," says her mother. "He's a barman."

"Oh," says Rufus, with an amused smile. "A *barman?* That's . . . nice."

"It's certainly helpful," trills her mother. "Especially tonight, when the original barman we booked got ill."

Rufus turns and studies Dominic as Emma cringes. "He looks very American," he says finally. "All good looks, big muscles, and white teeth."

"Thanks," Emma says guardedly, unsure if this is a compliment.

"Not at all who I would have imagined you with," Rufus continues, turning back to face her.

"Couldn't agree more," says her mother.

Emma closes her eyes just for a second, reminding herself to breathe deeply. "You need to stop, Mother," she says, her voice shaking with fury. "I've already had enough of your digs at Dominic. If I hear you say one more thing about him, if I hear you dismiss or refer to

326

him disdainfully one more time, we will both leave. I swear to you this is not an empty threat. It will take me five minutes to pack my suitcase, and we will go to a hotel for the remainder of this trip. Dominic is the best man I have ever known, and if you can't see that, if you are only capable of judging him by where he's from, or how much money he does or doesn't have, you will lose both of us."

Emma's voice is low, quiet, and resolved. Rufus has already backed away, leaving this to the two of them. Her mother stares at her before opening her mouth.

"First of all," says her mother, flustered but doing her best to save face, "I do not like the way you are talking to me. Secondly, this is not about Dominic, this is about you. I know you think he's the man you're going to end up with, but let me tell you, marriage is no piece of cake. It's one of the hardest things you will ever do, and it's hard enough when you marry someone from your own background, let alone someone from another world. I don't care that Dominic is American. I don't care about that. He may be a nice man, but he's from a completely different class. He's a barman, for heaven's sake. He doesn't understand your world, and you can't possibly understand his. I am delighted that you are having fun, Emma, but I do not think this is the man for you. He is not the man you are going to marry." She recovers her composure and steps back. "And frankly, darling," she adds, in a louder voice, "he's not exactly PLU, is he?"

Emma's heart is pounding as she stares at her mother. *PLU. People like us.* The most ridiculous

327

epithet ever invented. It was the absolute worst thing her mother could have said.

"*You* weren't *PLU*," says Emma, with a bitter laugh. "But you seem to have conveniently forgotten your roots. I've had enough. The guests will have to help themselves to their own drinks."

Turning on her heel, she strides to the bar, takes Dominic by the hand, and leads him upstairs to pack.

Emma never thought it would come to this. She never thought she would have to make a choice between her family and her man, but her mother has given her no option. Even if Georgina were to knock on the bedroom door and apologize, Emma isn't sure it would make enough of a difference.

Life is so easy when you are young, she thinks. You can say and do almost anything, safe in the knowledge that an apology will make everything better. The older you get, the more impact those harmful words and deeds have. Once said, those words cannot be unspoken.

Her mother is not the type to apologize. She has fallen out with friends over the years, and once crossed, she writes people off forever. Those few who have managed to stay in her inner circle have long joked that her parties are the most fun because they are always filled with new people, that you are unlikely to see the same faces three years in a row.

Emma is fighting tears as they both fill their suitcases. She still hopes her mother will come up, say something, apologize, ask forgiveness, at least try to stop the two of them leaving. But she knows such a gesture would be out of character.

No one is in the house as they carry their luggage down the stairs.

"Are you sure about this?" Dominic pauses in the entrance hall to look at her. "You're sure you want to just leave without saying goodbye? You're sure you want to fly all the way home without resolving this?"

"I'm sure," she says, on the brink of tears.

"Emma." He steps forward and reaches out for her arms, holding her steady. "Your parents aren't young. And they're set in their ways. Think about this. Anything might happen to them and you would never forgive yourself if you left now, like this. I understand why you're so upset, but you're going to feel better if you can find a way to forgive her."

Emma closes her eyes and shakes her head. "I can't right now. Maybe I'll feel differently in the morning, but right now I can't even look at her."

"Okay." He nods after a long pause. "I get it. Is there a place nearby for us to stay?"

"I already called the Summer House. They have a room."

"Let's go, then." He picks up both suitcases and walks through the door. With one last look behind her, pained by the very real possibility that she and her mother will never resolve things, that this may be the last time she comes here, Emma walks down the steps.

They are getting into their car when they hear a shout. George approaches, running from the side of the house, concern on his face.

"Where are you two off to?" he says. "Aren't you staying here? Isn't it too early to leave?"

Dominic puts the bags down and starts to walk back to the house. "Hi, George. Emma will explain. I left my phone upstairs." He disappears inside.

"I'm so sorry." Emma turns to George. "My mother and I had words, and . . . it just doesn't feel right to stay here any more."

"Did she tell you she thought *Dominic isn't PLU?*" He does a shockingly good imitation of her mother.

"Please tell me she hasn't been saying that to everyone? Please don't make this worse than it already is."

"She hasn't." George lays a reassuring hand on her arm. "I just know Aunt G. It's her favourite phrase. She doesn't realize that one's only supposed to use it ironically. She treated Dominic like a servant. I'm so sorry, Emma. I saw it happening, but I didn't know how to stop it. For what it's worth, I am thrilled you both came. I think Dominic is wonderful in every way, and I think the two of you are perfect for each other. And I don't think you should give a stuff what anyone thinks, least of all your mother. I love her, don't get me wrong, and I couldn't be more grateful to her for taking Henry and me under her wing in the way she has, but I think she is completely wrong about this."

Emma's eyes fill with tears. "Oh, George," she says. "Thank you. You have no idea how much better you've made me feel."

"Trust me, I've had to deal with all kinds of crap now that I'm engaged to Henry. Everyone always

330

thought I was gay, and all my friends think Henry's a secret lesbian."

Emma composes her features in a way that she hopes conveys surprise.

"No one understands what we're doing together, but honestly, Henry's the most amazing girl I've ever met. She makes me laugh every day, and she's kind, and sweet, and huge fun. We are going to have an amazing life together, and I really have fallen completely in love for the first time in my life. I know everyone thinks this is a disaster waiting to happen, but I don't care what they think. Henry and I will prove them wrong, just as you and Dominic will prove your mother wrong. Besides, your mother's the greatest snob in the world, so really, you should automatically discount everything she says."

Emma throws her arms around him in a tight hug.

"You should come and see us in America," she says. "Seriously. Any time. Thank you for saying everything you've said. And I didn't think you were gay," she adds.

George pulls back and shakes his head with a smile. "Darling, everyone did. I don't believe you for a second, but I forgive you. We would love to come and see you and the very hunky Dominic in America. I'll email you when you get home."

"What was that about?" Dominic has found his phone and come back to the car. He looks questioningly at Emma, who is sitting in the passenger seat waiting for him, frowning.

"George was amazing," she says, recounting what he said to her.

"Very amazing, you're right," says Dominic. "He's not who I thought he was."

"I'll tell you one thing I'm sure of: he's genuinely in love with Henry. When he talked about her, he went all mushy. It was sweet."

"I love that he said no one approves of their match. What the hell does anyone know? The only people who matter are George and Henry." He pauses. "And Dominic and Emma."

"Yes." Emma nods as her mother's words once again echo in her head. "You're right. Let's go. I need to get out of here."

CHAPTER
TWENTY-NINE

The view from the hotel dining room stretches across the fields. Emma gazes out the window. She never misses England when she is in America, does not give it a second thought. It is only when she is here, driving through pretty country lanes overhung with a canopy of green, winding through villages of old stone houses and thatched roofs, gazing out of windows onto rolling fields and meadows, that she misses it.

Their table is quiet; there's only one other couple here, on the other side of the room. Dominic is tucking into a full English fry-up, and Emma is sipping coffee to chase down the painkiller she had taken earlier. The tears she shed last night after leaving the house in the wake of her fury left her with a pounding head, and she is only just starting to feel human again.

"Isn't that your father?" Dominic says through a mouthful of pork sausage.

Emma turns, as Simon sees her and gives her a cautious wave. She waits for him to come and join them, but instead he walks in the other direction. She excuses herself from the table to find him sitting on a bench outside. When she sits next to him, he takes her hand and squeezes it, and she lays her head on his shoulder, saying nothing, as the tears threaten to spill yet again.

"How did you know I was here?" she says eventually.

"I have friends in high places," he says with a small smile. "I took you tea in bed this morning, only to find you'd disappeared. Your mother then told me what had happened, and I knew there were only a couple of places you could have gone. Come home, Emma. You still have three days before you're supposed to leave, and we both want you to come home."

Emma shakes her head. "I'm sorry, Dad. We're leaving today. I changed the flight. We're being picked up after breakfast."

Her father's face falls, suddenly looking old, older than Emma has ever seen him.

"You're leaving? Already? Oh, Emma." He shakes his head. "We can't end your trip like this."

"Daddy, I'm sorry. I am. But Mum said terrible things last night. I couldn't stay. I just can't do it."

"She didn't say any of those things to hurt you." Her father sighs. "She thought she was helping."

"Helping?" Emma snorts. "I don't need helping. I brought Dominic to England with me to meet you because we have something really special. When was the last time you met someone I was dating?" Her father says nothing. "Exactly. The last boyfriend of mine you met was Rufus, because nothing since then has been serious enough to warrant my introducing you. But this is. I know he isn't what she expects, I know he doesn't meet her ridiculously high, snobby standards, but her values are completely messed up. She'd rather I marry

334

some pompous, entitled banker who installs me in a mansion with a live-in housekeeper and a subscription to the yoga club to keep me busy while he spends his weekdays in the city sleeping with whoever he wants."

"That doesn't sound like a bad deal, actually," her father says, after a pause.

Emma can't help but laugh. "Right. Because that's really what every mother wants for her daughter. Daddy, the things that are important to her are not important to me. I've made money, I've lived in that world, and I don't care about any of it. I've found a really good man in Dominic, and you know he's a really good man. He's solid, and calm, and he has huge integrity. He does everything he says he's going to do, when he says he's going to do it. Daddy, I lived in New York City for years and pretty much all the men I met were players."

Her father raises a questioning eyebrow.

"They played around," she explains as he gives her an understanding nod. "They would say they would call and wouldn't, or would show up late, or would cancel at the last minute, or things would seem to be going fantastically well until I discovered they were dating three other women at the same time as me. Dominic doesn't have a dishonest bone in his body, and he makes me happy. He loves me, and I love him."

Her father sits for a while, nodding. "Do you have good conversations?" he asks eventually. "Is he intellectually stimulating? Does he find you intellectually stimulating?"

"We talk about everything," she says. "Does he have a degree? No. Is he sophisticated and well travelled? No. But he cares about people and is devoted to his son. If I need intellectual stimulation, I can get that anywhere. I can join a book group, or go to lectures. One person can't be expected to fulfil all your needs; that's just unreasonable."

"True," says her father, now turning to face her. "My darling girl, I want you to be happy. All I have ever wanted was for you to be happy. I am sorry that what your mother said was so insensitive and wounding. But" — he takes a deep breath — "I can't say that I entirely disagree with her."

The colour drains from Emma's face.

Simon puts his hand on her arm. "I think he is a wonderful man," he says. "And I can see that he makes you happy. I am just asking you to consider that you are from two very different worlds. Your mother is, as you know, inclined to believe that class is the single most important issue, but I take a different viewpoint. You were raised here in Somerset. You've lived in London. You're an English girl through and through. I have supported your time in New York because I believe adventures are good for the soul, and the time to have adventures, to explore new territories, is when you are young. But once you decide to settle down, you have to come home."

Emma stares at her father. "Daddy, I never planned to come home. I'm happy in America. Westport is my home now. I know you don't want to hear it, but I feel more at home there than I have ever felt here."

336

"But you and Dominic do come from very different worlds," her father says eventually, struggling to find the right words that will make her understand. "It seems you're compatible now, but in the long run that can be very difficult. It isn't as easy as you think."

"We are compatible," says Emma, relieved that her father can see that. "And yes, we do come from different worlds, but we can create our own world for the two of us. We already have."

"I just want you to be sure," says her father.

"I am sure," she says. "We are sure."

"You have to find a way to make up with your mother." Simon sighs. "I'll talk to her, of course, but you know how difficult she can be. I'm not sure you should fly back to the States without having spoken to her."

"I have nothing to say to her." Emma is resolute. "I'm sure I'll feel differently over time, but not today. She treated Dominic like a servant, because she believes he *is* below her . . . I'm not speaking to her today. Not yet."

Her father gives a small smile. "I know where you get your stubbornness from."

Emma looks at her watch. "Daddy, they'll be here to pick us up any second. I have to go." And with that, she stands up to give him a hug goodbye.

CHAPTER
THIRTY

Emma looks out the window as they leave the airport on their way back home. She looks at the weeds growing through the cracks in the sidewalk, the back-to-back traffic, the looming grey buildings lining each side of the highway, and a warmth spreads through her body. *Almost home*, she thinks, instantly comforted by the familiar sights and sounds. Home.

Dominic is quiet next to her, humming something, tapping his fingers on the steering wheel, a smile on his face. Emma shoots him frequent glances, knowing how excited he will be to see Jesse, days earlier than planned.

They pull off the highway, wind their way along Bridge Street, down Compo, pulling up in front of their side-by-side cottages. In the driveway is an unfamiliar old station wagon, at least twenty years old, the type of long, bulky car that few people drive these days.

"You ready to meet *my* parents now?" Dominic hesitates on the front path after unloading the suitcases from the trunk of the car.

Emma is about to answer when the front door is flung open, and Jesse tears across the yard. "Daddy!" he yells, flinging himself into his father's arms.

Emma stands back, watching them both, hoping Jesse might say hello to her, might have missed her, but he is far too busy chattering away to his father. He crawls all over him, kissing him, reassuring himself that his father is back, that he's not going away again.

"Say hi to Emma," Dominic says eventually.

Jesse turns and gives her a dutiful smile then a wide grin. "Hi!" He waves, and Emma laughs in relief, turning to walk next door to her own little house. But as she does so, she sees Dominic's mother emerge.

She is wearing a floral apron over beige trousers and a brightly coloured shirt. A short woman, she is well padded underneath the apron, and weighed down with copious amounts of chunky gold jewellery. Four large necklaces of varying lengths fall between her substantial bosoms; she wears large clip-on earrings and oversized rings. It is her hair that is the most extraordinary thing, standing high above her head, sprayed into a rock-solid beehive, accessorized by a large sparkly ladybird hair slide.

"Dominic!" She walks over and gathers Dominic in her arms, covering his face with kisses, leaving lipstick imprints all over his cheeks.

"Hey, Mom." Dominic squirms ever so slightly but allows himself to be kissed before pulling away. "I'd like you to meet Emma."

She turns, surveying Emma up and down. Approvingly, Emma hopes.

"Okay," she says, looking at Dominic with a nod. "Okay." Turning back to Emma she says, "Call me Nonna. Everyone else does. Come in. I just made fresh

339

cannoli for your father and Jesse, but there's more than enough for you. This kid." She gestures to Dominic while looking at Emma. "There's nothing this kid loves more than Nonna's homemade cannoli. How 'bout you, Jesse? What do you think of Nonna's cooking?"

"Good!" says Jesse, who is too distracted with the delight of having his father home to focus. They all laugh and enter the house.

"Hey, Pops," says Dominic. "This is Emma."

At the table, Dominic's father is reading the paper and nursing a cup of coffee. Instead of looking up, he merely grunts, and reaches over for a cannoli from the plate that sits in the middle of the table.

No one speaks.

"Sit down," says Dominic's mother, pulling out a chair for Emma. "You want some coffee?"

"Emma only drinks coffee in the mornings," says Dominic. Emma reddens, not wanting to put anyone out, not wanting to appear different in any way. "She drinks tea in the afternoons."

"I'm fine," Emma says quickly.

"Tea?" says his mother. "Very fancy. We only got coffee in our house. Are you sure you don't want some? Just a small cup? Go on." She sets a cup of coffee in front of her.

Emma doesn't mention that there is tea in this house; she knows because she bought it herself.

"You know who came to see us?" Dominic's mother says. "Stacy! I didn't know she was back in town. She came over and took Jesse out the first day we were here.

She looks great. And she's doing really well, making a ton of money in real estate. It was good to see her."

Dominic shakes his head. "You didn't check with me before letting her take Jesse out?"

His mother shrugs. "What's to check? She's the boy's mother. And she was leaving, so she wanted to get some time with him. I think she's really turned a corner. She says she's coming back to town."

"Oh man," Dominic mutters under his breath as Emma reaches over and takes his hand, giving him a supportive squeeze. *Don't say anything else*, she thinks.

"It will be like the old times," his mother says. "Good to have her around again. Sweetie, take a cannoli," she says to Emma, who is staring at her, aghast at her insensitivity. "No cannoli? I also got Italian cookies. Here." She gets up from the table and pulls out a large round tin from the pantry, opening it to reveal chunky cookies stuffed with jam and dusted with icing sugar. "Try one."

Emma shakes her head. She feels sure that the comments about Stacy were deliberate, intended to let Emma know she will never be relevant in their eyes, that Stacy is the true heir to the throne.

"I'm fine," says Emma.

"Just one," says Dominic's mother. "A small one."

"Leave her alone," roars Dominic's father, the first words she has heard him speak. "For Christ's sake, she says she doesn't want anything to eat."

Emma watches Dominic's mother's face fall. "Maybe just a small one," Emma says, reaching for the tin.

"Thank you for staying with Jesse," Dominic says, changing the subject. "I know he's had a fantastic time, right, Jesse?"

Jesse makes a face, then quickly plasters on a smile and nods when he sees his grandmother look at him.

"I fattened him up," she says proudly, reaching over and pinching his cheek. "He was all skin and bone when I got here. You like Nonna's cooking, don't you, sweetie?"

Jesse nods, squirming away from her hand.

"Will you shut up about food?" says Dominic's father, shaking his head. "All you talk about, all the goddamn time, is food. What you're gonna be cooking, what we're gonna be eating, what we haven't eaten. Jesus Christ. It's enough to drive a man crazy."

"Why don't you shut up?" says Nonna, her own voice rising. "Why you always got to ruin everything? I feed my family because I love them; that's what you do for the people you love. What do *you* do? Sit at the table in your undershirt, sweating, talking shit, putting down everyone around you."

Dominic's father sits back, pushing the newspapers away. "Putting down everyone around me? Dominic, do you see me putting down everyone around me?" He doesn't wait for an answer. "No, I ain't putting down everyone around me. Just you, because you drive me fucking crazy."

"Language!" says Nonna.

"Ah, shut up," he says, going back to his paper. "Everything you say gets on my last nerve."

342

"You should try living with you," spits Nonna. "It's enough to drive a woman to suicide."

"Is that a promise?" says Dominic's father.

Emma gulps her coffee down in one and pushes her chair back. "I'm so sorry," she says, "but I have to get going. It was so nice to meet you."

"I'll help you with the suitcase," says Dominic, also standing up. They are outside quickly, and Emma turns to Dominic. "Good God," she says when they are safely out of earshot, when they can no longer hear Dominic's parents bickering. "That was fun."

"Yeah. Welcome to my childhood. At least it didn't get physical."

"That was *awful*. Why are they even married? They hate each other!"

"Old-school Catholics. Divorce isn't allowed. But yeah, I think they've hated each other for years. I also think they couldn't survive without each other. It's a terrible, angry, screwed-up marriage, but they completely depend on each other. If my mother died, my father would go to pieces, I swear."

"Please tell me we'll never treat each other like that." Emma is now serious, putting down her suitcase outside the front door as she turns to him.

"We will never treat each other like that," he says. "Since Jesse was born, I have lived my whole life determined to be nothing like them." He leans in to kiss her.

"And what was all that about Stacy? Was that some passive-aggressive dig to make sure I know they prefer her?"

Dominic laughs. "They hated Stacy! That's the least of your worries. It's just my parents being my parents. Ignore them."

With that, Jesse bursts through them, pushing them apart, running into the house with Hobbes.

It is a relief for Emma to be on her own for a bit. Dominic has asked her to come back for dinner once his parents are safely out of the way. His fridge and freezer are now, apparently, filled with food. Emma knows that after dinner she will stay over, as she has done so many times before, but she needs this quiet time to think.

She doesn't like the comments Dominic's mother made about Stacy. She doesn't like that Stacy is back, either, although she's trying to like it, to welcome it, knowing it's good for Jesse.

She doesn't like that suddenly nothing is as straight-forward as it was before.

Her mother's words reverberate around her brain, as do her father's, even though she tries to push them aside. Their words are now tangled up with the ones spoken by Dominic's parents: who they are, what they said, how they treated each other. It was unsettling to see them, especially given her parents' concerns.

She had thought her parents wrong about her and Dominic. She hadn't thought their different worlds mattered. Emma corrects herself: she *doesn't* think it matters. And yet . . . meeting Dominic's parents . . . She cannot help but wonder if her mother and father are right.

344

Emma has no frame of reference for any of this. Dominic's mother and father are unlike anyone she has ever known. She has no idea how to talk to them, or what she would ever find in common with them other than Dominic himself. She tries to imagine what would happen if she and Dominic got married — if, say, her parents threw them an engagement party along the lines of the party they have just thrown for George and Henry.

She imagines Dominic's parents with her parents, with their friends, in their house. She imagines her mother's face listening to Dominic's father shouting that his wife drove him "fucking crazy".

It would not be pretty. She shakes her head to clear it. She has to stop thinking along these lines. She has no idea who Dominic's parents really are. Or how to behave around them. She thought she and Dominic could create a world of their own, a world in which it didn't matter where they both came from, or how different their backgrounds were. But what if she was wrong?

What if they did get married? she wonders. She is beginning to imagine it, the tiniest of thoughts, floating at the very edge of her brain. There is no rush, but isn't there only one real outcome for a relationship such as theirs, a relationship that is so easy, so filled with kindness and love?

They could get married here, she thinks. Perhaps on a country farm, lanterns hanging from branches, someone playing guitar, friends sitting on hay bales scattered through an orchard. That farm in Redding where they went the night Dominic kissed her; that would be perfect.

Or something small. Unassuming. Maybe they wouldn't invite their parents at all. Maybe they would just take the train into New York on the spur of the moment and get married at city hall, with no one present except Jesse.

There would be little point in trying to combine their two families, but perhaps, if they did throw a proper wedding, and the parents were there, they could figure out a way to manage it all.

It's only one day, she thinks. Anyone can put up with anything for one day.

But there is another nagging thought that she can't quite get rid of. What if she is wrong? What if George is wrong? What if their worlds *are* too different for them to find a way through?

She cuddles Hobbes, hoping for some comfort. A couple of days ago it felt like she didn't have a care in the world; now her head is spinning, her thoughts tumbling around. Is she making a terrible mistake? Should she end it now, before they are too entrenched?

But . . . but . . . they are so happy here. With their little side-by-side houses in Westport, by the beach, with Jesse. They are so happy in their own little world. And that world includes other people who like them both. Sophie and Rob like Dominic. They don't think he's *beneath* them because he doesn't work in finance, isn't hugely wealthy, isn't ambitious in the same way they are. All his friends seem to like her, to accept her.

It doesn't bother them that she's English; they don't think she's a snob.

She considers this for a long time, telling herself how silly she is for thinking this is going to be anything other than great. She hopes that any nagging doubts will soon disappear.

Not long after, Dominic knocks on the door. The coast is clear, he tells Emma. His parents have gone home, and dinner is ready.

She has no appetite, but she follows him next door and sits at the kitchen table, pushing her food around her plate, uncharacteristically quiet.

"Are you okay?" Dominic asks after Jesse has finished and gone upstairs to put his PJs on. Emma is quiet as he pours her a glass of red wine, as she wonders how to voice the jumble of concerns in her head.

"I'm fine," Emma says, in the way all women say they are fine when it is quite clear to everyone they are not.

"Something's the matter." There is a look of concern on his face. "What is it?"

Emma pauses. Should she share her concerns with him, or is that unfair? How can she tell him that meeting his parents has brought her own parents' words, their worries, flooding back? She can't help but wonder if they are right. Is it too much to expect them to find the middle ground for the rest of their lives?

Jesse appears suddenly in the doorway, now in his pyjamas. "Emma?"

"Yes, sweetie?" She is grateful for the interruption.

"Will you put me to bed?"

Tears well up in her eyes. She turns to hide her reaction, but Dominic can see how affected she is by the power of those six words: *Will you put me to bed?*

"Of course." She blinks hard and gets up from the table, heading to the kitchen sink so she can pretend to get busy washing up. "Just give me a couple of minutes, okay?"

Jesse heads back upstairs as Dominic slides an arm around Emma's waist.

"Wow," he says. "I told you he'd come around eventually."

"You did." Emma nods. For now, her other concerns have retreated into the background.

This is more important.

"What do you want me to read tonight?" Emma walks over to the bookshelf as Jesse climbs into bed.

"The book you bought me," he says. "The one about the anteater who eats the aunt."

Emma is surprised. When she bought him Roald Dahl's *Revolting Rhymes* earlier that summer, he had expressed no interest in it whatsoever. She told him this was her favourite writer when she was a child, and offered to read him a couple of the stories, but Jesse had said no, throwing the book on a chair and going straight back to his Minecraft game on Dominic's computer.

As far as she was aware, he hadn't even looked at the book, but now it seems she was wrong. She opens it to

"The Ant Eater", and starts reading, complete with exaggerated accents, both English and American, much to Jesse's delight.

As she reaches the middle of the story, she feels a small hand slip into hers, and she stops, just for a second, to enjoy the spontaneous affection.

Dominic walks past the bedroom door and hesitates, leaning against the door frame for a few seconds to watch them, his eyes alight with love. Emma pauses, thinking that Jesse will ask his dad to take over, but he doesn't. He lets her continue.

As she finishes the story, Jesse wriggles down, into the curve of her body, the perfect fit. He rolls onto his side, as she spoons him, tucking his small frame into her own. He takes her arm and pulls it over him, never letting go of her hand.

They lie there for a few minutes, before Emma gently pulls her hand away.

"Good night, Jesse," she whispers. She stays where she is for a few seconds more, listening to him breathe.

"I love you," she whispers, because that is what his father says to him every night, the last thing Jesse hears before he goes to sleep.

But he doesn't say anything back. Jesse is already fast asleep.

Not an hour later, Emma crawls into Dominic's bed, snuggling into his outstretched arm as Jesse had snuggled into hers.

This is what it's all about, she thinks.

Love. Commitment. Family. The superficial stuff is irrelevant. Stacy is irrelevant. His family background is irrelevant. Cuddling with Jesse tonight was transcendent. *I am going to make this work*, she thinks. *No matter what*.

CHAPTER
THIRTY-ONE

Emma walks around Terrain, wanting to buy something, unsure exactly what that something might be, or indeed, if there is anything here that she really needs. The retail space is gorgeous; she could move a bed into a corner of the shop and live here happily for the rest of her life. She wanders around slowly, trying to decide whether to purchase a marble cloche, a gorgeous cheeseboard, the distressed wood tray.

There are plants everywhere. Emma has never been good with indoor plants, invariably killing them within a month. She sees dozens of terrariums on display, but she's pretty sure she would kill whatever plants are kept inside those, too.

She is meeting Sophie and Teddy for tea in the café, but Sophie just texted her to say that she's still waiting for her mother, who is stuck behind a school bus, hence Emma's impromptu shopping interlude.

She pauses by a row of cool Wellington boots, tries on a French quilted jacket that she probably wouldn't ever wear. She fingers scarves, moves slowly along the glass jewellery cabinet, walks to the front of the shop and picks up every candle, smelling it, until she hears her name.

"Emma!" Sophie is bustling through the shop's displays, her hair loosely pulled back in a messy bun, immaculate in tight jeans, a white T-shirt, ballet flats. She is wearing no make-up but looks stunning. Behind her is her mother, Teddy, elegant in similar clothes, a cashmere cardigan, the same huge smile as Sophie.

"You both look so gorgeous," says Emma, hugging them.

"I'm so sorry we're late," says Sophie, as the three of them walk to the café counter to order tea.

"My fault, I'm afraid," says Teddy. "We timed it horribly. I always forget about the school buses. I don't know why they don't pull over. They used to, when I first moved here. When Sophie was in school, the drivers always let you pass."

"The driver on *my* route always lets me pass," says Sophie.

"It must be because you're young and beautiful. I sat behind him almost the entire way to your house to pick you up, with a huge line of cars behind me. I only minded because I knew I was going to be late, but there was nothing I could do. I turned on NPR and listened to a fascinating interview with Terry Gross. The woman behind me was not happy, though. She honked a number of times."

Sophie rolls her eyes. "That's probably why he didn't let any of you pass. Frankly, if I were a bus driver and had a woman behind me, honking, in a Range Rover, I'm pretty sure I wouldn't let her pass, either."

Startled, Teddy looks at her daughter. "How did you know it was a Range Rover?"

Sophie just shakes her head and laughs, turning to Emma. "Have *you* noticed the daily uniform in town?"

"Lululemon clothes, straightened hair, and a Range Rover? That uniform?"

"That would be the one."

"No," says Emma, shaking her head. "I can't say I've noticed." And all three laugh.

They take their teas to a table and sit down, shrugging off jackets and slipping them onto the backs of their chairs.

"It's so chilly now," says Teddy, rubbing her arms and warming her hands around her mug of tea. "I'm always surprised when the temperatures start falling again every September."

"We're practically in October," says Sophie. "I saw Christmas decorations in a shop the other day, which made me feel ill. Much too early."

"I completely agree." Teddy rolls her eyes. "They put them out earlier every year. Soon we'll be looking at garlands and tinsel in July." She turns to Emma. "Sophie mentioned you just got back from England with Dominic. How did that go?"

"It was . . . " Emma pauses. She can't lie. She can't say it was wonderful. She can't not say that they cut their trip short because of the way her mother treated Dominic, because of the things her mother said. She sighs. "It was interesting," she says eventually. "And kind of awful, if I'm honest."

"What happened?" asks Sophie in alarm.

Emma tells them the whole story. She tells them about England, about her parents, about her decision to ignore them and her belief that they didn't know what they were talking about until she met Dominic's parents. She tells them how she's realized that he *does* come from a very different world, and that while she knows what she has found with Dominic and Jesse is very special and worth fighting for, she cannot get rid of the sinking feeling that her parents may be right.

It is a relief to talk about this. It has been pent up inside her for days, and it has started to put a wedge between her and Dominic.

When Jesse asked her to read to him, requested that she perform the nightly routine that by rights used to belong to his father, she thought she could push her fears aside about there being too many differences between them for it to work.

Her doubts are not so easily dismissed.

It isn't that she wants a big life, or more money, or — heaven forbid — the trappings of the life she left behind in New York; it's that she was raised with museums, and art galleries, and theatre; she was raised with horseback riding, and ballet, and hunts. It isn't that she wants any of that today, but that she has spent her life thinking that she was supposed to want those things, supposed to end up in much the same life as the one in which she was raised.

"What do you think?" she asks finally, her worried eyes moving from Sophie to Teddy, and back again. "What do you think I should do?"

"*Do?*" Teddy frowns. "What do you mean?"

"Should we carry on, or should I leave now before anyone gets too hurt? It worries me that we're so different. I don't care that he's a bartender and a carpenter. I've never cared about that stuff, but" — she pauses, embarrassed to admit this, but seeking advice from people she trusts — "is it okay that he doesn't have any ambition? It's not like he's dreaming of one day opening his own bar, or becoming a master carpenter and founding the number-one cabinetry installation company in Fairfield County, with a team of fabulously talented men working for him. Is that okay? He's really happy exactly where he is, and although part of me loves that about him, I don't quite understand it." She sighs and buries her head in her hands. "God! I can't even believe I'm saying this. I never thought any of this would matter. One of the things I love about him is that he's not competitive with anyone. He's more comfortable in his skin than any man I have ever met."

"Why do you think that is?" asks Teddy.

Emma pauses to think. "He says he wasn't always like this. I think it's because he made a deliberate choice not to be like his parents. I think part of making any choice as deliberate as that must give you a sense of peace."

Teddy peers at her, mystified. "And isn't that the same as the deliberate choice you have made to leave your old life behind and follow your heart? I don't see what the problem is."

"That's all true." Emma nods. "I have made a deliberate choice and in so many ways I am happier than I ever thought I could be, or would be. But what if all that isn't enough?" She muses out loud. "Even though he is making a deliberate choice to be something other than his destiny now, don't we all turn into our parents over time? How can we avoid following that pattern as we age? We make choices about how we want to be seen in the world, but as we grow older don't we all forget to hold those constructs up, don't we all start falling into the patterns of our youth? Doesn't our essence always win out? And if so, what's Dominic's essence?" She pauses for breath, unaware of the tinge of hysteria in her voice. "And that's not the only thing. We're so different. He likes sports, and beer, and bars. I like books, and theatre, and good wine."

"No, you don't," says Sophie, laughing.

Emma stares at her. "What do you mean? Of course I do."

"You don't. I mean, who am I to tell you what you like and don't like, but I've known you for quite a long time, and I've only seen you drink pinot noir and Whispering Angel, which is good but not that good, and vodka. Secondly, when was the last time you went to the theatre?"

Emma sits back. "I am *desperate* to see *Hamilton*."

"But when was the last time you went?"

"A while ago," says Emma sheepishly.

"A year? Two years? More?"

"Maybe a couple of years." Emma attempts to brush over it. "The point is, I want to see *Hamilton* and I can't bring Dominic with me because he hates the theatre."

"First of all, isn't *Hamilton* mostly rap?" says Sophie. "It's not exactly Arthur Miller. I'm pretty sure he'll love it. Everybody loves it. Secondly, if you really think he'd hate it, take someone else. Take me! Take my mom!" Teddy nods her head enthusiastically. "So what if he doesn't like theatre?"

"I really like theatre," says Teddy. "I'd love to see *Hamilton*."

"You're missing the point," says Emma, as Teddy beams a benevolent smile upon her.

"I don't think so, my dear," she says gently. "I think we very much get the point. The point is that you're terrified that Dominic is not who he appears to be, even though all the evidence suggests he is *exactly* as he appears. And, you want him to be just like you, to want the same things you want, to like doing the same things you like doing, to fulfil all your wants and needs."

Emma looks at her. "When you put it like that, it sounds completely crazy."

Teddy nods. "It does, doesn't it?"

"But it isn't unreasonable to want to have the same aspirations. The same likes and dislikes. Isn't that what good relationships are based on?"

"In my experience," says Teddy, "good relationships are based on kindness. On putting the person you love before yourself. On thinking of what you can do to make that person happy. Good relationships require kindness, commitment, and appreciation. I think you have all of those, do you not? Despite what you just said about being frightened of him becoming like his parents, you're not really worried about that, are you?"

Emma hesitates, thinking. "Maybe not," she says eventually. "But if your lifestyle choices are different?"

"They aren't so different, though, are they?" says Sophie. "You both love your homes, the beach, leading a pretty quiet life. It's not like one of you wants to be out at fancy restaurants every night while the other is a hermit. You care about your friends, and Jesse. Isn't that the stuff that matters?"

"You don't think the other things get in the way? You don't think my parents are right? That we are from such different worlds, that relationships are hard enough, that throwing two people together who come from such different places means their union is destined for disaster?"

"I don't think that." Sophie looks at her mother. "Do you?"

Teddy shakes her head. "That's what friends are for," she says. "You don't have to watch football games with Dominic. I'm sure he's got lots of friends who can hang out with him for that. Just as you have people who can go to the theatre with you."

"Not that you actually go to the theatre," mutters Sophie, shrugging as Emma shoots her a look.

"He is a wonderful man." Sophie leans forward. "You cannot throw this away because of some ridiculous, superficial reason. You're more worried about being judged by other people; that somehow they will think Dominic isn't good enough for you, which means that you're worried you're not good enough."

Teddy looks at her daughter approvingly.

"She's right," she says to Emma. "Even though it may be difficult to hear. The Emma who is worrying about what people think, or how you might be judged,

358

isn't the Emma I've come to know this summer. I've known you a while, and the Emma you have become, the Emma I have gotten to know since you met Dominic, is my favourite Emma of all."

"*She's* right," says Sophie. "The two of you are great together. And think about Jesse. He's attached now. There is more at stake than just the two of you."

Emma nods. There is a long pause before she asks, "You really don't think we're going to turn into his parents?"

Teddy lets out a bark of laughter. "I hardly think so, Emma. It is true that we often re-create our childhoods. However dysfunctional they may have been, we experience those feelings as 'home', and re-create them in some form in our adult lives. But it is also true that we have a choice, and if we are lucky, and aware, we seek out the very opposite, which is exactly what Dominic has done, and what you are doing now."

As Emma listens, she feels the weight of anxiety lift for the first time since she and Dominic left England. "I do love him," she says, and she smiles her first genuine smile in days.

"I know," says Sophie. "This is all about your parents. You moved across the Atlantic to get away from them. You moved because you didn't have anything in common with them. You didn't want the life they had, and you didn't want the life they wanted for you. That you are only now paying attention to what they think is craziness. From what you've always told me, your mother doesn't want what's best for you, she wants what's best for *her*, right? Doesn't she want whatever will somehow elevate her status in the world?"

"Thank you for the reminder. You are absolutely right."

"I know. So can we just forget about your parents and move on?"

"Okay," Emma says carefully. Then, "Yes!" Her friends have told her it's okay to trust her instincts; they've confirmed for her that her choices are good.

"Shall we ask if they have champagne?" Sophie laughs. "I think it would be entirely appropriate at this point to celebrate the first day of the rest of your life."

That night, Jesse has a sleepover at a friend's and Dominic is out meeting a potential client before heading to work at the Fat Hen, leaving Emma alone. It's so rare these days, it feels luxurious. She cleans the kitchen and is about to go upstairs and jump in the shower when she checks the time.

It is too early to turn in for the night. She could run to the bar and have a quick drink with Dominic, surprise him. Excited at the prospect of his face when he sees her unexpectedly, she checks her hair in the mirror, shakes it out, adds some lip gloss, then picks up her handbag and slips out the front door.

The parking lot is jammed with cars. She circles a couple of times before two people walk out of the bar, making their way slowly to their Honda at the back. She waits patiently, waving a thanks when they pull out, manoeuvring her way into the spot.

The place is heaving. She weaves her way through, excited to reach the bar, to see Dominic in his element, so much louder, more outgoing, gruffer than he is when he is not working a crowd. He has described it as acting, talked about having a "bar persona", much like a stage persona, explained that as soon as he walks through the doors of the Fat Hen, he turns into Dom rather than Dominic. Dom, who flirts with the ladies, who winds up the men, who is quick with his hands, and with the queue, to ensure he gets the biggest tips of any of the bartenders there.

There are two girls leaning on the bar, with their heads tilted and waterfalls of hair falling over their shoulders. Even from a distance Emma can see them flirting with Dominic. They are what she would have once presumed were exactly his type. He is laughing with one of them, a blonde, and when she turns her head Emma recognizes her at once. The woman he was seeing when Emma first moved in. *Gina.*

She stands stock-still, heart pounding. She rarely thinks about what happens at night when Dominic is not with her, about what he is doing when he is at work. Of course he flirts, she knows he flirts, but it's always felt a bit abstract to her. She's never considered the possibility that it would be with former girlfriends.

Emma is not the sort of woman who is inclined to surreptitiously pick up a boyfriend's phone when he is in the shower to scroll through texts, checking to see what he is up to. She is very well aware that if you snoop, you are unlikely to be happy with what you find.

And you won't be able to do much about it without revealing the snooping, anyway.

She remembers a man she used to work with who would regularly scroll through his boyfriend's phone. One morning he came to work almost in tears, having discovered an email confirming a brand-new subscription to Grindr.

There was no other evidence of cheating, no other indication that his boyfriend had done anything but sign up for the sake of curiosity. All the women at work had gathered around to offer their opinions. Most of them believed the boyfriend had probably signed up just for fun, to see who else in the area might be on it. After all, there were at least three men in the office who were married but rumoured to prefer playing on their own team.

He didn't know whether to confront his boyfriend or not. The consensus among the women at work was a resounding no. Far better to say nothing — because opening that particular door was bound to be a disaster. It would be different, they all said, if he had found evidence of a date, or an intimate text — something concrete. But subscribing to Grindr alone was definitely not grounds to reveal your despicable nature as a snoop.

Emma trusts Dominic. She certainly met her fair share of untrustworthy men while living in New York. It has never crossed her mind that Dominic was anything like them. In fact, the whole point is that he's not. She doesn't think for a minute that he would do anything to betray her.

From where she is standing, she can't hear what is being said, but she can clearly see Gina leaning across the bar, showing off her spectacular cleavage and laughing as she says something, her right foot, encased in the highest of heels, sexily rubbing up the back of her left calf.

Dominic moves closer to her to hear what she is saying, then stands back with a smile, a shrug, and a shake of his head. At that moment, he looks up and sees Emma. His eyes light up as he waves her over. Gina turns to see what has caught his attention, and irritation washes over her face as she recognizes Emma.

"The tenant, right?" says Gina, as Dominic leans over the bar and gives Emma a long kiss on the lips, pulling away, then coming back for one more.

Emma can't help turning to Gina with a happy smile when Dominic finally steps back. It's not something she does very often, but right now it feels oh so extraordinarily good to be here, with Dominic, who is so clearly in love with her.

"The tenant." She smiles. "Right."

ACT THREE

CHAPTER
THIRTY-TWO

Autumn is upon them for good before they have noticed it's time for the seasons to change. One day the trees are green and lush, the next they are multiple shades of red, orange, and gold, the leaves drifting into the streets and covering up the last vestiges of summer.

With the changing seasons comes a routine that makes Emma feel settled and secure. And happy. She and Dominic have not talked about officially moving in together, and yet they seem to have moved in together. Most of her clothes are now at his house, and it has been months since she spent the night in her own, next door.

She still has her office there, though. The redecorating she did for Lisa has led to more clients, more work, and she has now redone the living room in her cottage as part showroom, part conference room.

She put up a Nobilis wallpaper that looks like bleached-out horizontal planks of wood. An L-shaped cream sofa is piled with tan and orange cushions and a large orange mohair throw. The coffee table is simple, a low square orange shagreen table with a Perspex box resting on top, and the latest interior magazines in neat piles for inspiration.

She painted the window frames a glossy chocolate brown, and had cream linen blinds made. Dominic boxed around the ancient, ugly fireplace with MDF, which Emma then faux-painted to look like limestone. Above the fire-place hangs a round, polished wood mirror, and hanging on the walls are abstract paintings in shades of orange, red, and brown.

Dominic wasn't at all sure of the colour scheme. "Beach houses should only be blue," he had said.

Emma hadn't wanted to point out that the colour scheme of the house when she moved in was everything *but* blue. Brown, salmon, and a grungy floral had been the order of the day when she first walked in. Now that it is finished, Dominic tells anyone who will listen that it is the most beautiful room he has ever seen, and Emma the most talented woman he has ever known.

"We should move in *here*," he says one evening, walking through the front door to say goodbye before he leaves for work. He no longer needs a regular sitter; every night Emma is next door at his house, at the house that is really now their house, where she puts Jesse to bed.

Jesse can still be difficult. When he is tired, or feeling overwhelmed, he sometimes reverts to blaming Emma for everything that is wrong in his life. Sometimes she hears him shouting at his father, "We don't need her! I hate her! Emma has ruined everything!" She is still wounded by those words, even though she knows he is just a child, he doesn't mean it. And it passes. It always passes.

368

It is clear he doesn't mean it when he snuggles into her in bed. It is clear he doesn't mean it when he tucks in beside her and pulls her arm over his small body.

Emma hasn't whispered "I love you" again, although there have been many times when she has wanted to. And she believes he may be on the verge of loving her, too.

Stacy seems to have dropped off the face of the earth. She sent Dominic a couple of texts when she first got back to Florida, and said she would come back towards the end of October. But October is almost gone, and there has been no word from her. Emma is starting to relax into the routine they had before.

"Well, we *could* live here, I suppose," she says to Dominic. "But you don't really want to live here. It's much smaller than your house. We'd all be on top of each other. You just want to live somewhere stylish."

"Who'd'a thunk it?" Dominic laughs, shaking his head. "Me, wanting to live somewhere stylish."

"I could redo your house, you know," says Emma. "All you have to do is say the word and I will gladly take on the project." She smiles. "No charge, of course."

"You're hired!" Dominic says with a laugh. "I want you to, of course, but I also kind of like it the way it is. Maybe in the spring, when you move in officially, we can do it."

Emma stares at him. "What?"

"We can do it in the spring."

"Hang on. Did you say when I move in?"

"I did."

"I'm moving in? Since when? Am I part of this decision?"

"I'm telling you now." He moves over to the sofa and sits. "Unless you don't want to?"

"I just hadn't thought of making it official. I thought things were pretty good as they are."

"Things are great. But you're sleeping at my house every night anyway. And you're already using this house as your office. Why not move in for real? When we get married, you're going to be living there anyway."

Emma can't breathe. "What did you say?"

Dominic speaks very slowly, as if he were talking to a small child. "I said, when we get married, we're going to be living together anyway, so we may as well live together now. Or in the spring. Whatever."

A slow grin spreads itself on Emma's face. "Are you proposing?"

"No!" Dominic frowns. "When I propose it won't be like this. I'm going to have champagne, flowers, a ring . . . the whole damn thing." He watches her face, nervous now. "That is the plan, though, isn't it? We are doing this, aren't we?"

"Doing what?"

"This. The whole thing. Living. Together. Marriage. All of it. This is it for me, Emma. Do you feel the same?"

Emma never wanted to marry Rufus. She hadn't thought she wanted to get married at all. But in the past few months, she has been happier than she has ever been.

"Yes," she says now, twining her arms around his neck as she kisses him. "I feel the same."

CHAPTER
THIRTY-THREE

"Snow!" Jesse bursts into their room, waking them up.

Dominic groans, turning over in bed. "Jesse, it's six thirty-nine in the morning. Go back to sleep."

"But it's snow, Dad! It's really snowing outside."

Emma rolls over with a stretch. "They did say snow was coming."

"But not a lot, right? Just a couple of inches?"

"There's tons of snow!" says Jesse, running to the window and opening the blinds. "Look!"

Outside is a blizzard of white. Emma puts her feet on the floor and shivers, wrapping her arms around herself. It's late November, too early, surely, for a serious snowfall.

Jesse grabs her hand and drags her to the window. As she stands there, a huge smile creases her face, and she's filled with childlike joy at the sight of the fat, fluffy flakes swirling outside. She squints at the pots in the garden. There's probably at least eight inches already.

"This is serious snow, Dominic," she says, turning to him.

"Three inches?"

"At least eight. Maybe more. And it's coming down fast."

"Aw, shit," he groans, covering his face with the pillow. "That means serious work."

"Work?"

"Who do you think is going to be shovelling and clearing the snow? We had a huge snowstorm a few years ago and the roof collapsed. I'll have to clear it off the roof if I don't want a repeat of that experience. Maybe I'll call my buddy Glenn. He has a snowplough on his truck, and he can do the driveway. So much for a lazy day."

"Dad? Dad?" Jesse dances up to his side of the bed. "Can we build a snow fort? Please? You said you would build a snow fort with me the next time it snows."

"I never said that," says Dominic. "When did I say that?"

"You did. You always say that. Will you? Can you get up now? Can we build a snow fort now?"

"We can't build a snow fort until it stops snowing," says Dominic as Jesse's face falls.

"Can I go and play in the snow, though?" he says finally. "Until it stops snowing?"

"Sure," says Dominic.

"Do you have snow boots?" asks Emma. "And snow clothes?"

"I have boots!" says Jesse. "And jeans."

As Jesse runs out of the room, Dominic pulls Emma in for a cuddle. "He'll be fine," he says. "He'll come in when he's wet and cold."

"You're tough." Emma snuggles against him. "I really think he should have a hat and gloves, though. And snow trousers. I don't want him to freeze."

"I know. We have the hat and gloves, but we don't have snow pants that fit him. We'll get a pair this weekend, okay? Look, don't worry. I guarantee he'll be back inside asking for hot cocoa in about five minutes." Dominic groans. "Oh God, I hate the snow."

Emma is shocked. "How can you hate the snow? I love the snow! It's the best thing about living here. Look at those gorgeous fat flakes. It's magical!"

"Yeah, the first snowfall is cool, I'll give you that, but then there's the work, and the weeks of filthy snow and gravel and sand piled up on every sidewalk. Ugh. Give me summer any time."

"I can help you," says Emma. "With the shovelling."

"Nah. You can make the cocoa, though." Dominic smiles, pulling her in for a kiss. "Do we have time for . . . "

Emma laughs softly as she moves a hand up his thigh, behind him to cup his buttock and pull him in. "We always have time for that."

"Where's Dad?"

Jesse played in the snow for almost exactly five minutes, just as Dominic predicted. He has had his cocoa, made popcorn, helped build a fire, and is now watching a movie. He's itching to go out and build a snow fort, but the snow has not yet stopped.

"Dad's shovelling snow," Emma says. *Like he's been doing the past three hours*, she thinks to herself. She has to admit that she had no idea how much work this involved. They don't have snow in England, not proper snow, like here. She remembers the occasional light dusting when she was young, and going sledging — sledding, they say over here, she reminds herself — on flattened empty road-salt bags, feeling every bump as they careered down the hill, shrieking with excitement.

"Want me to get him?" she says, pouring the leftover cocoa in a travel mug to take out to him.

"Yeah," says Jesse, already re-immersed in his movie. "Tell him to come help me build a snow fort."

"It's still snowing." Emma laughs. "He did say not until the snow stops falling. But I'll tell him."

Emma puts her coat and boots on, and finds a hat lurking in the back of the hall wardrobe. The only gloves she can find are Dominic's yellow deerskin work gloves, so she puts them on and steps out the front door, pausing to take in the sight.

The blanket of quiet takes her breath away. The snow is still falling — smaller flakes now, not as wet and heavy — but they're swirling in the wind, and there is absolute silence. The roads have been ploughed, but the tracks have long since been covered over, and every tree branch has a thick duvet of white.

Dominic has shovelled the path to the driveway. He has been meticulous, leaving straight lines on either side. Emma walks up the path, stepping over the short picket fence dividing their two houses, following footsteps in the snow around to the back.

Through the garden gate, she pauses for a minute, her eyes trying to adjust to what she sees. Everything is white, apart from a black shape on the ground, covered in a thin dusting.

She moves closer, her brain not computing what that shape is, the only thing that shape can be. It is only when she reaches it that her heart stops, and she sinks to her knees next to Dominic, lying still, in the soft, soft snow.

CHAPTER
THIRTY-FOUR

It's going to be fine. It's going to be fine. It's going to be fine.

How could it be anything other than fine?

Emma rocks back and forth in the snow, waiting for the ambulance to arrive, holding Dominic's hand, an unnatural calm coming over her; this is not how she would ever have expected to react in the face of something so potentially terrible, but she is almost numb.

She had phoned Sophie, her voice shaking with fear, to ask her to come and take Jesse. She told her briefly what had happened. Dominic must have been shovelling snow from the roof; he must have slipped and fallen. No, there was no blood. Yes, she was sure he was just unconscious; he was breathing. The ambulance was on its way. Jesse shouldn't know anything, not until they knew what was going on.

Emma keeps rocking, keeps murmuring.

Please be okay. Please be okay. Please be okay.

She senses a movement, and her heart leaps as Dominic stirs, then opens his eyes. Emma sinks with relief before bursting into tears.

"Ah, damn it," he says, struggling to sit up. "That'll show me, climbing on the roof in this weather. I slipped. Thank Christ it's snowing. It cushioned me."

They both pause at the sound of sirens. "I called an ambulance." Emma is almost giddy with relief. "I didn't know what to do."

"We can tell them to leave." Dominic stands. "I just have a headache. I'm fine."

The ambulance medics arrive and check his vitals. He seems fine. They declare him possibly the luckiest man in the world. He has what they describe as an "epic" bump, and just to be on the safe side they're going to take him in to the ER. Just in case.

"I don't need to go to the ER," says Dominic.

But Emma insists. He must go, she says. He should let the experts check him out, check to make sure everything is fine. Reluctantly, he allows her to lead him to the ambulance.

Sophie pulls up just as they are about to close the ambulance doors. She can hear Dominic arguing with the paramedics inside. She leans her head through the doors.

"Aren't you supposed to be dead?" Sophie asks him.

Dominic extends his arms. "It's the second coming."

"That's funny. But not really. Are you okay?"

"I'm fine. But your friend here" — he looks at Emma with a tender, if exasperated smile — "is making me go to the ER, just to be sure."

"So I'll take Jesse?" Sophie looks at Emma for confirmation, and Emma nods from inside the ambulance as they close the doors.

Despite the snow, they get there in no time. The roads were empty, and the ambulance had four-wheel drive. There is no wait today. Dominic is brought straight into an examining room, where he's looked over and declared to be extraordinarily lucky.

"I do want you to have a CAT scan," says the doctor, a young man, too young, thinks Emma, to be a doctor. "Just to be on the safe side. We want to be certain we're not missing anything. I'm sure everything in there is absolutely fine, but let's not leave any doubt."

"I'm sorry to have to tell you that nothing in there is fine," says Dominic, "according to my girlfriend."

The doctor laughs.

"I really do feel okay, though," says Dominic. "Can't I just leave? I can come back to the hospital if the headache gets worse."

"We need to make sure the headache isn't a sign of anything more serious," says the doctor. "With any luck, after the CAT scan you'll be good to go."

Emma sits in the waiting room as Dominic is taken upstairs, scrolling through her phone, exhausted suddenly from the surge of fear, adrenaline, and relief that has swamped her system.

There is a knock on the door. It is the young doctor. "Mrs DiFranco?"

Emma is about to explain they are not married, that her last name is Montague, but it is irrelevant. His face is serious, far more serious than it was earlier. She nods, more terrified than she had been before.

"Your husband is out of the CAT scan, but now he's being seen by the neurosurgeon. During the scan we found a small tear in one of his arteries, and some bleeding around the outside of the brain."

Emma stares at him. "What does that mean? You can stop the bleeding, can't you? He's going to be fine. Isn't he?"

The doctor's face is grave. "He's going to need surgery, and the neurosurgeon is on his way down to come and see you. He'll explain the procedure in more detail, but essentially it involves drilling a hole in the skull to try to evacuate the haematoma and relieve the pressure."

Emma nods, numb. "Can I see him?"

"He's being prepped for surgery. But he's not conscious." He takes a deep breath, as if he doesn't want to convey more bad news. "I'm afraid he lost consciousness during the scan."

The surgeon speaks to Emma briefly, but as soon as he walks away, she realizes she hasn't heard anything he said. Words flutter around her brain like confetti. *Haematoma. Herniation. Burr hole.*

But then a fragment of their conversation comes back to her. He mentioned — she is sure of it — that *the prognosis was better given that Dominic had had a lucid period.* Hadn't he? Had she imagined that?

She is shivering, so she puts Dominic's coat on to keep her warm, and in his pocket she finds his phone. She scrolls through his contacts, looking for his parents' number. Dominic may not be close to them, may only see them sporadically, but they need to know what's happened.

They arrive an hour later, moving slowly down the corridor, fear in their eyes. They seemed so intimidating the one time she had met them, but here, under these fluorescent lights, walking so tentatively down the corridor, they look frail and frightened.

"Mr and Mrs DiFranco." Emma gets up from her chair in the waiting room. They turn to look at her blankly, with clearly no idea who she is.

"I'm Emma. I'm the one who phoned you. We met a few — " She stops. It's not important. "Dominic is about to come out of surgery." She explains what the doctors are doing, removing the haematoma, drilling a hole in his skull to relieve the pressure, while his parents stare at her like rabbits caught in headlights.

She doesn't tell them that she has spent the past hour looking up epidural haematomas on her phone. She doesn't tell them that she is terrified. She keeps thinking of one phrase that loops over and over in her head: *Without prompt medical attention, an epidural haematoma carries a high risk of death.* What does *prompt* mean? she has asked herself over and over again. The ambulance came as quickly as it could, given the snow. Was it prompt enough? *Please, God, let it have been prompt enough.*

She has no idea how long Dominic had lain there in the snow before she found him. Had it been five minutes? Had it been longer?

She won't think about it. She can't.

"Is he going to be okay?" says his father.

"They haven't said. They did tell me it was good that he was conscious after his fall. But I'm sure he is going to be okay," says Emma, as tears spring into her eyes. "He's so strong."

His mother nods, just as the surgeon strides down the corridor. "Are you the parents?" He walks over and shakes their hands, then gestures to all of them to follow him into a tiny private curtained space off the main waiting room.

"The operation went well," he says, as Emma closes her eyes in relief. "We drilled a hole in his skull and seem to have successfully removed the haematoma and brought down the swelling. Mr DiFranco has been taken up to the ICU and we will be giving him medications called hyperosmotic agents, which will further reduce any residual swelling."

"Can you tell yet whether there will be any brain damage? Any seizures, or paralysis?" Thanks to her iPhone, Emma knows enough to ask this.

"It is too early to say," he says. "The next twenty-four hours are crucial."

He offers a few more details to Dominic's parents — what a haematoma is, how it happened — as Emma sinks back onto the hard seat, drawing her knees into her chest and hugging them. She rests her head on her knees, and turns away from Dominic's parents and the doctor, as silent tears trickle slowly down her cheeks.

The ICU is quiet. There is a different doctor on duty now. Emma wanders around the hospital corridors, eventually circling back to the waiting room. Dominic's parents sit there numbly, nursing cardboard cups of lukewarm coffee, which they aren't drinking.

In the early hours of the morning, a nurse pushes the door of the waiting room open.

"He's awake," she says. "Would you like to see him?"

Emma jumps up, then hesitates. His parents should go first. She'll accompany them if they invite her.

But they don't invite her.

Emma sinks back into her chair, stung. *They don't know me*, she tries to reassure herself. *They only met me once, and so briefly. They have no idea what I mean to Dominic, what we mean to each other.*

She stops the nurse by placing a hand on her arm as she is about to head out of the waiting room. "May I go in afterwards?" she asks, so quietly that Dominic's parents won't hear.

The nurse nods with an understanding smile. "Of course."

Ten minutes later, Emma is sitting next to Dominic's bed, holding his hand, as tears of relief course down her face.

"I thought you were dead," she says, attempting to smile through her tears. "For the second time in twenty-four hours."

"I'm just tired," he says. "You don't need to cry about it," and he squeezes her hand.

"How does your head feel? Are you in pain?"

"It's not so bad," he says, closing his eyes for a second.

"I can't believe this happened."

"I know. The random nature of life. But you're going to be fine."

"Thank God you found me."

"You have no idea how many times I've thought that since we got here. Promise me you will never get up on a roof ever again."

"That's really not something I have to promise. I'm not even going to stand on a chair after this. How's Jesse?"

"He's fine. Sophie's been texting me. I'll tell her to let him know you're fine. He's sleeping over at her house."

"And what about you? What are you doing?"

"I'm sleeping here. I'm not going to leave you, Dominic."

"You should go home. You need a good night's sleep. I'm more worried about Jesse. I bet the little guy's scared."

"Want me to bring him to see you tomorrow?"

"Not yet. I don't want him freaked out by all the hospital stuff. Maybe in a couple of days, when I feel a bit stronger."

"Okay." Emma can see he's getting tired, his eyes drifting closed every few seconds. "I love you," she says, and she leans forward and kisses him, sitting next to the bed for a few minutes until he is asleep.

Emma is so exhausted that she has to blink furiously all the way home just to stay awake. She doesn't even remember the last time she was out driving at four thirty in the morning. The streets are deserted and silent, and the streetlights cast warm pools of light on the snow. *This is so spectacularly beautiful*, thinks Emma, driving slowly and carefully. Her first proper

384

New England snowstorm. If only she were able to enjoy it.

She'd spoken briefly with Dominic's parents before leaving the hospital. They seemed as numb as she was, didn't seem to hear when she said she would take care of Jesse; too fragile and overwhelmed. As was she, but she had too many responsibilities, with Jesse, to give in to those feelings.

As Emma walks in the door of her cottage, Hobbes immediately curls around her ankles, looking up at her and mewing pitifully. She feeds her, makes her way slowly up the stairs, and pulls her clothes off before collapsing into bed.

CHAPTER
THIRTY-FIVE

There are no texts from Dominic when Emma wakes up. She feels a surge of worry before remembering the signs at the hospital saying no cell phones allowed.

Poor Dominic. His mobile phone — the one she'd found in the pocket of his coat and used to call his parents, the one she'd so carefully, returned to him when that kind nurse took her in to see him — is probably in a plastic bag in a cupboard somewhere, uncharged. She makes a note to herself to take his charger with her when she goes back to the hospital.

She checks her email, scrolls mindlessly through Facebook and Instagram before realizing with shock that it is almost nine in the morning. She had no idea it was so late, although she was up half the night, didn't get to bed until nearly dawn. She shakes her head to clear it. Things will get back to normal eventually.

She phones the hospital to see how Dominic is, but they won't give out information by phone to anyone other than family. *I am family*, she thinks, but she can't prove it, is too tired to have this discussion. She will go to the hospital as soon as she can.

Texting Sophie that she is coming to get Jesse, Emma jumps in the shower, swigging water straight from the tap to swallow a couple of ibuprofen, hoping they'll stop the pounding headache that comes with no sleep.

The streets are busier today, the roads no longer blanketed in white, but ploughed and already dirty. The Post Road is filled with traffic. Business as usual.

At Sophie's house, she gets out of the car and hops up the path. It may not in fact *be* the path, for there are a couple of feet of snow covering Sophie's entire front yard. She feels guilty leaving tunnels of footprints in the perfect white blanket, and she pauses in front of the house, looking up at Sophie's roof, where more thick snow sits, undisturbed, as perfect as a picture postcard.

Why did Dominic need to shovel snow from the roof? What was so important about our crappy roof on our crappy house?

She has to spend the day with Jesse, even though the only place she wants to be is with Dominic. It's not fair to leave Jesse, who must be so worried, even though he isn't showing it, with Sophie for the whole day. He needs to be with someone he trusts, someone with whom he feels safe.

With any luck, by the time she gets to the hospital, hopefully mid-afternoon, his parents will have left. If they were vaguely attentive to her yesterday, it was only because she knew more than they did when they arrived. But she is no one to them. At best, a temporary girlfriend to their son. A tenant. No one permanent.

Thank God the nurse let her in to sit with Dominic last night. Otherwise, Emma never would have seen him.

Wasn't it only in movies that they refused to let you see the patient if you weren't family? she thought last night. Clearly, given that they refused to tell her anything when she phoned, it happens in real life, too.

She told the nurses outside the ICU that she was his fiancée, surreptitiously slipping the Russian wedding ring — a gift from her parents on her twenty-first birthday, which she always wore on her right hand — onto the third finger of her left. It was almost true. They both knew they were going to get married. Not having formalized it yet didn't make their commitment any less meaningful.

Those nurses let her in to sit with him last night. Whoever answered the phone today wasn't having any of it.

Sophie's porch door is always open. Emma walks in and slides off her boots, and as Sophie comes from the kitchen to greet her, Emma starts to cry.

"I'm sorry," Emma wails, as her face crumples.

"Are you kidding?" Sophie takes her friend in her arms and holds her tight. "Let it out, honey. It's going to be okay. Jesse's upstairs watching TV. He won't hear a thing."

When Emma's sniffles start to subside, she pulls away as Sophie reaches over to grab a box of tissues.

"I'm so sorry," Emma says again. "I'm just so tired."

"Have you slept at all?"

"A little, yes. But I feel like I've been hit by a lorry. I think it's an emotional hangover."

"I can't believe what happened. It's horrific. What do they say? How long will it take for Dominic to be released from the hospital?"

Emma tells her that when she left last night, or earlier this morning, things had been looking better. She doesn't know precisely what his recovery will entail, but the surgery had gone well.

"There's something I have to tell you," Sophie says with a grimace. "I was so worried about Dominic, about what would happen to him, that I phoned your parents."

"My parents? Good grief, Sophie, why would you do that?"

"Because I thought things were looking really bad. I thought you might need them."

"What did they say?"

Sophie's shoulders slump as she looks up at her friend. "They booked a flight right away. They're on their way here."

Emma shrugs. She's too tired, too worried to continue to harbour a grudge against her mother. She'll sort it all out later. "Well," she says, "it wasn't necessary, but I can see you thought you were doing the right thing. It's fine," she adds, as she sees Sophie's distraught expression. "Honestly. Don't worry about it." She peers at her friend. "When you say on the way here . . . when, exactly?"

"Rob's gone to pick them up from the airport. They should be here any sec — " They both turn at the sound of a car.

Sophie looks miserable. "I'm sorry, Emma. I know you haven't spoken to them since your trip, and I would never have done this if I'd known Dominic was going to be fine."

They both go outside, and Emma says nothing. She watches the car pull up, then park, watches Rob get out and pull suitcases out of the boot, watches the back door open. First her father, and then her mother get out of the car, blinking at the searing light outside.

"Darling!" Georgina drops her coat and rushes over, putting her arms around her daughter as Emma starts to cry.

Jesse bounces along in the backseat, a tall furry black hat on his head, his face almost entirely hidden by the strap in front of his nose. He is not strapped into his car seat because Emma hadn't taken it out of Dominic's car, and he is excited to be going to the Bluebird Inn for Texas French toast and chocolate chip pancakes, excited to be with new people who not only have shown up unexpectedly but have brought him a toy London bus, a black cab, and the Beefeater hat, which he may never take off.

Emma has promised him he can have whatever he wants, in a bid to keep him happy and distracted. Her parents are doing an excellent job on very short notice. Georgina, in the backseat next to Jesse, is telling him stories about their farm, which seem to entrance him. She even has photographs from home stored on her phone, and she and Jesse are swiping through them, as she patiently explains who all of the people are and what they do on the farm.

She is talking to Jesse in much the way she talks to everyone else, as if he is a friend she has bumped into in the village shop and is filling him in on local gossip. Emma keeps shooting glances at Jesse in the rearview mirror, convinced he must be bored, but he is smiling beatifically at her mother and happily looking at the photos.

They park in the old filling station next door to the restaurant and make their way inside, taking a table by the window. Jesse proceeds immediately to snap off the heads of two of the geraniums in the window boxes before her mother tells him to stop. Emma watches nervously, waiting for him to throw a tantrum, but he seems transfixed by Georgina and immediately does what she says.

"We'll talk later," her mother had said earlier, when Emma had finished crying and stepped out of her mother's embrace. "I want to hear about Dominic. Daddy has a very old friend who's a top surgeon at Yale, and he's already left him a message. We're going to get him the best help possible."

"Thank you," Emma says gratefully. "I think he's in good hands, but it will be nice to get a second opinion."

"That little one is wonderful," says her mother now, watching as Emma's father takes Jesse's hand in the parking lot and leads him carefully around the idling cars to keep him busy while they wait for their food to arrive. "I understand so much better now. I'm sorry, Emma, for what I said."

"You don't need to apologize," says Emma, realizing it's true. There are far more important things at stake than what happened in England; she forgave her parents as soon as she saw them get out of Rob's car.

The food arrives soon after. Jesse delightedly digs into his chocolate chip pancakes, demanding that Emma's mother try some. Emma watches them with a tremulous smile, the first smile she has been able to muster since she found Dominic lying outside on the ground in the snow. It is quite clear that Jesse adores her mother. It is the very last thing she would have expected, that her difficult, judgemental, occasionally imperious mother would be an object of adoration in the eyes of a small boy. But there is no doubt that Jesse is smitten, and her mother, seeing herself reflected so beautifully in Jesse's adoring eyes, is smitten in return.

Emma would never have thought to phone her parents for comfort. But they are here, and she is comforted. The small mountain of carbohydrates on the table, drowned, as they are, in maple syrup, is comforting, too. Sitting at this table feels like a slice of normality in a world that has otherwise turned upside down.

"What's your name?" Jesse says, mid-chew, looking at Emma's mother.

"Georgina," she says, pausing thoughtfully. "How about you call me Gigi?"

Jesse nods, then glances at Emma's father. "What about him?"

Emma's mother furrows her brow in thought.

Jesse spears another piece of pancake. "Can I call you Banpy?" he asks Emma's dad. "My friend Dylan calls his grandpa Banpy, and I think you'd be a good Banpy."

Emma's father beams. "I don't see why not," he says to Jesse. Then he turns to his wife with a happy shrug. "Well," he says, "I didn't expect this!"

"Instant grandchild!" Emma's mother is beaming just as brightly. "What an unexpected delight. And entirely worth the wait, if I may say." Georgina gives Jesse an impromptu hug. Clearly he didn't follow their exchange, but he hugs her right back.

"Do you know when my daddy is coming home?" Jesse asks as they wait for the bill.

Emma takes a sip of coffee to stall for time, casting an anxious glance at her parents. But they can't answer this question for her. Taking a deep breath, she says, "I don't know. He's had a big fall and they have to make sure he's completely fine before they let him come home. It may be a little while, but I can hopefully take you to see him in a couple of days when he's feeling a bit better."

"Can't I go and see him today?" says Jesse.

"Not today," Emma says. "Today he's just sleeping, resting to get better."

Jesse stops wriggling and looks Emma straight in the eye. "What if he dies? Will I get to go and live with my mom?"

Emma is struck mute. She can't think of a thing to say.

"Jesse, don't say that, darling," says Emma's mother calmly. "I don't think he's going to die. It was a serious bump on the head, but the doctors think your father is going to be fine."

Jesse shrugs an okay, but the rest of them can hardly breathe. Emma gives her mother a grateful glance.

She is not equipped for this. She has no idea how to talk to a small child about serious stuff. What if something terrible did happen? How would she explain it? What would she say, after she has already told him his father will be fine? She forces the thoughts away and turns to the waitress to take the bill.

Once they are in the car and Emma is driving them all back home, she thinks again how glad she is that her parents are here, that they can babysit, allowing Jesse to sleep in his own bed tonight instead of at Sophie's. She is almost starting to breathe normally when Jesse mumbles something behind her.

"What, darling? I can't hear you." She turns the radio down.

"I want my daddy." Jesse's face crumples as he starts to cry. Emma's mother immediately puts a large arm around him and holds him close, kissing him on the head.

"I want Daddy to come home," he says, his whole body heaving. "I want to see him."

"I think we can go and see him tomorrow," Emma says, although she's sure that tomorrow will be too early. "I'll ask the doctors later. Why don't we all go home now, and you can introduce Gigi and Banpy to Hobbes, and maybe Banpy will even help you build a snowman." She looks at her father helplessly, and receives a nod in return.

"Gigi can make hot chocolate and cookies, and I'll be back home before you go to bed tonight. How's that?"

Jesse is still crying, more softly now.

Emma reaches back and squeezes Jesse's hand. "What about . . . if you sleep in our bed tonight? With me? On Daddy's side?"

Jesse looks up and nods. When Emma starts to pull her hand back, he clamps his on top and holds on for dear life, and that's how they drive, all the way home.

Back at the house, they decide that Emma's parents will stay at Emma's, while she stays with Jesse at Dominic's. Not surprisingly, exhausted by the events of the last few hours, Jesse cuddles up with Hobbes on the sofa and falls asleep. Emma finds she can no longer keep her eyes open, either, and her mother sends her upstairs to bed. Her legs are so heavy that she barely makes it up the stairs.

She crawls into bed, asleep almost as soon as her head hits the pillow. When she wakes up, staggering out of the deepest of slumbers, she's deeply disoriented. What time is it? she wonders. What day? The bed smells of Dominic.

Something is wrong; it takes her a few seconds to remember what it is. With the realization comes the worry, weighing on her chest. She lies there for a while, before remembering that Jesse is home and must be downstairs with her parents.

How long has she slept? Is Jesse still napping? She has to get up. She starts to stir, then sinks back into the pillows with relief as she hears Jesse clambering up the stairs. He appears in the doorway clutching Hobbes in his arms, before climbing onto the bed and depositing Hobbes on her chest.

"What have you been up to?" she asks.

"Banpy and I started to build a snow fort but it got too cold so he says we can't carry on today, but maybe tomorrow. And we watched *Harry Potter* one and two," he says.

Emma sits up. "Have I been asleep that long? Oh God." She looks at her phone. It is a lot later in the day than she realized. She is desperate to get to the hospital to see Dominic.

She puts Hobbes aside, but before she even fully rises from the bed, Jesse turns to her and says, "Nonna called. She said she's going to come and pick me up so I can stay with them. But why can't I stay here?"

Emma stills. Why would Dominic have made a decision like that without telling her? Jesse doesn't want to go; of course he doesn't want to go. But Emma can't do anything about it until she's talked to him. She supposes it's understandable for his parents to want Jesse to stay with them while Dominic recovers. They certainly don't want their grandson to stay with a woman they barely know, a woman they have shown no interest in getting to know.

But she can't do anything until she's talked to Dominic.

"Sleepovers can be fun," she tells Jesse. "Nonna will probably make something delicious for you. I'll talk to your dad today, and I'll probably pick you up tomorrow."

"But I want to stay here with Gigi and Banpy."

Emma smiles. "They'll still be here tomorrow. You'll have lots and lots of time with them. Lucky you, that everyone wants a sleepover with you."

Jesse shrugs miserably, downcast. "I said I wanted to stay home but they said I can't. I have to pick my five favourite toys to take with me, and anything I don't have, they'll buy me."

"That sounds like fun," Emma lies as Jesse scuffs the carpet with his foot.

"I really don't want to go." His voice is threatening to break.

"I know," she says, reaching out an arm as he snuggles up next to her, laying his head on her chest.

"I want to stay with Hobbes, too," he says.

"It won't be for long," says Emma. "I promise I'll look after Hobbes for you. And while you're with your grandparents, your dad can get strong and healthy."

Jesse thinks about it for a while before nodding reluctantly.

"I love you." Emma kisses the top of his head, squeezing him tight.

"I love you, too," says Jesse, not seeing the single tear drip down her cheek, which she quickly wipes away.

Emma jumps in the shower, but before she's finished, Jesse bursts in. She yelps, and grabs the curtain to make sure she's covered.

"Bye!" he waves from the doorway. "They're here!"

"Wait. Don't they want to speak to me?"

Jesse shrugs, but before Emma has a chance to say anything else, he has disappeared from the doorway. By the time she's thrown on a robe, they have gone.

"Did you talk to them?" she asks her mother, who is cleaning up the kitchen.

"I tried, but they weren't very interested. They barely said hello."

"I'm sorry. They're not my favourite people."

"No," says her mother. "I thought they were terribly rude. And now Jesse's gone. I was so enjoying him." Her face is so downcast that Emma puts an arm around her shoulders to comfort her, in much the way she had been comforting Jesse earlier.

"Probably it's just for one night," Emma says. "I'll talk to Dominic about him coming back tomorrow."

"I do hope so," says her mother sadly. "I have to say, I'm rather enamoured with him."

"He clearly feels the same way about you," Emma says with a smile.

But already the house seems oddly quiet. Things feel strange, and wrong. She tries to convince herself that there is a silver lining to Jesse's absence. She can focus on going to stay with Dominic at the hospital, and get a really good night's sleep.

398

Besides, she thinks wryly, surely it will motivate him to make a speedier recovery.

Showering has made her feel more human. She throws in a load of laundry, pulls on tracksuit bottoms, and fills a tote bag with toiletries, clean clothes, and a cushion. Now that she doesn't have to get home for Jesse, she can stay at the hospital all night. They may not find a bed for her, but she doesn't care. She *will* stay all night. She will stay as long as she is able, until Dominic is better.

Kissing her mother and father goodbye, she walks outside, grateful for the bracing cold air that instantly wakes her up.

When she arrives, she finds the hospital quiet downstairs, but the ICU oddly busy for early evening. She is buzzed in and puts her tote bag down in the waiting room before heading over to the nurses' station, stepping out of the way to avoid medical personnel walking quickly down the corridors, barely noticing they are about to run her over.

"Dominic DiFranco? Is it okay to see him now?" she asks.

The nurse looks at her blankly, as if she hasn't spoken.

"I'm here to see Dominic DiFranco," she says again. "I know it's not visiting hours but I've been home all day looking after" — she pauses — "our son. Can I go and see him? I can see you're all very busy here, but I've been waiting a long time and I'm worried."

The nurse falters. "Take a seat in the waiting room," she says eventually. "We'll be right with you."

Emma considers pushing through the doors and going straight to Dominic, nurses be damned. But she has never been a rule-breaker, and finds herself meekly following orders.

How odd, she thinks, that a hospital waiting room should feel familiar to her, should feel almost . . . homey. *Better get used to it*, she thinks with an ironic laugh. *You may be here for a very long time.*

She gets out her book and her cushion, crosses her legs on the chair, pulls her phone from her bag, prepared to fill the next few minutes with mindless activity. She hasn't checked her email for ages.

The door is pushed open just as her phone lights up. It is the neurosurgeon from yesterday, his face grave as he comes to sit down next to her. She smiles at him, relieved he is here; no one understands better than him what Dominic is dealing with.

He doesn't smile back. "I am so sorry," he says softly, as the smile slides off Emma's face and she stares at him in confusion.

He is so sorry for *what*?

He looks at her cushion, her book, her tote bag, closes his eyes for a second before looking back at her. "Has no one called you?" His voice is soft.

"About what?"

He takes a deep breath. "We don't know why this happened, but in the early hours of this morning Dominic had another catastrophic bleed. This one, unfortunately, caused a herniation of the brain stem."

Emma looks at him blankly.

"The brain stem controls heart rate and bleeding. When it is compromised, the damage is irreversible. This second bleed was fatal."

"I don't understand. What are you saying?" The fog is rolling in, but it hasn't reached her brain, not yet. "I'm so sorry," she says. "I don't understand."

He reaches over and places a hand over hers. "We did everything we could. Dominic passed away this afternoon. I am so sorry for your loss."

CHAPTER
THIRTY-SIX

Emma doesn't remember getting home. She doesn't remember being asked who should drive her home, doesn't remember suggesting that her mother was the person to call. She has no idea that a nurse sat with her until both her parents showed up at the hospital. She has no idea that her mother cried all the way there, and all the way back, silent tears streaming down her face as she drove her daughter home.

Emma has no idea that when they got home, her mother wrapped her in the cashmere throw which had been draped over Dominic's sofa to hide the years of stains from Jesse's TV dinners, and had poured all three of them big tumblers of scotch, which they downed in one.

Emma has no idea that she couldn't stop shaking, couldn't speak; that the only sounds coming out of her mouth were very quiet whimpers.

She didn't cry. Not then. Her parents managed to get her up to her bedroom, where she lay down between Teddy and Sophie, who gathered her in their arms and held her until she fell asleep.

She wakes up sobbing, but she can't remember why. Once she has started, she can't stop. Her mother bursts into her room, and takes her in her arms as she wails, her whole body shaking.

Two days later, she leaves her bed and comes downstairs. Her mother watches her anxiously, settles her on the sofa like a small child and makes her milky, sweet tea, just like the tea everyone drinks in England when they are cold, tired, or sad. Emma doesn't speak for a while, merely sips the tea, staring at the floor.

"Mummy?" Emma looks up at her. "What am I going to do?"

Her parents cancel their flight home. They tell Emma they will stay as long as necessary.

Despite their presence, the house feels empty and sad. She can't bear not having Jesse there, can't bear the loneliness. She has written to Dominic's parents, begging, pleading to see Jesse, but there has been no response.

Emma hears from AJ that Stacy has returned to take custody of Jesse, that she is now planning to stay for good. She is Jesse's mother. Surely she is the best person for Jesse to be with now that his father is gone. Given that no one seems to be allowing Emma to be with him.

Emma's life isn't a life she recognizes, and isn't a life she wants. She doesn't shower, doesn't eat, wanders around the house aimlessly, picking up things. Almost everything she touches, even the tiniest of objects she has never noticed before, contains memories of

Dominic. She can't believe she is never going to see him again.

It doesn't make sense. She sits at the kitchen table for hours, gazing out the window at nothing, vaguely aware of her mother's attempts at conversation. But Emma can't engage in conversation. Not yet. How can he have been here, how can her life, *their* life, have been fine? And now gone? How can he no longer be here?

Six months ago her life was full, and busy, and happy. She had moved out to Westport to start afresh; how can it be that in a few short months everything about her life had changed so utterly, become so much more than she ever thought it could be, and now it's gone? It's so much worse than if she had simply stayed in New York, unhappy. Now she has even less than she had before, when she didn't know what it was she was missing.

As the funeral approaches, she has to pull herself together. AJ has kept in touch, made sure she knows when it is, where to go. She hasn't been consulted about any of the arrangements. She probably wouldn't have been any use, even if she had been asked. His parents have made all the decisions.

On the morning of the service, Emma stands under the shower for forty minutes, letting the hot water wash over her, willing it to wash the grief away. But nothing helps. Looking at his bottle of shampoo, she finds herself sobbing. Anything can, and does, set her off.

As she sits in the bathroom, looking at her wet hair in the mirror, her face is almost unrecognizable, her skin so pale it is almost grey. She has dark circles under her eyes, and however much she tries, she can't see any life in them. She dries her hair and brushes it back into a chignon, slips on a black dress from her city days, wondering why it is so big.

In one of the drawers downstairs is a huge pair of black sunglasses, left by someone once upon a time, long ago. Emma puts them on to hide her eyes, and stuffs her bag full of tissues from the boxes that Teddy has left on every surface.

She feels completely cried out, but she isn't. Every time she thinks the tears have run dry, they come again, in great racking sobs. While she is opening a can of cat food for Hobbes, or locking the front door, or in the shower, looking at a bottle of shampoo.

She keeps hoping this nightmare will be over. It's only the beginning, she knows, but if she thinks that, if she looks into the future and sees her life stretching out ahead of her, without Dominic, she may not have the strength to carry on.

CHAPTER
THIRTY-SEVEN

The funeral is packed with people Emma has never seen before. Here and there she sees a few familiar faces, but she keeps her eyes down, too frightened to speak, too frightened that if anyone approaches her, all that will emerge will be a howl of pain. Her parents leave her as they find seats, and she looks around, blinking, like a newborn child emerging into the world for the first time.

There is a cloud of grief in the room. Emma has been to funerals before, of course. Her grandparents, several aged aunts, a business colleague who had been battling cancer for years. But their deaths had been expected. People were prepared; they gathered to celebrate lives well lived. Those funerals were filled with moments of solemnity and sorrow, but also lovely stories, sometimes levity, a recognition of the impermanence of life.

But this? This is something completely different. She sees Dominic's childhood friends, and his friends' parents, his former teachers, many regulars from the Fat Hen, and all the bartenders in town. She sees Gina, AJ, and Joey, and in the front row, as if she has always belonged there, Stacy. There are so many faces, so many people, so much sadness.

At the entrance there is a huge poster of Dominic, smiling his killer smile, a familiar twinkle in his eye. It looks to be a couple of years old, taken on a boat. Emma smiles when she sees his face, ten times bigger than life, immediately feeling the tears.

Another easel holds a poem. During the eulogy, Dominic's father tell the mourners it had been Dominic's favourite when he was a child.

Emma hadn't known that.

There was so much she hadn't known. She had always thought of them creating their own world, in their own bubble. And they had done exactly that. They had had six months in which to build that world, and it had been special, glorious. It didn't matter that so few of these people knew who she was and what she'd meant to him. It mattered only to the people they loved.

She sits next to her parents, and they hold her hands. The tissues in her handbag go untouched.

AJ gets up to speak. He tells a story about meeting Dominic in kindergarten, on the playground slide. He pushed him off, and then Dominic returned the favour, and they've been best friends ever since. He recounts the trouble they got into when they were young. He shares stories about their drinking games, and how they played on the railway tracks when they were still too young to know better, and how Dominic always got away with everything because everybody just loved him so damn much.

"Dominic was . . . oh boy." AJ shakes his head, blinking away his tears before going back to the notes he's brought with him to read from. "I can't even believe he's not here," he says softly. "Dominic was one of the greats. He was a really loyal friend, and he was an amazing dad, right, buddy?" He looks over to Jesse, sitting in the front row between Dominic's parents and Stacy, heartbreakingly unlike himself in a tiny suit and tie; his little face devoid of all expression as he fidgets and squirms, staying still only when he hears his name.

Jesse looks at AJ with a big nod and a sudden, unexpected grin. AJ gives him a double thumbs-up, and Jesse gives him one in return.

"He loved that kid with all his heart. And he loved Emma." AJ looks over to where Emma is sitting. "Emma was the great love of his life. Every time I saw him during these past few months, he said he finally had the family he always wanted."

AJ doesn't take his eyes off Emma's while he is speaking. He's saying this for her, and he's saying this to her. She can't tear her eyes away from AJ's, can't see that everyone is leaning forward to see who she is.

"Dominic loved bartending at the Fat Hen. He loved building shit even though he wasn't very good at it." There is a low murmur of laughter. "Oh, come on. Everyone knew he wasn't very good." AJ smiles at the memory, shaking his head as the crowd laughs. "He may no longer be with us, but these past six months were the happiest of his life. He left us too early, but he left us happy. I know he was happy."

Emma's body shudders as she bites her lip, her whole body heaving in a bid to keep the sobs in. She didn't expect this to happen, doesn't want to embarrass herself in front of all these people she doesn't know.

The tears stream down her cheeks as she meets AJ's eyes and nods her acknowledgement, understanding, and thanks.

It is irrelevant that Dominic's parents never thought to contact her on the day he died. That they showed up to whisk Jesse away, not giving a thought to her. It is irrelevant that Jesse is sitting between his grandparents and Stacy, three people he barely knows, three people who don't know him nearly as well as she does, who haven't tucked up behind him in bed and read him Roald Dahl. It is irrelevant that most of the people in this room have no idea who she is, or indeed that she ever existed.

But they know who she is now, thanks to AJ. And they know that Dominic loved her. She just doesn't know what's going to happen to her now.

After the service, Emma waits at the edge of the room while everyone lines up to pay their respects to Dominic's parents. As the crowd shuffles and sways, she can just about see the top of their heads. She has to queue up and do the same herself. Her parents are waiting for her in the car. She has assured them she will be fine.

She can see that Dominic's parents are heartbroken. Broken. Their faces pulled down with grief. Although they smile and thank people, Dominic's mother looks as if she is about to keel over. Whatever residual anger

Emma has been carrying about the way she's been treated dissolves.

When the crowd shuffles forward, Emma sees Jesse, standing between Dominic's parents, scuffing his foot along the floor as he always does when he's unhappy, or uncomfortable. Emma's heart feels like it has a vice around it. She stares at him, and he looks up, straight into her eyes, and freezes.

"Emma!" He races towards her, a six-year-old bullet, and jumps into her arms as he clutches her tight, sobbing into her neck, his arms and legs wrapped around her like a limpet.

Emma carries him to a chair at the side of the room and sits him on her lap, his arms still tightly around her neck, as she rubs his back and kisses him all over.

"I want to go home," Jesse says, between the hiccups and sobs. "Take me home, Emma. I want to come home with you."

"I want you to come home, too," Emma says. She didn't even realize, until this moment, just how much she has missed him. It seems he hadn't realized, either. "Maybe for a sleepover? Maybe for the weekend?"

"No!" Jesse shouts, pulling back. "I want to come *home*. Forever."

"I want that, too, Jesse, but I don't know what's going to happen. I may not be living there any more. I don't know what's going to happen, but I'll try to find out, okay? I'll try to figure this out for you. I'm sorry this is so hard, sweetie. Are you with your mom?"

Jesse nods, and she can see the confusion in his eyes. Stacy may be his mother, but he doesn't know her. She

410

may be his mother, but there's nothing familiar about her. She may be his mother, but that's just a word to him. She isn't a place to call *home*.

"I'm with Stacy a lot of the time, but I'm also with Nonna and Papa a lot, because Stacy isn't used to having a kid and they're helping her out until she gets used to it." Jesse looks utterly miserable.

"Let's just sit here for a while," Emma says. "I'll talk to them."

She waits until almost everyone has gone before approaching Dominic's parents.

"I am so sorry for your loss," she says, as they stand there. Silence. "I'm Emma," she reminds them . . .

"Thank you," says Dominic's father eventually, turning to speak to someone else.

Emma waits for Dominic's mother to say something, to open the door to . . . something. Anything. But she doesn't speak. She just nods and looks to the next person, to anyone else who will rescue her.

"I want to talk to you about Jesse," Emma says. "I know he's living with Stacy now, but I thought you could talk to her. Maybe he can come and have a sleepover with me? I'd love to see him. It doesn't have to be overnight. Maybe just a day. I could give her a break. And I think he needs to see his home. Where he used to live, with his dad. I don't think it's good for a child that young to be torn away from everything he — "

Dominic's mother raises her hand. "Not now," she whispers. "I can't do this now."

"She's threatened," Sophie says, having materialized at Emma's side and pulled her away. "She can't stand anyone else having had her son's love."

"But they weren't close. Why should she care? He's dead, for God's sake. Is she really so awful that she wouldn't care about her grandson?"

"Maybe jealous? Insecure? Possessive? And grief-stricken after losing her son. However she's behaving now, we have to forgive her."

"I promised Jesse I'd talk to her about having him for a sleepover."

"Give her a few days to deal with this. That poor woman. Imagine losing your son." Sophie shudders. "I can't. As a parent, it's unimaginable."

But what about Jesse? Emma thinks. *What about being six years old and losing everything you love in one fell swoop? Isn't that unimaginable, too?*

"Emma," Sophie says, "why don't you just ask his mom directly? Isn't he supposed to be living with her?"

"Yes, but I heard he's spending a lot of time with the grandparents."

Sophie turns her head. "Irrelevant. That's Stacy, isn't it? Go and talk to her."

Emma looks stricken. "Here? Now?"

"There's never going to be a good time. Do it now."

"You're Dommo's girlfriend?" Stacy says, as Emma introduces herself.

Emma nods. *Dommo?* She had never heard him called anything other than Dominic or Dom.

"I wanted to ask about Jesse. We'd grown very close. I know he's living with you now, and I'd love to spend some time with him. Maybe have him for a sleepover on the weekends? I thought maybe it would give you a break . . . "

"Jesse talks about you a lot," Stacy says gently. "I can tell that he loves you. I think, in time, it's a great idea, but right now I'm trying to get to know him myself, and I don't want to confuse him, and I don't want him to feel torn."

"I don't think he'd feel torn," says Emma. "You're his mother. No one can ever replace you, I know that, but it might be healing for him to have something from his old life, something that he associates with his dad . . . "

"No," says Stacy. "Not right now. I'm happy to talk again in time, but right now I need to strengthen my connection with him, and I'm not willing to do anything that might jeopardize that. If you want to give me your number, I'll get in touch when things are a little more settled with me."

Emma feels a lump in her throat, and swallows hard as she nods. She has no power any more, no say. At least Stacy has expressed a willingness to allow it in the future. She takes Stacy's phone and taps her number into it, and the two women nod at each other as Stacy turns to go, leaving Emma feeling lonelier than ever.

Emma is almost out the door, aware that people are staring at her, wondering about her, when she feels a hand on her arm. She turns to see someone who looks vaguely familiar, a man about her age, attractive, with glasses. She can't quite grasp who he is, until he introduces himself.

"The real estate agent," she says. "Of course. Jeff. I do remember you. We met that night at Artisan."

"I never did call you, I know. I heard you and Dominic . . . well. That's irrelevant. I'm so sorry for your loss, Emma. He was truly one of the greats."

"Thank you."

"I just wanted to say, if you ever want to talk, or need a shoulder to cry on, I'm around."

Emma tries to smile, is about to move away. But there's something else he clearly wants to say. He lays a hand on her arm. "I heard you talk to Stacy. Maybe this is none of my business, but I heard her say she doesn't want you to see Jesse right now. Stacy has no idea what being a mother is like. She's doing what she thinks she has to do to try to establish a bond with the kid, but you'll be seeing him soon. I guarantee it."

Emma blinks away a tear. "How can you be so sure?"

"Because Stacy isn't cut out to be someone's parent. She never has been. You need to wait for Jesse to come back. He will. It's just a matter of time."

Emma stares at him. She hopes he's wrong. She also hopes he's right.

CHAPTER
THIRTY-EIGHT

Her mother has told Emma that she will be happy again. Her mother has told her that although she may never stop missing Dominic, her grief will become a part of her, and his memory will lodge into her heart for the rest of her life. The pain won't go away, but it will become more bearable in time.

All Emma knows is that life will never be the same again.

Over the past couple of months, she has finally been allowed to see Jesse, who is shuttling back and forth between Dominic's parents and Stacy. Stacy hasn't yet found a job here, and she can't afford to leave Florida until she has secured something in Westport, so she shuttles back and forth. Jesse stays with his grandparents, albeit reluctantly, when she is not here.

Emma took him to the children's museum, and Shake Shack for a burger; he shook and clung to her when she tried to drop him off, begged her to let him come home. She tried to explain, as gently as she could, that it wasn't up to her, but she would try to see him as often as she could.

She is working again, no longer sleeping the days away in a fog of loss and pain, exhausted by grief. She is putting one step in front of the other, pretending to live a life, going through the motions, getting through each day as best she can.

One morning — it's a Tuesday, she thinks, but how can she be sure when the days and nights all blend into one another, each interchangeable — the phone starts to ring.

Emma does not often pick up the phone these days. There is nothing left to say. But on this particular Tuesday when the phone rings, Emma answers.

"It's Stacy. Jesse's . . . mom. I want to talk to you about Jesse. Are you able to meet me at the Sherwood diner in an hour?"

CHAPTER
THIRTY-NINE

It's late morning, and the diner is quiet, the early rush of businessmen and housewives in for breakfast having passed.

As soon as she walks in, Emma sees Stacy in a booth by the window. She slides in opposite, across the table, ordering tea from the waitress, wondering why she's been summoned. Maybe she's found a place to live in Westport, Emma thinks. Maybe she's coming back for good.

She stares at Stacy, looking for a glimpse into Dominic's life before she knew him. It is the first time she has seen her properly, close up. She is pretty, but weathered. *She has lived a hard life*, thinks Emma.

"How's Jesse?" Emma asks.

Stacy nods. "He's good."

There is a long pause. Emma decides to broach the subject head-on. "Have you moved back here for good?" She struggles to keep her voice from trembling.

Stacy tilts her head. "I've been splitting my time. I had planned to move back, initially, after Dominic died ... but I've got a lot of commitments in Fort Lauderdale. It's kind of hard to extricate myself."

"What about Jesse? Are you taking him to Florida with I you?"

Stacy shakes her head. "Dominic's parents have him a lot. They've been pretty good, although they're not so young and I know it's been a strain."

She takes a breath. "You know, I came back to Westport because I wanted to do the right thing by Jesse. I thought it would be straightforward, that I could just rebuild a life here. But I'm discovering it doesn't work like that. This is hard for people to understand, but I have a life in Florida, a good life, and a business, and it's hard to start all over again in a town I left because I didn't want to be here any more."

"But you're willing to sacrifice that for Jesse? I think that's wonderful," lies Emma.

"I thought I was willing to sacrifice that for Jesse," corrects Stacy. "But I haven't changed, and my feelings about this place haven't changed."

Emma's heart sinks. "You're taking Jesse to Florida."

There is a pause. Stacy shakes her head.

Emma frowns. "I don't understand."

Stacy's eyes fill with tears, which she blinks away by looking at the ceiling. "I can't. I'm not cut out for this. I want to be in his life, I do — he's a terrific little boy — but . . . I never wanted to be his full-time mother. I've tried so hard to do it, to be the replacement parent, but I can't."

"These things take time." Emma attempts to soothe what she presumes is a case of frazzled nerves, panic at what this means for Jesse; the weight of ensuring he is stable and happy, suddenly crushing. She isn't sure

418

what Stacy is saying, but it can't be good for this child; he can't be abandoned again. "It's a huge adjustment for everyone. You're going to be fine, I'm sure of it."

Stacy shakes her head. "No. I haven't come by this decision lightly, Emma. It has been five months since Dominic died, and I have given it my best shot. Jesse is a great kid, and he deserves to have a mother. A full-time mother. I may have given birth to him, but I'm not his mother. And I may be good at the fun stuff, but not the everyday grind."

Emma just stares at her.

"I know you think I'm a terrible person. Everyone will think I'm a terrible person, but I'm not. I'm just not mother material. I'm like the favourite cool aunt. You, on the other hand, *are* mother material. You're the one Jesse wants. He talks about you all the time, asks when he can move back in with you. You're the one he wants to be with."

Tears spring into Emma's eyes. She had no idea Jesse felt the pang of loss as intensely as she does.

Stacy takes a deep breath. "I want you to have legal custody of Jesse. If you want him." A shadow of doubt crosses her eyes. "I may have given birth to him, Emma, but I'm not his mother. You are."

Epilogue

Emma sprinkles chocolate chips on top of the egg-soaked bread before carefully sliding it into the pan. She fries the French toast, flips it, then lifts it onto a plate. Two pieces for Jesse, two pieces for her.

"Birthday breakfast!" she calls, as Jesse, who has been up for hours, runs into the kitchen.

"Can we eat it in front of a movie? Please, please, please?" he begs. "For a birthday treat?"

Emma never allows Jesse to eat in front of the television unless they are having a designated "TV dinner". She narrows her eyes. "What movie?"

"*Star Wars?*" he says hopefully.

She slumps in disappointment. "Again?"

"*Harry Potter?*"

"Okay," she says, as he whoops, grabbing the plate to take into the living room. "Be very careful," she shouts, following him in to drizzle maple syrup over his toast and squeeze up next to him on the sofa pretending to be engrossed in a movie whose dialogue she can recite line by line in her sleep.

She watches him from the corner of her eye. He is completely relaxed, engrossed in the film for the nth time despite the numerous times he has seen it.

Lately, strangers have been telling them they look alike. It's not remotely true, of course. They look nothing alike, Jesse with his dark, birdlike features, and Emma, who is all peaches and cream, fair complexion, and wide-set eyes.

"You look like your mom," people say. The checkout lady at Fresh Market, the sales assistant in the Gap, the woman who helps them in the children's section of Barnes and Noble. Emma always holds her breath, wondering if Jesse will pipe up that she isn't his mom, but he says nothing, just looks at Emma, who merely smiles, relieved she doesn't have to explain.

She may not be his mom, but she is beginning to feel like she is. Everything in her life has changed, and all of it now revolves around Jesse. She makes him breakfast in the morning, walks outside with him and waits on the little bench for the school bus to come and pick him up. She goes grocery shopping for his favourite foods to pack for lunch, and slides them into his lunch box with a silly drawing on a Post-it, every day.

Before, and she only ever thinks of it as *before*, Emma had spent her days trying to find design clients. Now she has joined a shop in town as their resident designer. She has a steady flow of regular clients recommended by the shop.

She makes sure she is always done with her work by the time the bus comes home, and always at the bus stop to greet Jesse when he hops off. She brings him inside, sits with him at the kitchen table, makes him his snack and listens as he tells her about his day.

She hadn't particularly wanted to be a mother, but now that she is Jesse's legal guardian, she has embraced her role as fully as anyone can. She structures her day around his wants and needs, things that need to be done at school. She used to judge the kinds of women who gave up full-time careers to have children, move out to the suburbs, and throw their lives into micromanaging their children's lives. But here she is, doing the same. And loving every minute of it.

Everything stops for a class party, a book reading, a Poetry Cafe in the school library. Her heart expands when Jesse stands up in front of everyone and reads aloud a poem he has written about summer, his eyes scanning the crowd of eager parents, his body unclenching as he spots her face, shooting her a quick grin and an almost imperceptible wave. She will be talking to some of the other mothers afterwards, and will feel something against her legs, a small arm winding around her body, and there he will be, not always looking at her, not always talking to her, but always, always claiming her as his.

Jesse bounces on the sofa and puts his plate on the table in front of them.

"When are my grandparents coming over?" he asks, as Emma looks at her watch. Dominic's parents, *Nonna and Papa*, see him occasionally, but they cannot seem to forgive her for raising their grandchild, even though it was what both Jesse and Stacy wanted, even though they confessed they were too old to raise him themselves.

Emma has tried to include them. She invited them for tea just after Jesse moved in with her, wanted to make them know she wouldn't get in the way of their relationship. She had made a proper English tea, hoping they would be seduced into liking her, or at the very least, accepting her.

She served petits fours, cucumber sandwiches with the crusts cut off, and smoked salmon on tiny rolls. She made buttermilk scones and served them with blackberry jam and proper English clotted cream that had her shriek with delight when she stumbled upon it in the refrigerator at Balducci's.

She had tried to express her love for their son, and then their grandson, with food, in much the same way she knew they had done with Dominic. But it had been a disaster.

Dominic's parents had sat uncomfortably at her table. They had answered her questions, but seemed to want to be anywhere other than there, in her kitchen, in a house that would always be their son's.

During the forty-five minutes they were there, they said almost nothing, both of them looking at their watches, clearly wanting to leave. When they did finally leave, Jesse asked what was the matter with them. Emma had no answers; she didn't know what to say.

She had tried and tried, sending emails, extending invitations, but there was no response. Dominic hadn't wanted a relationship with them; now she understood why. Their own discomfort in themselves, in their lives, in their skins, made everyone around them uncomfortable, too. That was why Dominic barely saw them, she realized. That was what made it all so difficult now.

Stacy has gone back to her life in Florida. She sends the occasional text, sometimes a photograph of herself. Just yesterday, Jesse received a big box of birthday presents. He thinks of her as a distant but loving aunt, just as she wanted.

The grandparents Jesse is asking about are *her* parents. Her sometimes difficult, self-absorbed mother and her diffident, quiet father have embraced Jesse, and embraced grandparenthood, with a joy and enthusiasm she could never have anticipated. From the moment they became Gigi and Banpy, they had forged an unbreakable bond with him.

The last time her parents came to stay, at lunch one day her father nibbled his sandwich, leaving the crusts in a neat pile on one side of the plate. Jesse did exactly the same. Emma implored him to eat his crusts, but he pointed to her father's plate. "See? Banpy does the same. That's where I get it from. It's not my fault."

"Are you telling me it's a genetic trait?" Emma burst out laughing.

"Yes," said Jesse, even though they all knew he had no idea what she meant.

Emma looks over at Jesse, now glued to the television screen, occasionally reaching over to take a bite of his French toast.

"Gigi and Banpy should be here in about half an hour," she says. "They just went into town to get some stuff for this afternoon. And Sophie, Rob, and Jackson are coming, too. They wanted to see you before the party. I think they may have a small something for you."

Jesse turns to her, his eyes wide. "Do you think Gigi and Banpy have gone to get me a birthday present? Do you think it's a go-kart?"

"I very much doubt it," she says, although knowing her parents, they will have indulged him and bought him exactly what he asked for. "Although who knows. They do spoil you. Maybe, if you're *very* lucky, they got you *Star Wars* Lego."

Jesse squirms excitedly. "I hope it's the *Millennium Falcon*, Mom," he says. This is not the first time Jesse has called her *Mom*. The first time it happened, she thought she had misheard. The second time it happened, she thought it was a mistake. This is the sixth time he has now said it.

She has ignored it up until now, but she can't ignore it today. She puts her plate down and moves closer to Jesse on the sofa, thinking about how to choose her words, what best to say.

"Jesse, can we talk about you calling me Mom?"

Jesse says nothing. She sees him swallow as he stares pointedly at the television screen. She picks up the remote control and mutes the volume.

"Sweetie, look at me." He does so, reluctantly, as if he is embarrassed, as if he were trying on the word, was hoping to just slip into the habit with both of them pretending they hadn't noticed.

"I just want you to know, that if you do want to call me Mom, it's completely fine with me. You know how much I love you. And even though I haven't known you for your whole life, I know I'm going to be with you for the rest of our lives." She pauses. Is she saying the wrong things? She feels stupid for not knowing what to say, for not knowing how to say it.

"The thing is, I didn't give birth to you, which you know."

"Stacy's my *tummy mummy*!" He grins at the babyish term Emma had come up with.

"Right. Officially I'm your legal guardian, but as far as I'm concerned, you're my son. And I'm your mom. Forever. If you want to call me Mom, I would be honoured." She watches Jesse, who keeps staring at the television, then looks briefly down at his empty plate.

"Okay," he says, grabbing the remote control and turning the volume back up. "Mom? Can I have another piece of French toast?"

Emma takes his plate and heads into the kitchen. This is not what she ever expected her family to look like. She would give anything to have Dominic back by her side. But Jesse is her family now. There is no doubt about that. And she is his mother. No doubt about that, either.

As she makes her way back to Jesse on the sofa, the Rolling Stones drums in her head, "You Can't Always Get What You Want". She gives Jesse the plate, kisses him on the top of his head, and curls up next to him. There is no doubt that Jesse is what she needs.

Acknowledgements

As always, there are tremendous numbers of people to thank:

First, my brilliant team at Pan Macmillan. A huge thank you to Geoff Duffield, Jeremy Trevathan, Katie James, Catherine Richards, Charlotte Williams, James Annal, Anthony Forbes-Watson, and everyone else on the team — I consider myself the luckiest author imaginable to have such a creative and clever publisher.

Thanks always to my wickedly wonderful agent, mentor and friend Anthony Goff. To Leslie Gelbman, Louise Moore, and Dan Mallory for their sage advice and excellent taste.

For their help and guidance: Stacy Bass, Valerie Fischel, Wendy Walker, Glenn Ferrari, Randy Zuckerman.

To dear friends and my early readers: Patti Callahan Henry, Elin Hildebrand, Dani Shapiro, Lisa Lampanelli, Sharon Gitelle, Nicole Straight, Jerri Graham, Russ Hardin.

To brilliant Gus Walker, titles whiz.

And always, always, to my ever patient, beloved family, Ian, Max, Harry, Tabitha, Nate, and Jasper. And to my husband Ian, who showed me what it was to fall in love.